GREEK
MYTHOLOGY
EXPLAINED

Published by Mango Publishing, a division of Mango Publishing Group,Inc.

Art Direction: Morgane Leoni

Illustrations by: Front Cover & Odysseus Artwork by Robert Crescenzio • Lamia & Artemis by Theo Shaw-Taylor • Bellerophon by Joel Holtzman • Medusa by Mattias Fahlberg • Icarus by Markus Stadlobe

For permission requests, please contact the publisher at:

Mango Publishing Group
2850 Douglas Road, 4th Floor
Coral Gables, FL 33134 U.S.A.
info@mango.bz

For special orders, quantity sales, course adoptions and corporate sales, please email the publisher at sales@mango.bz. For trade and wholesale sales, please contact Ingram Publisher Services at: customer.service@ingramcontent.com or +1.800.509.4887.

Greek Mythology Explained: A Deeper Look at Classical Greek Lore and Myth

ISBN: (p) 978-1-64250-802-4, (e) 978-1-63353-897-9
Library of Congress Cataloging-in-Publication number: 2018956618
BISAC—FIC010000 FICTION / Fairy Tales, Folk Tales, Legends & Mythology
HIS002010 HISTORY / Ancient / Greece

Printed in the United States of America.

GREEK MYTHOLOGY EXPLAINED

A Deeper Look at
Classical Greek Lore and Myth

MARIOS CHRISTOU & DAVID RAMENAH

CORAL GABLES

CONTENTS

Throughout history, storytelling has always played an important role in every culture. Once spread, a good story can capture countless imaginations and provide an endless amount of entertainment. But perhaps more importantly, it can also educate and instill moral values into an entire generation. Mythology is one of our oldest forms of storytelling and even to this day it influences individuals all around the world. One of the great things about mythology is that it's ever changing because the primary way these tales were told was through word of mouth. As the stories travelled across cities, states, and countries, details were changed to alter their meanings. Acts of heroism may have been embellished to create excitement and over time they became stories within stories, each having numerous interpretations. Often these stories resemble a summary of disjointed events rather than an in depth structured retelling. Characters can sometimes lack a real distinct personality in the original accounts of these tales and we don't get a true sense of their motives and aspirations. In *Greek Mythology Explained* we've remained true to the source material whilst filling gaps and exploring what really drives these characters and stories, creating a truly engaging experience.

BETWEEN SCYLLA & CHARYBDIS

I. Together We Are Whole

Odysseus winced, one hand at the helm of the ship and the other clutched around his skull. He could still hear the song of the Sirens they'd encountered a few nights prior, and like the ringing of tinnitus, it was there whenever the waves quietened. He still wasn't sure what was real and what wasn't, for those seductive she-devils had done a number on him, hovering at the edge of the ship and singing their bittersweet songs. He'd made sure the rest of the crew had stuffed beeswax in their ears so they couldn't hear it, but he'd willingly chosen to listen, because he was curious as to whether the tales were true.

Indeed, they were true and he'd have gone falling for any one of them if he hadn't had the crew tie him to the ship's mast, unable to move. He'd screamed for them to free him, but maybe it was just as well they hadn't heard him. Still, his head was on fire and it hurt to even think for more than a moment. He sure had no intention of hearing their songs ever again, that was certain. He shook his head free of the thoughts. After all, he needed his wits about him now.

'Can I interest you in a drink, sir?' Eurylochus stood beside him, calm as you'd like, slowly filling up a glass with red wine.

If he had to tell his first mate 'no' again, he'd probably shove him overboard. He didn't like to drink when onboard. The last time he'd done that he'd nearly rammed the ship against the shore and marooned the whole crew. But that didn't stop Eurylochus from trying.

'No, thank you,' he gently pushed the glass away and Eurylochus looked at him with his flat, emotionless face and just shrugged, knocking it back himself.

Odysseus supposed he couldn't blame him given their situation now. This voyage was certainly shaping up to be an accursed one at best.

The ship moved slowly, carefully inching forward as they let down the sail for a moment's breather. A streak of white light was strewn across the rippling blue waters, courtesy of the raging sun above, bringing with it a heat that had most of his men pacing about the deck shirtless and sweating. But Odysseus couldn't enjoy any of the grand weather, nor did he suspect his crew was as they gathered before him in an orderly sort of cluster—about as orderly as they got anyway.

'It seems like we have two choices,' Eurylochus was saying as he slurped the wine and pointed over to the right where a sheer chalk-white cliff towered over the ship.

There was a scar-shaped crack in the cliff wall and out from that crack spilled what Eurylochus had called Scylla. And by the gods, was it a beast. It had to have been at least twice the size of the ship with six serpent-like heads that were moving as erratically as the waves, never still. From this distance, which wasn't necessarily far at all, it looked as if every head was hysterically laughing at them, bobbing left and right as its razor-sharp teeth snapped open and closed. In amongst those six heads, however, was the haggard, misshapen head of a giant woman who looked dazed for the most part, eyes rolling back, languidly moving left and right. But that wasn't even the worst of it. Its body was a misshapen thing, all a sickly green colour with the sagging, wrinkling skin of an old woman.

'We either sail past dear Scylla over there,' Eurylochus said. 'Or we sail past Charybdis over there on the left.'

Charybdis wasn't much of a looker either, but at least it looked natural, conceived by nature herself. Odysseus hadn't considered it a monster at all, but Eurylochus had gone about naming it and since then it had stuck. To Odysseus, it was a gigantic whirlpool in the near distance sucking in the waves and anything else that was within its reach. Odysseus had to keep touching the helm, pulling the ship on course as it was gently tugged towards the water beast.

Odysseus breathed in deep that salty fresh air and found himself coughing it all out. The crew's combined stench met him instead, an invisible cloud of unwashed flesh, sweat, dirty rags and god knows what else. If they survived this, he'd have them all thrown in the sea with soap and wouldn't let them back on until they were a sight more dignified. You wouldn't catch him sweating and prancing about the ship half-naked and stinking. Even now in the heat, he stood in his captain's uniform with barely a drop of sweat on his brow.

But he'd save the discipline of the men for the ones that survived. There was no use parting wisdom on dead men now, was there? He glanced at Scylla and the six heads were still glued to him, their green eyes burning with an impatient rage. The old woman's head that sat atop the beast may as well have been asleep at this point; there was barely a twitch on her wrinkled, rotten face. Then he glanced over to Charybdis and saw the violent splashing of water as it whirled around and around, never stopping. It was like trying to choose a way to die.

'Are you sure I can't interest you in that wine, sir?' Eurylochus gave him a nudge.

Odysseus didn't even look at him this time as he harkened at the crew, 'We have a dilemma.'

The crew stood to attention at his voice and the ones who were cowering at the edge of the ship at the sight of the two monsters refocused their attention on him.

'As you can see, we have to pass through these narrow waters with Scylla on our right and...' He stopped to look at Eurylochus.

'Charybdis,' he supplied.

Odysseus rolled his eyes, 'Charybdis.'

'Which one is worse?' someone called out from the deck below.

'Scylla will no doubt tear our ship to pieces,' Odysseus announced before considering the giant whirlpool. 'Charybdis will....well, it will also tear our ship to pieces.'

The crew made a resounding moan.

'But if we go through Scylla first,' Odysseus stroked his chin in thought. 'We might be able to sail through. Unlike Charybdis who will suck us in, hold us in its grip and never let go.'

He didn't say much else. He watched as the crew considered both avenues, perhaps the most thoughtful he'd seen them since they'd repelled the sirens. A few lines of hardened faces glanced up at him with grizzled respect, nodding to him as if they weren't fussed about which decision he'd make, because they'd stick by it either way. The others were a bit more hesitant, some of them chewing their nails and shaking in their sandals, their steel swords rattling against the wood of the deck.

'Shall I have the men raise the sails?' Eurylochus asked as he pointed at Scylla.

'Hold on,' he lifted his hand. They couldn't go about sailing in the path of Scylla with a good chunk of them soiling themselves. No, he'd have to do something to raise their spirits. He'd have to—

'Maybe we should give them some wine,' Eurylochus suggested. He must've sensed the same fear amongst the men. Wine wasn't going to do anything but make it worse in the long run.

'Men!' he beckoned as loud as he could, grabbing every inch of their attention. He'd seen old captains give speeches to their men before and somehow, those strings of words were enough to give the men the feeling of iron skin whereby nothing could harm them.

'Men!' he shouted again. 'We're tired, we're hungry, we're burning up and we're all about done with this voyage, I imagine. But we're close to the end. In fact, the end is just beyond one of these two monsters before us. I know you're feeling low, you're feeling weak, you're feeling like our fate hovers above us. But if you can just give me one last push, one last fight, I promise you I will deliver us all home.'

The men cheered, but it wasn't enough. Not just yet. Maybe because he didn't believe it himself. Maybe because he knew deep down that not even half of them were going to make it through this one. Certainly not all of them.

'I promise you,' he added, 'I promise you that, despite our weakened, subdued states, we will find our home. We're going to give it all we have here and now as each and every one of us will emerge as legends of tomorrow.'

That got them perked up a little more. Most of them had stopped their shivering, and the ones who were cowering in the decks below were finally spilling out onto the main deck, eyes glossy with hope.

'This is our life! The water and all who inhabit it will bow before us and we will fight until the sun sets because it's all any of us have ever known, wouldn't you agree?'

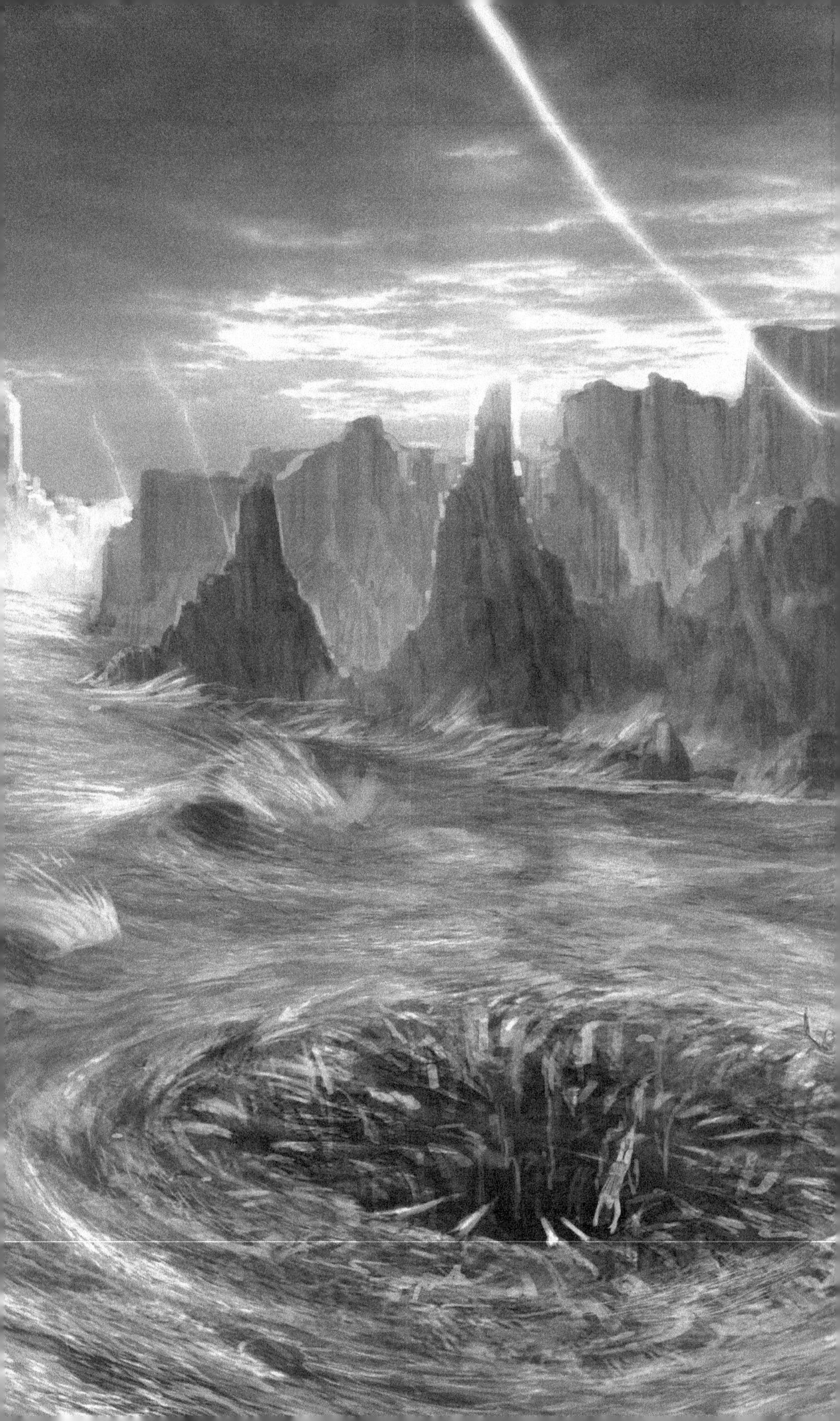

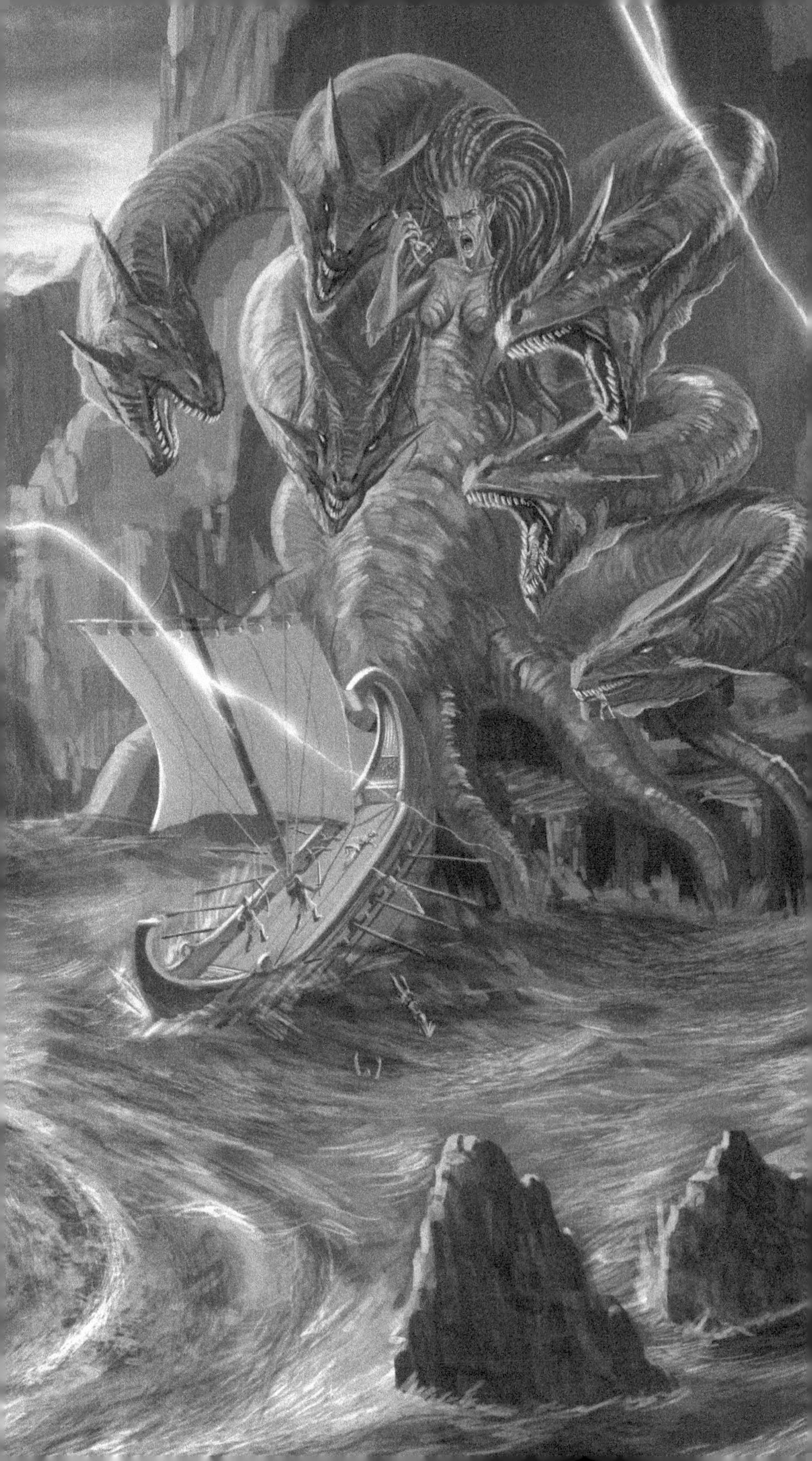

III. Charybdis Inhales

They weren't sailing anymore. You couldn't call being dragged in by a sucking monster sailing. Odysseus peered over the edge of the boat and saw the way the water was surging towards the whirlpool. It wouldn't be long now before they were caught in the centre of the vortex, spun around helplessly and then...well, only the gods knew what came next.

'We're just going to sail right through it?' Eurylochus was by his side, that same uninterested grey look on his face. Almost as if he regarded the whirlpool with as much enthusiasm as he had regarded Scylla.

'There isn't much else we can do, is there?' Odysseus said. He glanced back at Scylla, still sitting there between the crack in the cliff with its laughing heads, watching them head towards Charybdis. 'Unless you want to go back and fight her?'

Eurylochus regarded Scylla for a moment before shrugging his shoulders, 'Maybe we should—'

'If you even mention the wine, I'm going to slap you,' Odysseus warned him and that had the first mate clearing his throat and marching off down the main deck.

There were only a dozen men left over. Perhaps not even that what with the ones lying on the floor, some of them still and some of them twitching. Groans echoed out amongst the ship and those who were standing were bleeding by the bucketload. One man was even missing an arm as he stared blankly into the ocean.

Maybe I should give another speech, Odysseus thought. But he was no speech giver. He'd stolen his last speech from his captain before him, but even that same captain would've probably given up on the sorry bunch down below. The ship had certainly seen better days. Large chunks of the hull had been bitten off by Scylla and huge, jagged bits of wood stuck out in various places. One mast had collapsed against the main deck, squashing a man beneath it. The boom of the ship was crooked, and if Odysseus wasn't mistaken it looked as if an amputated hand was clasped around it. The shrouds were tangled around the masts, one of them ripped and billowing in the breeze. You could hardly call this a ship anymore, just a drifting slab of wood with a crew that was either dead or dying.

Charybdis was upon them faster than he'd liked. The boom of the ship hovered over the whirlpool first. Then the beak of the ship descended into the water, quickly followed by the keel until the entire ship was brought forward, lulled in by Charybdis. Odysseus grabbed hold of the chains that had been slung onto the deck and wrapped them around himself, tied up his arms and held on for dear life. He could hear Eurylochus rummaging around for something, but he didn't dare look as he kept his eyes focused on the dark spinning void at the centre of Charybdis.

For just a moment, it seemed like they might've sailed through unburdened. But Charybdis was merely playing possum. They were wrenched to the side and the entire boat was taken asunder for a moment. There was a collective scream, but the freezing water cut them off, shocking Odysseus and the men to the bone. Something about cold water made fear spread faster. Odysseus held onto the chains but he was spinning through the water now, unsure which way was up. He opened his eyes, but the water made everything blurry as he was tossed around, spinning round and round as the chains unravelled about him.

He saw the ship for a moment beneath him. But then it was gone, ripped away and stuffed somewhere, leaving him to be whipped around the water. He shut his eyes again. It was all he could do as he held his breath. Something slammed into him. It might've been another body for all he knew as he grabbed his own neck, clawing at it for air. He could feel the bubbles like needles going up his nose. He was beyond dizzy now, barely even awake as Charybdis took him round and round in a horrible, silent torture. There was a throbbing in his ears, but there was nothing else. There was no light anymore. Even as he opened his eyes, only the dark awaited him.

For some reason, death by Scylla didn't seem too bad as Charybdis spun him faster and faster.

IV. Washed Up

Odysseus could hear the waves as he came to, coughing up his lungs as he rolled onto his side. Seagulls gathered high above, singing the same song they always sang as he spat out water. The light was too bright as he opened his eyes, so he had to hide beneath his forearm until his sight adjusted. He touched the ground, tentatively at first until he realised that he was sitting atop a mound of rock, occasionally splashed by the spray of the waves.

He spun onto his back with a shriek and went for his sword only to find that it wasn't at his belt anymore. He had lost one of his boots and was left staring out into the ocean, alone. Well…not entirely alone. Scylla was still there in the distance, its heads dancing to a silent tune. Charybdis was nearer, still feasting on everything that came into its path and swirling it around and around. A wide array of flotsam bobbed along the waters that Charybdis failed to devour.

Amongst the wreckage, Odysseus noticed one man hanging onto a large chunk of wood as he drifted towards him. Eurylochus wore the same uninspired face he had always worn and merely looked inconvenienced by the outcome of such a devastating loss.

'That went well,' he muttered as he flung the bit of wood away and climbed up the rocky mound. There really wasn't much room up here for the two of them, but Odysseus budged as much as he could.

'Are there any survivors?' Odysseus asked.

'Probably not,' Eurylochus shrugged.

Odysseus sat there in silence, listening to the growl of Charybdis and the song of the gulls. Surely there hadn't been an attack like this on a ship before. Indeed, it was rotten luck to begin with—to be caught between both Scylla and Charybdis in the first place—but Odysseus felt as if he was owed a break by now, surely?

'You shouldn't blame yourself,' Eurylochus put a hand on his shoulder.

Odysseus made a slow glance at it, 'I *wasn't* blaming myself.'

'Oh,' Eurylochus said. 'Because it is kind of your fault.'

'Yes, thank you, Eurylochus. Your support in this time is most appreciated,' Odysseus snapped. The nerve of his first mate. Why, he would've shoved the man off the mound of rock if that didn't leave him entirely alone. Strange things happened to a man left alone at sea. Odysseus had heard tales of such things and had no intention of living them out himself.

'Won't be too long now anyway,' Eurylochus nodded at Charybdis.

Odysseus frowned. Just what was this idiot on about now?

'The ship will come back up,' he said when he found Odysseus' eyes on him. 'Charybdis always exhales what she inhales.'

'What?' Odysseus shook his head in disbelief. 'What do you mean she exhales?'

'Exhales,' Eurylochus said and gave him a demonstration by puffing out his mouth. 'Like a breath.'

'A breath?' Odysseus narrowed his eyes at the man.

'Yes, the ship will be up again in a minute once she breathes it out. I thought a captain of your experience would know that much,' Eurylochus made a pompous sound.

To Hades with it, Odysseus started rolling up his sleeves. Even if it meant spending eternity alone, he wasn't about to hear another word out of Eurylochus. He went to grab the man by the throat, but then there came a rumbling sound deep from within the whirlpool.

'Told you,' Eurylochus said, who either had no idea he was about to be throttled or didn't give much of a care. Odysseus suspected it was the latter.

A wooden block emerged from the whirlpool and hovered in the air for a few moments before crashing down onto the water. At first it was just an ambiguous wooden shape, but upon closer inspection, Odysseus realised it was indeed the ship. At least...what was left of it.

The sails were all but gone—just a thread or two flicked by the wind around the one remaining mast. The wooden bannister around the outside of the deck was half chewed off, and it didn't look like the rest of the ship was in any better condition. There was now a gaping hole in the hull of the ship from which water began to flood the lower decks. Still, it was nudged towards them by Charybdis like the wicked host it was, having its fun and then sending them on their way, worse off than when they entered.

'You may as well keep it,' Odysseus shouted at the beast. How in the gods' names was he supposed to sail in that thing approaching them?

'It can't be as bad as it looks, can it?' Eurylochus shrugged.

Odysseus turned to look at him and almost ended up going to strangle him again.

They managed to climb aboard once more, and for once, Eurylochus was right that it wasn't as bad as it looked.

It was much worse.

There were more holes in the ship than just the one in the hull. The ship had large wounds from where Scylla had drilled its heads through, and even now, water was filling up in the cracks, rotting the wood and weighing it down. In fact, the only reason the ship was moving at all was because Charybdis was pushing them away. There was only one mast on the ship and even that had a crack along its base, threatening to fall with the slightest push.

Odysseus paced around the main deck and was about to make his way downstairs to the cabins to inspect the damage. But they had already been flooded and the severed head of a crew mate bobbed gormlessly in the water.

'Confound it,' Odysseus hissed. 'The ship is full of holes, the sail has been ripped away, we have no food, the cabins are flooded and all of our crew are dead!'

'It's quite the predicament, sir,' Eurylochus intoned. That was when Odysseus heard him filling a chalice with wine again.

'Where did you get that?' he demanded. Of all the things this fool could've found, he managed to find wine? Of course he did!

'It was lying around,' Eurylochus gave a limp shrug. 'Can I interest you in a drink, sir?'

He held out the chalice, full to the brim with red wine with the faintest hint of grape. Odysseus looked at it for the longest of moments, remembering that last time he'd taken a drink or two on deck, which resulted in him marooning the entire ship. He'd sworn he'd never drink again, did he not? He looked around at the ship and felt it gradually begin to sink as it moved further and further into deeper waters.

With a huff, he shoved the chalice out of his face and reached for the bottle, snatching it from Eurylochus' hands and bringing it close to his mouth. He stopped to look at Eurylochus for a moment, waiting to hear some wisecrack or some comment about him going back on his word. But damn him, he'd earned a drink, had he not?

He chugged down the contents and didn't stop until it was empty.

The wine would lift his spirit, albeit a slight. It hardly seemed worth rescuing the few men who submerged from the waters, but he and Eurylochus helped the stragglers back to the ship—or at least, what was left of it. Still, he was alive, wasn't he? Why, he'd gone against the many heads of Scylla and made it through the abyss that was Charybdis and he was still here. That had to mean something, did it not? Just like his encounter with the Sirens, he was left fatigued but a small part of him couldn't help but crave the next encounter. He licked his lips, still salty from the water and paced his way over to the edge of the ship. He didn't know where the current would take their lifeless, crippled ship and nor was he sure of what would happen as they drifted. The only thing he could be sure of was that his Odyssey was far from over.

THE STORY OF SCYLLA AND CHARYBDIS EXPLAINED

For fans of Greek mythology, it's likely you would have heard of Odysseus and his voyage. For those less familiar, Odysseus was a legendary Greek hero and king of the island known as Ithaca. The majority of knowledge we have regarding Greek mythology comes from ancient literature written by a handful of renowned Greek and Roman poets. One of these poets was Homer who wrote both *The Iliad* and *The Odyssey* which became key pieces of literature in relation to Greek mythology. In both of these poems, Odysseus assumes a key role, with *The Iliad* taking place during the Trojan War and Homer's *Odyssey* focusing on the journey of Odysseus as he attempts to make his way home after the war.

Our story takes place during Odysseus' encounter with Scylla and Charybdis at the tail end of his epic journey as he attempts to return home. They had just escaped the island of the Sirens with Odysseus choosing to be tied to the mast in order to hear the Sirens' call. The crew, with the use of beeswax as earplugs, were not affected by the Sirens' call while their captain begged and pleaded to be released into the Sirens' clutches. The call itself is maddening and Odysseus was the only man to ever hear it and live to tell the tale. It's likely it took its toll on Odysseus, leaving him far from his best when his next encounter took place.

When travelling in between the island of Sicily and mainland Italy, Odysseus and his men found themselves needing to pass through a narrow strip of sea known as the Strait of Messina. To the left of their ship was a giant whirlpool, the monster known as Charybdis. To their right was the six-headed beast Scylla, who had been responsible for the death of hundreds, if not thousands, of sailors. Before realising the situation, their ship was already being pulled in by Charybdis, making turning back impossible. Odysseus and his crew were faced with the dilemma of whether they should veer left into the path of Charybdis, where the ship would be sucked into the whirlpool, or steer right, where it's likely Scylla would smash their ship into pieces. Odysseus, knowing that turning into Charybdis would guarantee that the ship would be destroyed, chose to take his chances with Scylla and sailed close to her cliffs.

Upon seeing the ship, Scylla emerged and began her vicious onslaught on Odysseus' ship. The ship itself would not have been armed with cannons and the weaponry we've come to expect from the pirating era as this story took place thousands of years before. With that said, even if the ship had been armed, it's unlikely that any weapons of the time would have been enough to deal with a monster the size of Scylla. With the ship in pieces and dozens of his men dead, Odysseus had no choice but to steer his ship in the direction of Charybdis in the hope that what was left of the ship and his men would survive the encounter. As expected, the entirety of the ship was sucked into the whirlpool and Odysseus was left stranded on a rock hanging onto an olive tree for dear life. The ancient Greeks believed that Charybdis was cursed with an unquenchable thirst and would have to drink from the ocean three times a day. During these times of day, Charybdis would inhale enormous amounts of water, but because of the curse placed upon her by Zeus, she would have to exhale and release all the water that she had swallowed. It was only when Charybdis eventually exhaled that Odysseus' ship was released. Odysseus climbed aboard and began searching for what men he could save, knowing that with a ship in pieces and with only a fraction of the crew alive, their journey home would be even more perilous than before.

At first glance, this portion of Odysseus' story seems like little more than a hero's battle with two enormous monsters. Although that is correct to a certain extent, there is some deeper meaning that can be abstracted from the story. Scylla and Charybdis may be the title of the story, but it's also a Greek idiom that describes being in a situation where you have to choose between the lesser of two evils. It's quite similar to the modern phrase 'between a rock and a hard place,' which refers to a situation where you're faced with two equally undesirable outcomes. This underlying theme is definitely one that can be applied to us as individuals even to this day. Most of us will come across situations similar to that of Odysseus. Now, of course, it's unlikely that we will be choosing whether to face an enormous six-headed monster or a whirlpool that destroys everything in its path, but we will have choices and outcomes we're not particularly fond of. Sometimes the choice or outcome we desire may not be plausible and we can only do what we think is best, leaving us stuck to choose between the lesser of two evils.

LAMIA

I. The Last Dance

Lamia held the small velvet box close to her heart as she all but skipped back to her palace. She wondered what lay inside ever since her beloved Zeus handed it to her, but she vowed not to sneak a peek until she returned home. It was more thrilling to wonder on what sort of marvel he had adorned on her, the anticipation of soon knowing making her stomach swoon. Perhaps it was some fine trinket, or some relic of old? For all she cared, it could've been a pauper's scrap but she would cherish it forever nonetheless, merely because it was a gift from her Zeus.

Dark clouds began to gather around the precipice of her gilded palace, but not even the sight of such a ghastly formation could dampen her spirits. Thunder rumbled through the sky at her approach, rolling across the air like the beating of drums. It reminded her of Zeus' laughter and that put a dreamy smile on her face. Rain began to fall, the sound of it beating the ground, making what sounded like the hissing of a hundred snakes. But still, her smile remained and she caught a glimpse of it in a puddle as she strolled down the cobblestoned streets, every inch of her serene and perfect. The wind nipped at her and a chilly breeze made her surrender a shiver. The thought of Zeus kept her warm.

Her palace stood before her, a charming and yet bold arrangement of spires and age old stonework. Even against the greying sky, the palace maintained its regal stature with flags flapping rapidly at the precipice of each dome. Tall windows were set on its face and long silk ribbons sauntered down the front and sides of the palace billowed gently by the wind. Her servants moved in like cavalry to greet their commander, falling to their knees before her. She gave them each a brilliant smile, for how could she not? She had been a kind and just queen after all.

Her subjects flocked to her and a great few of them were blocked by the guards who swooped in not long after her servants had. They chanted her name, tossing roses and violets at her feet as she offered them all a regal wave of her hand. A thousand voices echoed their love for her and a cacophony of whistling, hooting and clapping never ceased to dazzle her ears. She set her sights on them all and breathed in deep their every cheer and shout like they were feeding her, filling her up like sunlight to a plant.

Young men blushed at the sight of her, waving kerchiefs or shoving one another out of the way to get the best sight of her. Some women stood with their hands clasped at their chest, admiring her beauty as she passed them by. An old man dropped to his knees upon her approach, but she laid a gentle hand on his shoulder and asked him to rise. Indeed, she was his queen, but she always respected her elders. The old man said nothing, but he grinned from ear to ear as she helped him back to his feet.

A small girl came running into her arms. She was dainty and wore a yellow dress as bright as her giggle. Her mother appeared in the crowd distressed, but Lamia smiled and the mother relaxed. She gave the girl a peck on her forehead and handed her back to her mother who sounded off with apologies and a hundred pardons. Lamia gave the woman's shoulder a reassuring squeeze and told her not to worry.

Two boys, no older than ten years of age, were trailing behind her, tossing flowers at her feet. She gave both of their heads a ruffle before scooping up a handful of the flowers and placing them in her hair. The boys looked at each other for a long moment, as if they had been touched by a goddess, before they broke out into red faces and laughed their way back into the throng.

Still her name was sung into the air and despite the drizzle of rain, her people did not waver. A band assembled somewhere in the sea of citizens, and a fanfare broke out across the bevy, inciting clapping and dancing. She took the arm of a young lad and pulled him into a dance and while he, a mere peasant, was unexpecting of such an honour, he did not disappoint. She spun around with him for a few rotations, twisting and frolicking to the tune of the band, before she was taken up by one of the boys from before. After that, she was dancing with a trio of merry women who could not stop proclaiming how beautiful she was. Lamia would tell them to look at their reflections more often if they wanted to see beauty.

In a few hours, the whole town was dancing and the streets were filled with music, laughter, the clinking of glasses and the songs they spun of her. She would've wanted it to last forever, but then all good things came to an end, did they not? As she pondered on that thought, her advisor grabbed her quite firmly by the wrist.

'She's here,' he muttered in her ear, distress painted on his face.

Lamia gulped, 'She is?'

'In your chambers,' he nodded like he'd just seen a ghost. 'We can have the guards try and—'

'Nonsense,' Lamia placed both her hands on his quivering shoulders. 'I will go.'

She clutched the box Zeus had given her and looked upon her subjects once more, if only to capture this moment in her memory forever. Something in her gut told her that there wouldn't be a moment like this again.

She made her way back to her chambers.

II. The Wrath of the Gods

'Do you think you're beautiful?' Hera bit off each word like any response other than 'no' would be heresy.

Zeus told me I was, Lamia would've said if she had even a fraction of Hera's power. In fact, Zeus said it more than a dozen times—mumbled it out of his wet lips each time she took his seed. But she knew better than to say anything of the sort to the raging goddess who now stood in her chambers, her eyes twitching with rage. All she could do was hang her head low, her knees drawn tight against each other in hopes that her docility would appease the furious goddess.

'*You* and my husband!' she screamed loud enough that the paintings on the wall rattled. If the rest of the palace didn't know about her tryst with Zeus, they most certainly did now.

'Yes,' Lamia spoke, her voice barely spilling out over her lips. She knew it was a mistake to engage Zeus, and while she heeded the warnings of her advisors, in the end she could do nothing to resist him as he swallowed her up in his arms, lifted her high into Olympus and had his way with her. *It will be just the once*, she had told herself. A mere clandestine encounter beyond the ears and eyes of anyone except herself and Zeus—a secret they would share with only each other. *It will be just the once*, she had told herself.

'How many times?' Hera demanded, a vein in her forehead now throbbing like a contorted worm.

Lamia took a deep breath, 'More than a dozen.'

Hera's eyes widened, her nose scrunching up as she bared her teeth at Lamia. The admittance of that truth looked like it physically pained Hera as she wrapped one arm around her stomach, her expression like that of a caged animal pissed on by its captor.

'Your betrayal has cut me deep,' Hera clenched her fists and Lamia wondered how long it would take a goddess to beat the brains out of her.

'Zeus betrayed you too!' she shot back before she clamped her mouth shut, wishing she hadn't said a thing at all.

Hera recoiled at that, her hand hovering gingerly about her heart for a moment, no longer a fist. It was as if she had only just now realised that her husband was just as much to blame as Lamia was. But then that fire returned to the goddess' eyes, a green inferno lighting up within the depths of her pupils.

It was a fearsome sight as Hera's entire face began to contort. She was screaming in fury, spit spewing all over the floor. The blazing glow in her eyes was matched only by the pulsing of the veins down her arms. Lamia thought to run, but where could she go? Even as a queen, she could not hope to hide from Hera's vengeance. Lamia pressed up against the door, too afraid to try to open it and so she took to shrinking up against it instead.

The wind howled through the windows in tune with Hera's almighty roar. Lamia found herself pinned to her spot, unable to do anything as Hera leered at her. The goddess' breaths were like that of an angered dog, throaty and deep. Her shoulders were bunched up, every inch of her tense and ready to rip limb from limb. Lamia squeezed the gift Zeus had given her between her sweaty palms if only for the modicum of relief it brought her.

'Just do what you came to do.' Lamia tried to sound brave, but the desperation was evident through her cries. She wanted to live. Truth of the matter was, she wanted to see Zeus again. She wanted him to storm into her chambers now, fend off Hera and swoop her up in his arms the way he'd done so many times before.

But Zeus didn't make a grand appearance. He probably wasn't even watching.

'You think he'd come for you?' Hera hissed like she'd read her mind. 'He's probably with some other mortal harlot right now, insolent girl.'

Lamia felt a sharp twinge in her heart at those words. Perhaps because they were probably true. Zeus' appetite knew no bounds. If Hera couldn't sate him, what hope did she think to have? She wondered if he even meant the things he'd said—whether any of it meant more to him than just a night between the sheets. It had to have meant something, hadn't it? She looked down at the box and watched as a teardrop dampened a spot of the velvet lining.

'This is what he does,' Hera snapped. 'I thought you might be wiser to his ways, but I see now you are no different.'

Hot tears were streaming down her face now. Zeus had to have loved her. He said it to her, had he not? The thought of him saying it to someone else just as easily made her chest tighten and she suddenly found it harder to breathe.

'Shed no tears.' Hera relaxed all of a sudden, the fire in her eyes dying as quickly as it came about. She folded her arms across her chest and took a slow, deep breath. She no longer looked at Lamia but instead outside the window where the rain began to fall. 'We've all shed enough for him.'

'Aren't you going to kill me?' Lamia asked.

Hera looked at her for the longest moment. Lamia knew in that hardened stare that she already made up her mind. She wasn't hesitating, she just enjoyed prolonging that suspense—enjoyed watching Lamia squirm for life. Lamia's fingers tightened around the box. A part of her wished to open it now—to know what her beloved had bestowed upon her before abandoning her to this fate.

'No,' came Hera's voice, her eyes now set on the box as if she meant to pry it out of Lamia's hands. 'No, I'm not.'

No? Lamia didn't understand. She deserved to die for this, didn't she? Hera never stayed her hand in the past when confronting Zeus' concubines. It didn't make sense for her to do so now. Could it be she realised that Zeus was part of the problem at last? Could it be she had finally taken enough from him that she could take no more? Lamia knew that if she was Hera, she wouldn't have been able to stomach this many affairs.

'You're not going to kill me?' Lamia ventured, trying to hide the hope in her voice.

'I'm not going to kill you,' Hera's voice came again, a wry smirk appearing on her lips. '*They are.*'

They materialised from the air itself, bringing with them a black smog. Two creatures no bigger than a pair of foxes began to take form right before Lamia's eyes. Both creatures hooted like wild baboons at the sight of food. They had pointed ears that twitched as they moved to stand on two hooved feet. Their arms were stubby and pilose—two unkempt, dwarf-looking spawns with bulbous heads and misshapen features.

Lamia squeezed Zeus' box close to her, but it was no box at all anymore. Instead, there was a glistening knife with a deadly razor edge. One of the creatures galloped after her and shrieked from its bloody lips. Before Lamia could get the knife up, the creature crashed into her chest, taking her to the floor. She felt its talons grab her throat the moment they landed. She gasped, placing her hand against the creature's grimy face, trying to push it off. But the creature just snapped her hand with its maw, its eyes fixed on her with a chilling grin. For just a moment, she thought she knew those eyes. But then she rammed the knife into its head and watched them fill with blood.

The creature made a sad sort of croak before it crumbled to one side. Lamia didn't realise she was holding her breath. She let out a terrified gasp before wrenching the blade out of the creature's skull and backing up against the wall. Hera was laughing, perhaps now in a more manic fashion than before. Lamia didn't even know why she was fighting. Even if she could kill the last creature, Hera would finish her off with a mere flick of her fingers.

The last creature went berserk at the sight of its fallen ally. It began screeching at her in a horribly alien sort of sound. It began galloping towards her, saliva spilling out of the side of its mouth like a waterfall. Its face was knotted into one ugly, maddened expression. Its jaw hung open and several rows of teeth could be seen seated in the void of its mouth.

Lamia managed to step out of its way and it went crashing into the wall with a loud thump. Before it could regroup, Lamia made her move. She drove her knees into its spine, pinning it to the ground as she set her entire weight upon it. Then she lifted the knife up high and plunged it into its back. It let out a long, residing groan, but Lamia didn't stop. She ripped the knife out of its back and brought it back down again, grinding bone and flesh against the blade. Blood splattered in her face, some of it getting in her eyes. Still, she drove the blade into the creature, each stab weaker and weaker until the weapon slipped from her grasp and went skittering across the floor.

Hera's arms were around her stomach, hunched over in a fit of breathless laughter. She sucked in air, brought herself up to a standing position and wiped a tear away. She couldn't seem to compose herself as she turned from mighty goddess to a giggling girl.

'What's so funny?' Lamia screamed at her.

Only then did Lamia realise that the creature beneath her had long, dark, silky hair just like hers. The creature didn't have talons anymore, which confused Lamia. Instead, it had small human hands like those of a child.

Lamia knew those hands.

She let out a horrified shriek as she fell off of the body and landed beside it. Just ahead of her, she saw the gaping hole she made in the head of the other creature; now just a blue-eyed boy in a puddle of blood.

The knife began to change shape and in the blink of an eye it returned once more to the shape of Zeus' box. This time, Lamia didn't feel herself reaching for the box because she was transfixed on the massacre before her.

Her children were dead.

III. The Child Killer

A day would pass before they stripped Lamia naked and ushered her out of the palace doors and into the mob that awaited. What were once worshipping folk now became a current of vile faces, every one of them spitting and screaming at her as she stumbled through the street.

'Child killer!'

'Zeus' whore!'

'Monster!'

She tried to hide her shame, but hands grabbed at her from all directions, yanking and shoving her off balance. She collapsed into the dirt more than a few times, her body now cut and bruised from head to toe. She wasn't a queen anymore. She was less than dirt in the eyes of her people. She was nothing.

'Sinner!'

'She-devil!'

'Murderer!'

She shoved her hands over her ears as she ran, but she couldn't block them out. She could never block them out. The same way she couldn't block out the images of her children lying there in their own blood. The mob threw things at her—mud and rotten fruit for the most part but soon faeces and gods knew what else. Her hair was damp with piss and her lips were swollen from where she hit the ground and bashed her mouth. She was bruised from where her own guards groped, slapped and struck her like she was a common harlot and not their ruler.

'Evil witch!'

'False queen!'

'Child killer!'

She could see the forest in the near distance and knew they wouldn't follow her in there. She herself didn't wish to wander into the marshlands for fear of the harsh terrain and the wild beasts who roamed it. Then again, could those beasts be any worse than the ones that surrounded her now? Her feet were sore from blisters and her ankles ached from where she had been kicked and tripped by a dozen different men and women.

'Murderer!'

'Wicked queen!'

'Child killer!'

She tried to explain to them that it was Hera's doing, but they would not believe her. Even now she pleaded with them and begged them to heed her words. But they could no more understand her than a pack of wild dogs could. She was bleeding from the nose now and the lashes on her back were stinging as if a thousand wasps descended upon her. One man spat in her face, grabbed her by the hair and laughed as he yelled in her ear.

'Child killer! Child killer! Child killer!'

She managed to break away from him and limped her way off of the cobblestones and onto the grasslands. The mob must've realised her intentions because they began making hissing noises and hooting in the air at her. They soon stopped giving chase and the last line of their entourage would spill away, albeit reluctantly.

'Child killer! Child killer! Child killer!'

Their chant would chase her into the woods, and while she promised herself she wouldn't look back, she did. Her palace was shrouded in shadow as the red sun began to retreat beyond the horizon. Her subjects were now nothing more than ambiguous shapes with pitchforks and lanterns barricading her from returning to her own home. They'd all betrayed her, and while she knew she couldn't blame them, she couldn't help but clench her fists as she heard their chant fill her ears once more.

'Child killer! Child killer! Child killer!'

In her hand was the box Zeus had given her. It was all she had left of him. In fact, it was all she had left of anything. She didn't open it. In fact, she daren't think she would ever open it, for it would forever remind her of what had happened. But to part with it was too great a thing. It was all she had now.

'Child killer! Child killer! Child killer!'

She turned her back on her people and descended into the depths of the woods, knowing full well that someday, somehow, she would have her vengeance upon them all.

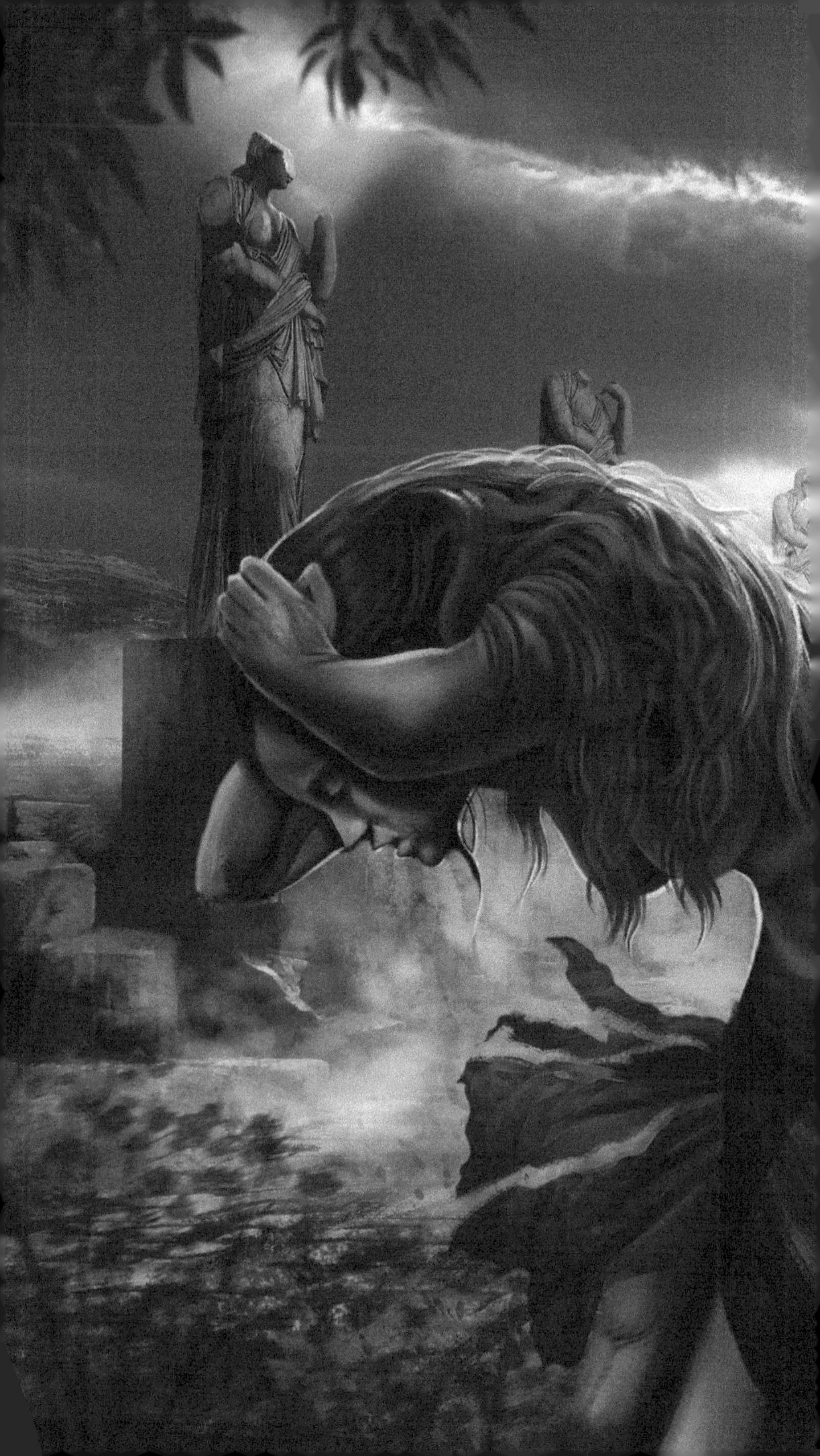

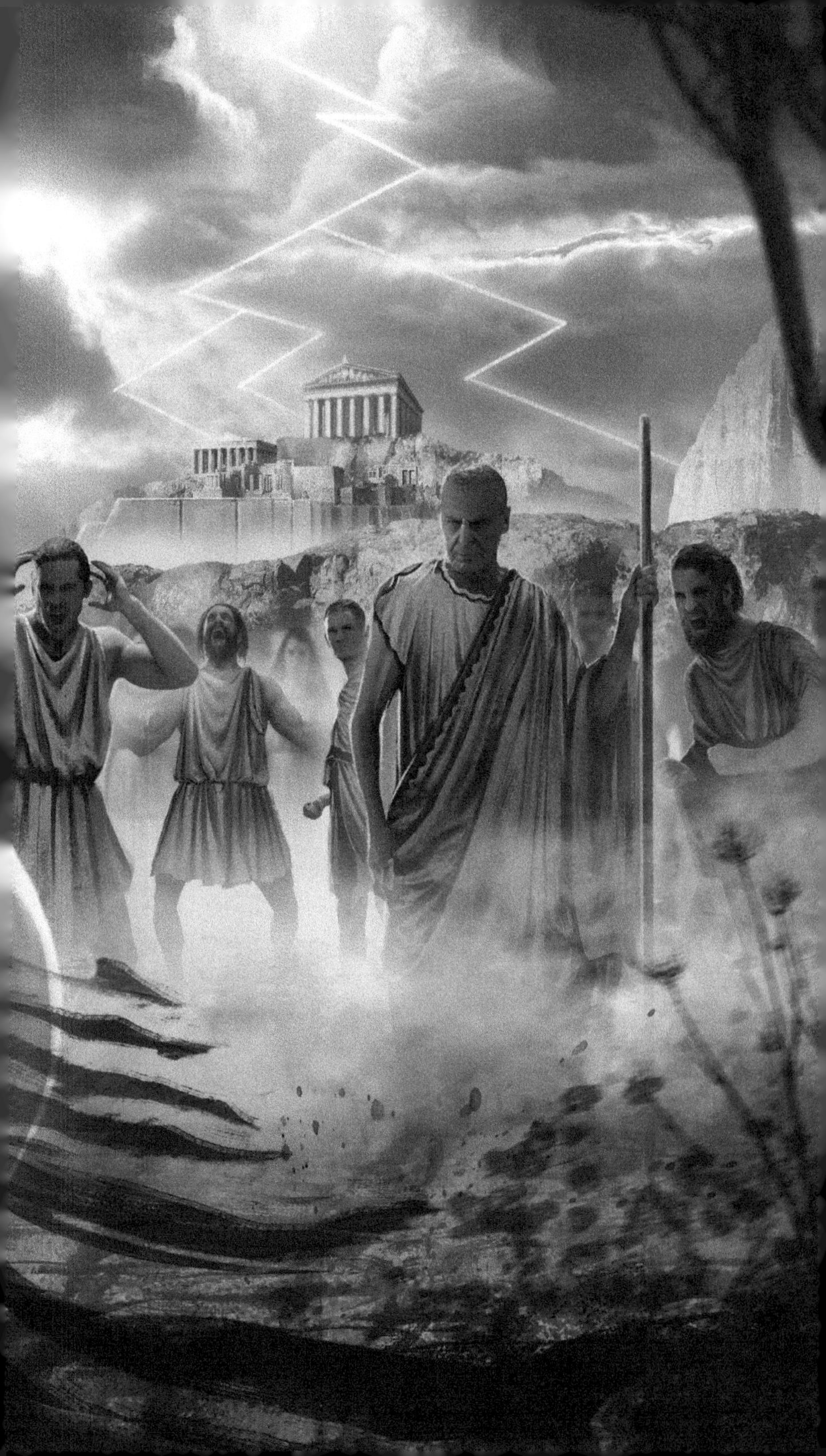

IV. What Lies In the Woods

The nights were the worst.

The daylight didn't seep out of the forest as the sun retreated. No, the woods themselves were simply plunged into darkness in the blink of an eye. It wouldn't have been the first time she went sprawling onto the ground, bashing her knees against the hard dirt and, as luck would have it, hitting her head too.

Panic set in as she lifted her head. Her heart rate quickened and she had to slam her hand over her mouth to halt her anxious breaths. The monsters out here had acute hearing after all. With the daylight gone, she was left blind. Nothing terrified her more.

But at least the darkness brought some relief. She could see nothing, and therefore, she could see nothing that would remind her of her past. Sometimes, she even shut her own eyes as if it would somehow make the dark all the more prominent.

She scrambled on her hands and knees, careful not to make too many loud noises for fear of the creatures descending upon her. She'd done well to avoid them thus far, but deep down she knew it would not stay that way. Her stomach rumbled as she curled into a ball at the base of what she hoped was a tree. If it was anything else, it could go right ahead and consume her and put an end to her miserable life. It didn't change the fact that she was hungry though, and her stomach wasn't in the mood for playing the quiet game.

The wind whipped at her and rustled the leaves of the trees, making them hiss all around her. She would've been colder if she was still naked, but thankfully she found an old sheet marooned on a high branch and climbed to claim it. She wrapped it around her like a dress, but her arms were still exposed and suffered from cuts, bruises and a severe case of goose pimples. Her nose was running, but she had to keep using her hand to wipe it despite desperately wanting to blow it. If she made such a sound in the thick of the night, the monsters would surely come for her, wouldn't they?

She heard one of them circling her just the night before. It might've been a wolf what with its snarling and growling, but for just a second she caught glimpse of its yellow eyes glowing in the shadows. Whatever it was fled in the other direction, and though she was sure it gave chase, she would stumble down a steep hill and manage to escape its clutches. Such luck wouldn't shine on her forever though.

She didn't want to hug onto Zeus' box, but hugging that seemed better than hugging herself. She laid her head against the dirt and surrendered tears and sobs for the sixth or seventh night in a row. By the gods, how many nights had it been? She pined for her kingdom, pined for her people, pined for her children, and ridiculously enough, found herself pining for Zeus. She stared up at the night sky—an endless black sheet with the faintest smudge of stars staring back. Why would Zeus allow her to suffer like this? He told her he loved her, didn't he? He looked her in the eyes with a face as serene and pure as anything she'd ever known. He wouldn't have forsaken her like this...would he?

This is what he does, Hera's words sunk into her like the fangs of a viper. No, maybe Zeus had indeed forsaken her; that thought made the tears flow even more. She clutched at the box for dear life, hoping that he would come charging down from the stars, but just like the previous nights, he didn't show. She felt stupid for thinking that he would.

There was a snap of a branch and Lamia nearly shrieked. She couldn't see anyone at first, only the endless void that the woods had become. But then there was an ambiguous shape swaying just ahead of her, hardly trying to be discreet like she was. Its eyes came into focus: two green eyes that glowed like Hera's. The light from its eyes gave birth to the misshapen form of its face, but any details or expressions that the creature possessed, Lamia couldn't see. It skulked ahead of her and its feet must've been wet, for they squelched in the mud. Whatever it was breathed like something was stuck in its throat, a low throaty wheeze escaping its lips. It swung its arms about in a languid fashion, but if she wasn't mistaken, they sounded like the beating of heavy wings. Its head snapped left and right as if it was looking for something. Lamia got a sinking feeling that it sought after her.

It moved like a drunk stumbling out of a tavern, but those eyes were not the type to take lightly. It wasn't a tall figure as far as she could see, but it had a large globular head that swung back and forth. Lamia didn't move—didn't even wipe the drop of fluid dangling by her nostril. She shivered at the sight of the creature which now prowled about the area, occasionally pouncing on something and tearing at it with its maw. She desperately wanted to wipe her nose, desperately wanted to let out a sob and desperately wanted to be free of all of this. The creature stormed this way and that, pacing and kicking dirt in frustration with its massive claws. It was stabbing at the ground before drilling its own face against it, hooting and screeching. Its tantrum showed no signs of stopping until its head snapped in her direction and its eyes made the slightest squint.

It was looking at her.

At first, Lamia just stared back. Surely it couldn't see her. Surely the darkness concealed her well enough that she remained invisible to the sights of the creature. But then the creature made a rabid grunt at her and a new excitement came over its body as it galloped towards her, large black wings flapping with excitement.

A harpy, then.

She pushed up off the ground and ran with her hands out in front of her. If she hit a tree, she would be done for. The harpy stormed after her and she could hear its footsteps thumping behind her. It had a crazed growling to it now, its wheezing and snorting all the more pronounced as it gave chase. Lamia didn't look back. She couldn't look back. A part of her wanted to just lie down and accept her fate, but the fear of confronting it made her legs move by themselves.

She tripped over a low log and pitched onto her face. If there was pain, she didn't feel it. Not yet. She scrambled onto her feet and charged onwards. She could feel it on her heels. She was sure she could feel its breath on the back of her neck as she moved. She darted around a tree, but before she could run another step her chest tightened. Her thighs were on fire, cramps were squeezing at her calves and her heart was thumping so much so that she thought it might burst.

She could hear the creature come to a stop as well. Its teeth were snapping at the air as if it was trying to taste her scent. She straightened against the tree, certain that the creature was on the other side and momentarily oblivious to her whereabouts. But it wouldn't stay that way at all. No. Lamia slowly turned around, got her foot into a crevice of the tree and began to hoist herself up, one inch at a time. She managed to get herself high enough that the monster couldn't reach her, but given its tenacity thus far, it would certainly find a way. Blasted thing could fly, after all.

She bit down on her lips, suppressing even the slightest of breaths for fear the harpy would hear her. It wandered beneath her, head on a swivel as it searched for her. It growled with every twist of its misshapen head, slashing the shrubbery with its wings as it grew restless without its prey. She wanted to close her eyes, but fear had her eyes fixed open wide.

A drop of sweat fell from her brow and for that moment, time seemed to slow. That clear drop fell through the air, and while she thought to reach for it, she was not quick enough. It bounced off the harpy's head.

The creature screeched like it was stung. It spun around with its giant wings, black feathers spewing everywhere as it began to swing at the air like it had been descended upon by a thousand flies.

Please don't look up, Lamia begged silently. *Please don't look up.*

She took one last look at the night sky and asked Zeus, or whoever would listen, *Please.*

The creature went still all of a sudden. Lamia thought she could see its block-like shoulders shifting as it caught its breath. She was sure it was going to look up and devour her. If she was honest, a part of her wanted it to just be all over so this nightmare could end and she could finally rest. But the creature didn't give her such satisfaction. It merely moved off with a strop and disappeared into the shrubbery.

Lamia would sleep in the tree that night.

V. Facing Fear

It took weeks to assemble, but the shelter Lamia constructed out of branches, barks and rocks served well enough to keep the cold out. She started a small fire in the centre of what she supposed was her home now: a mix-match of odd rocks and the bindings of misshapen wood. She laced the branches overhead and the thick leaves served as a roof against rain. But it would not serve against the harpy who materialised along with the night.

She woke at the crack of dawn every morning since her first encounter and sought to put as much distance between herself and the monster. But sooner or later, it always found her, and by now, she was tired of running. She'd fashioned a spear out of a slender bit of wood and spent the past few days sharpening the point in the hopes of jamming it right through its heart. But she'd seen the hide of the creature up close more than enough times now and she knew it had thick, callus, armour-like flesh. It would take more than a thrust from her weakened body to draw even a drop of a blood, let alone kill it.

She held her hands up against the fire and felt the warmth consume her. Fire kept the creature at bay for some reason. Each time it came at her it would stop short of the flames, eyeing them with reverence before seeking to put them out. Lamia used fire more than once against the creature, assuming it wasn't raining. Most recently, she held a flame-lit torch up to its maw which made it scamper back, but it had gotten around her and managed to give her a nasty scar for her efforts. Lamia touched the wound across her chest and winced.

The night came in the blink of an eye and the woodlands were flooded by the dark. Lamia's small fire quivered but remained burning. She sat cross legged with her back to the strongest of the makeshift walls and laid the wooden spear in her lap, waiting for the harpy to come. She closed her eyes and thought only of the darkness, for it was the darkness that now came to bring her peace. She no longer pined for Zeus, nor her family, nor her people. Even the faces of her children slowly seeped from her memory, now just vague visions that belonged to someone else. Indeed, she still felt a pang of distress and she could still feel their blood on her fingers, but the night kept her mind busy and the creature kept her on her toes.

It ambled its way into her sights, out from the shrubbery and into the open space before her. It moved rather delicately at times, trotting forward on its talons with a slow nod of its vulgar, human face. Sometimes it looked controlled, perhaps even arrogant in its approach. But very soon it would descend into a mad beast hell-bent on devouring her and anything that stood before it.

It stopped short of its advance once it noticed the fire which evoked the first signs of its rage. It foamed at the mouth and dark quake lines began to etch their way onto its face. Before long, it was screaming at the fire, pointing and thrusting its wings at it as if it had no place in the dark. But like always, it turned its attention upon her and that gave birth to the rest of its anger.

The creature exploded towards her, hovering a few inches off the ground as it screeched. Lamia drew forth the spear, still unsure how to hold the damn thing. She decided to grip it with both hands, took what she hoped was a formidable enough stance and held her ground. She couldn't stop herself from shaking as she allowed herself to glance at the trap. One thin line of wire awaited the creature as it swooped towards her. Lamia held her breath.

The worst thing would be for the creature to fly over it. Then there was nothing but the fire that could save her and even that was dwindling. The harpy wouldn't cower from a mere cluster of flames, no. It would stamp them out before doing the same to her. She gripped the spear tight—as tight as she had once gripped Zeus' box which now sat in the dirt, nearly forgotten. She kept her sights on the wire. The creature came flapping towards it and was too enraged to consider her ploy. It sailed over the wire safely and Lamia's heart sunk.

But its talons were not so lucky.

The creature went down in a mess of its own wings, an unshapely black shape crashing on the ground. Lamia wasted no time rushing it. It thrashed on the ground even more crazed now that it was unsettled, and that caused Lamia to hesitate a moment, for where was she meant to stab? In the end, she chose randomly, driving the spear down into the harpy's ribs. The creature roared at her, splotches of green blood coming away with the wood and melting it with a resounding hiss. Smoke billowed from the spear and it didn't take Lamia long to realise it was now void of use. She plunged what was left of it into the creature's sternum, but it smacked her with its elongated wing and sent her flying against one of her walls.

The flames weltered, only mere embers remained. Lamia didn't have time to assess the damage her body sustained. She heard a ringing in her ears and the world was tilting as far as she could see, but she had to get to her feet. She used the wall to help her balance and grabbed a handful of rocks, lobbing them at the creature who too struggled to regain its balance.

'Come and kill me then!' she roared at it and realised she hadn't spoken a single word since her banishment. Her voice sounded different, even to her. The tone and pitch and everything else in between was hardened, husky, and nothing like the sweet silk she had once known.

The creature was holding its side, green pus leaked from its wound. It made a strange sort of pained grunt but then began licking its lips as if it tasted something nice and wanted more. It made a brief glance at the fire before turning back to her. Lamia was sure it was smiling. It was one of the first times she truly got to gaze upon its ghastly face. Its eyes were no longer green, but sunken in and void of any colour. Its maw was lined with fangs, dripping with both saliva and blood. Lamia clenched her own fists, and for the first time, despite her jittery bones, she stepped before the fire.

The creature merely smirked before limping its way back into the shrubbery. She wouldn't see it again for nearly two decades.

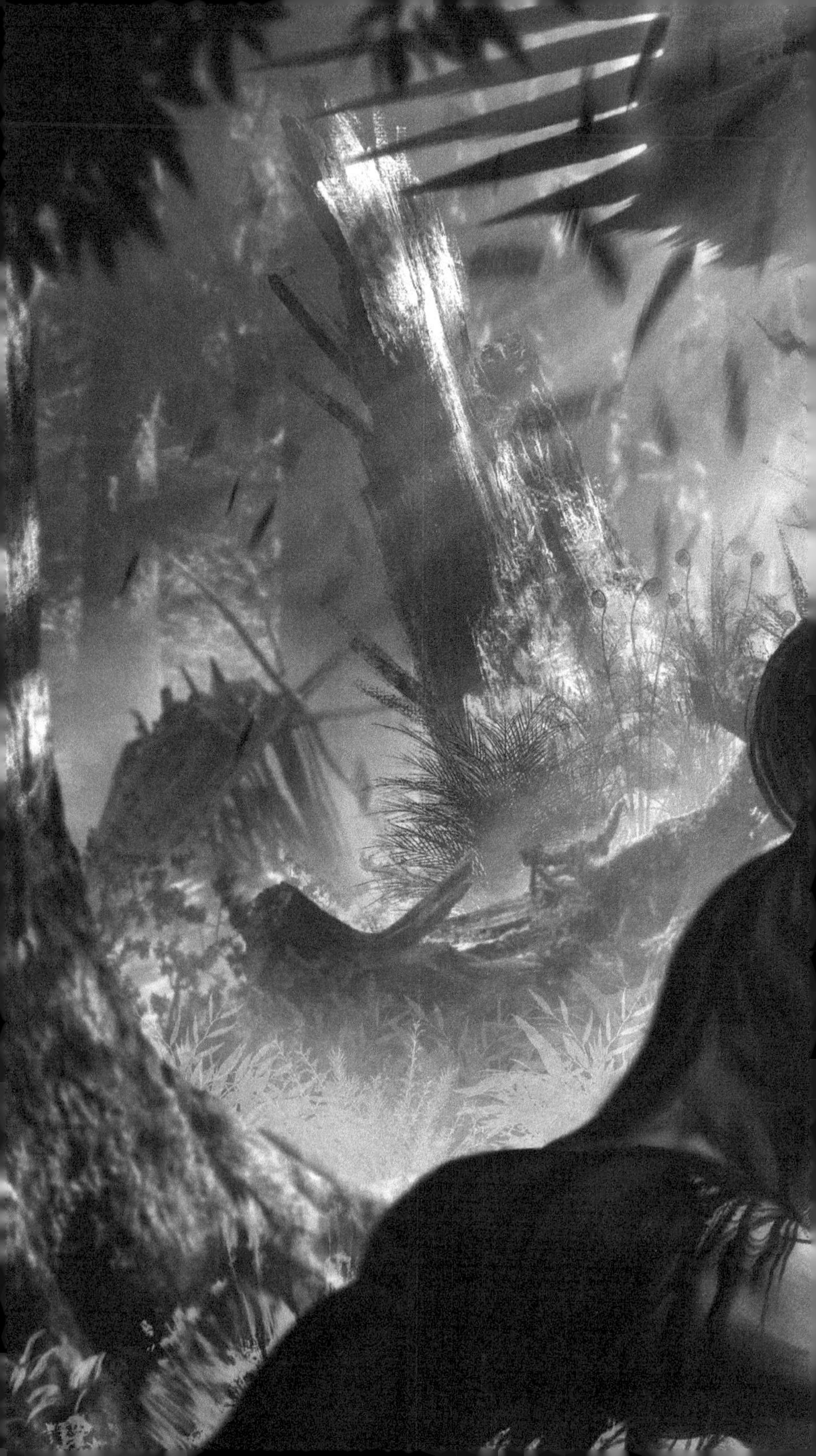

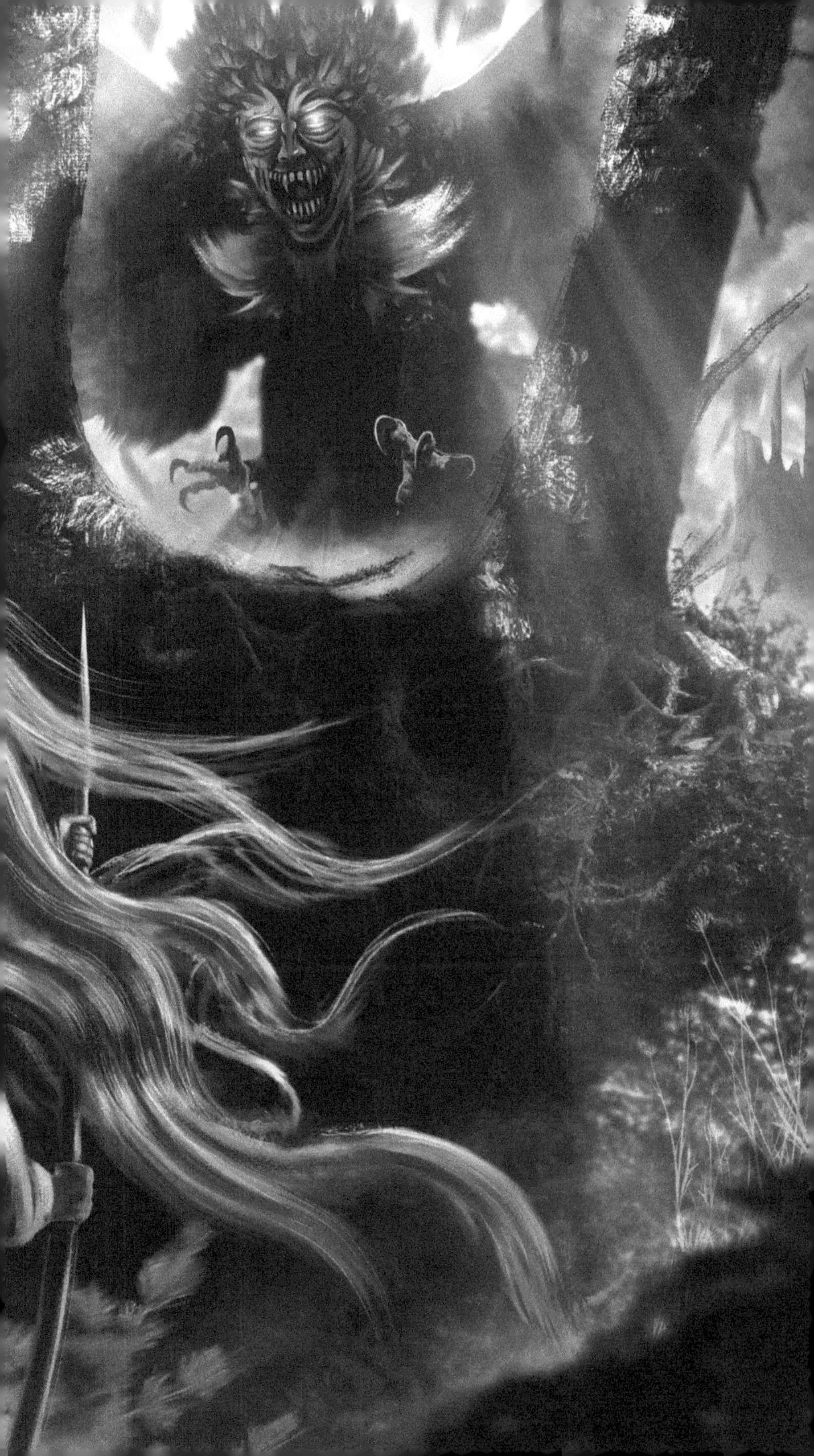

VI. The Survivor

Lamia gutted the fish with her bare hands, scooped out its innards and set it over the fire. It might've looked like a meagre meal, but it had been months since she ate anything that wasn't a plant or an insect. The fish was still wet, but the flames saw the searing of its flesh and before long it was browning, the smell of it bringing her back to the kitchens in her palace. At least, she was sure she had a palace...or maybe it was someone else who had a palace? She remembered being someone far greater than the shell she since became, but she couldn't remember who that might've been. Still, there was something anew born unto her, a lone survivor in the woods. *Her* woods.

Indeed, the other wild beasts here feared her. She would hunt them sometimes, skipping through the trees like an ape before descending upon them with her teeth. She'd eat them while they still clung to life, too hungry to start a fire and roast the flesh. As soon as night fell, they would cower from her and seek refuge in whatever crevice they could find. But Lamia knew every inch of these woods, and they could no more hide from her than they could beg for their lives.

The bloodlust that consumed her was not present tonight though. Tonight, she wanted nothing more than to merely enjoy the meal before her and perhaps spend the night sleeping as opposed to watching. Twenty years might have passed, but she still remembered the harpy that came for her upon her arrival. She had gone looking for it in fact, but never once did it turn up.

Either it was gored by another creature, or it too was hiding from her now that she ruled the woods. Something in her gut told her otherwise though. Something was different in the air tonight. There was an insidious throbbing throughout the atmosphere that she hadn't felt before, and the scar at her front began to burn.

She got to her feet and made her way into the same open space where she last wounded the creature, only to find it waiting for her. At first she felt nothing, but then there was a tremor in her heart and she remembered feeling the adrenaline that this monster sewed inside of her.

She killed creatures twice its size, but this one felt personal. Perhaps it was the scar that it had inflicted upon her, wounding her flesh so that no man would ever look upon her again, not that such a notion was of want to her now. Maybe it was the fear it had once instilled in her that made her want its blood all the more. She was glad, for now she could save the fish for a snack instead.

Lamia grabbed the two wooden spikes she made and marched her way from the fire and into the creature's path. A crimson glow surrounded them, and for the first time, Lamia could see the creature for what it was—a demonic spectre with flesh as black as ink. It twisted its body to show her the wound she gave it all those years ago, and while it paled in comparison to the one it gave her, it still looked nasty. Lamia took the wooden spike and shed the fabric on her body until she stood stark naked before the creature. Its eyes immediately focused on the sickly scar that trailed its way down her chest, across her bosom and down her stomach.

She didn't feel the cold anymore as she kicked the shreds of fabric away from her feet. She was more animal than human now anyway. What use would modesty be to her now? She was the woods now—or at least an integral part of it. It was her domain, just like she once ruled over the domain of somewhere else, some many moons ago. But this was different. Here, she needed no subjects, no rules, no policy, no decorum. All she needed was blood and there was plenty to go around.

The creature stormed towards her and Lamia saw a moment of confliction in its face as she in turn stormed towards it. It wasn't expecting such a bold move. Perhaps it had waited until she was old so it could catch her all the more easily, but it hadn't counted on her becoming stronger. The harpy made an uncertain lunge for her, but Lamia drove her foot into its knee and sent it off balance. It landed on its side and Lamia mounted it, readying to drive the wooden spike through its head. But the creature screamed and smacked her with the back of its wing, taking her off her feet.

She rolled with the fall, ignoring the pain as she got to her feet. The creature self-righted too, though it stopped to regard her once more as if it was contemplating whether it had the right person or not. Lamia grinned and rushed it again, this time driving her shoulder into its gut. It went down to the ground with her, its wings flailing and clawing at her. She elbowed it in its jaw and brought one of the spikes down to its head. But again, the creature was faster and managed to use its talons to shove her off.

Lamia fell backwards, but rolled to get to her feet. By the time she did however, the creature pounced and got its talon around her neck. It began to rain and that made Lamia regret shedding that bit of fabric, but there was no time to lament. The creature lowered its head against hers and she could smell its warm, rancid breath. She stabbed it in its sides, feeling the spikes enter its flesh as hot liquid poured out of the holes. The creature whined, but it squeezed her neck tighter.

Streaks of blue lightning lit up the clouds; there was a rumble through the air as if the sky burped. The creature screeched at the sound, its eyes widening as her breaths became harder and harder to take. Still, Lamia drove the spikes into the creature until its blood melted the wood much as it did the spear she once used. Before long, she was only pummelling the creature with her fists, each strike weaker than the last.

Again the lightning flashed, but this time it lit up the entire wood long enough so that the creature relinquished its hold on her. Thunder roared through the sky and Lamia took that moment to drive her knee into the creature's back before wrenching it to the side. She struck the creature with her fists, using them like hammers as she battered its skull. The creature cried out, but it didn't take long for it to lift her up off her feet and fling her into the dirt once more.

Lamia didn't get to her feet as quickly as she would've liked. It was a good thing the creature was still shaking off her blows, because she struggled to catch her breath. Her throat was on fire from where it nearly crushed her neck with its hands. She sucked in as much air as she could, but every breath hurt and had her choking. She tried to stand, but she slipped in the muck, now slippery from the rain, and found herself on her face again. She rolled onto her back, reaching for her spikes only to remember that they were stuck in the creature's side or otherwise melted. Her hand found purchase on something else: a tattered box that she once cherished.

The creature drew Lamia's attention away from the box as it made it to its feet. It had an uneasy stance, like it was painful just to maintain an upright position. It slugged forward with one unsteady claw, dragging the other one along like a useless tail. Its sides were leaking that same green blood, and it looked as if it was melting through its own hardened flesh what with the smoke hissing off of its body. It lifted its long feather and pointed at Lamia and with the snap of its teeth, the muscles in its neck tensed and it was screaming bloody murder at her.

Until a bolt from the sky silenced it.

One quick zap and the creature snapped its jaw shut. It wavered to one side and then to the other before it hit the floor in one unfulfilling thump. Smoke billowed from the gaping wound on its back from where it was struck by the sky. Its leg made one final twitch and then it was devoid of all life, just the way Lamia always intended. But it didn't feel right. She looked down at her hands and felt the bloodlust burn stronger, for the creature was not slain by her own hand.

She began scratching at her own palms in frustration. The killing of that very creature would've brought her more relief than death itself. But no, it had been robbed from her just like her previous life, her throne, her children and everything in between. She tugged at her hair, or at least what was left of it, and screamed at the creature in some blind hope that it would get up and she could finish it her way. But it was done.

'Lamia?' A deep voice came from behind and she spun around, grabbing the nearest rock with the intention of beating whoever it was to death. The bloodlust would need to be sated by something, after all.

She was about to lunge at the new entity but found herself stopping short. For some reason, she remembered him, and his mere presence sent a chill down her spine. Though she couldn't say it was a bad chill. Her body began to tingle in his wake, her heart beat faster and faster and with it brought the strangest feeling of elation.

'Lamia,' he said and this time took a step towards her. 'I've been looking for you.'

'Z-Zeus?' She tried his name on her lips and knew that it fit him.

Zeus smiled and she had to all but stop herself from falling before him, a slave to his charms once more.

'What has become of you?' his smile vanished from his perfect mouth and in its stead was a horrible sort of disgusted look.

'What...what do you mean?' she stammered and looked down at her scar. Was this what he meant? She knew she had to have been older and she couldn't have had the flawless look he once knew, but surely a scar would not have him looking so repulsed. He loved her, had he not?

'Have you not seen for yourself?' he pointed at the box.

The box was tattered. It all but fell apart in her hands as she lifted the lid and finally gazed upon what lay inside. She remembered thinking it might've been otherworldly riches or some trinket belonging to the gods. But what lay inside was neither of those things. She carefully pried it out of the box and held it between her fingers like a child holding a dagger for the first time.

It was a plain brass amulet.

Lamia shrieked. Truly, the amulet was a pretty thing, but it was her reflection that she couldn't pry her eyes from. She saw her face—not the face she remembered, but instead, something odious and dreadful. Gone was her beauty and her youth; what remained was not a gorgeous queen but an unremarkable crone. Her forehead was riddled with dark, splotchy spots and chasm-like wrinkles were sewn into her face. Her eyes were sunken, much like the creature's, but she also had deep bags that looked like clouds filled with dirty rainwater. Her face was gaunt, the skin stretched over the bones in her cheeks making for a constant, unflattering expression. Her lips were dry with bloody scabs and her teeth were all but rotten, some of them even missing. Even her hair had thinned to the point that she could see her scalp amongst the greying.

'Zeus,' she cried out. 'Why didn't you come for me sooner?'

He didn't answer. He took a step back as if he'd seen enough and wanted nothing more than to leave. He looked conflicted for the first time, but he stayed a little longer. Lamia supposed he owed her that much, did he not?

'I had no use for you,' he told her and those words cut her harder than anything in the woods could've done. 'I still don't.'

This is what he does, Hera's words danced around her once more.

'Then why are you here?' she snapped at him. 'Haven't you hurt me enough?'

He spread his hands out before him as if trying to appease her. 'I've come to offer you revenge against those who turned their backs on you.'

'*You* turned your back on me,' she hissed.

'Be that as it may,' he spoke, 'I am not the one who banished you here.'

'What will revenge bring me?' she glanced at her reflection once more. 'It will not bring my people back. It will not bring my children back. It will certainly not bring my youth back.'

'Your people betrayed you. Your children were a tragic casualty. But your youth...I can see to it that you are reborn.'

'How?' she dared to ask, though she wasn't sure she wanted the answer.

A grim smile came upon his lips as he made his way towards her. For a moment, she felt for her wooden spikes, and if she still had them, she'd have probably jammed them into his perfect face despite the thousand lightning bolts that would disintegrate her after. He extended his hand, and just like that, she felt herself drifting towards him. His fingers found her scar and his cool touch sent a warmth into her that she longed for. He trailed his finger down the length of the wound, both eyes fixed on it like he'd never seen such a thing in his life.

Then his finger left her and she felt cold again as he knelt down to the corpse of the creature. He dipped the same finger into the green pool of blood that amassed around it.

'What are you doing?' Lamia went to take a step back, but Zeus grabbed her by the wrist and rubbed the blood between his finger and thumb.

'I can't bring back your people, nor can I bring back your children. But I can at least grant you your beauty. At least for now.'

'How?' she tried to pull back as he brought his now blood-dripping thumb close to her lips.

'Close your eyes,' he told her and dripped the blood down her throat.

She felt nothing at first, staring up blankly at Zeus' face. For just a moment, he looked like he was studying her eyes the way he once did, dreamily falling into them as he had once plunged his lips against hers. But there was no such kiss this time as the corner of his lips began to twitch into a cunning smile.

She lurched away from him. Perhaps her instincts from having lived in the forest for so long were now overactive. Or maybe they were just right. She felt a spasm go through her sternum and the blood from the harpy that slithered down her throat burned like a warm spirit. Before she could cry out, she lost control of her legs and fell. She hit the ground hard, but she rolled with the fall, trying to distance herself from Zeus. Whatever he had done was darkening her sights.

She thrashed on the ground, teeth locked together as she clenched her jaw, tighter and tighter as if it might quench the pain. But it didn't. She let out one resounding scream into the night and that had the owls storming out of the trees, taking to the skies. Lamia wished she could join them, but she was bound to the ground, her legs unresponsive as she tried to kick.

'It's almost done,' Zeus said.

What's almost done?

She grabbed hold of her legs, but where there should've been her skin there was instead scaly flesh. Her heart skipped a beat and she looked down, opening her eyes just wide enough to see the reptilian hide that covered her legs—a thick serpent's body that was rippling and rough to touch.

Her skin was changing colour. The lower half of her stomach becoming a mix of green and brown with strange symmetrical shapes. She thrusted her hands upon her stomach, touching where her thighs used to be in disbelief. It was like touching leather, for it was horribly smooth.

She was breathing hard as she rolled onto her stomach, dragging herself across the soil, clawing at anything as she crawled away from Zeus. But Zeus was merely laughing now, and that same bawdy laughter that had once been music to her ears was now like two fists battering her at either side.

'What have you done to me?' she roared back at him, but all of a sudden he was gone and only his laughter remained as it thundered through the forest.

She scraped her elbows against the rockery, dragging her large, cumbersome snake-body along with her. She tried to get to her feet, but there were no feet to get to. She glanced back, saw the end of the snake's tail that was all black and shining and quickly looked away. It felt as if her legs had been tied together, but the more she reached for them, the more panicked she grew.

A cataract awaited her at the entrance of a rocky alcove just a few yards from the harpy's lifeless body. She couldn't see her reflection clearly, courtesy of the running water, but she could make out her sunken expression just like before, except now there were fangs and venom dripping off her lips. Her eyes were red like fire, her tongue now just a long stem narrow enough to fit through her dagger-like teeth.

'Why, Zeus?' she howled into the air. 'Why this fate?'

His laughter still echoed around her, but she could hear his voice from somewhere deep in the forest. 'You wanted revenge, didn't you? Now you have the power to take it.'

'Not like this,' she roared. Now her voice was dark, sinister, and came with its very own hiss from her tongue. 'Not like this!'

'You're resourceful, dear Lamia,' Zeus snickered, his voice echoing against his own laughter. 'You'll figure out how to make it work for you.'

'Zeus!' she cried out for him one last time. 'Don't leave me like this!'

But then his laughter came to an abrupt end and she was left alone in the darkness with nothing but the rustling of the trees and the trickling of the water.

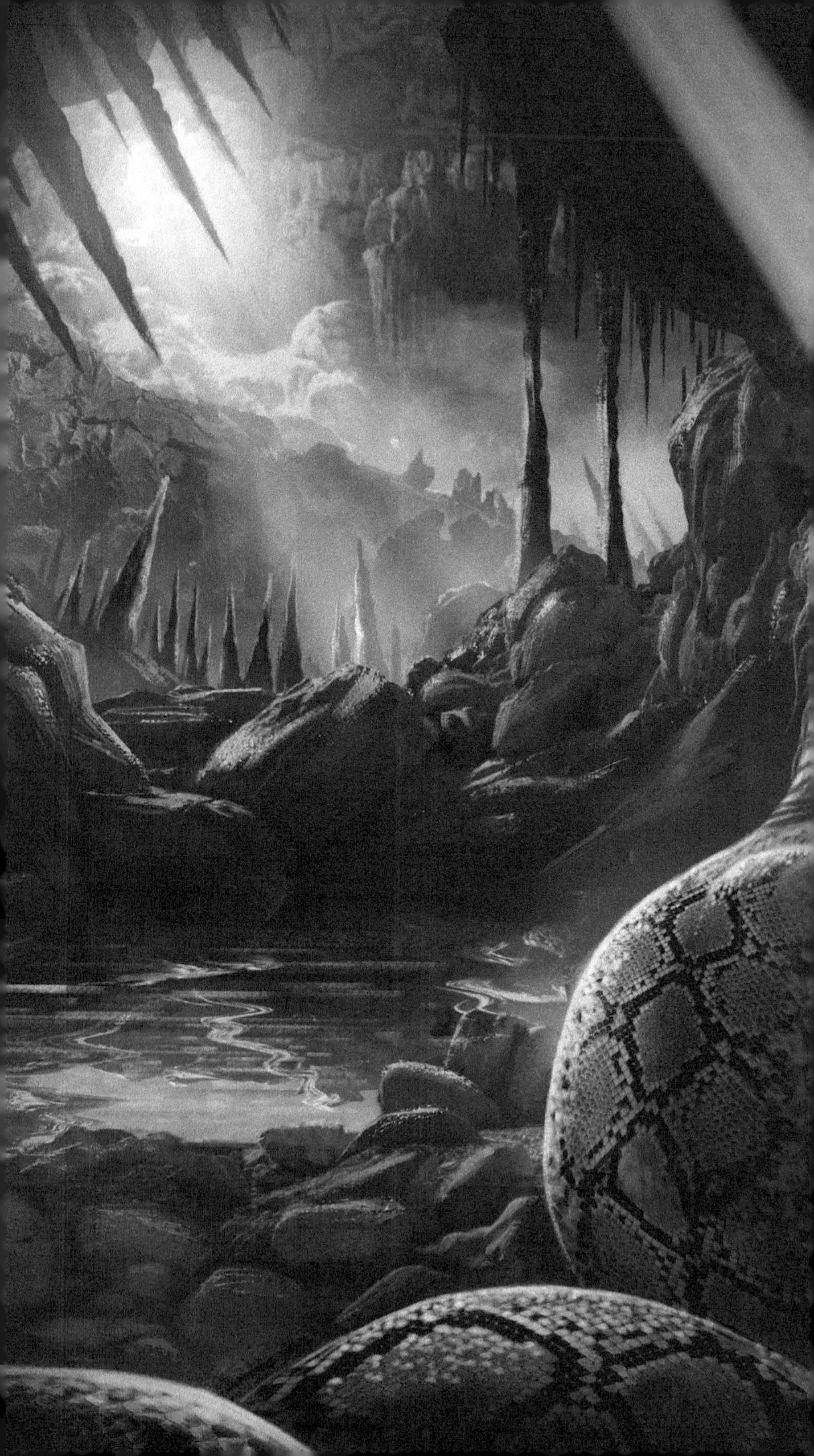

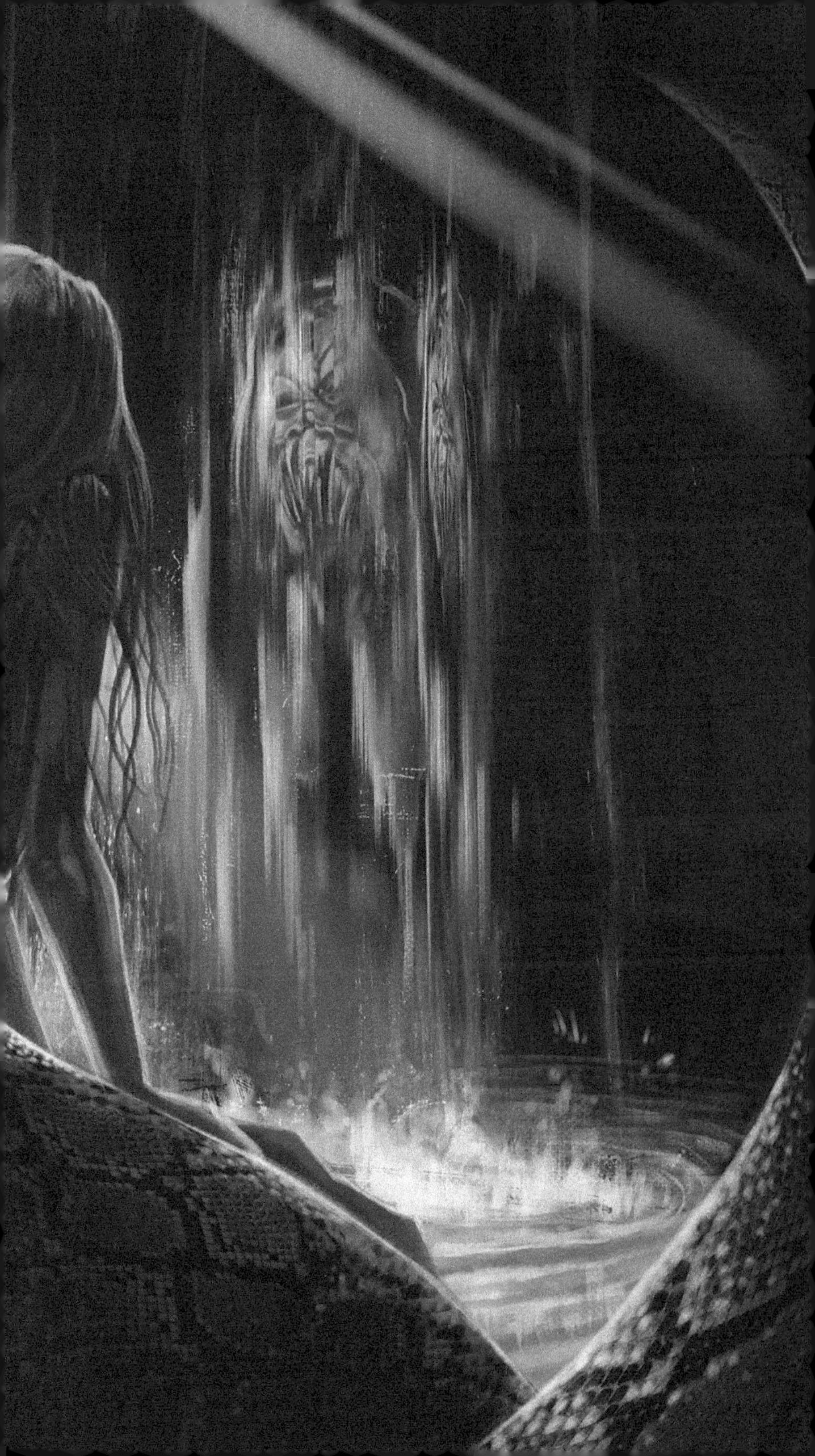

VII. The Woman She Became

The crone drained the chunk of meat of its blood, pouring every bit of the red juice into a bottle. She'd need all she could get, for the creatures of the woods were all but slain, which meant blood was becoming scarcer and scarcer. It was the price she paid not only for her vanity, but for her own mix of potions and elixirs that the folk in town were increasingly more interested in.

The birds were chirping outside in the trees and the crone would've smiled if half of her face wasn't numb from having slept face down on her desk two days prior. At least the birds were happy. For now. She'd poisoned the seeds she'd left out for them, and just like the last time, she would soon hear their lifeless bodies thumping on the roof. She'd drain their blood later, weak as it was.

The concoction was almost complete. She became so adept at making it that she was sure she could do the entire blend in a matter of minutes with one hand tied behind her back. It took a lot of bargaining with the gods, but she obtained what she needed, and before long, she was producing her tonics solely by herself. Business picked up in the last fifty years and she did not go a week without at least one customer stopping by. She knew she would've had more if she lived closer to the city, but out here in the woods suited her just fine. The crone didn't think she could stomach the city. Not after what happened.

She could see a faint reflection of her face in the pink brew as she slowed the stirring of her spoon. She caught a glimpse of her wrinkled chin, a sprout of fine hairs on her upper lip and a gaunt, sunken space under her eyes. Then she began quickly stirring the spoon again, forcing her eyes shut as she tried to fend off the image of what she had become and what she did to get here. But, even with her eyes closed, she could see it like it was yesterday—could feel the blood drip between her fingers.

There came a knock at the door and immediately her eyes snapped open. Her nose twitched and she found herself sniffing at the air as if she could determine who was there by mere scent. She could smell his heart, that much was true, but she could not determine his age. If he was too old, his blood would not satisfy her needs. Old blood was even weaker than the birds'. But if he was young...

She gathered her stinking robe from the stand and slipped into it as nimbly as she could without stumbling over. Her old bones had certainly seen better years, but she could still manoeuvre around the room, at least at the rate of a half-starved cripple. She pulled the hood of her robe over her brittle hair and wiped away the gunk that built in the corner of her eyes. With a shaking hand, she reached out and opened the door.

'Uh...hello?' a young man stood at her door—not the youngest man, mind you, but young enough to be foolish in love. He had that boyish, innocent glow about him like he'd blush at the sight of a bosom. His face was hairless, and though he appeared nervous, he retained energetic eyes that were wet with adventure.

'Can I help you?' she croaked.

The young man gulped and pulled at the collars on his shirt before fidgeting with his cuffs. 'I'm looking for a potion.'

The crone smirked. None of these foolish men were looking for a potion. No, they were looking for *the* potion. The young man began to redden in the face and soon he was taking a step back, his hands jittering by his sides.

'Who sent you?' she demanded.

'There was a man my acquaintance used to know named Ron. He said you were able to make a potion that made women fall in love.'

'Ah, Ron!' The crone tried to picture him, but found she could not. When you were over two hundred years old, faces and names blurred into one messy puddle. 'I trust he and his beloved are happy?'

The young man hesitated a moment, 'Actually, Ron went missing about a year ago. His love was so stricken with grief that she took her own life.'

'How terrible,' the crone bowed her head. 'Love is often the thing that hurts us most, is it not?'

The young man shrugged his shoulders.

'And yet, here you are about to request the same potion to achieve the same goal.' The crone looked him up and down. 'Don't you see that love will burn you? You're young, boy. Perhaps come back to me when you've had some more experience with the trials of life.'

She moved to close the door, but the young man got his foot in the way.

'Please!' he begged. 'You're my only chance. My love is soon to marry another man, but I wish to be with her more than anything. He does not even love her, nor does he treat her with the kindness that she deserves.'

'Such is the way of things,' the crone tried to close the door but he was persistent. 'We all long for the things we cannot have.'

'I will do anything!' He refused to budge and the crone could see the turmoil in his eyes, could hear the desperation in his voice and knew right there that she had another customer.

'Anything, you say?' she allowed the door to slowly swing open.

The young man nodded fervently. 'Anything!'

She held out her bony hand and gestured for him to enter her small hut. If he had his reservations, he didn't show them openly. In fact, he seemed almost all too willing to wander into the warmth that her old sanctum provided. Then again, they were all eager, were they not? Every customer she ever had would scuttle into her shop as if she was offering shelter from a firestorm.

'You must've travelled far,' she made her way around her table, 'I don't see a horse with you.'

'I walked,' he said with half a smile.

'All this way?' the crone was surprised.

'As I said, I would do anything.'

'So it seems,' she gave him a wavering look before reaching for one of the empty bottles on the desk.

'Your potions can really make her fall in love with me?' the young man asked, hopeful. His eyes lingered on the mixing bowl.

'Yes,' the crone replied. 'Which is why you should consider whether this woman is truly worth your time. Once taken, the spell cannot be reversed.'

'Why would I want to reverse it?' the young man laughed.

The crone smirked, 'You'd be surprised.'

The young man withdrew a slight at that, but it didn't stop him from speaking. 'They say that you can create all kinds of potions.'

The crone didn't like hearing about *them*. They'd spun tales about her for the past two hundred years, but never did she allow herself to succumb to their hurtful words. They'd hurt her enough with their actions. Still, sometimes she grew intrigued to learn about what version of the ghastly crone in the woods they were tooting now.

'Is that all they say?'

The young man's knees were rocking and he went back to fiddling at the buttons on his cuffs. He couldn't look at her when he spoke, but he managed to utter, 'They say you're a sorceress.'

'A sorceress?' The crone snorted. That was a sight better than what they said in the past.

'Yes, they say you can make a man turn invisible and that you can make him fly if you give him the right potion.'

The crone smiled in agreement, even though none of those things were true. It would not do to have the young man lose faith, not now at this critical point. She had him right where she wanted him. It was always so simple when it came to the youth—so eager to fall in love. This foolish boy walked gods knew how many miles and was here in the middle of the wild woods, conversing with a questionable looking crone about potions. It all sounded ridiculous even to her, and yet, the man before her overlooked it all.

'All of my potions are grand,' she said with a modest tone as she began pouring the mixture from the bowl into a bottle. 'Just a few sips of this and the woman you seek will be yours forever.'

'Is that all that must be done?' the young man asked as he leaned over the table, closer to her work.

The crone raised an eyebrow up at him, 'It's as simple as that.'

'You have my eternal thanks,' the young man bowed his head. 'How can I repay you?'

'I'll tell you what—how about I give you this one potion for free?' the crone said.

'For free?' the young man frowned. 'Why would you do that?'

'Why, I can see that you are clearly in love with this woman who does not love you in return. It pains me that it is always the ones we want the most who end up wanting us the least. So, I seek to remedy that pain you feel.'

'I...I have money,' the young man was about to turn out his pockets.

'I refuse your money!' the crone slammed a stopper into the bottle and tossed it at the young man.

He almost failed to catch it, but once he had it in his grasp, he wasn't letting go.

'All I have to do is get her to drink this?' he asked.

'Correct.'

'What's in it?' he asked.

'Do you really think I would so easily speak of my secrets?' the crone snorted. 'Now, be gone with you.'

The young man stood in the doorway with a grin on his face. 'Thank you so much! But there must be some way I can show you my gratitude.'

'Tell your friends about my business,' she bid him farewell. 'I get awfully lonely.'

'I promise I shall,' he bowed his head.

'And don't forget to return that bottle,' she demanded. 'Your failure to do so will taint the spell.'

'It will?' the young man considered the ordinary bottle in his hands.

'Yes,' she lied. It was the only way she could get him to come back.

'Then I will see you in a few evenings time,' he nodded and hurried his way back into the woods.

VIII. The Price of Youth

The crone grew weary of waiting for him. Several nights would pass where she sat in her creaking chair, gently rocking by the open window with nothing but the yellow moon for company. The wind whistled as it sauntered through the open window, and the crone pulled her cowl around her neck a little tighter. As she did, she caught a glimpse of a velvet box living amongst vials, bottles, bowls and spoons that she had yet to wash. It had been a while since she last laid eyes upon it. The sight of it made her old heart clench, and where it once somersaulted with excitement, it now merely twitched like a toad being prod with a stick.

She stood up from her chair in a huff and stormed away from the box. She stopped short of one of the bottles on a shelf, and for just a moment, considered it. The bottle was brown, scratched and incredibly unremarkable in comparison to the more kingly, patterned bottles that she collected from the gods. This one she labelled Youth, but the word itself seemed strangely foreign when she really thought about it. She remembered trying the potion for the first time many moons ago—remembered emptying every drop of it onto her tongue—and thought nothing of it until she touched her face.

What was once callous, wrinkling skin was now smooth and soft like it had been in the days since passed. The pains in her joints were banished, leaving her free to move and dance just like she was known to do before... before the incident. She was beautiful again the way she once was. But it didn't last long.

She pulled out the stopper of the bottle and breathed in deep the aromatic essence of the potion. It put a smile on her face and she couldn't remember the last time she had generally smiled. But it wouldn't be long before her smile wavered and she found herself submitting a pained sob. It smelled like her daughter.

She swung her head around at the velvet box and stared at it with anguish. She didn't know why she still kept the damned thing, because all it represented was pain in its most hurtful form. She would've thrown it out, but then a part of her believed she deserved this. She deserved to suffer, perhaps more than anyone. Even now, with the gods fading into the background of her reality, she still bore their curse.

She took a long swig from the bottle. She couldn't say why. Perhaps she became so skilled at torturing herself that now it was second nature. It trickled down her throat, warm and sharp like whisky, but sweet too as it brought that old familiar feeling of respite. She didn't feel it immediately, but soon she felt the weight of her body lightening, felt her bosom regain its previous plumpness and felt the stiffness in her legs evaporate second by second. She drew her tongue along her teeth, surprised to find that they had all returned and without the shield of rot too. The podgy bulge on her stomach began to shrink, and as she drew her fingers over her face, she could no longer feel the chasm-like wrinkles.

There came a sharp knocking at the door before she could glance at her newly invigorated self. It was too late for a customer now, surely? She reached for the wooden spike under the table but knew that if there was a crone hunter out there, he wouldn't knock. They never knocked.

'Who's there?' she barked, but her voice sounded different now, all serene and unburdened by phlegm.

'I'm here to return the bottle,' a voice replied. 'I was here a few days ago.'

The crone raised an eyebrow. She was sure he wasn't coming back, but he wouldn't be the first to return to her days later with the empty bottle. If they had any sense they'd take her potions and never come back. But she would have no fun that way. She wanted them to feel love, wanted their lovers to feel it too. But more importantly she wanted them to feel the absence of it and the void in between.

She pulled the door open and saw him standing there in the dark looking most pleased indeed. He held his jaw tight, suppressing a sickening smile no doubt. His cheeks were full of colour, and where he was subdued and desperate a few days prior, he was now alive with passion and confidence. He may as well have been a different man at this point, all debonair and certain like the sun could plummet and he would catch it.

'I trust the potion worked,' she said with her cowl still tight around her face.

'It did!' he rejoiced and handed the bottle out for her to take. 'I slipped the potion into her tea and by the evening she left her husband to be and professed her love for me.'

'I didn't doubt it would work,' she smiled from within her cowl. 'Shall I be expecting your friends before long?'

'You have my word,' the young man inclined his head. 'I told my closest friends who will definitely pay you a visit soon. They were reluctant at first because...well, because of the stories but—'

'The stories that I am a sorceress?' the crone asked.

The young man stopped to scratch his neck and it was the first sign of uncertainty he'd shown since his arrival. 'Yes, that. I also learned that they have a name for you, actually.'

'What might that be?'

The young man frowned, 'Your voice sounds different than I remember.'

'What do they call me?' the crone ignored him.

'Lamia,' he cleared his throat. 'Supposedly, the story goes that she was once a beautiful queen but she went mad and killed her children. The legend states that she fled to this very forest to prey on the vulnerable, but they're just tales to scare children.'

'Yes,' the crone licked her lips. 'People like to talk, don't they?'

'Yes,' the young man agreed. 'I should be going now.'

'Won't you have a spot of tea with me?' she reached out and grabbed his arm. 'I get awfully lonely in the night.'

The young man hesitated and glanced back the way he came through the trees. He didn't say anything at first as he kept glancing back down the way, probably impatient to get back to his lover now that he had her all to himself.

'I'd love to,' he pulled his arm away. 'But it's late and I have quite the journey. Please, allow me to reimburse you for your labour. I have money.'

'Are you sure I can't tempt you?' she purred and began to loosen her cowl.

'Yes, I must be going...' he trailed off as she grabbed a fistful of her dirty robe and began to lift it up her leg, revealing her spotless thigh.

'What are you doing?' he stammered, though he couldn't reposition his gaze as he took in her bare legs. She sheared the robe and let it slip off her shoulders as it landed softly around her feet. She supposed he was expecting the old hag he'd seen before, but the look of desire on his face and the bulge in his pants said he was pleasantly surprised to find her as she was.

She snatched the cowl off her head and threw it to the wind. Her dark hair cascaded down her back and she shook her head from left to right, for it had been so long since she was blessed with the feeling of hair like this. The young man was hypnotised at the sight of her, and just like her worshippers hundreds of years ago, he could do nothing except breathe in every inch of her.

'Are you coming in?' she slipped her hand around his arm and didn't need to do much more persuading beyond that.

It was clear by the way he ravaged her neck that he no longer saw the old, wretched woman she had become. No, he saw the beautiful woman she once was with enticing eyes, slender arms, soft skin, long legs and sweet lips. He lifted her without much hassle at all, not unlike how Zeus lifted her and threw her down onto his numerous mattresses made of exotic animal skins. She moved to grab him, but he was faster, pushing her down and plunging his mouth over her breasts. She gave a breathy moan and he grunted in response, long forgetting about the woman he had left behind in the city. But that was no surprise. The crone knew she had the beauty to rival the goddesses and that no mortal man could resist her. Not even Zeus kept away, after all.

He pulled her closer, spreading her legs and wasting no time in having his way with her. Zeus was always impatient like that too, but she submitted all the same. He slipped himself in, pinning her arms above her head as he began to thrust into her, kissing her neck as he did. She got her fingers in his hair, bit down hard on his shoulder before surrendering another moan. She hoped Zeus was watching, hoped he watched all the other men she took to spite him for abandoning her. This was her revenge against him—the thought of him going insane at the notion that a mere mortal man was devouring her instead of him. But that thought didn't last long, because deep down she knew that Zeus didn't care. He'd probably forgotten her name by now.

She grabbed the young man's hair and wrenched him to the side. He went over with a grunt, and though he gave some resistance, he soon deferred to her as she mounted him and began to sink herself onto him. He had the face of Zeus now, much like her victims always did. She would try hard in the beginning to visualise his handsome, beautiful features on these lesser boys—her prey—but now it was automatic. Her eyes saw Zeus beneath her in all his chiselled glory, glistening with sweat, that lustful hunger in his eyes. She saw his face begin to contort like she remembered and felt his breath begin to quicken as she pinned his chest.

He groaned, teeth clenched as he grabbed her tightly by the hips. His eyes rolled back, his entire body beginning to convulse as he lost control of himself, spilling his seed into her the way he'd done a dozen times before. She wondered then if Hera was watching as she reached for the knife. She wondered which she'd be more outraged by: the seduction of her husband or his demise. Zeus flopped beneath her like a fish yanked from the bowl and thrown on the floor. His head shook from left to right, his legs kicking as she trailed her fingers against his sweating chest. He let out one final puff of air before going still, one arm hung lifeless off of the bed.

She plunged the spike into him.

Ironically enough, it brought him to life. He screamed and it was strange, because she never heard Zeus scream before. He tried to shove her off, but she was quick enough to get the spike in and out of him a few more times. Blood was splattering everywhere, just like it did when she murdered her own children. Just like then, she didn't stop stabbing him as blade met flesh, the sound of skin and sinew being torn and squelched, filling the room to accompany her own maddened growls. Zeus' head flopped back against the pillow, his eyes wide with horror.

She slipped off of him and the fiery thirst for blood that took her dropped her just as suddenly. She tried to gain her balance, but she ended up hitting the floor, drenched in his blood. She pushed herself up, but her hands slipped in the red pool beneath her and she went crashing into it. She spat blood as she rolled onto her back and found his lifeless hand dangling in her face.

She hissed at it and smacked it away, only to notice the mottled patches return to her skin. The sickly colour was back on her arms and the sagging of her flesh was as evident as it ever was. The pain in her joints returned with a vengeance and she soon began to feel as old as the forest itself. She rolled onto her side, face down in the young man's blood, and begun to suck it up with her lips. No, it was hardly dignified but her inner core called for it, longed for it, and so she sipped, if only to regain her strength. She came up for air a moment later, gasping and wiping her mouth as the pain began to subside.

She glanced over at the young man's corpse once she got to her feet and watched a moment as his blood leaked off of the bed and trickled onto the floor. Perhaps the worst part of these exchanges was the disposal of their bodies. But she had no time to waste. His friends could arrive at any moment with the hopes of obtaining the same love potion and she'd want to be good and ready to take their lives too.

'Your love will miss you,' she snickered as she began to restack the bottles she knocked over. 'She will long for you, pine for you and wonder why you never came back for her. The same way my Zeus never came back for me.'

She grabbed what she thought was the last bottle only to find it was the velvet box that Zeus had given her. She remembered how excited she was, skipping her way back from Olympus, eager to know what lay inside. Now she despised it, for she knew the brass amulet inside could only show her how ugly she had become.

She clutched the box tight—as tight as she did when she thought Hera might've pried it from her hands. Then she screamed and threw the box across the room with such a force that it burst open. She swooped down low to retrieve the brass amulet and soon found herself laughing in hysterics as she held it before her face. Her teeth were blackened again, every inch of her face stained and creased like chewed gum. Her eyes were milky red and her hair was once more a tussle of thin strands all brittle like the branches of a tree. She set it down on the table and sunk to her knees in a fit of tears.

IX. Lamia's Revenge

Yon was crying.

Kroy couldn't really blame the poor lad, though. His younger brother had hurt his knee pretty badly during the fall and while he was able to walk on it, the massive gash made it hard to do so.

'I know it hurts but the more you cry, the more chance the creatures will hear us and come after us,' Kroy teased. He knew how scared Yon had gotten when their father told them the story of a monster in the woods that sought the blood of children.

'It's not funny, Kroy!' Yon snivelled. 'Father wouldn't lie about those sort of things.'

'It's just a stupid story to get children scared,' Kroy gave his brother a squeeze at the shoulder as he guided him along. Though, the way his father told it was rather chilling, like he'd seen the creature himself.

'We shouldn't have gone off by ourselves,' Yon shook his head. 'Now we're lost and father is probably worried.'

'There's nothing to worry about,' Kroy smirked. 'So we're lost. We'll find our way. Just try not to bleed anymore, eh? Lamia might come for you!'

'Shut up, Kroy!'

Kroy laughed. But his laughter wouldn't last very long. Night fell upon them sooner than they expected and still they were traversing through the woodlands with the howling of wolves in the distance.

'It's your fault,' Kroy cursed. 'You're bleeding all over the place. The wolves probably smelt it a mile away.'

'This is your fault!' Yon snapped back. 'Father told us to stay put but you dragged me along.'

'Yes, but I didn't tell you to fall over and stab your knee, did I?' Kroy argued.

'Sometimes I really h—'

'Look!' Kroy rejoiced. 'We're saved.'

Ahead was a hut sitting by its lonesome, shrouded by creeper. Smoke billowed from the chimney on the roof, and as far as Kroy could see, an orange light glowed from the window.

'I don't know about this,' Yon wiped his nose, 'it looks spooky.'

'Well, we have to find somewhere to stay,' Kroy said. 'Unless you want to be out here when the wolves find us.'

Yon sighed and then nodded.

Kroy started slowing down the closer he got to the hut. Sure, he'd given Yon the big talk about not being scared, but something about the building made him hesitate. It might've been the weeds that defecated the front of the house like scratches on a face, or maybe the fact that there was someone actually living out here. Who in their right mind would live here?

'Maybe you're right,' Kroy gulped. 'Maybe we should...'

The door creaked open and there in the doorway stood a tall figure with a long robe draped around it. Yon grabbed hold of his brother and Kroy wasn't ashamed to grab his brother back—perhaps one last embrace before they were hacked to death. But if the figure meant to kill them, it showed no signs of it. In fact, as it moved towards them, Kroy couldn't say he'd seen a more beautiful woman.

'Boys?' the woman marched her way towards them. 'What are you doing out here? It's dangerous!'

Kroy couldn't find his tongue straight away. He'd seen pretty women before, but this woman was...well, he couldn't quite find the words for her. She looked stern with her hands fixed upon her hips, but Kroy could tell there was concern in her kind eyes.

'We got separated from our father,' Kroy finally said. 'I'm Kroy and this is my brother Yon.'

'Hi,' Yon squeaked.

'That's a nasty cut,' the woman shook her head at Yon's knee before the wolves called again, and she looked up startled. 'Quickly, get inside!'

The boys didn't argue and hurried in to the warmth of the woman's hut. She shut the door behind them and lingered there a moment as she listened for the wolves.

'They won't bother us here,' she turned around. 'Now let me see to that bleeding, shall I?'

Yon slipped into a chair and the woman went about assessing the damage. She wiped away the blood which trickled down his leg and then set to washing the knee with a rag and some hot water.

'It stings,' Yon flinched.

'Yes, but you're brave aren't you?' the woman smiled at him and Yon made a giggle like he was falling in love with her just as much as Kroy was.

Kroy wasn't going to be upstaged by his younger brother though.

'I was getting ready to fight the wolves,' he said and rolled up his sleeves.

The woman laughed, 'I'm sure you were. You look very strong, Kroy.'

'I am,' he nodded.

She finished patching up Yon's leg with a bandage and then gave his hair a bit of a ruffle, making him giggle even more.

'Your father must be awfully worried about you two,' she gave them both a stern look. 'If it wasn't dangerous out in the dark, I'd help you look for him now.'

'You won't make us go out there again, will you?' Yon asked.

The woman smiled, 'Of course not, children. You'll have to stay here until morning. But maybe you boys ought to think about listening to what your father tells you to do.'

Kroy was relieved to hear that he could stay. Not only because he got to stare at her a bit longer, but also because he didn't know if he could keep his pretense of bravery up in front of Yon. Still, he'd be lying if he said he wasn't worried about his father. Knowing how foolhardy he was, he might've even gone out looking for them in the dark.

'Don't worry,' the woman pinched his cheek. 'I'm sure everything will be okay.'

Kroy felt at ease because of that and the woman's radiant glow made him feel safe as he sunk in the seat next to Yon.

'You boys must be hungry. I can cook up something, if you wish?'

Both Kroy and Yon's stomachs rumbled at the mere thought of food and the woman chuckled in response. 'I guess I'll set the table for three today then.'

The leg of lamb she made was a succulent thing and each bite Kroy took made his tongue dance with excitement. Even Yon cleaned his plate and he never cleaned his plate, even when they had pudding. He sat back in his chair with his hands over his stomach and could honestly say that he could not eat another bite. It was perhaps the best meal he'd ever eaten in his life. What was it one of his father's friends told him? Find a beautiful woman who can cook and pinch yourself, because you're probably dreaming.

So Kroy did pinch himself, but he didn't wake up.

'What are you doing there?' she asked him.

'Uh...' Kroy stammered. 'Nothing.'

'You never told us your name,' Yon said and Kroy could've kicked himself. How could he not have asked her name by now?'

'It's...' the woman hesitated, like she'd forgotten. 'It's Sylvia.'

Kroy yawned. That meal certainly made him drowsy all of a sudden. He stretched his hands above his head and sank lower into his seat.

'Why do you live all the way out here?' Yon asked and Kroy balled a fist. Why was his brother so naturally gifted at saying the right things? Kroy would have to work on that.

'I just...choose to live away from the hustle and bustle of the city,' she explained and took a sip from her water.

Kroy went to do the same but realised he'd already finished his glass. He would've gotten up to refill his glass, but he felt rather comfortable in his chair. For a moment, he felt his eyelids begin to droop.

'Don't you get lonely?' Yon asked.

'I have visitors,' Sylvia winked and Kroy noticed her hands move underneath the table.

'What about a husband?' Kroy stammered, he realised his speech was slurred and he was swaying from left to right all of a sudden.

'Kroy?' Yon sounded concerned. 'Kroy, are you okay?'

Kroy stumbled out of his chair and hit the ground hard. No, he wasn't okay. His eyes were wrestling against him and while he tried to stand, he felt as if his weight had tripled. Yon stormed over, but his voice was becoming faint. He saw Sylvia step out of her chair with something in her hand, and unlike Yon, there was no urgency to her movements.

'Kroy! Kroy!' Yon was shouting in his face, but Kroy couldn't move his mouth to speak. He knew that leg of lamb had been too perfect, for now he felt his stomach churn in rebellion. He grabbed hold of his brother, tried to use him as a crutch to get to his feet, but he couldn't. Beyond him, he saw Sylvia approach...but it wasn't quite Sylvia anymore.

'Run,' he told his brother, but Yon just looked at him with a perplexed face.

'Run?' he shook his head.

Sylvia didn't have legs anymore, no. She had the body of a serpent, all yellow and green with scales that glittered in the light from the fire. She no longer had footsteps, of course, but merely the dragging of her fleshy tail against the floorboards. He saw her fangs oozing with venom as she lifted a wooden spike and aimed it at Yon.

'Run, Yon!' Kroy told him.

'I don't understand,' Yon grabbed him tight.

'Lamia,' Kroy croaked before she drove the spike into Yon's back and out through his chest.

...

By the time Kroy came to, he half expected to wake up to the playful prods of his younger brother. Or maybe to the rougher shakes of his father making him rise to do some chore or other. But no, this time Kroy woke to the sound of dripping water and a dark room lit only by a few candles. He blinked a few times and was quick to find an escape at the top of a set of stairs where a door stood ajar. However, getting to those stairs would prove difficult, for he was tied to the chair in which he sat.

'Hello?' he croaked and suddenly he got a flash of his brother's face, he saw the anguish in his eyes as a wooden spike was rammed through Yon's entire being. No, it had to have been a nightmare, surely?

'Yon?' he called his name, but his brother didn't answer. As far as he could tell, he was alone in the room. That is, until he saw the shifting of a figure as it slithered across the room.

That beautiful woman was gone—replaced by this almost hairless crone who scooted about the room on her serpent body. She moved fluidly enough, like an actual snake like his father explained, but her wrinkled chest and her bony arms were human. Her face was less so—all bunched up and sagging, drooping off of her like slime. Her nose was crooked, her eyes misshapen and hollow. Kroy pulled at his restraints.

'I wouldn't bother with all that,' she snickered, no longer the voice of the woman who lured them in, but instead, something far more infandous. It sounded as if talking pained her in some way, and her long tongue draped out of her mouth, making it difficult to understand her.

'Who are you?' Kroy barked, but he knew who she was. His father painted her in enough detail.

'Lamia,' she smiled, her fangs dripping with something red. 'But you knew that already, didn't you?'

'What do you want?' Kroy pulled again at his restraints, feeling for the knot as he worked away at it.

'You know the story,' Lamia smirked. 'It's true. I seek the blood of my victims, and with it, I regain my youth. But did your father tell you the story of why I really do this?'

'Because you're evil?' Kroy guessed and supplied a sarcastic sort of smirk of his own for all the good it would do. He wouldn't show Lamia that he was afraid. If he wasn't brave, then how could he tell Yon to be brave?

'Evil?' Lamia recoiled. 'You're the evil ones. You in your city—my former kingdom! It was you who cast me out. It was you who did this to me. For that, I take vengeance on any and all who dare step into my woods.'

'Where's my brother?' Kroy spat. He'd seen his father spit when he was peeved and thought it looked rather intimidating. Lamia didn't seem phased by it. She dipped her finger into a raw slab of meat on the table nearby and licked the trail of blood that came away with it.

'He's here,' she grinned before dabbing her finger in the pool of his guts again and taking a slow lick.

Kroy vomited on himself. It was about all he could do. That mess of bloody meat on the table couldn't have been his brother, could it? The room filled with Lamia's laughter, but it made Kroy work at his restraints all the more. He refused to accept that his brother was gone. Yon was an annoying child at times, but he didn't deserve to die. Kroy would've given his life for Yon's at any given moment, isn't that what big brothers were meant to do? Protect their siblings?

'That's not my brother!' Kroy shouted and he would've kept shouting it, but then, Lamia lifted up Yon's head and tossed it at him.

Yon's bloody head rolled to a stop before his feet. Kroy couldn't speak after that, but instead took to making a strange wailing sound that was alien even to him. His younger brother's mouth was fixed open and there was a stupid, gormless expression on his face. His hair was drenched and part of his neck bone was sticking out, still intact.

'I pulled his head off,' Lamia said, as if it needed saying. 'I'll be saving his blood for a rainy day—for when more foolish children come wandering into my woods. Your blood...I might use yours now and go in search of your father. Tell me, is he a handsome man?'

'Shut your mouth,' Kroy hissed as he managed to free one of his hands.

'You have fight, boy. I like to think my son would have been like you—loyal and fierce.'

Kroy needed something. He needed a weapon, or a strategy or something other than blindly rushing the creature and fighting it head on. His father was right, he was just a boy. How could he hope to stand up to the monster which now stood before him? He looked at the stairs again and knew that if he was quick enough, he might've been able to make it to the door. What other choice did he have?

'What's the matter? Don't you find me pretty anymore?'

Kroy freed his other arm and the rope that bound him fell to the floor. Lamia wasn't stupid. She caught sight of it straight away and her mouth twisted with anger. She lunged at him, but Kroy darted to the side and grabbed the first thing he could get his hands on. It was a sturdy enough box, velvet and small but heavy enough to stun her if his aim was true.

'Let go of that!' she exploded at him.

Kroy looked at it, and while it didn't seem all that special, he obeyed her...by throwing it with all his might and catching her right between the eyes. She stumbled backwards with a screech and went crashing into her cabinet, spilling its contents and shattering glass. Kroy was sure he saw an amulet fly out of the box, but he didn't stay long enough to find out. Without looking at his brother's remains, he darted up the stairs and slammed the door shut behind him. He hurried across the hut, wrenched the front door open and descended into the cold darkness outside.

He didn't dare look back as he sprinted away from the hut. The wolves had gone silent, which was a good sign, but there were other predators in the woods too. Still, they paled in comparison to Lamia. Kroy was sure he'd rather face a bear than her. He ran endlessly until his legs would carry him no more and his lungs were on fire. Even then, he scrambled on hands and knees, hoping that somehow the path he was on would lead him back to his father.

Eventually, he would sink to his knees and suck in air through his mouth and his nostrils. He was sobbing now, not just because he was going to die out here, but because he failed his brother. Yon would still be alive if he hadn't dragged him away from the camp. Heck, none of this would've happened if only he'd listened to his father and stayed put. He glanced back the way he came and couldn't see any signs of Lamia giving chase. As far as he could see, the woodlands were still if not for the hooting of an owl somewhere in the trees.

He set his hands on his knees and hunched over, still catching his breath. He knew he couldn't stay here for long. Who was to say Lamia wasn't going to come speeding her way out through the shrubbery? No, he had to find a way out. He turned on his heels to keep running, but found his breath was caught in his throat. Although, it wasn't the only thing stuck in his throat.

Lamia's fangs sunk deep.

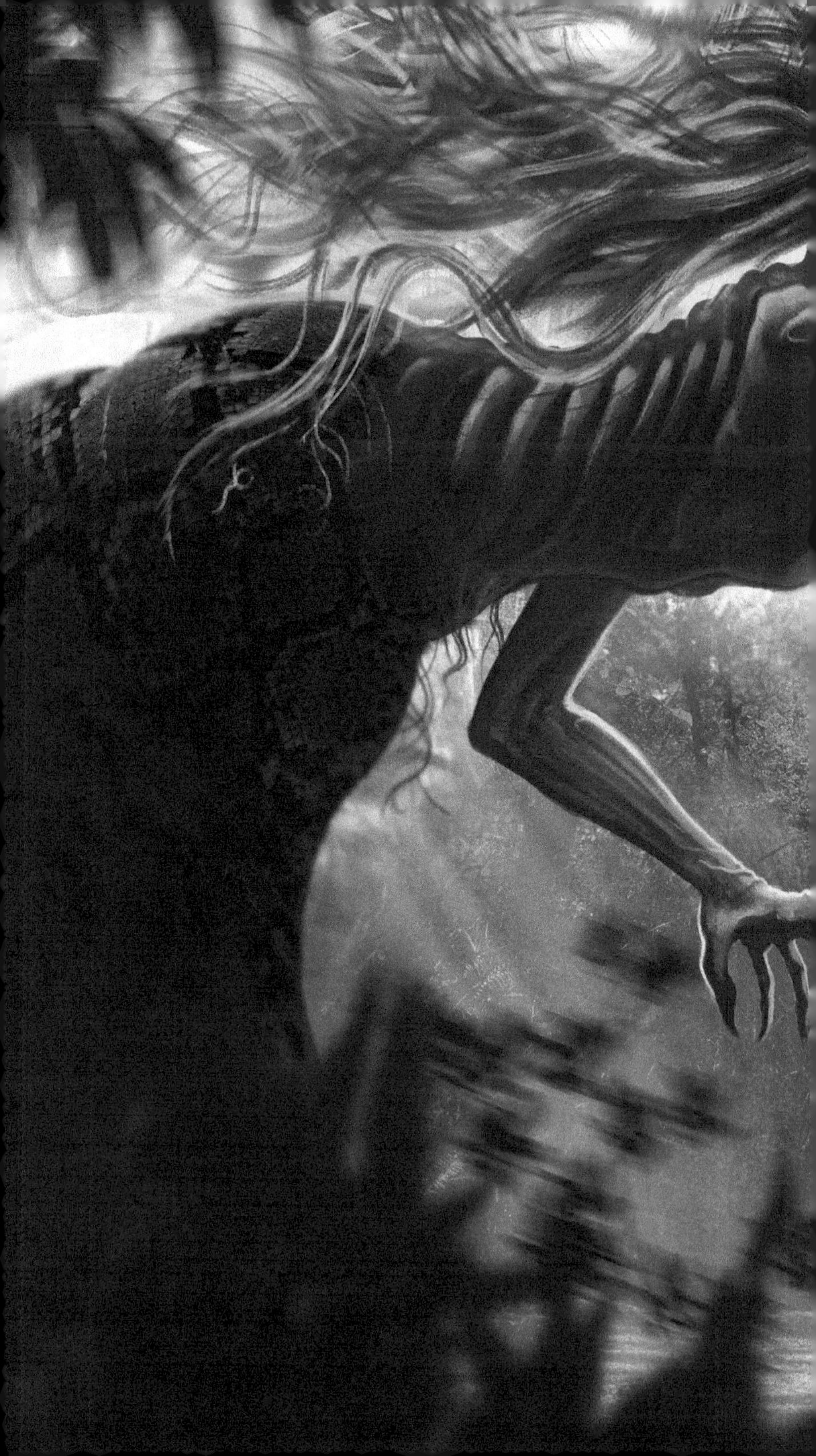

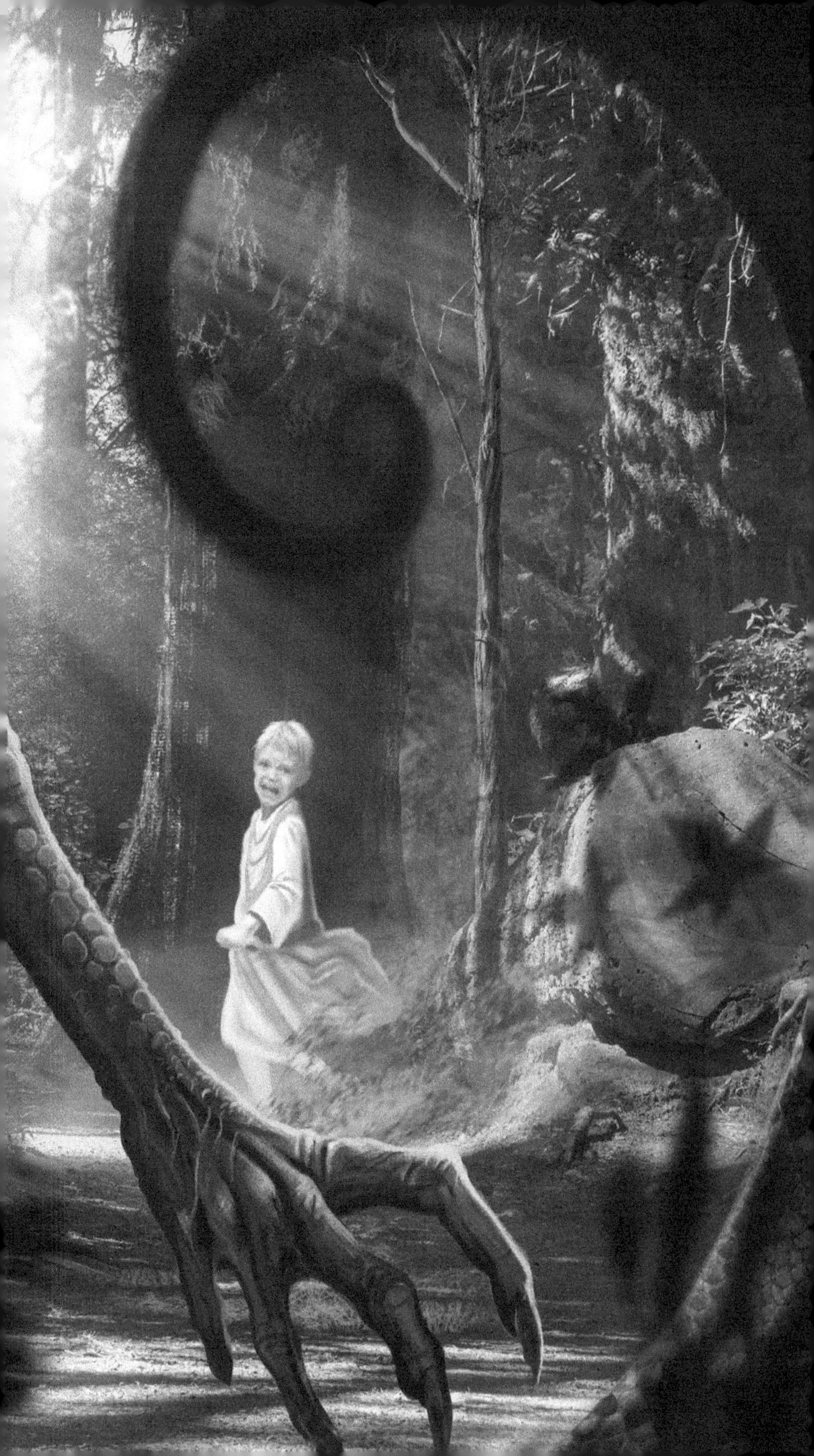

THE STORY OF LAMIA EXPLAINED

The story of Lamia was told throughout Ancient Greece and most commonly served as a cautionary tale primarily told to children. Parents would often tell their children that if they misbehaved or went out after dark, the grotesque monster Lamia would kidnap and devour them, seeking revenge for her own lost children. She became quite an iconic figure with many variations of her myth still told today.

Lamia was the daughter of Poseidon, the god of the sea, which would technically make her half-human and half-god, but she was never regarded in the same manner as the other heroes and demigods of Greek mythology. There were some women who displayed powers one would expect from a demigod. But it was fairly common for the female offspring of a god and a human to possess a radiant beauty that set them apart from other mortals rather than manifesting godly attributes. Lamia was however thought of by many as a queen. The exact region of her rule was somewhat debated, but there are some accounts that point to it as the region we know today as Libya. This was mostly due to the fact that the Greek poet and historian Dio Chrysostom told tales of half-women half-snake creatures called the Lamiai, which closely resembled the descriptions given to Lamia herself. These creatures were attributed as the 'Libyan myth,' hence the belief that Lamia ruled over the region of Libya before she was turned into a monster.

Throughout Greek mythology, whenever mortals showed any hubris towards the gods, they were made an example of and Lamia, like many before her, fell victim to the wrath of Hera. The numerous affairs of Zeus are fairly well documented. But of all his wives, Hera appears as the most resentful and for good reason: once she learnt of Lamia having her husband's children, she intervened either by killing Lamia's children or by tricking Lamia into killing them herself. The latter was quite a fitting punishment in Greek mythology as it was common for gods and goddesses to manipulate mortals into committing terrible acts. Simply killing the children would have only galvanised Lamia and the people of her kingdom, but by forcing Lamia to commit the murder herself, there would be greater psychological and political repercussions. This not only led to a lifetime of blame and self-hate, but Hera was able to turn the people who once worshipped Lamia against her. Taking her children and her kingdom from her was not enough, and in some variations of the myth, it was Hera who then turned Lamia into a hideous monster, making an example of her. This version is brought into question as it can be argued that making an example of Lamia in this way achieved very little. The infidelities of Zeus would continue and the consequences of angering him were far worse than Hera learning of the affair.

In another version of the story, after being exiled, Lamia grew old. When her beauty faded, Zeus appeared, offering her immortality and the chance to exact revenge on all those who had wronged her. Some may wonder why Zeus didn't just make Lamia immortal and restore her beauty, instead choosing to turn her into a monster. The answer to that is quite simple: many of the Greek gods, especially Zeus, didn't care and often mortals served as not much more than entertainment. Zeus could have punished all those who wronged Lamia, but as controversial as it may seem, he instead chose to give Lamia the power to do so herself. In some versions, Lamia was cursed by Hera to never fall asleep. Zeus would show some compassion to his former love, taking pity and giving her the ability to remove her own eyes and finally fall asleep. What Zeus actually transformed Lamia into has somewhat changed over the years, with many believing Lamia to have the upper body of a women and the lower body of a serpent—a figure that is still often described as being alluring and seductive, quite similar to how many viewed Medusa once she had been transformed, despite that not really being the case.

In later depictions, the term Lamia was pluralised to Lamiae referring to a group of vampiric demons who would lure men into their bed to later feed on their flesh and blood. There are also some depictions of Lamia being a monster of the sea because of her father Poseidon and his association to the sea. This belief was further fuelled by Lamia being the potential mother of Scylla, the enormous six headed sea monster, and Akheilos, the lipless shark, a human who was also transformed into an animal after unsuccessfully challenging the goddess Aphrodite to a beauty contest. Some believed that Lamia herself could have been a shark as some variations of her name roughly translated to mean 'Lone Shark' or 'Dangerous Shark'.

Much like the crone in the story, there are accounts of Lamia becoming what the Ancient Greeks believed to be a sorceress—what we would consider a modern day alchemist. She would brew potions and concoctions that would mask her true appearance to men. They would not see a hideous creature with the tale of a serpent, they would only see a young, beautiful woman. Under this guise, she would seduce these young men and convince them to marry her, only to murder them shortly after and feast on their blood. Her exact motives for this form of seduction aren't particularly clear; we can assume that, in this almost vampiric form, the only way to sustain herself was through drinking blood. However, the entire ritual of seducing young men and then breaking their hearts and murdering them does not seem to be done out of necessity but out of enjoyment. Lamia is essentially recreating what she had previously experienced, but this time she doesn't play the role of the heartbroken, she instead assumes the role of Zeus. Some might say that this was her attempt to exact revenge on Zeus and all men in general.

Lamia became an iconic figure to the ancient Greek people as she was one of the many examples of what could happen to those who offended and angered the gods. Her story was told throughout Ancient Greece and is still told even to this day as a way of frightening children into good behaviour. Lamia can be seen as the Greek equivalent to the boogeyman. However you choose to view the story of Lamia, whether it's as a demonic monster who would devour children or as serpentine seductress who murdered young men out of resentment for Zeus, there's no denying that her story has all the elements of a compelling narrative. Love, heartbreak, betrayal and revenge are all themes that can be found in her story. The myth of Lamia is arguably one of the most interesting and emotional journeys within Greek mythology.

BELLEROPHON

I. Confession

King Proetus sat in his obsidian throne, staring down impassively like he'd rather have been somewhere else. Even as Bellerophon took a knee before him, Proetus merely regarded him the way he regarded his servants. Bellerophon couldn't blame the man, though. He probably had a thousand cases like this a day.

'Speak of your crimes,' Proetus droned, swinging one hand lazily out before him.

'Murder,' Bellerophon replied without hesitation. He'd had enough time to think on what he'd done and knew mincing words at this point was a waste of time. Proetus' face remained dormant and still, but it was his wife Stheneboea who shifted in the seat beside him.

'Murder?' she leaned forward with a purring to her voice. 'You do not look capable of such a thing.'

Bellerophon wasn't sure whether that was a compliment or an insult. Queen Stheneboea made a twitch of her red lips, the corners of her mouth suggesting a coy sort of smile. He'd heard tales of her charms on his way to Argos, but the stories had not done her beauty justice. Bellerophon allowed himself a moment to eye the shape of her legs which were plentifully exposed courtesy of the fashionable slit on her dress. He looked away when he felt the stirring in his pants, keeping his eyes fixed on King Proetus, for he was a man of honour, was he not? He would not be swayed by such foolish urges. It's what had gotten him here in the first place.

'Who did you murder?' Proetus mumbled, scratching at his stubbly beard.

'My brother,' Bellerophon spoke honestly and even to his own ears it sounded apathetic. He'd relived the moment over and over again in his head to the point that confessing it out loud meant nothing. He'd tortured himself at the thought of it for so long that now he was numb.

'Your own brother?' Proetus frowned, perhaps the only sign that he had any interest in the matter at all.

'Yes,' Bellerophon confirmed.

'Why?' Stheneboea gasped and made a show of crisscrossing her bare legs before her. Bellerophon didn't look, if only out of respect for Proetus. Though he noticed a few guards loitering at the sides of the room who could do with readjusting their gaze.

'I don't remember,' Bellerophon shrugged, it was the truth. 'I was drunk and we had an argument. The next thing I know, I was covered in his blood.'

No one spoke after that. King Proetus remained stoic, but at least he looked more awake having heard that bit of information. Still, it was Queen Stheneboea who was stroking her chin with her thumb and forefinger as if she was to decide his fate.

'And what, pray tell, do you think your punishment should be?' King Proetus sighed.

'Death,' Bellerophon said simply. 'I have robbed my brother, my family and the world of a life. I accept my fate with open arms and make no excuses for my misfeasance.'

'You're an honest man, for a killer,' King Proetus noted.

'I only speak what is right,' Bellerophon replied.

'It would be a shame to execute a man who speaks so earnestly,' Queen Stheneboea touched her husband's arm, and just like that, life was born into his face once more.

'I have executed men for lesser crimes,' Proetus replied, though he sounded unsure of himself now as he succumbed to his wife's lustful glare.

'Perhaps,' Stheneboea began and tilted her head at Bellerophon, supplying a slow wink, 'we should grant him a second chance.'

Bellerophon felt his heart do a flip. No, he didn't deserve a second chance, but yet he couldn't deny the feeling of relief—even if it meant living with the curse of his brother's blood forever on his hands. He lowered his head all the same, waiting for King Proetus to come to the right decision and announce his execution.

But he didn't.

'Fine,' he said with another wave of his hands. 'Guards, offer this man a cot for the night in the cells and see him on his way in the morning.'

'No, you mustn't—'

'Bellerophon,' Queen Stheneboea cut him off. 'We have made our decision. Be thankful for our kindness.'

'But—'

Two burly guards flanked him on either side, carrying a shield and spear each. They both had a mean look to them like they hated their jobs and hated life more. Together, they slammed the butts of their spears on the ground and grabbed Bellerophon by the arms.

'You heard the king, did you not?' one of them uttered. 'To the cells with you!'

Bellerophon opened his mouth to argue, but before he could, he was being dragged away. King Proetus was filling up his glass of wine, probably forgetting his face already. But Queen Stheneboea kept her eyes fixed on him, a salacious grin forming on her red lips.

Bellerophon looked away and fought the urge to look back.

II. A Man of Honour

The night came quickly.

Bellerophon stood by the window of his cell, both hands tightly wrapped around the iron bars as he stared out at the endless desert. The air was still, and there was nothing except the sound of a snoring guard further down the hall and a constant dripping that Bellerophon was beginning to loathe. In the morning, he would be free to walk the very desert before him, supposedly absolved of his crime. But deep down, he knew absolution would not be so easily achieved.

He tried to sleep, but he saw his brother in his dreams, all bloody and screaming, begging him to stop. He would've cried, but he dreamt the same dream a thousand times that he now felt nothing. He gripped the iron bars tighter, so tight that he was sure they loosened. He could've escaped if he wanted, but this was where he belonged. In fact, even this was too good for him. No, he deserved—

There came the sound of a door closing. Bellerophon swung around and saw an orange light chase away the shadows in the hall. It came closer and closer and was soon accompanied by the sound of footsteps. A figure stopped shy of the bars that kept Bellerophon enclosed and waited there for a moment before stepping closer. It took a moment for Bellerophon to realise who it was.

'I trust the cell is...' and she stopped to look around at it like it had personally insulted her 'satisfactory'?

'Queen Stheneboea,' Bellerophon went down to one knee, more so out of reflex than anything else.

'Rise,' she told him. 'This is not a formal visit.'

Bellerophon wondered what sort of visit it was meant to be then. It wasn't until she stepped closer, an inch away from the bars, did he realise what sort of visit this was. She didn't leave much to the imagination—nor was she particularly shy considering the snoring guard could've woken at any moment and seen her in such a gown. The fabric looked thin. In fact, it was thin enough that he could see her flesh underneath if he looked hard enough. The gown had lace patterns around the cuffs and was cut shamelessly high above the knee. She smelled divine.

'I'd like to thank you for pardoning me,' Bellerophon cleared his throat and tried to pull his gaze away from her, but couldn't. To be honest, he wasn't in the mind for thanking her at all. He had come here to die and nothing more.

'I'm glad you're in the mood for thanking,' she said, trailing her finger over her breast, down her stomach and slipping away. She had an all-knowing smirk on her red lips, like she knew exactly what he was thinking.

She pushed open the gate and Bellerophon took a step back. He would've reached for a blade if he had one on his person, but instead held up his hands like he was submitting to an assassin.

'You seem disturbed,' she giggled and made a subtle tug at the tassel on her robe. One side of the garment pulled to the left, exposing her a little more.

'Your husband,' Bellerophon croaked, back against the wall now as he finally looked away. 'I trust he must be wondering where you are at this hour.'

'The fool is asleep,' she reached out for him and Bellerophon took a deep breath, still not entirely sure what was happening. But it was painfully obvious, was it not? Only a fool like him would second guess the moment before him.

He felt her fingers in his hair at first, then they were caressing his jaw before slowly grazing against his lips. He didn't react, but instead found himself standing there like a dumb mute, frozen to the core. Her fingers moved down his neck and he shivered at her touch, though he couldn't say it was a bad feeling. She moved into him, pushing her bosom closer to his face before straddling him, a quiet purring sound escaping her lips.

'When I saw you this morning,' she whispered and grabbed his hands, placing them on her hips, 'I knew I had to have you.'

'Your husband is probably wondering where you are,' Bellerophon croaked, but in all honesty he was starting to forget what King Proetus even looked like. All he could focus on now was her bare chest and the sudden urge to plunge his mouth against it.

'Let him wonder,' she said by his ear, her warm breath exciting him all the more.

She began kissing his face, running her lips along his jaw before sucking at his neck. He should've pushed her off —should've used his strength and fended her off and out of the cell, but his hands were now gripping her tightly on their own accord. She nipped at him with her teeth and he grunted at the pain, fuelling the need to nearly bite her back. She grabbed his hair, pulled his head back and just looked at him for a moment, a mischievous look in her dark eyes.

Then she was kissing him, slipping her tongue into his mouth. He recoiled at first, but then he found himself kissing her too, a muffled groan escaping his mouth as she bit down on his lip. Something about that had him lifting her up by the hips. She squealed, but she didn't resist as she wrapped her arms around his neck, pulling him close, feasting on his lips. He marched her forward, her legs tightly drawn around his waist as he grazed his hands up her thighs.

Then he dropped her onto her ass outside of the cell and pulled the gate shut.

'What are you doing?' she growled at him.

'Go back to your husband, Stheneboea,' Bellerophon muttered and retreated once more to the window.

'You ungrateful fool!' she snapped, pulled her gown together in a huff and tied it back up. 'I offer you myself and you throw me away like this? I am a queen!'

'A queen without honour,' Bellerophon muttered again, 'is no queen at all.' This time he had turned his back on her and gazed out of the window once more.

'I saved you! My husband would've fed you to the dogs for your crime!'

'He should've,' Bellerophon said.

'You haven't heard the last of this!' Stheneboea grabbed the lantern and stormed out, leaving Bellerophon in the dark once more. A part of him wanted to give in to her. In fact, a part of him almost did. But above all, he was still a man of honour. He'd murdered his brother and disgraced his family, but he had to hold onto something. It was the only thing stopping him from slipping into madness.

He gripped the iron bars once more, watching the silver moon glistening against the dark sky. He was smiling to himself, for though he'd been pardoned, he was sure Stheneboea wasn't the type of woman who was used to hearing 'no'. Perhaps those dogs she spoke of were still on the cards after all. Perhaps justice would finally be served and he could rest at last.

He closed his eyes.

III. The Cost of Freedom

Sleep hadn't eluded him.

In fact, if Bellerophon was honest, he was having the best slumber he'd had in quite some time. That was until he felt hands grab him by the torso—not Stheneboea's hands this time, though—no, a pair of hands far rougher and belonging to one guard who reeked of garlic.

'What is the meaning of this?' Bellerophon demanded, but he had a reasonable idea. The guard tossed him into another, and before he could protest, he was being shackled by the ankles.

'King Proetus demands your presence,' the uglier, more scarred one yelled in his face.

'And I needed to be shackled?' Bellerophon demanded.

'After what you've done, scum? You're lucky the king hasn't let the dogs loose on you already.'

'And what did I do?' Bellerophon asked as he was shoved out of the cell.

He wouldn't get his answer right away. The guards marched him through the dimly lit cells, past the dozen other prisoners who may very well have seen Queen Stheneboea in her scandalous outfit the previous night. But it had been after midnight, and from what Bellerophon had heard, most of these sorry criminals would be put to the axe soon. No one would listen to them hark about anything now.

'Should've taken her offer, Hellerdaphone!' one of the prisoner's snickered, a squinty look on his gaunt face.

'It's Bellerophon, actually.'

'Whatever, your name is stupid!'

The guards shoved him onwards before he could retaliate. He was marched up a set of stairs and directed through the palace grounds where a bevy of mortified faces awaited him.

'Devourer!' someone shouted.

'Rapist!' shouted another.

'Go back where you came from!' a child had the nerve to shout.

Even the guard who had his hand rammed up against his armpit made a comment, but Bellerophon didn't catch what it was. He was too busy being pulled this way and that. The crowd, which had gathered before the palace, were orderly at least. They gave him a wide berth as he was ushered through the courtyard, past the water fountains and the eloquently cut bushes that he would've admired any other time.

'Enjoy it while you still can,' the guard grunted like he'd read his mind.

'You ain't gonna see daylight again, scum.'

'Wasn't planning on it,' Bellerophon replied as they entered the palace.

King Proetus' face was crimson and Bellerophon was sure he could see a vein protruding from his forehead. He had his jaw clenched tight, like he was holding back a mouthful of flames that would sear everything in sight. Beside him sat Stheneboea whose eyes were watery red, her mouth twisted into an unflattering shape.

'My king, my queen—'

'Silence!' Proetus roared, his voice thundering through the room.

Bellerophon fell to one knee all the same, for it seemed better than just standing there like a school boy about to meet the cane. Proetus was breathing so heavily that Bellerophon could hear the air being sucked up through his nostrils and back out again through his gritted teeth. Stheneboea, on the other hand, had pulled her knees up to her chin, hugging herself as she began to shiver.

She sure wasn't shivering last night, Bellerophon noted to himself.

'Defiler!' Proetus thrusted his finger in the air at him. 'We offer you salvation, and in turn you try and rape my wife?'

Bellerophon recoiled, 'I did no such thing!'

'Liar!' Stheneboea screamed. 'I have the word of a guard to prove it!'

'It's true!' one guard came storming out from nowhere. 'I heard some rustling during my patrol of the cells last night, but I had no idea this villainous man had his hands on our queen.'

'You were sleeping!' Bellerophon accused. 'I could hear you snoring long before she even came down to my cell to seduce *me*.'

'Are you saying that I, a queen, would lower myself into coming down to those vile cells to...to fornicate with you behind my husband's back?' Stheneboea hissed.

Bellerophon nodded, 'That's exactly what happened.'

'And to think I considered you an honest man,' Proetus remarked.

'I am,' Bellerophon defended, but he knew his words would fall on deaf ears. Truth was, he could see in the way Proetus' hand hung by his sword that he himself was ready to come charging across the room, swinging as he did. A part of him wished to confess to the crime, but that would not be just. He should've been put to death because of his brother's fate, not the false accusation of the queen.

'Slay him!' Stheneboea hissed from her throne, her words full of venom. 'He tried to defile me. Defend my honour and let his head roll.'

'Allow me, sire.' One of the guards stood close by and Bellerophon became very aware of the sword hung loosely on his shoulder.

'The honour should be mine, sire.' Another guard stepped forward, this one carrying a shining axe which he twirled in his hands. It sure seemed like the whole bloody kingdom wanted his head removed from its neck.

'King Proetus,' Bellerophon spoke up, 'while I cannot provide the evidence against your wife's words, I can only express my account of the events. I did not try to have my way with Queen Stheneboea, though I will not sit here and protect what shred is left of her honour. It was she who came down to my cell to seduce me, and upon not receiving my reciprocation, she grew tempered. King Proetus, I did not attempt to rape your wife.'

'Shut it, worm!' One of the guards moved his spear to strike him, but King Proetus raised his voice before he could.

'Hold your arm!' he yelled at the guard before turning a lingering glance at his wife.

'What?' she snapped at him. 'You don't believe this lowly dog, do you? He killed his own brother. Do you think you can trust a word he says?'

King Proetus made a slight squint of his eyes at his wife, but if there was any cause for suspicion it was gone before Bellerophon could interpret it. His hand moved away from the sword at his hip and nestled its way into the pocket on his robe. Where his face was an angry red before, it had now cooled allowing for the lines in his face to subside a slight. He glanced once more at his wife, regarding her demeanour with a twitch of the brow before shuffling back into his throne.

'What are you doing?' Queen Stheneboea barked at him. 'Will you not slay him after he put his hands on me?'

He gave her a long, hard look and to Bellerophon it seemed almost accusatory. 'The gods will not take such an outcome lightly. We gave him refuge. To kill a guest is to incur the fury of the gods, or did you forget that?'

'I...I...of course not,' Stheneboea stammered. 'The gods cannot be angered.'

'And so I am left with a predicament,' Proetus tapped his chin. 'I can't kill you without the gods disapproving. I can't imprison you again without the people of my land growing restless of your fate. So what am I to do with you?'

'Strike me down for the murder of my brother as I came here to receive,' Bellerophon proposed and even craned his neck forward, making it all the more easy.

'No, you have already been pardoned of that crime,' King Proetus declared before turning to Stheneboea. 'We must send him away. Perhaps your father would be better suited to taking his life.'

'My father?' Stheneboea's eyes flashed for a moment; that wicked grin was back on her face as she curled her fingers, making a fist at Bellerophon. 'Yes, my father will not hesitate to remove your bowels when he finds out what you tried to do with me.'

'Just kill me!' Bellerophon shouted across the throne room, but the guards were already dragging him away.

'See him escorted to Lycia,' Proetus ordered.

'No!' Bellerophon struggled. 'Do not let another man decide my fate. Take my life now for the murder of my brother and have this done with!'

'I will have a letter written to go with him explaining his fate,' Proetus was speaking to one of the guards, not even looking at Bellerophon anymore, like the parent who was ignoring the screaming child.

'King Proetus!' Bellerophon screamed all the same as he wrestled with the guards. 'Kill me! Do you hear me? Kill me!'

But once more his words may as well have been silent, for King Proetus was already scribbling something down on parchment. His hard expression remained intact, one eye fixed on the paper and the other wearily glancing over at his wife.

IV. Lycia

They'd stuffed him in the back of a rickety carriage and only bothered to speak to him when they came to a stop in the road—usually to offer him the chance to relieve his bladder. They'd given him a threadbare blanket, or at least, Bellerophon liked to think they had given it to him. Truth was, it was there upon his arrival with dark red blood stains and more than enough holes that it would now serve better as a fishing net. Still, he wrapped it around his shoulders to protect against the chilly breeze of the morning.

The sun might've shined, but Bellerophon wasn't in the mood to appreciate it. He watched the sun rise and fall three times since his banishment from Argos, but each time he looked at the golden sphere in the sky, it warmed him less and less. One of the guards had brought him a thin slice of veal to munch on and he savoured every inch of it, sucking the meat dry before passing it down his throat.

'No point feeding me,' he'd told them when they tossed the meat at him.

'You will not die before judgment has been cast by King Lobates,' the guard said. 'King of Lycia! Father of Stheneboea! The—'

'I know who he is,' Bellerophon cut him off and the guard diffused, shuffling back to the front of the carriage.

King Lobates would certainly send him on his way into the afterlife. Bellerophon didn't know what it was to be a father, but he knew well enough the rage he might've felt when faced with a man who attempted to rape his daughter. Bellerophon liked to think that he would've given the man the chance to plead his side of the story, but he wasn't sure he'd stomach it without going for his throat. King Lobates would probably nail him with a spear the moment his face appeared in his court.

'Perhaps I'll get the justice I seek here, then.' Bellerophon spoke to himself, but there came a long, resounding 'nope' from somewhere inside his head. When was it ever that simple?

They pulled into the city of Lycia, where all the rooftops appeared to be a sunburnt orange. The buildings were similar in size, some of them more regal looking with gables and billowing silky curtains. Others were decrepit with smashed in walls and broken windows. The first thing that Bellerophon noticed was the stark difference between the rich and the poor; one side of the street abundant with rich folk and nobles while the other littered with beggars and cripples.

The carriage pulled to an abrupt stop and the guards immediately shuffled out of their seats, their footfalls marching around the carriage before appearing at the back.

'Out you get,' one of them reached in and grabbed him by the arm, wrenching him out. Bellerophon almost tripped over his own feet he was pulled so hard, but he managed to land with his dignity, if not awkwardly. He was still shackled, his arms bound tightly in front of him and his ankles wrapped with a steel chain.

They marched him in the direction of a long marble stairway, flanked by eloquently designed statues of beasts and men alike. King Lobates' palace stood at the end of the stairway cordoned off by a golden gate that gleamed in the sunlight. Bellerophon imagined it was like walking up to Olympus, but to a lesser degree of grandeur. Still, the architecture of the building was a wonder with giant spires shooting into the air and large flags flapping dutifully in the wind.

But Bellerophon's attention was soon drawn to the subjects of Lobates, who for the most part scurried about like gutter rats. Men and women in rags and rotten garments clustered together, some with children huddled closely in packs. A few of them were hunchback with shoddy walking sticks to aid them on their journeys. Old men were slouched on the ground, some with flies orbiting their faces.

'These people are dying,' Bellerophon remarked.

'It's their own fault,' one of the guards shoved him. 'Scummy filth.'

Bellerophon caught movement in the corner of his eye and before he knew it, there was someone shouting something.

'You walked right into me!' one nobleman was ramming his finger against a man twice his senior. Bellerophon knew he was a nobleman because of the feather in his stylish hat and the exquisite robe he wore.

'I'm sorry,' the old beggar lowered his head. 'I wasn't looking where

I was going.'

'Probably looking for pennies, weren't you?' the noble carried on and it wasn't long before he was joined by some of his friends, all of which were dressed in a similar fashion.

'I...I'm sorry,' the beggar tried again. Now they were shoving him back and forth until one of the men grabbed him by the shoulders, swept his legs out from under him and planted him on the ground.

They all had a good laugh at that. They held their bellies with amusement, slapping each other's backs before kicking the poor sod while he was down. Even the guards on either side of Bellerophon supplied a grim sort of chuckle, like they knew it was wrong but quite enjoyed the show nonetheless.

'Hey!' Bellerophon called out and just like that, they all stopped and turned to face him.

'This isn't your fight,' one of the guard's reminded him. 'Keep your mouth shut until you're before King Lobates and then you can say what you want.'

But Bellerophon didn't listen. 'Leave that man alone!'

'And why would I do that?' the noble looked him up and down, realised he was in chains and strutted his way over. 'You think you're going to do anything to help in those chains?'

'Come closer and you'll find out,' Bellerophon challenged.

'Fool,' one of the guards nudged him, 'keep your tongue in its hole. I'd rather not have to protect a dead man.'

'I don't need your protection,' Bellerophon snapped.

The noble strutted his way over, smug and pompous like he was approaching a weary dog. He folded his arms in front of him before stopping just a step away from Bellerophon. He didn't say anything, but instead wore that arrogant smirk on his pink lips as if he'd already won the argument.

'Well then, show me, prisoner.' He spoke at last as he leaned in. 'I'll even let you strike me fi—'

Bellerophon drove his own head against the man's nose.

The strike was enough to have the noble reeling back, his nostrils spewing blood like a fountain. He stumbled over himself, hit the ground hard and sprawled on the floor, wailing. His friends stormed over, one of them with a knife in hand. The knifeman lunged, but Bellerophon stepped to the side and barged the man off course. A third man struck him in the face and Bellerophon had no choice but to take the blow once, then twice. On the third strike, he veered to the left and drove his foot so hard against the man's ribs that it sent him crashing against a wall.

The man with the knife came storming towards him again, the knife raised high. Bellerophon didn't think. He tensed his arms, felt the shackles around his wrists snap as he moved his arms to catch the man by the forearm. The attacker's eyes were wide all of a sudden, a shimmer of regret forming on his face before Bellerophon launched him onto his back.

That was when the guard grabbed him—one set of heavy hands tightening around his shoulder. Bellerophon snatched away, drew his elbow up and drove it into the side of the guard's head. He went down fast enough, his helmet rattling off his head as he hit the ground. The other guard went to strike him with the spear, but Bellerophon caught it with both hands.

'You're violating the law of Argos!' the guard roared at him, desperation in his pudgy face.

'We're not in Argos anymore,' Bellerophon smirked and wrenched the spear from his hands before snapping it over his knee.

The guard opened his mouth to say something, but looked too stunned. His eyes were bulging from their sockets as he grew red in the face, his breath panicked and strained. He took a few tentative steps backwards as he watched Bellerophon break apart the steel chain around his ankles with his bare hands.

'Impossible...' he gasped.

'Your duty is done, guard,' Bellerophon said as he brushed a bit of dirt from his shirt. 'I'll see myself to Lobates.'

Once more the guard opened his mouth to speak, but his words must've died on his lips because he took to clearing his throat instead. He rummaged through his pocket and pulled forth an envelope which he tossed at Bellerophon's feet. He said nothing after that, but he didn't take his eyes off him as he very slowly retreated back to the carriage. Bellerophon watched him climb onto his seat and continued to watch him until he whipped the horses and began to head back down the road.

Bellerophon snatched the envelope off the ground and scanned the front. It was addressed to Lobates, and Bellerophon could only imagine what scandalous things Proetus had probably written about him—how he'd seduced his wife and killed his own brother. Only one of those things he would happily die for.

He stuffed the envelope in his pocket and stepped over the guard he'd knocked out whilst sweeping a gaze at the noble with the bloody nose. One of his friends was rubbing his ribs from where he'd been booted, but the one with the knife hadn't gotten up yet. They studied him cautiously, perhaps a residual sense of hope still lingering that they could all subdue him if they rushed him together. Bellerophon was sure they didn't have the guts though.

But then the old man who had been originally hassled stumbled into his path, falling to his knees.

'You have my thanks, friend.'

'There's no need to mention it,' Bellerophon said and helped the old hunchback up to his feet.

'Not many folk 'round here anymore that would do what you just did,' he said, clearing his throat. 'You're a hero, you are.'

Bellerophon couldn't say what it was about that that made him feel suddenly...alive. Perhaps it was the appreciation in the man's eyes—all glowing and full of praise. Or maybe it was that feeling of power that now flowed through his body, that same power that had him punching his brother to death.

He shook his head free of the thought and inclined his head at the man, shaking his hand before bidding him farewell. He started his way up the stairs, prolonging his ascension as he took in one deliberate breath after the other. He imagined they would be his last few breaths, and he wanted to enjoy them before he paid the piper.

But it was never that simple.

V. A Simple Task

King Lobates sat on the throne, twirling one stubby finger through the mess of grey hairs on his upper lip. His eyes were bulbous things though sharp and piercing just like those of his daughter Stheneboea. But where she had the look of a devilish temptress, Lobates had the look of a seething bull. Even his nostrils would periodically flare in and out as he regarded Bellerophon, watching him like he'd seen him somewhere before and was trying to place his face.

King Lobates didn't say anything at first. Much like Proetus, he had that deliberately slow way of blinking like he had all the time in the world and then some. His throne was of more humble decoration to Proetus', with none of the lavish patterns and gilded armrests. He had a long obsidian chair that looked about as comfortable as the carriage that Bellerophon had come in. Several of the guards in this room stood to attention, each one of them dressed in burgundy armour and equipped to the teeth with spears, lances, swords and shields.

'You have my attention,' Lobates addressed Bellerophon, his voice thundering across the room, along the royal blue rug that stretched across the floor. If Bellerophon wasn't mistaken, he was sure the flames from the torches on the wall swayed to one side at his words.

'King Lobates,' Bellerophon went down on one knee and only then began to take note of the way in which the flames on the wall cast a crimson light throughout the room, enveloping Lobates and giving him a more threatening edge. 'I've come from Argos bearing this letter for you.'

King Lobates raised his bushy eyebrows, a hint of suspicion rippling across his face. He made a gesture at one of his guards and immediately, one of the lankier of the dozen stormed his way over to Bellerophon. He snatched it from his hand, gave him no more than a passing glance before spinning on his heel and marching back to deliver it to his king.

'Don't think that I didn't hear about that commotion outside, boy.' Lobates spoke in a grave voice as he twirled the letter between his fat fingers. 'They say you knocked out three men and one of your own escorts with barely a broken sweat.'

'Stories are exaggerated,' Bellerophon replied, though he thought back to how easily he had overcome them and couldn't help but remember that word the old man had used. Hero. Truth was, he had always been strong—strong enough to move boulders, strong enough to strike through wood and...strong enough to murder his own brother with just a few taps.

'They say you broke your own shackles,' Lobates tapped his sagging jowls.

Bellerophon didn't like the hungry way Lobates had begun to look at him, his eyes suddenly adorned with a certain shine.

'My restraints were...weak.'

'Witnesses say they were made of steel,' Lobates pointed out all matter-of-fact like. He seemed to enjoy having all the answers, but all the answers he needed were in that envelope he fidgeted with.

'They very well may have been,' Bellerophon said. 'But there is no use of such tales. I am sent here by King Proetus, your son-in-law, for crimes I committed against my brother.'

Lobates let his eyes slip onto the envelope. He seemed almost reluctant to open it, but once he did he scanned across it, mumbling the words to himself. Bellerophon lowered his head, half expecting the king to come barrelling out of his chair for the lie about his seduction of Queen Stheneboea.

Lobates lowered the letter and he fixed his gaze back on Bellerophon.

'You tried to rape my daughter?' he spoke in a chilly, calm voice.

'No,' Bellerophon replied, trying not to sound too off-guard by Lobates' demeanour. The man might've been boiling with rage on the inside, but he wore his face like he couldn't be any more at peace. 'The truth may not please you.'

'And my worthless son-in-law sent you to me because he didn't wish to incur the vengeance of the gods for murdering a guest?' Lobates muttered. 'And so now I must bear that burden, must I?'

'I did nothing of what I am accused of. My only sin is killing my brother,' Bellerophon spoke. 'If you strike me down for that reason alone, then the gods will not give you grief.'

Lobates gave nothing away. His face had the same emotion as a block of wood.

'Why should I believe you?' Lobates leaned forward, his voice growing steelier with each passing moment.

'Perhaps you shouldn't,' Bellerophon shrugged. 'Perhaps you should impale me now. But do it in the honour of my brother, not for your shameful daughter.'

At once, Lobates was on his feet, his cloak swishing in the air. His guards moved to mimic him, each of them fixing their eyes on Bellerophon as they reached for their weapons. Sounds of steel were drawn from their scabbards. Blades of all shapes and sizes hissed in the air. Bellerophon didn't know why he leapt to his feet and threw up his fists. It wasn't like he'd come here for anything other than death. But old habits died hard, did they not? Pretty soon, Bellerophon was eyeing each and every one of them back, welcoming the death that he was owed.

'Stand down,' Lobates told his guards and the words caught Bellerophon off guard. He swung around at the king, puzzled. 'I won't give you such an easy death, Bellerophon.'

'Then what will it be?' Bellerophon demanded, eager to have this done with. 'Hanging? Drowning? Burned alive?'

'No,' Lobates stroked his chin. 'You're a man of considerable strength, that much I can see. Even the way you hold yourself is something to be revered. Who are you, Bellerophon?'

Bellerophon looked around, but then he shrugged. 'I'm no one.'

Lobates descended down the few steps of his throne with his arms behind his back and strolled towards Bellerophon. The guards in the room all tensed, each of them leaning forward with their swords and their lances. The only sounds in the room after that were the creaking of metal and the nasal breathing of one guard to the rear. Lobates stopped short of him, the corner of his lips forming a smile.

'I won't hang you. I won't drown you and I certainly won't burn you alive,' Lobates said as he scrunched the letter up in his fist. 'But I will set you a challenge—a challenge that if you pass, I will grant you forgiveness for your crime.'

'I didn't come here for forgiveness,' Bellerophon snapped, and there in his mind flashed the image of his brother's mangled face, bloody and bruised and beyond any resemblance. 'Kill me where I stand and we can be done with this.'

Lobates was openly smiling now, his toothy grin wet with saliva. 'Fail this task, and I can assure you, the death you seek will find you.'

'Fine!' Bellerophon sighed. 'What is the task?'

Lobates glanced around at his guards. Bellerophon felt the tremor in their auras as they each took a shy step back, their weapons jittering in their arms all of a sudden. It was then the crimson flames danced all the more furiously as a gust of wind blew in from the windows. King Lobates leaned in close, so close that Bellerophon could smell the hint of lemon on his breath.

'Have you ever heard of the Chimera?'

Something gripped the room then. It may as well have been an invisible fist squeezing the walls together, squashing the space in between so that everyone felt a little more uncomfortable. Bellerophon could see it in the eyes of the guards, the baby-faced men with swords and the hardened, grizzly men with axes, each surrendering that look of shared fear. There was no fear in Lobates' face though, just opportunity sparkling in his eyes.

'I've heard of it,' Bellerophon replied, though even he felt a shudder in his spine at the mere mention of it. 'A creature so terrible that it breathes fire, does it not?'

'It breathes fire indeed, with the head of a lion and a goat, both. It also has the venomous head of a serpent. This creature has terrorised my lands for too long. My men will not go near it and the ones that did are now in the dirt,' Lobates explained.

'And what makes you think I will?' Bellerophon demanded. 'I might've been able to defeat three bullies and snap a chain, but defeat the Chimera? You have too much faith in me.'

Lobates' eyes narrowed, two slits on his face stabbing at Bellerophon. His smirk hadn't subsided though, but it did look all the more menacing as if he had Bellerophon backed into a corner.

'Do you not want absolution, Bellerophon?' Lobates' asked. 'All the crimes in your name will be cleared upon slaying the Chimera.'

'That's if I can slay it,' Bellerophon challenged.

'And what is the alternative? Should you fail, you will be met with the death you came here for, only at the claws of the Chimera.'

Bellerophon had to admit that much was true. The thought of standing before the Chimera made his knees weak. He preferred to simply take an axe to the throat, or be burned in a public display than to face off against an enemy that greater men had failed to slay. But, in the end, what choice did he have? Either he'd kill the Chimera or he'd be devoured and all would be as it should.

'Fine then,' Bellerophon accepted. 'Where is this Chimera?'

VI. Death Awaits

They'd stuffed him into an armour similar to that of the guards. A burgundy coloured breastplate sat tightly at the front, the paintwork already marred and dented by some other skirmish. He was strapped with a pair of greaves that felt loose, and upon closer inspection, Bellerophon noticed that one was larger than the other. A royal red cloak was draped from his shoulders. Bellerophon thought it was a bit too much, but Lobates had insisted. A helmet was dunked on his head, the same colour as the breastplate, only it stank of sweat and itched at the sides of his face.

Why am I doing this? Bellerophon asked himself, eyeing his form in the reflection of a shield in the dimly lit barracks. He liked to think he would have come up with an answer, but Lobates strode into the room flanked by two of his men.

'Ah'! Lobates sounded off as he looked Bellerophon up and down like a father inspecting his son's first suit, 'You look like one of my own platoon, Bellerophon!'

'I don't feel like it,' Bellerophon replied. Truth was, he'd never worn armour before and moving around in it felt clunky and slow. The greaves were heavy, pulling at his knees, and the breastplate weighed more than he liked, enough to have him leaning forward. It might've served as protection in battle, but Bellerophon didn't see the point of it if he couldn't move freely.

'Can I interest you in a sword?' Lobates gestured at the weapons rack on the wall. There was a selection of gleaming metals from traditional swords and spears to more unorthodox curved axes and outlandish daggers with serrated edges. Most were clean, but there were a few dirks and broad swords that were stained with blood, some of them encrusted with the stuff like algae on rocks.

'I'll take the spear,' Bellerophon shrugged, though he'd never held a spear before. It seemed like it would serve well in keeping the creature at arm's length, but other than that, what was he meant to do with it? Poke the damn thing to death? 'Best give me the bow as well.'

'The bow?' Lobates seemed surprised.

'At least I know how to use that,' Bellerophon said under his breath. He'd hunted in the woods with a bow before, even though shooting rabbits and deer was likely to be considerably different from shooting the Chimera.

Maybe I can rain arrows at one of its heads and catch it in the eyes, he thought. Though his optimism was cut short when he envisioned the flames from the Chimera's mouth engulfing the arrows and burning them to nothing.

'The bow it shall be,' Lobates clicked his fingers and one of his men moved in to retrieve it from the rack.

They shoved the bow in his hands and strapped the spear to his back along with a quiver of withered arrows that didn't look fit enough to hunt common wildlife, let alone a beast. He was going to die fighting the Chimera, that much was true.

And perhaps then I can rest from this world and leave it to—

'You will travel north of here,' Lobates approached him, wrapped an arm around his shoulder before ushering him out the door of the barracks. 'The Chimera was last seen at the far side of the volcano. It's said that it has chosen this spot as its home.'

'The far side of the volcano?' Bellerophon stopped. 'That's a thousand miles away.'

'Then you best be on your way,' Lobates gave that same sinister grin.

'You can't spare me a horse, or an escort of some kind?' Bellerophon tried. The distance was one thing, but travelling alone would certainly make the journey tedious.

'I have no such provisions,' Lobates was shaking his head and began marching faster, shoving Bellerophon out the front doors and back out into courtyard.

'You have an army,' Bellerophon reminded.

'And you have a gift, my boy,' Lobates said with a shady wink. 'Don't let me down, Bellerophon. Your life does depend on it, after all.'

'But—'

The two guards at Lobates' side slammed the doors shut and Bellerophon was left staring at them, mouth half open with the mind to punch them down. But where would that get him? Once again justice had eluded him and he was given the freedom to simply walk away if he wanted. An honourless man would've tossed the spear and bow away and ventured off into the world, forgetting the suicide mission that was the Chimera and done as he pleased.

But damn my morals, he cursed to himself and set his eyes on the horizon where the orange sun was just beginning to set and shadows rolled out onto the hills ahead, a black tide slowly creeping up upon the land. *Damn my morals, indeed.*

He descended down the steps, the armour clinking and clanking, each foot forward bringing with it a melody of metallic jingles. He certainly wouldn't be creeping up on the Chimera, that was for sure. He entered the throng of the civilians in the courtyard, most of them heading home from a day's hard labour. He shouldered his way through the mess of homeless and nobles alike, a dozen voices floating through the bevy all jumbled and nonsensical.

But there was one voice that stood out—a man shouted at him, grabbing at Bellerophon's gauntlets with meek, bony hands.

'Bellerophon!' his old, croaky voice sounded off. 'Are you one of Lobates' men now?'

Bellerophon looked down at the old man and realised he was the cripple he had saved from the noble.

'Temporarily, I suppose,' Bellerophon replied and carried on through the courtyard.

'But Lobates' men are corrupt,' the old man limped after him. 'You're nothing like them.'

If you only knew, Bellerophon thought to himself. He bet none of those men had slain their own brother.

'I'm going to slay the Chimera,' Bellerophon told him.

'You what?' the old man shrieked, sucked in a breath and started unrolling a fit of coughs. 'You're joking, aren't you?'

Bellerophon just gave him a dead look.

'You're not joking,' the old man realised. 'It breathes flames, you know? It has the head of two mammals and—'

'And I'm going to kill it,' Bellerophon cut him off. 'Or it's going to kill me. Either way, everyone gets what they want.'

'And what do you want, Bellerophon?' the old man was struggling to keep up now, his voice falling behind.

'Justice?' Bellerophon said, but even that word seemed alien now and further out of reach.

'It's a long journey to the volcano,' the old man shouted, his voice now almost completely lost in the bustle behind him. 'Stop off at the temple of Athena! I've heard men have found solace and wisdom there.'

Bellerophon gave a limp wave to the man. Solace and wisdom would've been all well and good a few years ago, but now the concepts of both were lost to him. Still, the temple would provide refuge in the form of shelter and perhaps warmth from the road. It was about all Bellerophon could hope for as he tightened his grip around the shoddy bow. He sure wasn't killing the Chimera at this rate and he couldn't decide what compelled him more. The fact that he was going to die, or the fact that he was okay with it.

VII. Athena's Wisdom

Weeks had passed, but Bellerophon couldn't say how many. He'd lost track after the first two sunsets, and beyond that, his focus was mainly on acquiring food and finding shelter from the occasional downpours. He'd rationed the arrows, shooting the prey that he knew he could hit before retrieving the arrows in the hopes that their integrity had not been compromised. In the end, he was down to a mere dozen arrows and he was sure the Chimera would take more than that. But he had to eat, did he not? There was no point battling the Chimera on an empty stomach.

Night was soon approaching; the skies darkened, bringing with them the faint flickering of stars and the emergence of the moon. The woods were alive with noises from the pitter patter of raindrops to the sounds of creatures buzzing and squeaking. Each footstep he took was a squelch in the mud, the armour still ringing out, surrendering his presence as if calling out for bigger predators to come and have a go at him. And it was cold too. Bellerophon hadn't counted on the icy winds this deep into the woods, as well as the mists floundering between the trees, chilling his skin and bringing him gooseflesh.

He was all but ready to stop by a cluster of rocks and build a fire when he saw the beige coloured structure between the gaps of the trees. He leapt forward, hurrying through the dense shrubbery, hacking away at most of it with his bare hands until he was standing before the rectangular structure, all polished and pristine. The moonlight passed over it, giving it an angelic, almost otherworldly sense, like it had fallen from Olympus itself and landed perfectly in the thick of the woods, unsullied.

The temple of Athena had four pillars at its front with several steps leading up to its main entrance. A triangular gable sat overhead with inscriptions that dripped with rainwater. Beyond that, there was an unremarkable wide space that served as the main room, but there was no lavish furniture nor godly gems or even a throne of some sort. But still, the structure reeked of a certain power that Bellerophon stopped to behold. If he was honest, he felt like he didn't belong there. This felt like an earthly retreat for the gods, and he was merely trespassing on their sacred monument.

He built the courage to set one foot on the first step, and just like that, a low rumble of thunder shifted across the sky. It was enough to make Bellerophon reconsider taking another step, but it was growing colder out here and the threat of rain would have him drenched for the fourth night in a row. It would be no good fighting the Chimera with an empty stomach and a cold to go with it. So he pressed on, one step at a time until he was by the pillars, staring into the vacant room.

'Hello?' he spoke, his voice all hoarse and raspy.

There was no response, only the echo of his voice until it was drowned out by the hiss of rain outside. He laid one hand on the pillar as he stepped inside and couldn't help but feel a subtle vibration suddenly seeping out of the pillar, into his palm and down his wrist. He was on his toes now, spear at the ready as if something was about to materialise from thin air and come at him. But nothing came. There were only the dark corners of the room, the whitewashed walls all perfect and spotless along with the marble floor, free of dirt and gleaming.

Bellerophon took his boots off and set them to one side before venturing further in. He glanced up at the low ceiling only to find more inscriptions, but it was too dark in here to make out what they said. Either way, he was in no mind for reading. His inner clothes were soaked through and he hoped the breastplate and the greaves did a better job at protecting him from the fire of the Chimera than they did from the rain. His eyes were heavy too, his joints and bones achy from a day's hard walk.

Solace and wisdom, he thought to himself as he allowed himself one last glance around the room. He could see how a man might've found peace being this far from the world, but the only wisdom he found was the decision to have a sit down. He parked himself in one of the shadowy corners, tore off his stupid cape and wrapped it around himself. But damn, it was still chilly and he clenched his arms around himself, embracing himself for warmth.

He wouldn't be far from the Chimera soon and still he had no real strategy or plan as to how he would slay the beast. Surely it would be more trouble than just ramming a spear through its heart, assuming it even had a heart. He would've pondered on it more but his eyes fell shut, and before long, his head was lulled against the wall.

Sleep came for him. But it did not come alone.

He knew he had to be dreaming because he wasn't in the temple anymore. In fact, he wasn't anywhere. An endless white space was laid out before him, above him, beneath him—everywhere! He frowned at first, his eyes slowly adjusting to the new surroundings before he was breathing heavy, his heart racing as he got to his feet and reached for his spear.

He spun around, spear in hand now as he looked left and right, hands clutched tightly around the metal pole, expecting something to come charging at him. But nothing came. Was he dead? Had he expired in his sleep? Perhaps the cold had truly gotten to him, or perhaps the lack of food. Maybe he'd been slain in his sleep by some thief or maybe he'd had his throat torn out by a wandering wolf. The thoughts consoled him and cooled his beating heart, for at last he would be at peace now.

His grip loosened around the spear and he let it clatter against the ground, expecting it to ring out. But it was silent. Was there no sound in the afterlife?

'Where am I?' he called out, only to find the words did not spring from his lips as they normally should have.

His head was on a swivel now as he searched for some answer, searched for someone, something, anything! He snatched the spear from the ground, heart starting to race again as he charged in a random direction, footfalls silent as he ran. Even the armour made no sound for once. Was this really death? An endless white bliss, yet surrounded by no one and nothing, forever trapped and alone with his own thoughts? Why, this was not the peace he sought after. In fact, no. This was Hell.

He kept running as if doing so would bring him, new surroundings, but instead the white space simply expanded before him growing further and further into the distance. There had to be an answer to all this, didn't there? There had to be some explanation, some clue some—

'Hmm, what's this?' a woman's voice sauntered its way to his ears.

He spun around, only to find her floating down from above as graceful as a petal billowed by the gentle nudge of the wind. Her dark hair sailed down her arms, gorgeous jet black locks that moved as if each strand was alive. She had gentle features with dark yet kind eyes that were earnest and compelling. She wore a smile on her face, one that didn't falter even for a second. If Bellerophon was honest, he had never seen a woman like her before.

'A hero, in my midst?' she tilted her head like she wasn't sure, but then she chuckled and began nodding her head, assuring herself of her words. 'Indeed, a hero.'

'Me?' Bellerophon spoke, his words suddenly audible. He didn't know why that made his heart swoon with a certain enjoyment. The old man had called him a hero and Bellerophon had to admit it had brought him a certain guilty joy. He was no hero. No. He was nothing but a murderer, an honourless man clinging onto his morals as if it would make a difference now.

'You are conflicted,' the woman noted and there was a brief drop of her smile. 'One side of you believes he is evil. The other longs to be good.'

'Who are you?' Bellerophon choked.

'It's not obvious?' the woman said. 'You are in my temple, are you not?'

'Athena?' Bellerophon gasped and fell to a knee immediately.

'No need for all that,' Athena waved a dismissive hand at him. 'It is so rare for me to have company here. Tell me, hero...what is your name?'

'Bellerophon,' he told her.

Her eyes immediately lit up, 'Bellerophon? Indeed, a hero after all. I know of you.'

'You do?'

'I know your father,' she said. Her smile dipped once more, but this time it didn't come back. A grave look came upon her face all of a sudden, and no longer was she serene and innocent as her feet touched the ground.

'I'm glad one of us does,' Bellerophon suddenly regretted dropping the spear as she began walking towards him with one hand behind her back.

'Bellerophontes he called you,' she bit off the name like it tasted foul in her mouth. 'But I confess, your version of the name is far less idiotic.'

'My mother told me my father was a nobody,' Bellerophon took a step back, his eyes still fixed on that hand behind her back.

'She in part was right,' Athena shrugged. 'But wrong at the same time. Enough about him. Tell me why you are here.'

He had an urge to keep his lips shut, but something about her approach made him speak freely, as if not doing so would have her carve the answers out of him all the same.

'King Lobates sent me to defeat the Chimera,' he said, the spear still set in his hands.

'Hmmm,' Athena touched her lip. 'You're being used, Bellerophon. Lobates simply wants you dead but is too cowardly to condemn a man to death by his own hand. I think he might sense your strength and does not want to test it.'

'My strength?' Bellerophon frowned.

'Oh don't be so foolish,' Athena chuckled. 'You have demonstrated strength beyond that of ten men throughout your life. Tell me, how do you think you killed your brother with a mere tap? How do you think you can break steel chains as if they were string?'

'I...I...'

'You're a hero, Bellerophon, but you also have your father's simple mind. You'll fight the Chimera, but know your worst enemy awaits you should you slay it.'

'My worst enemy? You mean Lobates?'

Athena smirked, 'Someone closer to home.'

That was when she sprang forward, arm outstretched reaching for him. Bellerophon lifted the bow; he would've fired off a shot if he hadn't noticed the golden bridle hanging from her fingertips. He was expecting a knife, but this? What was the meaning of this?

Perhaps she intends me to hang with it, he mused.

'Take it,' she told him. 'Or did you think you would simply walk up the side of the volcano to fight the Chimera?'

He took it hesitantly from her hand, but once he had it he held it limply between his fingers. He supposed he should've said thanks, but he would've preferred an enchanted dagger or some godly hammer. Even a plate of food would've gone down a treat.

'Your escort awaits you outside my temple. Use the bridle to tame him, and he will be a loyal companion—one who will help you slay your enemies and chariot your name to Olympus.'

'I don't understand,' Bellerophon started towards her. 'What am I supposed to—'

'His name is Pegasus.'

And then she was gone.

He awoke with a start, one side of his arm numb from the wall and the other flailing about, searching for the spear. He was drenched in sweat. He fumbled with the cape, tore at the damn thing all tangled about him until he was free of it. His breath was fast, his lungs sore as if he had been dunked underwater and was only just now breathing properly again. It was darker too, darker than it had been before. A slender ray of moonlight cascaded through the open entrance, making for a glowing trail across the temple floor. It was the only source of light.

Bellerophon got to his feet, grabbed the spear in his left hand and went to grab the bow with the other. But his arm was still numb, so numb in fact, that he hadn't noticed the golden bridle still sat in his palm.

'Impossible,' he said breathlessly.

There was a neighing outside, but that didn't make sense to Bellerophon. There were no wild horses in the woods, and no rider would dare bring one in given the harsh terrain. He grabbed his bow and slung it over his shoulder before creeping along the trail of moonlight until he was outside by the pillars again.

The moon looked like it had doubled in size; a giant ball dominating the sky, casting everything below from the grass to the trees in an enchanting, silvery hue. The rain had stopped and where it had been chilly before, it was now warm, though Bellerophon attributed that to the sweats he had during his sleep. The neighing came again, only this time it was more urgent, like it was calling to him.

Bellerophon scurried up the nearest hill where he heard the horse, crawling up on hands and knees until he reached the top. He looked down at the open space below where a small field and one shimmering white horse with the wings of a giant swan awaited.

Pegasus, Athena had called it. *A companion*, she had described it. But it sure didn't look like one. It dug its hooves into the grass, wiping them the way a bull might at the sight of red. It brayed at him with an aggressive whip of its majestic head, its silver crest wafting wildly with it. The nostrils at the bottom of its long face were opening wide, closing for a short time and then opening again, air puffing in and out as it grew more and more agitated. Its legs were like stalks, steady and planted. Bellerophon found his own were prone to the occasional quiver as he breathed in the beast.

He moved towards it carefully and only raised the bridle once he was close enough. But Pegasus watched his every move, its big black eyes glued to him, like it was daring him to take another step. Its wings began to twitch, his hind legs bending a slight as if it meant to take flight and ditch him before he could even tame it.

'Hello,' Bellerophon spoke, though his words came out of nerves. 'I'm Bell—'

Pegasus stormed forward, brayed harshly in Bellerophon's face and slammed its head against his breastplate. Bellerophon made a sharp cry before he was on the floor, the world somersaulting as he bounced in the grass, rolling to a stop. It took a moment for everything to stop spinning, but once it had, he kicked up onto his feet and grabbed hold of the bridle once more.

Pegasus saw him go for it though and the beast neighed again; this time it came with an unlikely roar. It stopped Bellerophon in his tracks as he saw the creature's wings expand, ivory-coloured feathers blossoming out from its sides. Bellerophon was in awe of its magnificent form until it slammed its wings together. Then a gust of wind wrenched him off his feet, stole away his breath and planted him on his face some dozen feet away.

Pegasus neighed victoriously while Bellerophon spat mud out of his mouth.

A loyal ally? He found himself looking back in the direction of the temple. He reached for the bridle as he rolled onto his back and sat up, this time a little less enthusiastically. Pegasus was pacing left and right, its eyes still fixed on him as it trotted here and there, prancing about all cocky and superior. If it was any more human, Bellerophon was sure it would be trash talking him.

He must've landed badly because the small of his back stung with shooting pains up the left side. Still, it would take more than that to keep him down. He lifted the bridle at Pegasus, flaunting it at the beast as if to show it what he intended. But Pegasus didn't care. The horse only seemed to want to fight as it galloped towards him, teeth now fixed in the shape of a violent smile.

Bellerophon met it head on, though he couldn't say how wise that was. The beast lifted its wings once more and beat them together, but Bellerophon lunged to the side as the gusts tore past him. He must've moved too fast for the horse, because all of a sudden Pegasus made a whining grunt and the confidence in its right eye melted.

Bellerophon swung the bridle at it, but Pegasus evaded it, plunging its head to the ground to avoid it. Bellerophon took that moment to charge it, but Pegasus was fast and got its front legs up to drill away his breastplate. It rang out through the woods, and though the breastplate was hardened steel, Bellerophon still felt the blows shake his entire inside. He grabbed a hold of the horse's right fetlock, sunk his fingers around the left ergot and tried shoving the horse over.

But Pegasus held its ground and shoved back, forcing Bellerophon down to one knee. He could feel the pressure in his shoulders, could feel sharp twinges going down his arms as he fought back, lifting Pegasus back inch by inch. The horse shoved its head against his and that's when they locked eyes, the pair of them growling and hissing as they fought for leverage. Bellerophon couldn't say how long they were locked in that stalemate, stuck in a frozen dance where neither of them would budge.

The spear glittered in the corner of his eyes, but he couldn't reach for it. Even if he could, Athena told him to break the horse, not kill it. Besides, Bellerophon wasn't sure slaying the beast was even possible at this point. His wrists were bending back and the same sharp pains were now shooting up his forearms. Something was bound to snap. He could feel it in his bones, quite literally. Pegasus must've known too for it was grinning again, its tongue poking out of its mouth.

So Bellerophon drove his helmeted head against the creature's snout. Immediately, Pegasus rolled back its head in pain and Bellerophon pounced on him, striking the horse with an open-handed thrust. Pegasus' eyes went lax for a moment and that was when Bellerophon reached for the bridle, untangled it and went to plunge it over the horse's head.

But Pegasus clapped Bellerophon in the head with its wing which sent him crashing against the grass again. A part of him wanted to stay down after that. He was bleeding from the mouth, the left part of his arm burning from skidding across the tough grass. He rolled onto his back with a groan, his hand blindly searching for the spear, or the bow, or the bridle. Whichever came first.

It was the bow.

'Fine,' Bellerophon croaked as he staggered to his feet. If Pegasus meant to kill him then so be it, he'd go down giving the beast something to remember him by. He grabbed a fistful of arrows, drew the bow back and sent out three shots at the beast. Pegasus grunted, unimpressed. It shielded its face with its wing as arrow after arrow plunged into it. Bellerophon moved closer and closer, each arrow meeting its mark, drilling into the wing of the creature. Though, as far as Bellerophon could tell, most of the arrows were snapping on contact.

He reached back for another arrow, only to find he'd used up a third of his quiver. He cursed and thought about lobbing the spear, but then he noticed that Pegasus was still shielding its face with its wing. So he grabbed the bridle and sprinted towards the beast who had only just now began to realise that the volley of arrows had stopped.

One eye appeared above its wing as it took in Bellerophon's approach. Realisation set in as it saw the golden bridle in his hand. It moved its wing to slash at him, but Bellerophon slid under it and came up fast to plunge the bridle down over its face.

Pegasus reared, but not before it planted its legs into Bellerophon once more, the impact taking him off his feet immediately and thrusting him through the air. He hit a tree hard, his head rocketing against the bark before he pitched forward, gracelessly crashing to the floor. Fruit cascaded down around him, branches and leaves raining down on him as he lay there, face down and barely breathing. He could hear Pegasus roaring to itself as it struggled with the bridle, but he hadn't the strength to look up at it.

He was sure he must've blacked out because all of a sudden, Pegasus was silent. He was sure he could hear it mulling about nearby, but then his ears were thumping with blood and he wasn't even sure which way was up. He managed to get feeling back into his hands, flexing his fingers in and out before he tried pushing himself up.

Pegasus was waiting for him, expressionless. The golden bridle sat perfectly around its head. Bellerophon smirked, then he chuckled and then he was laughing at the absurdity of it all. But laughing hurt his ribs and he stopped that soon enough before rolling onto his back.

'Are you not going to finish the kill, you stupid animal?' he grunted through the pain.

Pegasus appeared in his sights, its snout sniffing the top of his head. A flicker of annoyance appeared in the horse's eyes and it opened its mouth to reveal its teeth as it went for a bite. Bellerophon shut his eyes, his body rigid as he anticipated the moment those teeth sunk into his flesh. But instead, all that came was the wet tongue of the animal draping against his face.

'Blah!' Bellerophon smacked it away and shuffled to his feet in spite of the pain. 'What is the meaning of this?'

Pegasus made a whimpering sound as it trotted towards him, its head low as if it expected to be petted.

Bellerophon had half the mind to punch it. 'Oh, so now you want to be friends?'

The horse looked up at him with two glossy wet eyes and made the slightest nod.

'Accursed creature,' Bellerophon limped over to his spear and his bow and began collecting up any arrows he could. 'We could've saved a lot of time if you just came quietly.'

Pegasus neighed at him.

'Oh shut up,' he said as he grabbed hold of the horse's back and hoisted himself up. 'I'm the one with the broken ribs.'

Now what? he thought to himself as he took hold of the reigns and tugged left, then right. He hadn't the first clue about how to ride a damn horse, let alone one with wings.

'Yah!' he said in a loud voice. He'd heard men riding horses shout that a lot, perhaps it would get the horse moving.

Pegasus remained defiantly still.

'Athena said you would take me to the Chimera,' Bellerophon poked it atop its head. 'If you're not going to help me then you can just—'

Pegasus neighed, and all of a sudden, Bellerophon was clinging to its neck for dear life as Pegasus took flight. Its wings were beating by its side as they rose higher and higher, the trees soon beneath them as they hovered in the sky. Bellerophon found the courage to look down but wished he hadn't. He took hold of the reigns once he found the courage to let go of the horse's neck, and he adjusted himself until he was reasonably comfortable. Well, as comfortable as a man on a flying horse could get, he supposed.

The forest stretched out beneath him, the tops of the trees bewitched by the vibrant moonlight. Bellerophon took in a deep breath, mesmerised at the sight—mesmerised by the fact that he was this high up. He was laughing now, despite the soreness in his ribs as he held his hands out by his sides, feeling the wind against his face and sweeping by his arms. His heart was thumping fast, for he had never experienced such exhilaration. Was this what the gods felt like, staring down upon mortal men from such heights?

'Pegasus!' Bellerophon said, making his voice as heroic as he could before whipping the reigns. 'May we go onwards and crush the Chimera together!'

He imagined it would've looked rather mighty if Pegasus had soared across the sky...but it didn't.

Bellerophon cleared his throat before tapping Pegasus on the head again.

'I said,' he cleared his throat, 'may we go onwards and crush the Chimera together!'

But Pegasus merely grunted and made no indication that it was going anywhere.

Bellerophon sighed, 'Just fly that way, creature.'

And then they were off.

VIII. The Chimera

They'd flown for at least a day, but Bellerophon was surprised at how quickly the volcano sneaked up on them. In what seemed like the blink of an eye, the sky had turned black, courtesy of the ash and dirt being fired out from the volcano. More than once, Pegasus veered to avoid the flaming, molten rock that the volcano spat out. A grievous fog crept out of the crater and puffy black smog siphoned into the sky, blocking the sun and bringing the world to darkness.

Red lava spilled out of the crater, streams of the stuff leaking down the side of the volcano and pooling in various areas of the craggy land. Fires were spreading down below from where the molten rock projectiles were landing in the fields, destroying everything. It would make landing difficult, for the lava seeped along the grass, crawling in every direction, making for a deadly battleground.

Lightning flickered in the sky, the occasional bolt scaring Pegasus and making it buck and neigh. Bellerophon stroked the horse's head and whispered what he hoped would soothe the horse, but he wasn't sure it was having much effect. Lighting struck some of the nearby trees, cindering them and spreading more fire as if it was at all necessary. It was like the volcano and the sky were warring with each other, trying to outdo one another to see who could burn things the best.

Bellerophon eased Pegasus downwards. The last thing he wanted to be was struck by lightning when he was so close to the Chimera. They flew at tree level, but now Bellerophon found it hard to breathe as the smog and the embers caught in the back of his throat. He kept his forearm in front of his face, guiding Pegasus by the reigns with the other when he noticed movement on one of the volcano's ridges.

Six eyes stared up at him, one set golden, one set red and the other a cold blue. He knew the stories about the Chimera, knew them well in fact. But still, they could not have prepared him for the three headed demon that waited down below.

Its leftmost head was that of a lion, a golden mane surrounding its fuming face with long, sharp-looking whiskers and even sharper teeth. A fountain leaked out of its mouth, part of it clear like saliva and the other red like blood.

The rightmost head was that of a goat, eyes as fiery as the lava itself, emblazoned with nothing short of fury. Its horns were almost the size of Pegasus, two black horns that were noticeably misshapen on the account that it had probably rammed a few of its victims and inadvertently bent them. When it breathed, embers of fire escaped its mouth.

The final head was that of a snake, but it was attached to its tail and therefore moved freely above the other heads, its long tongue wriggling before snapping back. Its golden eyes were the most subtle with two black slits for pupils, waiting patiently for Bellerophon's descent.

As they drew nearer, Bellerophon noticed that one side of the Chimera's body was a burnt blondish colour while the other was a coal black. It had two front claws, both of which looked more than capable of crushing the armour plate worn around his chest. Its sinewy frame was even more intimidating with thick flesh along its arms and along its torso. It moved on all fours, one vicious claw at a time, prowling around a small caldera.

Pegasus touched down almost silently amongst the sounds of the bubbling lava and rocks that were being flung from the crater, soaring through the air before crashing in the distance with one mighty explosion after the other. Fires crackled all around, the flames themselves bickering as they spread across the grasslands. Then there was Bellerophon coughing, but even that was drowned out as the lion's head began snapping down with its teeth.

This is it, Bellerophon gulped as he reached for the spear. *Why am I doing this?* The answer still eluded him, but there was no turning back now. He hopped off of Pegasus and wondered whether the horse would ditch him now, ascend to the skies and forget all about him. Bellerophon wouldn't blame the creature.

For such a terrifying monster, the Chimera moved into his path in a dainty fashion. The lion's head still snapped this way and that, evidently disgruntled by Bellerophon's emergence. The snake remained calm, its head moving in a hypnotic fashion from left to right. The goat was poised, occasionally blinking with its vengeful eyes.

Bellerophon wondered which head would swallow him first. Maybe they'd feast on his corpse together, dividing him up so they all got a piece. He was sure the snake was smiling at him now, its tongue slowly gliding along its scaly lips. Bellerophon looked at his spear and then he looked at the girthy frame of the beast and couldn't help but feel like he should've taken the sword as well. Heck, he should've taken the entire armoury with him.

The beast was breathing heavier now, each head giving out an unsynchronised chain of breaths that each sounded horribly different. It began creeping towards him, strutting its way like an arrogant cat that had found a legless mouse.

Bellerophon readied his spear and called out, 'My name is Bellerophon!'

The Chimera didn't care. All it saw was talking meat.

'It is during this moment that your reputation will be sealed.'

Pegasus neighed impatiently and then darted back, giving the Chimera a wide birth.

'I hope you are one with your maker,' Bellerophon continued as he readied the spear at the Chimera. 'For I intend to send you to him!'

The Chimera lunged at him, its left claw whooshing in the air. Bellerophon dived out of its way, rolled onto his feet and staggered back against a craggy wall. The Chimera made no hurry to find him again as it turned its body around, each head none too flustered that it had missed its first strike. There would be plenty to follow, Bellerophon had no doubt of that. They stared at each other for the longest of moments, neither one of them sure of what move to make next. But the Chimera didn't stay dormant for long.

It was the snake that drew its head back as if it was looking up at the sky. Then, it opened its maw and swung its head forward, spewing a dark coloured acid. Bellerophon dived out of the way and damn near impaled himself on his own spear. He looked back, saw black acid bubble and melt away the rockery like it was butter. He grabbed the spear, shot up on his feet and took to encircling the beast as best he could, looking for an opening.

The Chimera lunged again, but this time Bellerophon met it with his spear, stabbing the flesh of its claw. The Chimera howled as it wrenched its claw back, but then the snake head snatched Bellerophon off his feet and tossed him like a doll. He rolled hard with the fall, hitting every sharp, jagged rock before stopping short of a pool of lava that had gathered. He could feel the heat from it against his skin and quickly scurried away from it.

The Chimera was already coming at him again, its feet sending up clouds of dust and dirt. Bellerophon took a moment to take a breath, lifted his spear and lunged head on to meet it. He caught the creature in the goat's jaw; that had it reeling back. The goat screamed and the Chimera swung around, perhaps the first sign of damage. However, its tail swept Bellerophon off his feet again, this time batting him straight through an assembly of rocks.

Bellerophon rolled with the fall, but it didn't make much difference. Tiny pebbles impacted his face, one of them nailing him right between the eyes. His arms were cut up, blood spewing out from a thousand different cuts, but he couldn't feel the pain yet. He couldn't see the Chimera anymore, for he was shielded behind one of the rocks, buying him some time to recuperate. His legs were shaking, his arms a mess of jelly as he fumbled for the spear again, but he couldn't find it.

He felt vibrations through the ground, tremors that jolted him left and right. Before he could move, the Chimera burst through the rock-shield with the horns of the goat and ploughed into him, barrelling him over a ridge. He cried out, but he didn't have much to cry about yet. He was falling, the ground rushing up to meet him until he slammed side-first into the dirt. It beat landing in lava, that was for sure.

The Chimera appeared above the ridge, staring down at him with giddy looking faces. The goat was bleeding, the wound from the spear would likely leave a scar on its mouth, but something told Bellerophon that the Chimera wasn't a vain beast. He struggled to get the bow off his shoulder, struggled even more to free an arrow from the quiver, but once he did, he fired upwards, catching the Chimera in the chest. The creature might've winced, but Bellerophon wasn't sure.

He tried to move off his back, but his body wouldn't respond. So Bellerophon was left to nock another, trying his best to get his shaky hands to line up the shot. He let the bowstring throng, but the arrow missed its mark and came straight back down, clattering uselessly by his side. He tried to get another arrow from the quiver, but he couldn't shift his weight to retrieve it.

That was when the Chimera roared, all of its heads raining growls down upon him as it stepped forward, lunged in the air and came crashing down on him. Bellerophon didn't shield his face. He lay there with his arms by his sides. He kept his eyes wide as the Chimera fell towards him. He welcomed death. He always had. He was going to be crushed.

Then, Pegasus rammed itself against the Chimera, knocking the beast hard into the side of a mountain. The Chimera was stunned for a moment, and Bellerophon had the nerve to hope that it wouldn't get back up again. But then its snake head floated upwards, eyeing Pegasus with venom spewing from its lips. It got to its feet and came storming towards Pegasus, but the horse was swift and managed to take to the air again. It kicked with its hooves, caught the goat in the face and almost turned the entire creature inside out. But then the Chimera struck with its claw, catching Pegasus on the side and forcing it to land.

It pounced on the horse, the two of them growling and biting at one another, kicking and slashing, neighing and growling. Bellerophon scurried to his feet where he found the corpse of one of Lobates' men, his armour plate crushed in and his head squashed into a bloody pulp. Bellerophon supposed if there was ever an omen, that was one of them. He wrenched the sword out of the dead man's hand and started up the incline in aid of Pegasus.

By time he got there, Pegasus was lying on its side, still breathing as far as Bellerophon could tell, but bleeding from a cut on its side. Something about that made him hate the Chimera and so when he found himself charging at the creature from behind, he didn't hold back. He leapt upwards, surprising himself at how high he had jumped before he readied the sword, swung it across the snake's neck and took its head off in one brutal strike.

Acid rained everywhere, the tail of the Chimera swaying back and forth like a deflated balloon before it sagged on the ground, leaking pus and dark greenish goo everywhere. The Chimera didn't react at first, but then it was rolling on the ground in a fit of pain, thrusting left and right before it flung itself over the ridge.

Bellerophon rushed over to Pegasus and placed his hands on the creature.

'Are you okay?' he asked, breathless.

Pegasus neighed weakly in response.

'Did you see that?' he said, smirking while panting for dear life. 'I'm winning.'

Pegasus groaned.

'Can you still fly?'

Pegasus nodded, though Bellerophon didn't like the look of that gash above its wing. He tore off his cape, tied it around the wound as best he could and hoped that it would ease the poor creature's pain in some way.

'I won't be long,' Bellerophon patted the horse and the horse neighed back as if it didn't believe a word he said. Bellerophon couldn't blame it.

The Chimera appeared again, climbing up the ridge as its two remaining heads greeted him. The goat's violent red eyes were something fierce, and when it breathed, flames came out from its nostrils. The lion was now gritting its teeth at him, shiny saliva flooding out from between the gaps of its fangs.

One down, Bellerophon thought, readying his sword. *Two to go.*

The Chimera mounted the edge of the ridge, but instead of staying on all fours, it now stood up on two, towering over Bellerophon like a giant. Bellerophon gulped, took two steps to the side and started running. He didn't know where he was going, but he couldn't face that thing head on.

Not like that.

It stamped after him, roaring at him as the ground began to shake with its every footfall. It became harder to keep steady, harder to keep on track with the ground shaking, and before long, Bellerophon was down on the ground, flapping about like a helpless fish. He dropped the sword and went to reach for it but found it kicked away by the Chimera. Before he could self-right, the Chimera plucked him off the ground and held him up, inspecting him the way a jeweller might've inspected a rare gem. It brought him close to the goat's side, its mouth now twisted in a grim sort of smile. Its warm tongue slithered out of its mouth and draped across Bellerophon's face, suffocating him for a moment before letting him free.

'Foul creature,' Bellerophon roared at it, but the Chimera merely giggled in response. It began toying with him, lifting him this way and that, shaking him up and spinning him upside down. Before long, Bellerophon wasn't sure which way was up anymore. The world began to distort, colours of red, grey, black and beige merging into one messy puddle. He puked over himself—tasted his own bile down the side of his lips—before trying to reach for the bow.

But the Chimera had him held tightly and he could only free the one arm. The other was trapped and no matter how hard he tried to wriggle free, the Chimera's grip was true. It snorted at him with its snout, made a sort of hee-hawing sound from its throat before bringing him closer and closer to its rotten mouth.

Bellerophon reached back and grabbed one last arrow from the quiver. He wasn't going to die, that much he had decided. But it was looking bleak now that he'd lost the spear, now that Pegasus was down and now that he couldn't reach the bow. What good was an arrow without a bow? He didn't have time to think anymore as his head neared the teeth of the lion. So he jammed the arrow straight in the lion's blue eye.

Blood exploded out of the creature's eye, soaking him through. The Chimera flinched back, screaming wildly as it released its hold on Bellerophon. But Bellerophon held onto the arrow as best he could, legs dangling, before he pulled himself up and thrust himself atop the goat's head.

The Chimera had one claw trying to nurse the wound at its eye, but its other claw came hammering down from above. Bellerophon dived between its claws, causing the beast to stun itself. It hit the side of a craggy wall, wheezing and violently shifting this way and that. But Bellerophon wasted no time getting a hold of the creature's horn, wrapping both arms around it like he was tightly embracing it before heaving with all his strength.

It didn't seem like anything would happen at first. In fact, this seemed like a pretty terrible idea. But then there was a crack and all of a sudden, the horn snapped off in his hands. The Chimera bellowed into the air, beating at its chest before bringing its hand down upon its head to flatten Bellerophon. But he was quicker, and used the horn the way he would've used the spear, stabbing at the claw each time it came down. Bloody holes appeared on the creature's claw, and before long, it stopped striking at him and took to manically shaking its head to be rid of him.

But Bellerophon held fast and turned the horn so the point was facing downwards. Then he drilled it straight through lion's skull, one inch at a time until he felt it drive through its fleshy brain, further down into its face, sinking the horn as far as it could go before the Chimera dropped to its knees. Then it pitched on its face, bringing Bellerophon crashing down with it.

He didn't even bother rolling with the fall this time. He didn't have to. His body bounced on its own accord like a lifeless toy, tossed this way and that before coming to an abrupt stop a few feet away from the Chimera. Everything immediately hurt, but he could do no more but scream at the darkening sky, his fingers curling with the pain until he had no more breath left. There were spasms of sharp pain down one of his legs, the other jittered all on its own accord. His arms seemed fine enough, with the exception of the cuts he'd received and the rain of blood spilling from his brow, getting in his eyes and drenching his face.

His breastplate was dented, a part of the metal digging into his abdomen. His spine was on fire, parts of his neck lit up with shooting pains, a thousand pinpricks across forearms with bruises, swellings and gods knew what else. His elbows were burned, parts of his legs smoking from where he must've been scorched by the lava and not realised it. *How does a man get burned by lava and not feel it?* he wondered to himself, but then his head began to hurt and the act of thinking became agony.

He tried to sit up but his chest was on fire and each time he tried, something in his body clicked and kept him down. The bow was in pieces by his sides, one of the arrows sitting precariously in his back, spearpoint first of course. He felt for the sword, realised the Chimera had kicked it away and realised he was done. Without any weapons, he could no more fight than he could stand up.

The Chimera stirred somewhere beyond his feet. How close, he couldn't say—close enough that it knew he was there. It sounded like it was in pain too, but it was shuffling, which meant it was still mobile, which is more than he could say about himself. He wondered if Pegasus was in the right frame to come and finish the fight for him, given that he had taken two of the three heads himself. It seemed only right that the horse do the last one. But when the goat's head appeared above him, Bellerophon knew he was on his own.

It still stood on its muscular legs, its shoulders bunched up as its chest rose and fell with each steady breath. Smoke was billowing out from its nostrils, the occasional flare of fire threatening to emerge from its mouth. *So it will be death by burning then*, Bellerophon thought. *I suppose there are worse ways to meet one's destiny.*

The Chimera tensed its arms and its breathing began to quicken, each breathy exhale coming with a pained grunt. What was left of its snaky tail still flopped about, but the head of the lion hung lifelessly like a dead bit of decoration. Bellerophon hoped the goat would enjoy the flies that would no doubt descend upon it. He hoped it would enjoy the rotten stench too.

There was a light behind the goat's teeth. He could see the orange glow building up as embers escaped from its nostrils. It was getting ready to roast him, just like in the stories. Its stomach was beginning to glow too, an orange, reddish bulge swelled at its gut. Its cold blue eyes grew wider with excitement, and then it slowly opened its mouth to reveal the furnace at the back of its throat.

Something clattered by his side. Bellerophon almost ignored it but was surprised to find the spear laying there beside him, as if someone had just tossed it at him. He looked up and saw the limping Pegasus neigh at him.

He didn't think after that. He simply grabbed the spear, didn't even consider aiming, but merely tossed it with all the strength he had left. He saw the mouth of the goat expand wide, saw the flames reach their full potential before they spewed out of its mouth.

But the spear caught the goat in the neck and immediately, the goat clasped its mouth shut, its eyes blinking, perplexed. The Chimera grabbed hold of the spear, realised it had gone through its throat and wasn't sure whether to yank it out or not. It began retching, blood spilling out from its mouth as its claws found their way around its own neck. It tried to do something—tried to pry the spear out or somehow nudge it away—but it was done.

It began thrashing about on the ground, its stomach lighting up with flames. Its claws hammered about at the ground more like a child's desperate tantrum than anything else, but the agonising grunts were undeniable. Its stomach burst into red and orange flames that were quick to embark along its legs, devouring its entire frame the way it had done to the grasslands. The Chimera tried rolling onto its stomach, but the spear got in the way, preventing him from even lifting up its final head. Pretty soon, the flame from its belly chased up its chest and before long, its head was engulfed.

Bellerophon couldn't keep his own head up after that as he let it hit the dirt. He stared up at the murky sky, half a smile on his face at having done it. The pain was nothing to smile about though, and pretty soon, he was wincing at every ache. He heard Pegasus trot its way over to him, the horse quietly braying as its hooves scrunched in the dirt.

Bellerophon smirked as it came in sight above him, 'Told you I'd kill it.'

He shut his eyes to rest.

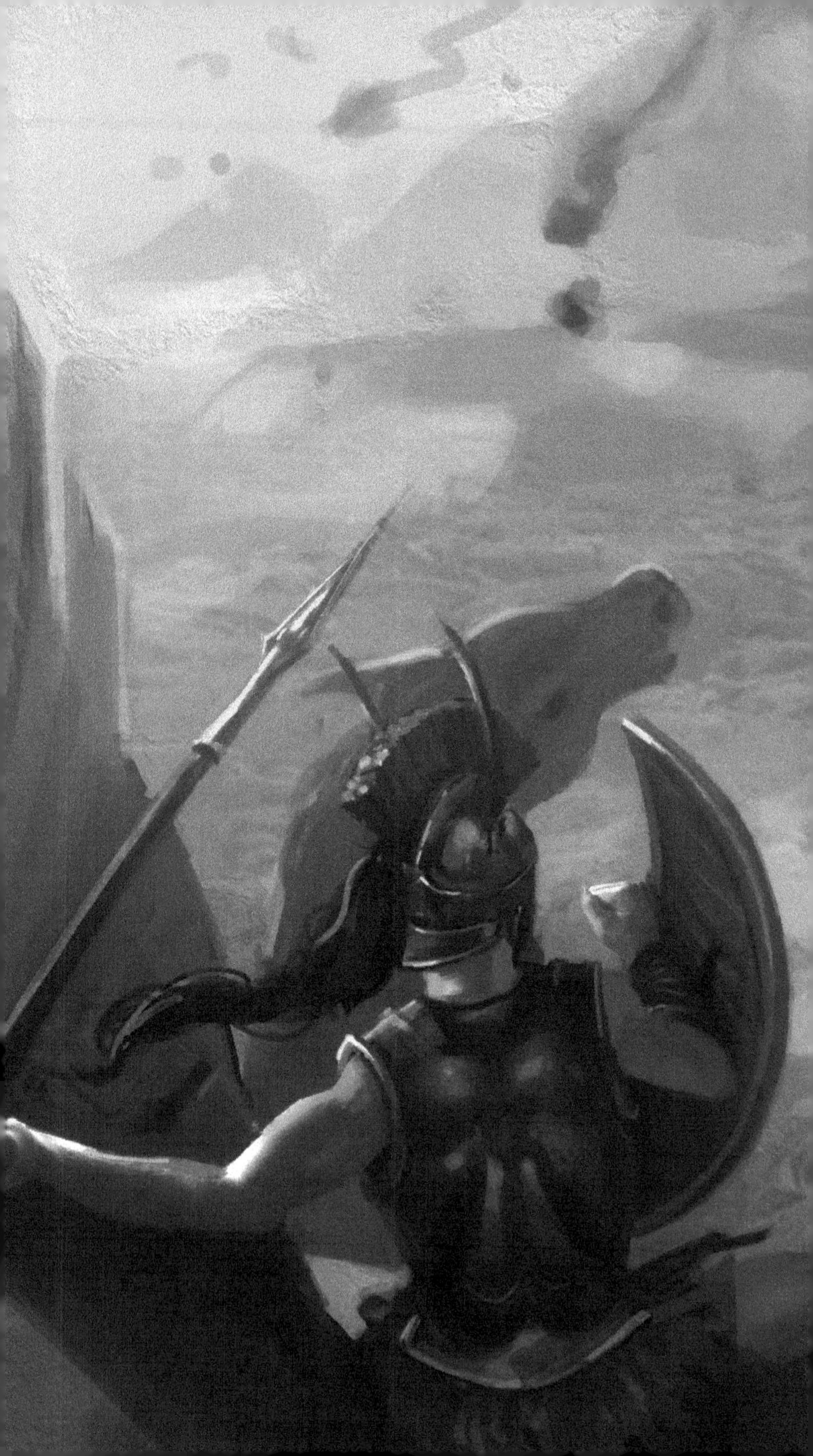

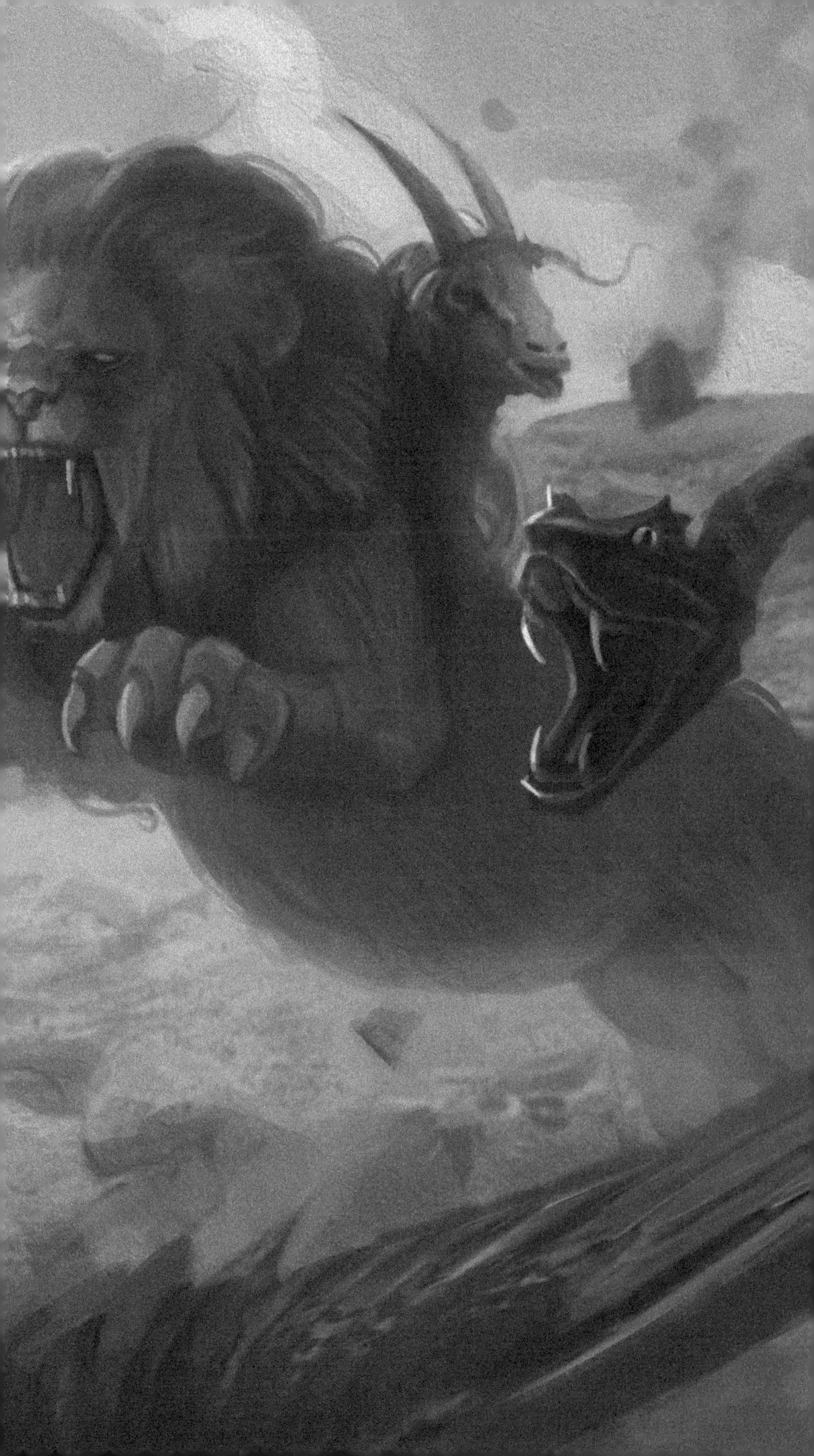

IX. A Hero Returns

Bellerophon swung the bag over his shoulder with one hand and guided Pegasus with the other, gently nudging him to descend. Beneath them sat the kingdom of Lycia, and Bellerophon found himself blinking in the sudden brightness as the clouds gave way to the morning sunlight.

He spotted the south side of the city first, an almost endless carpet of stone-walled houses, some fine and others decrepit and probably abandoned. To the north, Lobates' palace stood like an arrogant bully, casting its shadow amongst the other, lesser buildings. Green lawns broke up the monotony of the grey city and lofting towers belonging to regals and nobles served to remind the people just who was important and who was not.

As he and Pegasus drew closer to the main courtyard, Bellerophon noticed the crowd of people who had gathered there—a sea of faces, each with the same stunned expression. They were pointing manically, some of them tripping over themselves to get away and others tripping over themselves to get closer. As he got nearer, he could hear the excited buzz wriggling through the crowd, some of them in awe at the magical beast and others more sceptical of his mission's success. There was a prominent chant that rang out the loudest though, the chant of his name over and over again.

'Bellerophon! Bellerophon! Bellerophon!'

His cheeks went warm the moment Pegasus hit the ground, and suddenly he was very aware that every set of eyes in the vicinity were focused on him, smiles and cheers directed his way. Men and women were barging one another in the thick of the throng, trying to get the best sight of him and Pegasus. Small children zig-zagged in between the adults' legs, peeking a glimpse of him with wonder in their eyes.

The nobles were on one side, waving kerchiefs and lobbing their hats in the air in celebration, while on the other, the homeless rattled their can of coins, shouting words of encouragement from their toothless mouths. People were pouring out of the balconies on the higher buildings, waving and thrusting their hands as if trying to reach him.

'Bellerophon! Bellerophon! Bellerophon!'

All he could do was lift a weak, painful arm up at the crowd and wave back, but when he tried to smile his lips wouldn't comply. He was too shocked at such a reception, for he'd never had a reception like this before. Most people had looked past him, barely even spoken to him for that matter. Now, they were screaming his name and damn near biting at each other to get the best look at him. His cheeks were still warm, his armpits sweating and while he still sat atop Pegasus, he daren't not get off, for he suddenly couldn't feel his legs.

'Bellerophon! Bellerophon! Bellerophon!'

The chanting showed no signs of stopping. The people were enraptured by him, and if he was honest, he didn't quite want it to stop. A part of him wanted to soak this up, to bathe in the glory that was their adulation. But then he'd always known modesty, had he not? A part of him felt a pang of guilt for enjoying this so much, but had he not earned it? He'd killed the Chimera for crying out loud. He deserved to be recognised for that as a brave man at least, or a strong man or a...hero.

It was then that he felt a tugging at his arm, and there beneath him was the old cripple he had saved from the nobles. The old man was grinning with his blackened smile, his eyebrows wispy and almost faded, but visible enough because they were raised so high.

'I knew you'd do it, Bellerophon!' he shouted by his side. 'I told everyone who would listen that you'd come back victorious and here you are!'

'You did all this?' Bellerophon climbed down from Pegasus.

'Well...no,' the old man confessed, 'but I told them all you'd come back even though none of them listened to me. When they saw you flying in, they all knew!'

That was when Lobates' men came storming through the crowd, shoving people here and there, barging others to the floor and smacking the more rebellious with their shields. Upon seeing Bellerophon, they went for their swords, but as they did, Pegasus let out a mighty neighing sound that had them holding back. The crowd hushed into silence after that, the echoes of their celebration drowning out and into the air.

'King Lobates demands a report from your venture, Bellerophon!' one of the guards announced.

Bellerophon lifted the bag in offering, 'Take me to him then.'

It felt like an age since he had last been marched through the throne room like this, only this time he wasn't muscled in by two guards on his side. In fact, they'd given him a wide berth and even argued at the entrance as to who was going to walk him through. In the end, Bellerophon strode in himself and two of the guards had no choice but to double in after him. One of them could smell the contents of the bag, but he didn't question what was inside; he merely looked at it with a mix of disgust and uncertainty.

'Bellerophon!' Lobates greeted him, though he didn't get up from his throne. In fact, Bellerophon noticed a twinge of annoyance in his face, like he wasn't expecting to see him again so soon, if at all.

'My king,' Bellerophon lowered his head.

'My subjects normally kneel,' Lobates was quick to point out.

'I'm not your subject,' the words flew from his mouth and even Bellerophon was a little stunned that they had. A part of him felt the need to submit and kneel, but the other half was still burning with adrenaline, the memory of the Chimera in flames so vivid that he didn't see the need to kneel to anyone ever again.

Lobates let it slide, 'Your mission was a success?'

'It was,' Bellerophon nodded.

'And now you have a flying horse?' Lobates massaged his fat chin.

'A gift from Athena,' Bellerophon confirmed and he could see the muscles in Lobates' face twitch.

Lobates glanced at each of his guards for a moment, though Bellerophon couldn't say why. A silence ensued after that where Lobates began taking a key interest in the bag he held. Flies were drawn around it now, buzzing hungrily.

'Is that what I think it is?' Lobates pointed with his chin.

'It is,' Bellerophon confirmed.

There was a muscle working at the side Lobates' head now, 'Show me.'

So Bellerophon emptied the bag right there and then on the polished floor, which would need a great deal more than polish after this. The head of the snake spilled out first and landed with a wet thump, green stinking goo pooling around it. Then came the head of the goat, its mouth hung gormlessly open with both its eyes welded shut. Then came the head of the lion, but it was a black thing and hardened like rock, barely even a shape anymore—just an ambiguous burnt thing with teeth.

'I trust our business here is complete,' Bellerophon spoke, trying to appear like the stench didn't bother him.

A few of the guards were already choking, some of them dropping their weapons and darting out of sight. Some of them unloaded their guts there and then or stumbled over themselves to get as far back as possible. Only Lobates remained where he was, but he was shuffling uncomfortably in his throne like he'd just found needles in the seat. He'd gone a shade lighter too, his lips pursed in a most agitated way, as if this wasn't what he had asked for at all.

'I would've taken your word for it,' he cleared his throat.

'If that was true, you would've pardoned me when I said I didn't touch your daughter.'

Lobates got to his feet and took a step forward, one eye on Bellerophon and the other lingering on the mess of heads at his feet. Then, much to Bellerophon's surprise, he gave a stiff sort of bow.

'It appears my son-in-law was wrong about you, Bellerophon.' He said after clearing his throat. 'A deal is a deal. You are pardoned of all your crimes and may walk this world as you please once more.'

Bellerophon returned the bow with a curt nod of his head. He would've blathered about his appreciation for the king's decision, but he didn't see why he had to. As far as he was concerned, Lobates should've been on his knees, kissing his feet for his heroism. But far be it from him to say anything. At the end of the day, he was a man of honour, was he not? An honourable man didn't go about making demands or stepping out of line. Lobates was still the king after all.

With that, he turned on his heels and began making his way out of the room. His quest was complete, but the image of his brother's bloody skull still remained as prominent as ever. In fact, it hadn't changed much at all. Deep down, buried under the newfound heroism and that fresh feeling of power, the guilt presided. For a moment, he thought he heard his brother's laughter from above, a laugh that was both nostalgic and scornful at the same time. He clenched his fists, for even though he'd slain the Chimera, the justice he came for was still out of reach.

A young guard came storming past him, face shiny with sweat as he bolted for the king.

'My king! My king!' he was panting as he collapsed to his knees. 'The Amazons! They came at us in the woods and ambushed us. They've taken our squad prisoner.'

'Outrageous!' Lobates beckoned. 'Those animals have tried my patience for the last time!'

'What will you have us do?' the young guard panted.

'*You* will do nothing,' Lobates clicked his fingers and immediately two other guards seized the younger one by the arms. 'If your squad was captured, then why are you here?'

'I...I...I ran, sir.' The guard lowered his head.

'Coward,' Lobates clenched his fist so hard there was an audible cracking of bone. 'Throw this piece of dirt in the prisons. We'll execute him later.'

'No, please!'

The guards hoisted him up, and despite his kicking and screaming, they carried him easily enough with the most stoic expressions, as if they'd done this a hundred times before.

'Raise an army,' Lobates ordered one his guards. 'We'll storm in there and get our men back and crush those she-devils once and for all.'

'But sir,' the guard gulped. 'The men have expressed their concerns about fighting the Amazons. They are skilled warriors, brutal and cunning beyond our...well, beyond us.'

'What are you saying, man?' Lobates demanded.

'I'm saying that our soldiers are scared to fight them and therefore will not,' the guard lowered his head in shame.

Lobates' face scrunched up into a red ball of anger, 'Bellerophon! Do you hear of this cowardice?'

Bellerophon wasn't sure what he was meant to say. He didn't think he had right to say anything now that his obligation was fulfilled. All he had to do was walk out of those doors and he'd be free from Lycia, free from Lobates and Proteus and everyone else. He'd take Pegasus and fly far away from here, never to look back again in hopes of escaping that image of his brother.

But he spoke anyway, 'It's not my place to comment.'

'Fear them, yes.' Lobates hissed. 'But to cower and refuse to fight them? That is treason!'

'You are right, King Lobates,' Bellerophon noted. He had intended to look away and carry on walking. But King Lobates came rushing over to him, his fat bulge of a stomach swinging with him.

'You have won honour today, Bellerophon, and completed my quest to win back your freedom. But what if I offered you another task to win glory and riches and power?'

Bellerophon didn't like the wet look in Lobates' eyes, but he did like the sound of what he'd mentioned.

'Think about it, Bellerophon. You slayed the Chimera and now my people adore you. Imagine if you could slay the Amazons for me. The people will all but collapse at your feet. They already sing of you as a hero, imagine after this victory against those savages. They won't sing of you as a hero then, no. They will sing of you as a god!'

'A god?' Bellerophon's breath caught in his throat.

'Yes, my boy! A god!' Lobates wrapped his arm around him, using his other arm to paint a picture before his eyes. 'I'll grant you your own district in the kingdom and you'll be paid a handsome reward! We'll even give you your own stable for Peggard!'

'Pegasus,' Bellerophon snapped.

'Pegasus!' Lobates quickly corrected. 'Of course I meant Pegasus.'

A god, Bellerophon was staring down at his hands, the same hands that had killed his brother in a single tap and the same hands that had single-handedly brought down the Chimera. He was still reeling from the reception he'd received upon flying in with Pegasus, a hero's welcome. But he could only imagine what it would be like flying in as a god and how the people would lap up his every gesture. Why, it would be a glorious feeling that even now made him feel warm inside, made him giddy in the stomach and made his head all light with joy. If he was honest, he'd even forgotten about his brother for a moment.

'What do you say, Bellerophon?' Lobates gave his shoulder a squeeze.

His own district in the kingdom? Why, he'd be rich beyond his dreams, surely. With his own district he could do whatever he wanted. He could build his own home, or a tower with a hundred floors like the nobles had, with a green lawn and a massive fountain that people would adorn. He could still hear their chants outside, the ringing of his name as loud as the Chimera's dying roars. He was grinning now and that made Lobates grin with a slow nodding of his fat jowls.

'I'm going to need new weapons,' he told Lobates, but Lobates was already beckoning the order.

X. The Apple Never Falls Far

He zoomed across the sky, an army of one. He had no battle plan, no rescue strategy for Lobates' captured men, nor even a clue of how to navigate the island. Yet that didn't concern him. The Chimera had concerned him, but a bunch of women dressed in armour? It made Bellerophon laugh.

He could see their meagre city beneath him now, a small and marooned bit of land almost lost in the thick of the wild blue ocean. There were only a dozen buildings or so, most of them with straw roofs held up by clusters of wood. The occasional house was built of stone, but the craftwork was sloppy and Bellerophon could see several neighbouring buildings sloping to one side like a line of drunks.

Two effigies stood in the centre of the land, one of a woman holding a shield and the other a bow. Beyond that, there was a more significant building—a temple of sorts—that towered over the rest, one that had been built symmetrically with a golden disc for a roof. Bellerophon imagined that the leader of their tribe lived there, holed up in comfort like Lobates was, fat and too weak to do anything herself.

He could see the women now as he came in for landing. At the sight of him, they scuttled this way and that, gathering up bows and shields to give him a welcome he'd no doubt remember. Pegasus hit the ground and broke into a sprint along the grass, making headway towards what looked like a defensive line before the temple.

At least fifteen women in golden armour stood with their bows ready, some of them with swords and spears thrown in the mix, daring him to come closer and closer. Bellerophon obliged them, drawing Pegasus into a slow trot but progressing nonetheless.

They all had similar faces, strong jaws with a constant, murderous frown. Bellerophon was sure he could tell a joke and he'd sooner get an arrow in the eye than a laugh. They were of a burly frame too, some of them packing more mass than himself. They had legs the size of trees, arms like logs with rippling muscles—hardly women at all anymore as far as Bellerophon could tell.

'Speak of your business here, man,' the blonde one in the middle hissed at him. Not a single one of them looked like they were interested in what he was there for, in fact they seemed all the more eager to kill him as he removed his helmet. They didn't even bat an eyelid at Pegasus who Bellerophon could feel was becoming twitchy at the sight of all those weapons pointed at them.

'I must ask that you lower your arms,' Bellerophon announced. 'My dear friend here is not fond of violence.'

'You're lucky we didn't shoot you and your monster pet out of the sky,' another one piped up, one ginger-haired creature with hair on her upper lip. More hair than Bellerophon had, in fact.

'Well that's not nice,' Bellerophon hopped off of Pegasus. 'He has feelings as well, you know?'

'State your business,' the blonde one hissed again.

Bellerophon strolled his way in front of Pegasus, taking his time. He drew a hand over the creature's crest, gave him a little scuffle behind the ear to which the horse neighed in delight, before sweeping a glance at the Amazons.

'My name is Bellerophon,' he spoke and took much enjoyment when he noticed their hardened expressions suddenly weaken.

'Bellerophon?' A darker skinned one spoke, her sword now lowered. 'They say you slayed the Chimera.'

'I did,' Bellerophon blew some dirt off his knuckles. 'Alone, might I add.'

Pegasus neighed at him.

Bellerophon sighed, 'Well, I suppose I had some help.'

'What do you want, Bellerophon?' the blonde one seemed to speak for them all.

'I've come for Lobates' men, I suppose. The ones you ambushed and have taken hostage.'

'We did not take any men,' one of the women snapped, this one with shorter hair cropped at her chin. 'We would sooner gut them than take them as prisoners.'

'Tell that to Lobates,' Bellerophon shrugged.

'Is he here?' the blonde one piped up again. 'Just what I thought. Instead he sends his lapdog to do his bidding.'

'What did you call me?' Bellerophon snapped.

'Lapdog,' she said, only this time slower and with more venom.

Bellerophon twitched at that. He couldn't say why it bothered him so, but he felt his hand reaching for his sword. Maybe because her words were true. He was acting for Lobates, carrying out his errands like an obedient pup. Damn it, he'd slain the Chimera. He shouldn't have had to do anything more to earn the district in the kingdom he was promised. Lobates should've been on his knees, kissing his feet for having brought the monster down in the first place.

'Your words cut deep,' Bellerophon feigned a smirk, tried to play it off like he'd heard it before but he didn't think he was fooling them at all.

'Our weapons cut deeper,' the blonde woman shouted.

Bellerophon looked at Pegasus, 'Do you remember that thing you did to me when we first met?'

Pegasus grunted, nodding its head.

'Do it to them,' he commanded.

Immediately, Pegasus lunged forward, neighing like it had gone mad all of a sudden. Its wings were flapping. Terrible gusts of winds came out from nowhere. Without warning, it smashed its wings together. Bellerophon saw their eyes suddenly widen as a monstrous wind rushed at them. Some of them threw their shields up to block, but in the end, they were all taken off their feet and flown to the ground like dolls.

Bellerophon let out a fit of laughter as he watched them recuperate. One of them had hit the ground so hard that she didn't get back up. Another one looked like she'd hurt her arm, for she dropped her shield and was nursing it with her sword hand.

'You've done it now!' the blonde shouted.

'Give me Lobates' men and I won't fight you,' Bellerophon gave them one last chance.

'They aren't here!' the blonde screamed as she came charging at him, sword raised high. 'But you will pay for your disrespect with your life.'

Bellerophon drew his sword without urgency. He even had the nerve to catch his own reflection in the shining metal, observing all the little cuts and bruises he'd gotten from tussling with the Chimera. He smirked, saw one tiny cut on his lip and pressed his tongue against it.

'Die!' the blonde roared, not ten paces away now.

'I tried to,' Bellerophon whispered. 'It never worked.'

She swung high, going for the head. Bellerophon knelt beneath it and slashed at her thigh. She let out a howl, but she swung around to try and catch him in the back. But Bellerophon was quick. He lunged to the side of her and kicked her wound so that she fell to one knee. She swung back blindly. He smacked her wrist with his free hand so her weapon clattered to the grass. She looked back, eyes wide with fear all of a sudden.

He smirked at her. He liked to think of it as a mere gesture of appreciation for her bravery. Then put the blade in her back. She made a strange sort of gasp, her arms out by her side, fingers wriggling. The blade was bloody and she looked down at it sprouting out of her chest, her mouth wide with no noise except for some odd, throaty sounds. Then he wrenched the blade out and shoved a foot against her back, nudging her face first onto the ground.

'Next!' he called out.

They all ran at him. Spears were raised, bows were drawn, swords were swung, axes and daggers all sparkling in the sunlight. Some had shields. Some didn't. To Bellerophon, it didn't matter what they had. He wiped his sword under his armpit, took up a formidable enough stance and waited for them to come.

Pegasus wasn't so patient though. It stormed forward, trampling three of the fools who tried to stand their ground. Its hooves saw to the caving of their heads, and at one point, he saw the horse lunge down and rip out a throat in one bloody snatch.

The one with the ginger beard got to him first, swinging her axe at him. She went high at first, aiming for his head. But then she changed last minute and slammed it straight into his breastplate. He grunted and stumbled backwards. The woman was stronger than she looked, her eyes on fire with fury, her brows drawn together as foam escaped her lips. She went to pull the axe free, but it was stuck there in his armour. With that split-second distraction, she didn't see Bellerophon drive his sword straight through her neck.

She crumbled before him, blood spurting from her wound as her eyes went lax and she lay on the ground, coughing as she tried plugging the wound with her hand. But she was done. Bellerophon stepped over her and met the next one who was swinging another sword. She went for a slash at the abdomen too, but Bellerophon bounced his own sword against hers, throwing her off balance. She came back again, swinging with a diagonal cut. But Bellerophon moved to the side, grabbed her by the chin and twisted her head so fiercely that something clicked. She went down without a word.

The darker skinned woman charged screaming at him, but Bellerophon wrenched out the axe in his breastplate and tossed it at her face. His aim was true, because her scream was cut short as the axe sunk into her jaw, taking her off her feet and planting her on her back. He grabbed her shield, and not a moment too soon either.

The women with the bows began firing arrows at him, and he had to duck behind the shield, feeling the thud of the projectiles as they pummelled the wood. He began counting the thuds, three or four of them before there was a few seconds delay where they were setting up their next volley. On the next delay, Bellerophon lobbed the shield at one of them, catching her in the nose and taking her out. One arrow hissed past him, another thudding in his greave, causing him to buckle a slight. He was about to rush at them, but then Pegasus used its head to bash one of them so far she somersaulted off the island and landed in the water.

A dark haired woman who might've been pretty if she wasn't the size of a truck came from his side, striking with a spear. Bellerophon sidled out of the way, moved inwards before she could retract the spear for another stab. When she realised his ploy, she swung it at his head, but she didn't have enough momentum to catch him before he slid under it. He grabbed the arrow in his greave, wrenched it out and shoved it straight in her gut. She fell forward, momentarily embracing him as she coughed blood onto his shoulder. He grabbed her hair, threw her to the ground and collected her spear.

One of the archers shot him again, this time nailing him in the arm. He let out a growl before wrenching the arrow out in a bloody show and tossed it away. She tried to get another arrow from her quiver. By the time she did, he had lobbed the spear at her, hitting her in the chest and pinning her against one of the houses.

Pegasus had finished stomping the final Amazon, blood splattered all over its legs and over its mouth. It came trotting over, majestic as ever with its head in the air as if it hadn't just murdered a couple of women.

'You missed one,' Bellerophon noted as there was one woman darting up the stairs and into the temple.

Pegasus made a sound and shrugged.

'Keep watch,' he patted the animal on the head. 'I'm going to see if Lobates' men are inside.'

He headed up the steps two at a time, eager to be back to Lycia, where he'd fly back in with Lobates' men on the back of Pegasus. He'd have that hero's welcome again, no doubt. The people would adore him—rich and poor alike, all of them flooding to get the best glimpse of him as they bestowed upon him their praise. Why, he'd be more popular than Lobates himself. Not that the fat fool seemed at all at one with his people anyway, but it did make Bellerophon think how far he could really go.

He slowed his pace as he walked through the temple entrance only to find a grand chamber awaiting him. Silk curtains were draped from the ceiling and ceramic bowls of fire were lit in every corner. There was an odd sort of pattern on the floor, a myriad of colours all beautifully spilled to make quite a compelling symbol. Old statues were piled about the room—all of women of course, with heroic poses and threatening stances. Pots of gold were decorated around the room, treasure chests and old pots stacked here and there in neat little arrangements.

It wasn't until he got closer to the centre of the room that he noticed the woman who had fled, her strength all diminished as she crouched behind another woman. Tears were flowing from her eyes and she was snivelling like a scolded dog, blood splattered over her face as she winced behind the other woman.

'I tried, Hippolyta,' she sobbed, 'but he's too strong!'

'At ease child,' Hippolyta replied. 'I will handle things from here.'

Bellerophon assumed her to be the leader of the tribe, but where he had assumed she would be fat and incapable like Lobates, she was in fact slender and not without the meanest of glares. Lobates might've been able to draw his brows together real tight, but this woman seemed to simply exude disdain for him. She didn't hold her face in any particular way, but her blue eyes were icy cold. She wore fur around her shoulders with a strong looking carapace that was kept in place by a girdle that rippled with light.

'You have come here looking for something that is not here,' she snapped at him, and for some reason, her words had him taking a step back, like he was a child being scolded by his mother all over again.

'Lobates' men,' he found his voice, 'hand them over to me and no one else dies.'

'You fool! They're not here. What benefit do we have from kidnapping his men?'

'You tell me,' Bellerophon said and slashed the air between them with his sword.

'You don't want to do this,' she spoke gravely as she pulled out her own sword from its guard. 'You may have killed the Chimera, as they say, Bellerophon. You may have defeated my warriors. But I'm a very different story.'

'You can say that again,' Bellerophon snorted. 'Unlike your friends, you I wouldn't kick out of bed.'

Her eyes flared with anger. Within the space of a second she was upon him. She slashed with such a speed that he could only just meet her with his own sword. She pushed against him and just like that, he was already down on his knees, his back bending as he tried with all his strength to hold against her.

'Yield and I won't kill you,' she hissed.

Bellerophon grabbed her ankle, but before she could shake free, he ripped her off her feet. She slammed on her back, but she rolled to the side before he could plant the sword in her back. She wasted no time coming at him again, this time striking like a scorpion and going straight for his centre.

He smacked her sword away. She looked up with hesitation, a moment of uncertainty in her eyes. He brought his sword down upon her, but she grabbed it with her bare hand, ripped it from his grasp and snapped it over her knee. The sound of it echoed through the chamber and all Bellerophon could do was stare at her as she puffed air out her nose, her eyes becoming more and more emblazoned with fury. How she'd snapped steel like it was a twig, he couldn't quite say. Not even the Chimera had given him a look the way she did.

She lunged at him and before he could move, she drove a fist across his face, knocking him back against a wall. He crashed forward after that, hands and legs flailing as he tried to get back to his feet. As he did, he found her waiting for him. She drove her foot into his stomach, sent him spiralling into the ceiling and crashing back down. He landed hard, his face kissing the cold floor.

'Your arrogance will be your undoing,' she muttered as she stalked her way towards him.

Bellerophon felt his whole body light on fire. He couldn't feel his face. He'd never been punched like that before. He wasn't sure if he was missing teeth, but if there was ever a punch to dislodge them then that would've been the one. He lifted his head as best he could, tried to shut off the ringing in his ears but it only grew louder as she came nearer. He squinted up, saw that glowing girdle around her waist and couldn't help but wonder what it was.

'Get off my island,' she barked at him.

'I can't hear you,' he mumbled as he rolled onto his back.

'Get off my island,' she said again.

'Can't...hear,' he grunted, though the ringing was beginning to subside.

'I said,' and she leaned in close. 'Get off—'

He pummelled her right between the eyes with such a force that it sent her flying back. She crashed through one of the statues, breaking it in half. She hit the ornaments around the room, a massive crash echoing out as she hit the wall with a loud thump.

Bellerophon pulled himself up into a seated position and hissed through the pain in his abdomen. His midsection was on fire, every inch of his torso sore and bruised and no doubt bloody. He wondered what it would've been like without the armour—probably would've been dead, all things considered.

Hippolyta was on all fours, choking and covered in dust in the corner of the room. She was breathing hard, a stunned expression on her face as she held her head.

'You want to keep going?' Bellerophon winced as he got to his feet.

'You,' she grabbed onto the wall for support, 'you are not mortal, are you, Bellerophon?'

'Eh?' Bellerophon tilted his head. 'If I am not mortal, then what am I?'

'A demi-god,' came another voice from the temple entrance. A man's voice.

Bellerophon turned to see him standing in the entrance way, a tall and broad man whose presence seemed to demand attention. Perhaps it was the beard, a majestic thing, all mottled grey and thick enough to serve as a rug. Whoever he was, he wasn't wearing a shirt either, which Bellerophon thought was rather ridiculous. It wasn't exactly warm out.

The man had a muscular build, barely an inch of fat on him but instead chiselled muscle, his arms the size of Bellerophon's if you were to put them both together.

'Poseidon!' Hippolyta gasped.

Poseidon? Bellerophon nearly choked. It couldn't have been, could it? The man didn't seem to have any other expression but a cold disappointment as he regarded the pair of them, a subtle shaking of his head. Bellerophon noticed his legs were covered in dark blue scales, most of them wet with a noticeable sheen. Water dripped off of him as if he'd stepped out from the ocean itself a moment ago, but his white hair looked dry enough. Only then did Bellerophon take note of the trident strapped to his back, a golden weapon that was so large it would've probably pinned the Chimera with no real effort.

'Hippolyta,' Poseidon acknowledged her, but his eyes were set on Bellerophon, 'Ares sends his regards, girl.'

'I am happy to hear that my father remembers me,' she said, a hint of malice peppering her words.

Poseidon paid it no mind, his eyes still fixed on Bellerophon, 'You, boy, have been causing a lot of trouble.'

Bellerophon felt his knees go weak. It might've been from the lack of rest or the injuries from battle, but something about Poseidon's words went through him like a volley of arrows.

'First you murder your brother. Then you kill the Chimera. Now you've slaughtered a bunch of innocent women.'

'I wouldn't call them innocent,' he found his tongue and gave Hippolyta a sneer. He wouldn't have even called them women come to think of it.

'You're growing stronger, that much is true. With Pegasus you are now a formidable force—a worthy demi-god, perhaps worthy enough for Olympus itself one day.'

'What do you mean, demi-god?' Bellerophon took a step back. 'How do you know these things?'

Poseidon smirked, 'Isn't it obvious, boy? I am your father.'

'What?' Bellerophon nearly choked.

'I see you have your mother's brain though,' he said with a bawdy laugh. 'Did you never question why it was that you could do things that no other mortal could?'

Bellerophon thought back to his childhood and how he'd always been strong, how he'd lifted things above his head like they weighed nothing, how he'd beaten boys twice his age and size in fights. Then he thought about his brother and the way his head had exploded at the mere tap of his fist. Were Poseidon's words true?

'Why wouldn't my mother mention this?'

Poseidon shrugged, 'Do you think I know? Do you think I remember her? She is one of many. But you...boy, you are special.'

Bellerophon felt his eye twitch. He hadn't gotten to know his mother that well, but she'd tried to do right by him. Hearing Poseidon speak so dismissively of her had him itching to reach for the dagger at his belt. But then there was a strange sort of look in Poseidon's face, a fatherly sort of expression of pride as he began to nod slowly.

'She changed your name, I noticed. I named you Bellerophontes, but it seems her commoner ways robbed you of such a glorious title.'

'Bellerophontes?' he whispered it and suddenly began to wonder how different his life might've been had he been Bellerophontes, the son of Poseidon, and not Bellerophon, the nobody.

'Why are you here now?' Bellerophon asked him. 'All these years, why now?'

Poseidon picked something from his tooth and flicked it away, 'Your powers are almost fully unlocked. Your potential as a demigod is almost fully reached.'

'You mean he's not at full strength?' Hippolyta was rubbing her head.

'Not yet,' Poseidon's eyes flared blue. 'My son is merely scratching the surface of his true power. But instead of using that power to do great things...he wastes it serving children like Lobates.'

Bellerophon couldn't say what it was that made him feel suddenly ashamed. Poseidon's voice had turned grave, the appraising look in his face dwindling and becoming something close to regret.

'But I slayed the Chimera,' Bellerophon protested.

'Quite the achievement,' Poseidon said, 'for a mortal. You could bring Lobates' kingdom to its knees, boy, but instead you bargain with him for a mere district. Don't you see the man is using you? This errand you have embarked on is merely a ruse. There are none of his men here, Hippolyta speaks the truth.'

'And now there are good women who I must put in the dirt because of your foolishness,' she growled at him.

'I don't understand,' Bellerophon stammered. 'Why would Lobates send me here if there was no one to rescue.'

'In hopes that the Amazons would kill you,' Poseidon spoke like it was obvious. 'He sensed your power—knew you would only grow stronger and would one day rip the kingdom from his fat, worthless hands. He hoped you would die here.'

'And now he has come to confirm your corpse,' Hippolyta hissed as she spied from the window.

'What do you mean?' Bellerophon stalked over.

The grasslands expanded before him and the first thing Bellerophon saw was the corpses of the women he'd slain. Weapons were littered about the ground, the Amazons tossed here and there in various slumps, all of them still. Bellerophon felt a pang of distress, for he had ended their lives for what? To appease Lobates in the hopes of obtaining honour and glory? By the gods, he was Poseidon's son. He didn't need a fool like Lobates giving him orders. If he wanted a district in the kingdom, he would damn well take it.

Hippolyta was eyeing him intently, silently blaming him for the death of her people no doubt. He could see her in the corner of his eye, could feel the grief in her stare as her hand hovered by her blade. She should've plunged it into his neck. Bellerophon wouldn't have blamed her. But she hesitated, perhaps coming to the realisation that she may not have been strong enough to finish him off as she had originally thought.

In the distance he could see Lobates' ships as Hippolyta pointed out. Indeed, Lobates was coming to confirm his death, sailing with two large vessels, each flying the flag of Lycia. Bellerophon clenched his fists. He'd been used. He'd been played like a fool. Lobates was probably laughing his lungs out at how much of an idiot he was. It made Bellerophon shake with rage, his blood boiling as he felt his heartbeat quicken.

'What will you do now, Bellerophontes?' Poseidon approached.

'Watch,' Bellerophon snapped and stormed out of the temple.

Pegasus was neighing wildly as he emerged from the temple. It seemed like even the horse had clocked on as Lobates' men came pouring out of the ships, all of them armed to the teeth.

'There's more than fifty men there,' Hippolyta muttered, trying to hide the anxiety in her voice. But Bellerophon heard it. He'd be lying if he didn't feel anxious himself.

'I bid you both farewell,' Poseidon spoke behind them.

'You're not staying?' Bellerophon deflated.

Poseidon only grinned, 'I'll see you in Olympus, Bellerophontes.'

And just like that he jumped into the air, soaring higher and higher like he'd been shot from a cannon. Then he plunged into the ocean with a massive splash, feet first as he disappeared from sight. Bellerophon shielded his face from the blast of water that flew over him.

'Do you have a plan for what comes next,' Hippolyta sneered at him before uttering his name in a most unpleasant manner, 'Bellerophontes?'

A flank of men moved in from the left-most ship, another from the right. They marched in complete unison, like a colony of ants before conjoining to form one moving body. A sea of spears and swords. Further up on a raised chair was Lobates, a cocky twist of his lips as he oversaw his army, barking a few orders here and there. The fool was draped in armour from the neck down, a deeper shade of red from his men, but one that stood out all the more for it.

'I killed your people and they were innocent,' Bellerophon inclined his head. 'That will haunt my conscience along with the death of my brother for the rest of my days.'

'You didn't answer my question,' she snapped. 'Do you have a plan?'

He looked at her, took in her grieved expression and committed it to memory. He didn't deserve to forget this, much like he didn't deserve to forget his brother.

'I have a plan,' he nodded. 'Tell me how to right the wrongs I have committed.'

Hippolyta wasn't expecting that, her lower lip dipped and her eyes widened. Then she swung her head at Lobates' men, swept a glance at their approach and then pointed.

'Kill them and I won't hunt you for what you've done.'

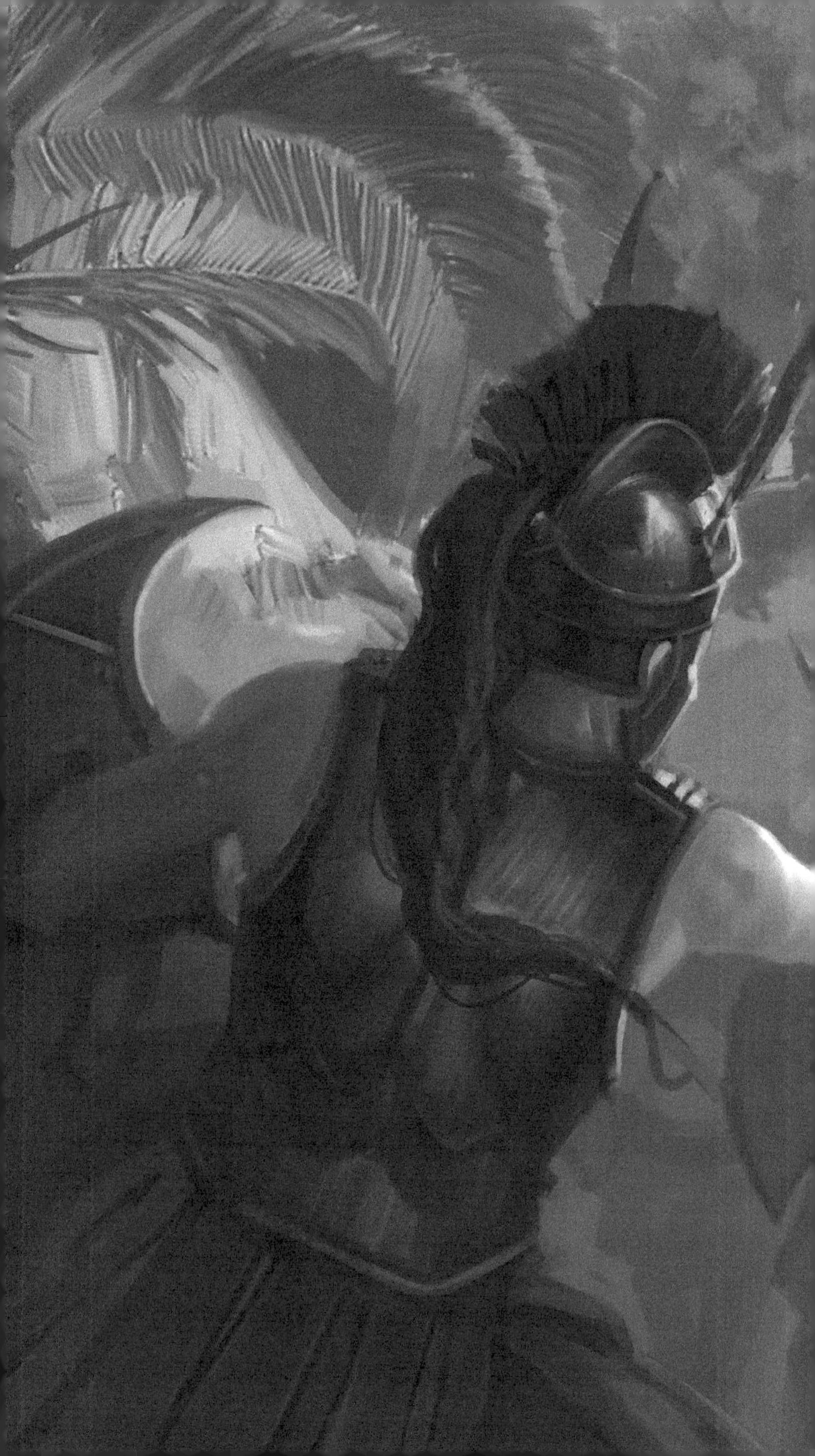

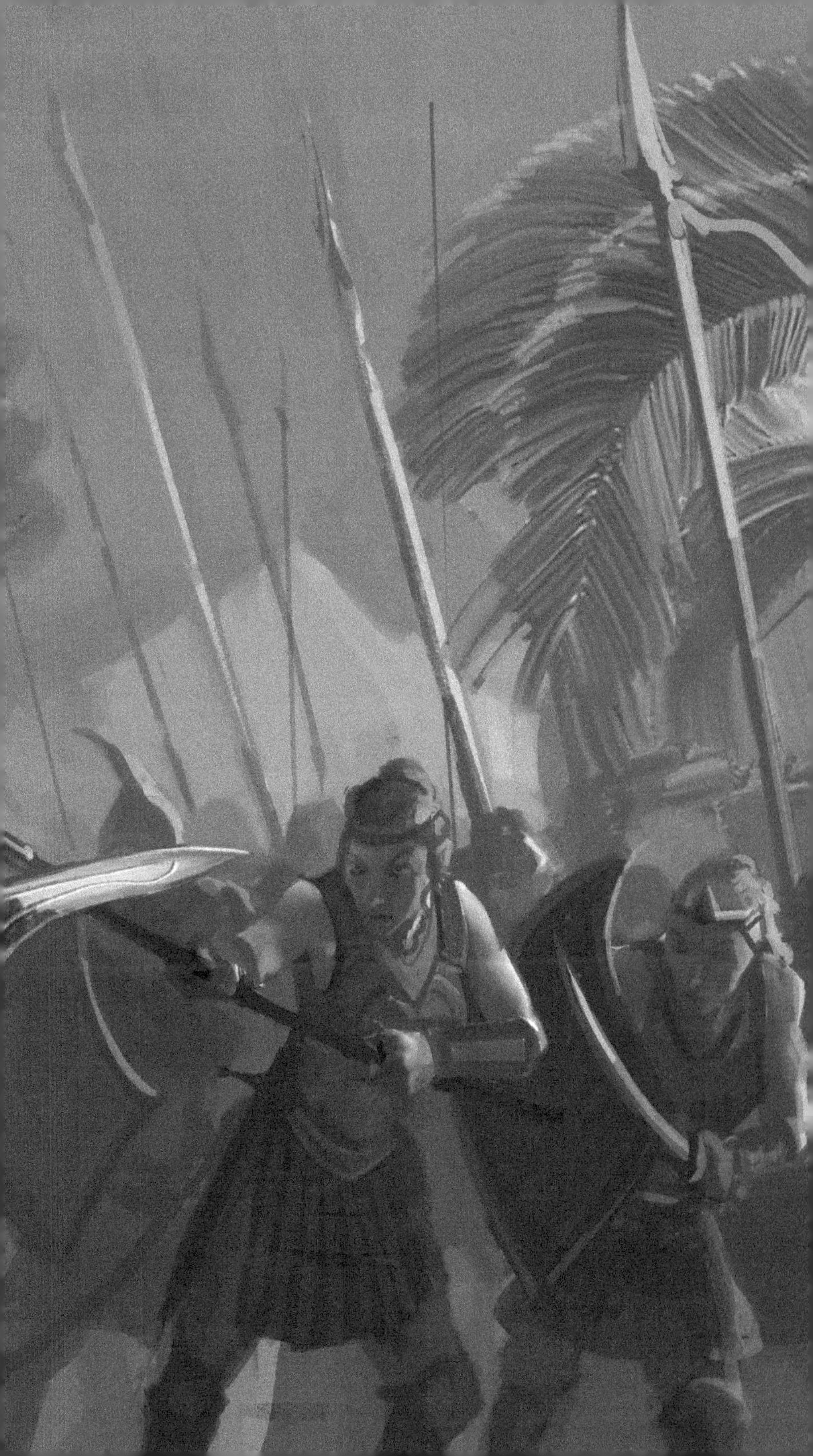

XI. The Army of One

Their footfalls echoed across the island, their heavy loads crushing the grass, stamping it flat. The rattle of their weapons rivalled the sound of the crashing waves until they came to a sudden stop, each of them eyeing him and Pegasus impassively. He had to give it to them, for if they were afraid, they didn't show it. But they soon would.

'I must confess,' Lobates called from the back of his army, positioned high up on a makeshift scaffold with two burly guards holding it in place, 'I had hoped the Amazons would do away with you. If I'm honest, I was hoping you would butcher each other entirely.'

'Sorry to disappoint,' Bellerophon shrugged. He grabbed a sword from one of the fallen Amazons, grabbed a shield too for all the good it would do for when fifty men came rushing at him.

'I had hoped the Chimera would kill you, but you've proven to be a stubborn one, Bellerophon,' Lobates shouted, his voice carried by the wind.

'My name isn't Bellerophon!' He shouted back. 'For the short time you are left breathing, you will address me as Bellerophontes!'

Lobates cocked an eyebrow, 'Why?'

'For I am the slayer of the Chimera,' he beckoned. 'The defeater of the Amazons!' he bleated. 'And the son of Poseidon!'

'Eh?'

And just like that, wave after wave smashed against the sides of the island. White foam hissed against the grass, water exploding onto the banks at heights of at least twenty feet. It made Lobates' men stagger left and right, their neat formation suddenly uprooted like a nudged chess board.

'I knew there was something off about you!' Lobates roared once the waves settled. 'I knew you had to be something more than mortal.'

'And yet, you still tried to manipulate me,' Bellerophontes clicked his knuckles. 'Perhaps you are not as wise you claim to be.'

'Wise enough to know you're not a god,' Lobates held his hands out. 'Wise enough to see you outnumbered.'

Bellerophontes couldn't help but smile as he scanned over the army. 'You didn't bring enough men to outnumber me.'

Lobates' face creased into a ball of outage. He thrust his finger forward, eyes wide with rage and roared, 'Kill him!'

They weren't reluctant in their approach at all. In fact, if they weren't so disciplined, Bellerophontes was sure they'd be tripping over themselves for a piece of him. But that would change soon. He spotted their features as they came close. Men with beards, moustaches, clean shaven and scarred. Men with blocky frames, swamped in leather and steel. Men with slender frames, some of them barely men at all with fine sprouting hairs on their chin. Men with spears. Men with swords. Men with the king's will embedded in their souls.

Dead men then. The whole pack of them.

The first man tried shoving a spear in his face. The metal gleamed. Bellerophontes heard the heroic scream pour out of his toothless mouth. It wasn't nearly loud enough to phase him. He smacked the spear aside with his shield, and the man's scream was cut short. Bellerophontes sunk the sword into his gut, didn't wait to see the realisation set in the fool's red face before ripping the metal out of him.

Blood sprayed out from his wound, caught the nearest man in the eyes and had him swinging like a wild savage, no form or grace. Bellerophontes parried his thrust and took him in the throat, ripping the blade out through his neck and sniggering as his head rolled off his shoulders.

Some shaggy haired man with a mean look swung a mace at his face, but Bellerophontes slipped underneath, slippery as a fish, danced around him and slashed at his legs, bringing him down to size. The soldier wasn't blathering after that, but he looked rather perplexed all of a sudden, staring up, wondering why his legs weren't obeying him. He didn't wonder long. Bellerophontes buried the pointy end of his shield into his head once, twice and then a third time. His flesh squelched and there was satisfying crunch of bone before his eyes went lax and he collapsed backwards—done.

They came in thicker groups now—a sea of soldiers all stabbing and slashing, more than thirty men all screaming and belting at the top of their lungs with one goal in mind. They moved with no strategy, but simply rushed him, tossing themselves at him like naive lambs before the slaughterhouse. Two men grabbed him from either side, one of them sinking a warm knife into his back and the other swinging an axe in his gut. Bellerophontes slammed his elbow into the poor sap on the side, laughed when his nose projected an arc of blood in the air, showering them in red. The other man was grunting, trying to free the axe he had planted. He looked up then at Bellerophontes, denial blossoming in his wet eyes, probably wondering how a man could take an axe to the gut and not feel something. But Bellerophontes had taken harder blows from the Amazons. He'd taken harder knocks from the Chimera. Even his brother had shown more heart. These mortals couldn't swing hard enough to hurt him.

He drew the knife out from his back. Then he plunged it straight through the struggling soldier's ear, shoving it down his ear canal, relishing in his scream as he lost his footing. He was trampled by his own men, some of them stumbling over him now, like a pile of worms all wriggling in confusion. One soldier swung a sword at him with enough strength to warrant the shield. Bellerophontes took it, the impact rocking the shield, sending vibrations up his arm and through his neck. He grinned at the man. A grin that disarmed him long enough for Bellerophontes to boot him between the legs and smack him with the shield. He flew in the air, the big man singing like a girl as he crushed a few others in the wild dash.

Shields bashed against shields, armour clanging against steel, voices of a panicked army spreading like disease. It all made Bellerophontes giddy with power, made every inch of him tingle and come alive like never before.

He lost his sword. Damn thing had gotten so slippery with blood it jumped out of his hand, probably glad to be free of his murderous grasp. So he swung with his fists, felt metal slice up his skin where one blade in particular entered his fist, cutting through the knuckle and grinding against bone. It tickled. He drove his other fist through someone's helmeted head—punched a hole right through the steel, shattering his temple as bits of the armament came flying off along with his teeth.

A ginger-haired man grabbed Bellerophontes by the throat and he let him, just to see what he'd do. He went for his chest with a dagger, a look of elation and glee on his face like he was imagining the bonus he'd receive for slaying the son of Poseidon. Bellerophontes cut his fantasy short, snapped his wrist with one sharp twist and made him stab himself through the eye.

That was when Pegasus made itself known, screeching in the sky as it soared above. Bellerophontes ripped the dagger out of the screaming man's eye, the entire eyeball dangling off it. He tossed it at another young soldier, almost certain he caught him straight in the mouth. But he'd never know. Pegasus slammed down hard on the bevy of soldiers, crushing them under its weight. There was a combined groan.

An awful melody of agony and cries segued into the sounds of battle. Arms and legs twitched on the ground, gritted teeth foaming with blood, one or two men crawling over comrades, one with a bloody spurting stump of a leg. Pegasus didn't let them go. It dived down with its teeth tearing out their throats with sick precision, more like a bird plucking worms from the soil, tossing their bloody lumps in the air before catching them in its mouth.

It moved about with a crazed sort of grin on its mouth, using its wings to barrel men off their feet. It used its head as a battering ram, heedlessly going from enemy to enemy as it swung its skull the way Bellerophontes might've swung a sword.

What was once a majestic creature was now a hellish beast, its coat more red than white. It stamped the injured men into oblivion, hee-hawing as it galloped across the battleground, squelching brain and guts under its hooves. Bellerophontes had never quite bonded with an animal before. He hadn't bonded with any one come to think of it. But he absorbed that monster's crazed grin, its mouth dripping with blood, and flesh making the Chimera look like a fresh kitten.

Bellerophontes felt his mouth was held in a strange way, his lips bloody and his mouth bruised, but the muscles were pulled either side of his face. He realised he had a crazed grin of his own.

A bony soldier who looked no more than fifteen made the roar of a cub, lifted his sword above his head and struck. Bellerophontes caught him by the wrist, tugged hard enough that he felt something snap. The boy froze, eyes fixed on his sword as it fell from his grip, unsure what was happening. But Bellerophontes knew. He wrenched the boy's arm out of its socket, waited for the boy to let out a wail of shock before beating him with it, savagely pummelling him until he stopped making sound.

Three men tried tackling him, one going for his legs and the other two rushing him with a mace and a club each. Before they could reach him, an arrow burst through one of their skulls, toppling him over. The other one stopped, glanced around back towards the temple before he was caught in the throat. He turned back around like he hadn't been shot at all, fixed a wide eyed look on Bellerophontes as he held out his hands, and reached for him despite the arrow in his neck. But then he began to gurgle, blood bursting out his mouth before he slipped onto his face.

Hippolyta looked mortified but she nocked another arrow, giving Bellerophontes a steely nod. That made two demigods and a winged beast against an army of fifty. It hardly seemed fair for them. It certainly wasn't fifty men anymore, several men were sprawled out on the ground, turning the grass red. Bellerophontes' nose was clogged with the smell of entrails and guts, the aroma of death itself wrapping him up in its sticky embrace. He remembered the feeling—remembered how it felt to pull away his steaming fists still wet with his brother's blood. It's why he had been haunted by the guilt all along. Not the act itself, no, but the euphoric feeling of utter superiority that rushed to him making him fierce, unstoppable...god-like.

It wouldn't be long before they weren't rushing him anymore, and in fact, they were falling back. Bodies were strewn across the battleground with only small pockets of grass still visible amongst the severed flesh. Bellerophontes wasn't even walking on grass anymore, he was stepping on bodies, some of them still alive, barely. Lobates was still barking orders at his men, his arms swinging left and right like a mad composer. But his men didn't seem like they were in the obeying mood anymore.

Arrows still rained from above and Hippolyta's aim was true, every shot meeting its mark. One of the guards had lifted a shield above Lobates' head, holding it up for him like an umbrella as he yelled at fleeing men. A few stragglers still came at him, some fools who weren't ready to pass on the glory they thought they could obtain. Bellerophontes punched a soldier through his breastplate, stopped the man in his tracks and reached in further in, moving past his armour, past his flesh, through his rib cage.

The man was screaming, his hands tightly wrapped around Bellerophontes' arm, trying to free himself. But Bellerophontes rummaged about for his heart, felt it beating for a moment before he wrenched it out. It was an odd shaped thing, a man's heart. It was warm to touch, all juicy and soft and squirting blood. The victim just stood there with a gaping mouth, sucking in breaths that weren't coming. Bellerophontes didn't see him fall over, but he heard him writhing on the ground a moment later. He tossed the heart in his palm, throwing it up and down like a ball. Then he leaned back and threw it as close as he could to Lobates.

Lobates saw it bounce at his feet and for a moment, it was clear he didn't know what it was. But then the realisation set in and his eyes were glaring up, jowls trembling as his men fled back to the ships. The guards lowered him to the ground and the bigger one with the shield over his head tossed it to the ground and did a runner.

'Traitors!' Lobates was shouting as Bellerophontes drew near. 'Traitors! Every single one of you!'

There was only one guard left beside Lobates by the time Bellerophontes was in speaking distance. He held out a long pike, warding him away. He must've been near enough Lobates' age, grey around the sides with blotchy skin. He had a hardened look to him, though the strength was seeping out of him by the moment as he began to digest the situation.

'Strike then,' Bellerophontes snorted at him.

The man gave one last look at Lobates, shrugged apologetically before tossing the pike on the ground. Then he was running back for the ship.

Lobates sighed and reluctantly turned his head to face Bellerophontes. He didn't hide his disdain, didn't quiver like a wet mess or try and beg for his life. Not just yet. He lifted his chest an inch, balled his fists and cleared his throat.

'I w—'

'You're going to have to make up for all my time you've wasted,' Bellerophontes glowered.

'Time wasted?' Lobates tried to smile, but it came out limp. 'How about the lives you've wasted here today?'

'The blood is on your hands,' Bellerophontes declared, which was ironic because his hands were literally caked with guts, his fingertips dripping blood as they spoke. But Lobates probably knew better than to point that out.

'What now then?' he barked, trying to keep a brave face that was melting away like wax under a flame. 'Are you going to kill me as well? Well, have at it then, Bellerophon!'

'It's Bellerophontes,' he hissed. 'And yes, you are going to perish.'

'I'm not getting any younger, boy.' Lobates threw up his hands in submission. 'You want me dead? Come on then! Strike me.'

Bellerophontes didn't move at first. He wanted the anticipation to sink in, for it to eat away at Lobates' core as he stood there, trying not to surrender a tremble. He held his mouth shut tight, creases in his cheeks becoming more prominent as he resisted the urge to beg for his life. He wanted to run, Bellerophontes knew that much. He could see it in the way his eyes jittered, but the fat man's running days were long behind him.

Bellerophontes lunged forward, quick as a cat, and sunk his hand into Lobates' shoulder, squeezing tight. Lobates winced. He looked like a turtle trying to shove its head down into its shell, or in this case, his gelatinous neck. He shut his eyes tight, lips drooping unflatteringly as he awaited the strike that would kill him, but it never came.

'Please!' Lobates cried out at last. 'Please, Bellerophontes! I can give you riches. Is that what you want? Riches for you to go on your way and live your life as you please.'

'I am living it as I please,' Bellerophontes grinned and began squeezing his cushion of a shoulder.

Lobates screamed and tried to break away, but Bellerophontes wasn't letting go. He sunk his nails into his shoulder, piercing the skin before he felt bone. Lobates struck him with a weak hand at the chest, but the man lost his balance and dropped to his knees, wheezing and wailing like a distressed child.

'What do you want?' Lobates screamed through the pain, his face all pink and sweaty.

Bellerophontes tapped his chin, 'More than a small man like you can offer.'

His fingertips pierced Lobates' skin like knives through the breast of a chicken, soft and moist. Lobates tried pulling away again, but he only caused more damage as Bellerophontes applied more pressure, tugging gently at the shoulder in a way that was not meant to be tugged.

'Stop!' Lobates screamed. 'Stop, I'll do anything!'

'Anything?' Bellerophontes quite liked the sound of that.

'Anything!' Lobates nodded.

'I want the kingdom then,' Bellerophontes decided. 'I want Lycia.'

'Done!' Lobates was quick to concede and so Bellerophontes released him, his hand coming away bloody. He wiped it on Lobates like he was a towel.

'You'll announce upon our arrival that you have submitted Lycia to me,' Bellerophontes instructed.

'It doesn't work that way,' Lobates was sobbing on the ground. 'You'll need to be married into the family.'

'Then you best find me a bride,' Bellerophontes grabbed him and hoisted him up to his feet. 'Anyone in mind?'

Lobates winced, though Bellerophontes was sure it wasn't over the pain. 'There's only one person you can marry that will make you eligible for my throne.'

'Well then you best introduce me,' Bellerophontes clicked his fingers and Pegasus came galloping up to his side.

'You've already met her,' Lobates growled, nursing his shoulder. 'My daughter, Stheneboea.'

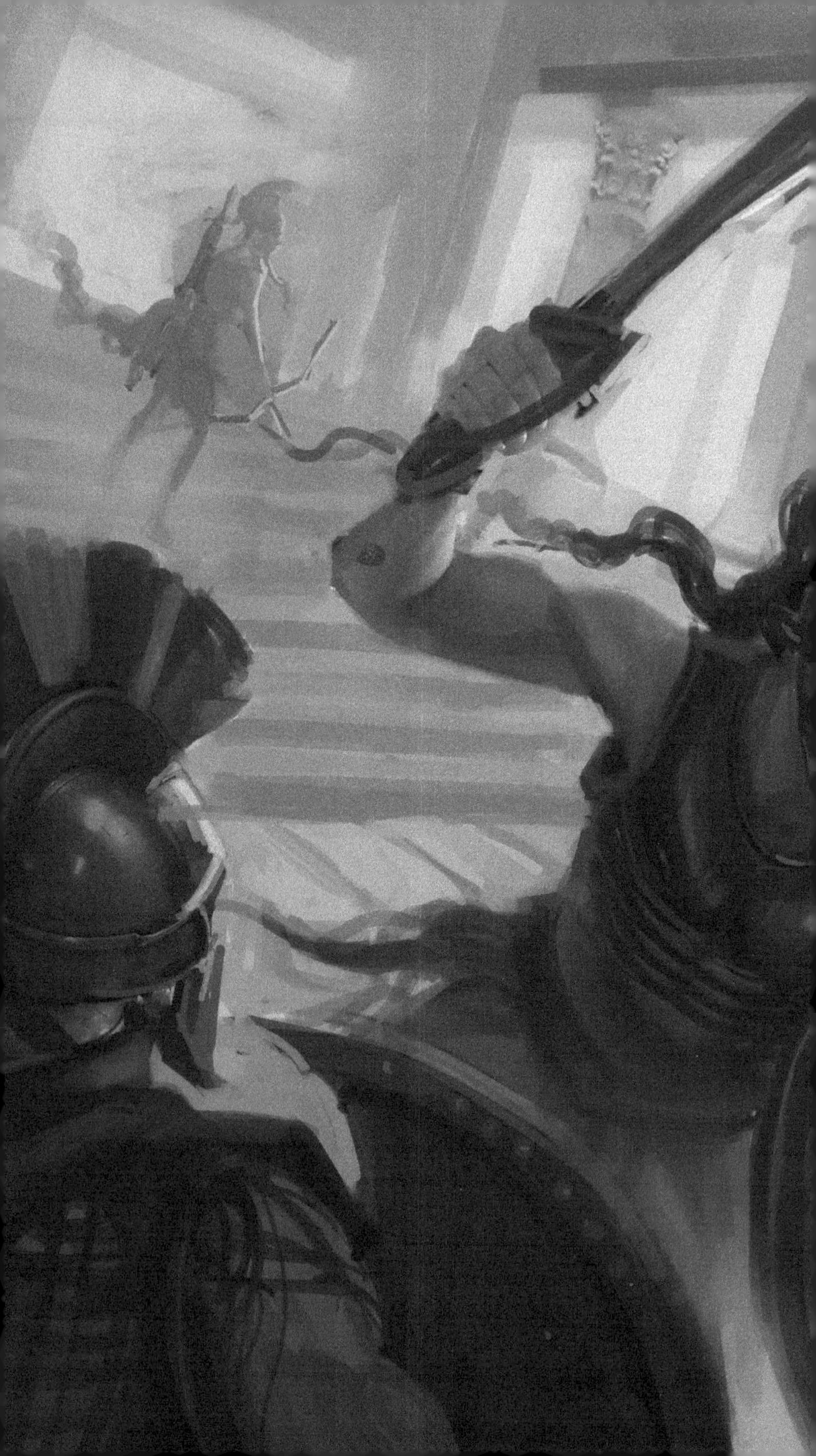

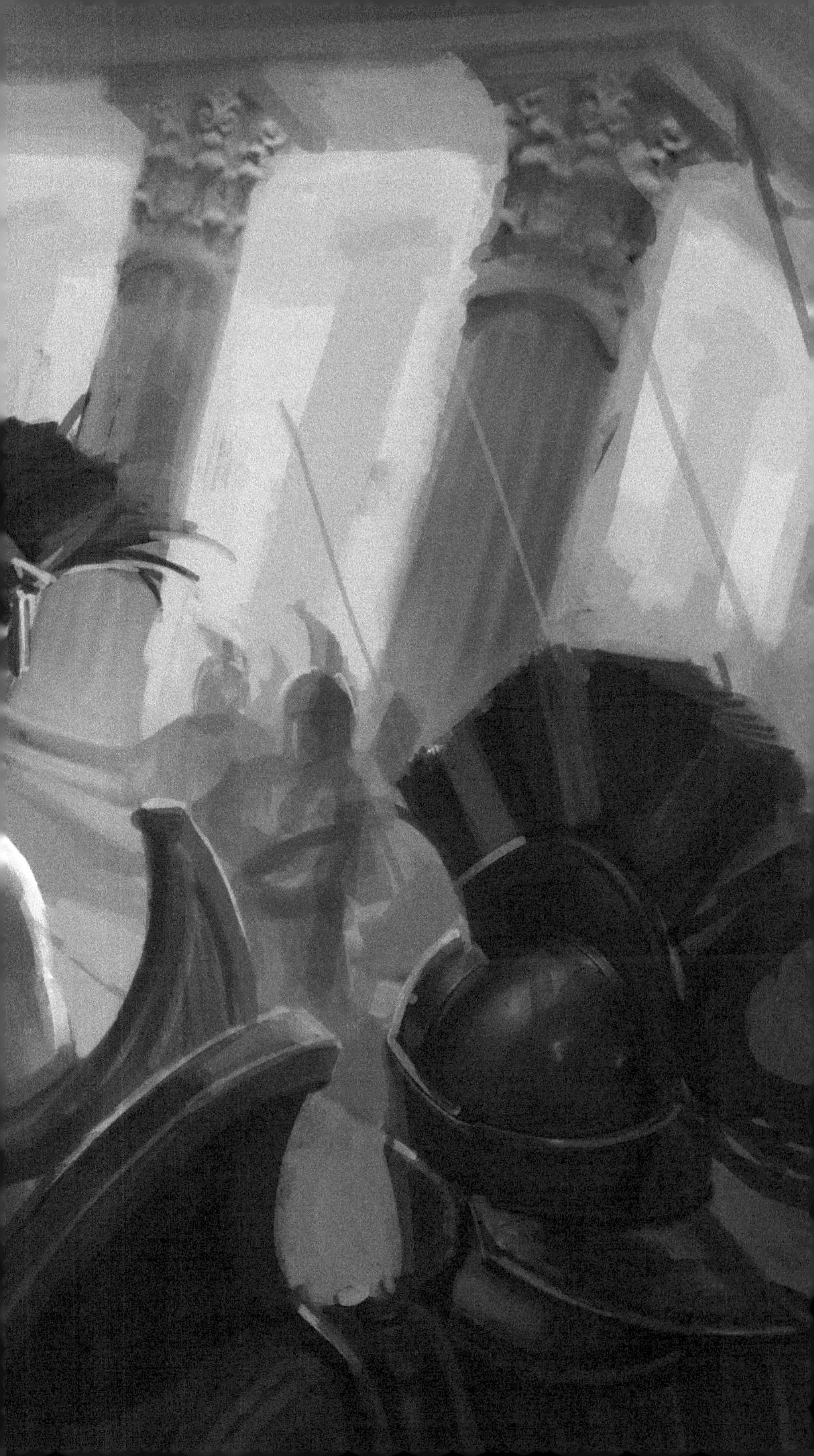

XII. Until Death Do Us Part

Bellerophontes revelled in the sunlight as it cascaded across his face. He was dressed in the finest silks: a royal blue fabric that the servants had whispered was spun by a woman who was part spider. Bellerophontes scoffed at the nonsense and had the servants dismissed for entertaining such ludicrousness. It wasn't the most comfortable garment. The belt made it either too tight or too loose. He wore a pair of block-shaped sandals to go with it. If he was honest, Bellerophontes would've happily married in his armour.

Crowds had gathered on either side of the courtyard, half of them poor and swathed with flies. The other half rich with exquisitely coloured clothes, men and women regarding him with sham-filled smiles and nervous bows. At least the poor lot were honest about their reservation for him. They'd heard about his gruesome dismantling of the army, and while they bowed before him, they did so out of fear.

Pegasus was playing with some of the children, but it wasn't long before their parents yanked them away, bowing before the horse too as if it would snap their heads off their necks. Then again, perhaps they weren't being over cautious. Pegasus eyed them with an icy coolness before he eyed their children, its tongue gracing its mouth.

'The queen!' People began to hark. 'The queen is coming!'

The orchestras around the courtyard began to play and a melody of acoustics and strings swept up the land, lulling it into even more pretence, a horribly beautiful pretence. People began to dance—those on the rich side of the courtyard sweeping each other up and doing what they could to forget that a cold-blooded killer was essentially taking their kingdom for himself. The poorer folk swayed side to side, eyes glued to their new king with a silent judgement. A part of him hoped it wouldn't remain silent so that he might crack a skull before kissing his bride.

A carriage was brought in by two black stallions that stopped short of the podium in which he stood. The door opened and Lobates came limping out with a hand resting on his shoulder. He took one look at Bellerophontes and looked away just as quickly, a grim sadness on his face. He offered up his hand into the carriage and a slender hand reached out to grab it.

Stheneboea was just as he remembered. A temptress of beauty, perhaps beautiful enough to warrant a visit from the gods. What she had been doing with a fool like Proetus, Bellerophon couldn't say. But she was here now, draped in a crimson gown, her slender arms bare but sparkling with glitter. She had dressed modestly, unlike the shameless garment she had worn to his cell that night. Her legs were concealed beneath her gown, but Bellerophontes was sure he'd be seeing them again rather soon. Her dark hair trailed about her shoulders and she offered up a teasing sort of grin, one that said *I knew I'd get you.* Bellerophontes returned it with a grin of his own.

'I present my daughter, Stheneboea,' Lobates said with all the enthusiasm of a dying fish.

Hardly a lady, Bellerophontes thought to say. *And she's presented herself enough without your help.*

'Bellerophon,' she curtsied. 'It's so nice to—'

'It's Bellerophontes,' he snapped at her so loudly that the musicians around the courtyard each skipped a note. 'I'm the son of Poseidon!'

'Bellerophontes,' she near stumbled backwards and probably would have if Lobates hadn't moved in to support her. 'Forgive my mistake.'

'Hmm,' he mumbled before taking her hand and yanking her from Lobates. She squealed, but if he'd hurt her she didn't show it. She fell onto his chest, giggling as she slipped a hand onto his lower back, the other caressing the side of his ribs.

'When you sent for me,' she whispered in his ear, 'I dropped that fool Proetus and came running immediately.'

'How could you not?' he trailed a finger up her arm. 'I am the son of Poseidon.'

'A complete step-up from my former marriage then,' she breathed heavy on his neck.

'Without question,' Bellerophontes said.

Pegasus came trotting up, gently beating its wings as if trying to upstage him. He gave the horse a scathing look and the beast rolled its eyes, silencing itself all the same.

'Before we are married,' Stheneboea purred, 'I was wondering if you would take me on a ride?'

'A ride with Pegasus?' Bellerophontes asked.

'Yes,' Stheneboea nipped at his neck. 'I promise I'll return the favour.'

He had to gulp then, perhaps the first time he'd been caught off guard in a long while. He had to hand it to her, she knew how to get around a man. But he would not be so easily fooled. He might've been Bellerophontes now, the son of Poseidon, but he'd always been strong in the mind. He wouldn't end up like Proetus, docile and at the whims of her beck and call. He wouldn't spare a brother-killer just because she'd taken a liking to him.

'Come then,' he pulled her to one side and helped her mount the creature.

'I strongly advise against this,' Lobates stormed over. 'That thing isn't safe, my dear!'

'Father, I'm in good hands. I have the son of Poseidon to protect me.'

'And who will protect you from him?' Lobates muttered under his breath.

Bellerophontes joined her on Pegasus. She grabbed hold of his waist, nestled her face against his back as they began to ascend, higher and higher. The music began to fade out and the cheers of the people were lost below. Pegasus climbed up, his wings beating fiercely as he veered left and right, the wind crashing hard against them. Stheneboea screamed with elation, laughing and gasping all at the same time. He bet Proetus hadn't been able to achieve that.

'Bellerophontes,' she exhaled as Pegasus slowed to a stop in mid-air, 'you certainly know how to impress a woman.'

'Of course I do,' he nodded. 'I am the son of—'

'When we are married, I will bore you many children who will go far and wide, conquering this world.'

He was about to reprimand her for interrupting him, but then he imagined the sight of his children—strong boys and girls who would mount the world the way he had mounted Pegasus. Why, the mere notion of it began to put a smile on his face.

But then he remembered Proetus' absent face for some reason and the gormless, lifeless look in his eyes.

'Why didn't you give Proetus children?'

'I...' she took a moment to glance down at the clouds, 'I wasn't able to—'

'So what makes you think you could carry my children, the grandsons of a god?'

'I'm certain that—'

'I do not tolerate lies, Stheneboea.' Bellerophontes spun around on Pegasus so he was facing her. 'I must confess that given our past encounter, I'm not inclined to trust you as my wife.'

'You needn't have such worries,' Stheneboea reached for his face. 'As if I would do anything to betray one such as yourself.'

Probably the same line you used on Proetus, rehearsed and rehashed to suit the receiver.

He stared into her perfect black eyes, took in her flawless face and wondered just why on earth he was doing this. He was the slayer of the Chimera, the defeater of the Amazons, the son of Poseidon. Not some pompous noble trying to ascend the social ladder.

'Why am I doing this?' he asked out loud. 'My power knows no bounds, and yet here I am, pandering to your politics. I can simply take this kingdom and marry no one.'

'Yes,' Stheneboea straightened in the saddle. 'But our traditions are very important to the people. Marrying me will guarantee your rule not just here, but in Argos too.'

'All very well,' Bellerophontes caught her hand before it could trail against his cheek. 'However, now that I am a fully-fledged demi-god who can take what he wants...I wonder what use I have of you.'

Her eyes widened and it looked like she suddenly became very aware that she was hundreds of feet from the ground.

'I will make an excellent wife for you,' she stammered. 'I'll dote on you, worship you, fall for you!'

'Fall for me?' he frowned. 'I daren't say there's ever been a woman who has fallen for me.'

'I will,' she grabbed his hands and shuffled closer. 'I'll fall for you.'

'You will?'

She nodded feverishly, eyes all wide and steaming with desperation.

'Prove it,' he said simply.

She hesitated, 'How?'

'Fall for me,' he told her.

And then he pushed her.

To her credit, she didn't scream. He peered over the side of Pegasus' rump and watched her descend, no look of fear, but more so a look of perplexity on her pretty face, like she wasn't sure what had happened. She reached for him with languid arms, the wind wildly ruffling her hair and her gown. The clouds swallowed her up after that.

Pegasus bucked with laughter and Bellerophontes had the right mind to join in. He guided the creature into a descent and he caught sight of her just in time to see her body explode on the ground in a bloody mess. Needless to say, the musicians had stopped playing and instead there came a mixture of horrified gasps, screams and general terror. Commoner and noble alike dashed about like a pack of wild animals, none of them too sure of where they were going as they trampled over one another.

Bellerophontes landed beside Lobates, the man so pale in the face it was ghostly. He didn't blink. He just stood there staring at the puddle of red in the centre of the courtyard, his beautiful daughter face down with her arms all crooked and her leg pointing in a way it wasn't meant to point.

Bellerophontes snatched a broom from one of the servants who was pinned on his spot before shoving it in the hands of Lobates. He accepted the broom absently, his eyes distant and watery, unable to understand what he'd just seen.

So Bellerophontes thought he might give him some direction as he patted him on the injured shoulder and pointed at the carcass, 'Go clean that up.'

XIII. Ambition

Bellerophontes sat on his throne, staring at the bowl of soup in his lap. He trailed the spoon through the green mixture and brought it up to his face before depositing it back in the bowl, scowling at it. Months had passed since he'd become king, yet the foolish cook still couldn't make a meal to his liking. He slammed his fists on the side of the throne before tossing the bowl to one side, not caring that most of it spilled on the floor.

'Servant!' he beckoned at the top of his lungs, so loud that the guards in the room were startled. He didn't know why he even kept the guards, for what could anyone do against him? He supposed he liked the decorative effect they offered though, several mean men in armour—the same men who'd cowered from him on the Amazons' island.

A man came limping out of a doorway on the side, his face gaunt and drooping. He'd lost most of his hair over the few short months, tufts of it still marooned on his head. Dark circles formed about his eyes, his cheeks unshaven and blotchy. Bellerophontes would have to speak to him about his appearance if he didn't fix up.

'You summoned me, my king?' Lobates sank to one knee.

'Servant,' Bellerophontes addressed him, 'send me the cook. I wish to yell at him for his idiocy!'

'You've already yelled at him this morning,' Lobates craned his head upwards. 'And the night before. And the night before that. I fear he might quit.'

'You fear?' Bellerophontes glowered. 'Servant, I think you have forgotten what fear actually is. Shall I bring Pegasus in here and show you?'

Lobates didn't react in that feeble, beggaring manner that Bellerophontes had become accustomed to seeing in his subjects. Instead, Lobates just looked up with a tired, drained expression like he was about ready to fall on his face and nap.

'No, sir,' he muttered, 'that won't be necessary.'

He got up off his feet and brought the cook in a few moments later.

'My king,' the cook lowered his head as if that was the only respect he deserved. Bellerophontes had half the mind to give him a lesson on how to receive a king, but that would wait until after he'd yelled at him a bit for such a disgraceful bowl of soup.

'Cook,' he started, 'the soup today was—'

'What now?' the cook sighed.

'Foul,' Bellerophontes snapped. 'The soup today was so foul that had I served it to Pegasus, I think he might've died.'

'Shame you didn't,' Lobates muttered under his breath. Bellerophontes would most certainly be speaking to him about his little wisecracks.

'What was wrong with it this time?' the cook sighed, folding his arms like he'd forgotten just who he was talking to.

'First of all,' Bellerophontes lifted the bowl, 'I don't like eating out of wooden bowls. What am I, a villager? I want ceramic! Secondly, you've put too much salt in the mixture. Anymore salt and I'd be...I'd be...'

'Salty?' Lobates finished for him.

'Hmm,' Bellerophontes nodded. 'Salty indeed!'

'Anything else, your highness?' the cook droned on, evidently not giving much of a care.

'Yes, actually!' Bellerophontes said and threw the bowl at him.

It caught him in the chest, the hot liquid soaked over his face and had him screeching with pain. Bellerophontes could do no more but laugh, laugh as he buckled backwards with steam and seaweed on his face.

'You spoilt brat!' the cook got to his feet and roared.

'Easy now, Cook.' Lobates tried shuffling him away. 'He is the—'

'Oh don't we all bloody know what he is,' the cook shouted before he started prancing around in mockery. 'Blah, Amazons, blah! I killed the Chimera. I killed the Amazons. My name is Bellerophon. Blah, blah, blah. Oh wait, no it's not. It's Bellerophontes—because that makes all the difference in the world. Blah, blah, blah! Oh did I not mention? I'm the son of Poseidon by the way! Blah, blah—'

'You dare mock me, mortal?' Bellerophontes leapt from his throne.

'I do dare,' the cook snapped. 'Also, I quit! I slave day in and day out for your dietary needs and it's never good enough. Tell you what, Mr Demigod, if you want a decent meal, why don't you bugger off to Olympus and get one then?'

Bellerophontes moved with such a speed that the cook didn't even throw up a guard. What kind of guard could a cook have anyway? Bellerophontes struck him across the face with an open palm, not the most devastating of strikes, but enough to have his head whipping to the side and his neck making an audible crack. His body collapsed on itself, knees going first before the rest of him followed.

'I'll get the broom,' Lobates wasn't surprised in the slightest. He barely even flinched.

Bellerophontes had never been spoken to in such a manner. Why, he was shaking. His breaths were coming so fiercely it was like he was on the battlefield again. But that cook was no threat, nor was he even a challenge. He was just a mortal fool with a weak mind and weaker bones. He was nothing. And yet, why did his words have Bellerophontes' heart beating so madly.

'Of course,' he suddenly realised, 'he's right.'

Lobates stopped in his tracks, 'He is?'

'Of course he is,' Bellerophontes was staring at his corpse. 'He's absolutely right. I've been a fool this whole time.'

Lobates cleared his throat, 'You have been a rather demanding king—'

'Not that, idiot!' Bellerophontes hissed. 'I should be in Olympus, not down here.'

'My lord, I don't think that's a—'

'Silence, servant!' Bellerophontes was already running towards the exit. 'I'm going to visit my father! Perhaps there I might find something decent to eat.'

He sallied on to Pegasus, grabbed the horse's reigns and whipped the beast into motion. Pegasus grunted and gained a bit of speed as he galloped through the courtyard before taking off into the air. Bellerophontes would've preferred for there to have been no clouds in the sky, but he was met with thick, black ones that were heavy with rain. It mattered not though, he would reach Olympus as was his birthright. *See you in Olympus*, Poseidon's words whispered about him and Bellerophontes whipped at Pegasus again, eager to get there.

Pegasus moved at such a speed that it wasn't long before he spotted it—a bloated mountain floating in the middle of the sky, surrounded by a misty cloak. Upon this mountain was a glorious arrangement of buildings, not at all like the shoddy and awkward assembling of buildings back in Lycia. No, these buildings were made of pure gold, every inch of them sparkling even with the shadowy clouds glaring down from above. Water spilled off the edges of the mountains, lakes and rivers festooning the face of the rocky terrain.

Spires shot out from the centre of the city, towers and monuments all built by the finest of builders, scraping the sky with almighty dominance, yet sleek and immaculate so as to be considered beautiful. Dome shaped buildings were littered here and there, some flying flags and others barren save for the statues erected there instead. A golden gate trailed the perimeter of the city, gorgons and otherworldly creatures made of clay set atop at various points, like guards to the kingdom.

There was a man stalking on the clouds at the edge of Olympus, his long white hair perhaps more splendid than Poseidon's, all radiant and full of life. His beard was a magnificent thing too, though lost in a shawl he wore around his shoulders. He was a girthy man too, like Poseidon, and he moved slow as he traversed across the clouds as graceful as any king.

Upon closer inspection, Bellerophontes noticed that the man had a goose in his hand that was flapping wildly for escape. He had his large fingers enveloped around its neck, though he didn't pay it much mind as it pecked at his wrist. By this point, he wasn't paying attention to anything at all except for himself and Pegasus who slowed to a stop.

'You're a long way from home, mortal.' The man spoke and when he did, his voice rumbled through the clouds as if it had come from above as well.

'I am no mortal,' Bellerophontes spoke. 'I am Bellerophontes, son of Poseidon.'

'I see,' the man grunted before turning his attention to the goose. 'I'll deal with you later,' he said before flinging it away. The animal hissed at him, but it wasted no time fleeing.

'I've come to see my father,' Bellerophontes spoke.

'Your father doesn't live up here, boy.' The man replied. 'Best you be on your way. This is no place for mortals.'

'Mortals?' Bellerophontes clenched his fists. 'I am no mortal, I told you already. I am Bellerophontes! The slayer of the Chimera, the defeater of the Amazons! The son of—'

'Be gone, insect.' The man waved his hand dismissively and then there was a flash of terrifying light.

Everything went white, then there was a thud in his spine. He was falling, that much he knew. The wind crashed agaist him, whipping at his silks and stealing his breath away. He found he couldn't move his arms, couldn't move his legs or even get his head to look left or right. All he could do was stare up at the man who grew further and further away, a blue sizzle of lightning in his eyes.

He got some life back in his arms, but not much as he flapped around for Pegasus. But Pegasus was just a sleeping mule now, its wings blackened from the lightning bolts as it descended past him, still as can be. The side of the mountain flashed past—grey rock, the occasional stray branch, a bird or two, patches of moss. He tried to manoeuvre in the air, but his bones were like jelly and he could barely keep his eyes open. His limbs flapped about uselessly. He would've screamed in hopelessness of it all, but the wind chased up his nose, taking away his ability to breathe.

The courtyard came up to meet him faster than he'd like. It hit him in the side harder than anything had before, rattling his head and his teeth and just about everything else. It punched the air out of his lungs and had him flopping about like a damned fish plucked out of the ocean. He didn't think he'd ever stop bouncing off the concrete, his head and face cut up and bloody, his bones broken, limbs all mangled and out of place. When he finally came to a stop, his body twitched and with every moment there was pain, agonising pain that had him screaming into the air.

None of them came to his aid. He could hear them pointing and gasping, some of them shrieking in horror and others running to get away from the sight of him. Some were laughing and he would've stormed up to them to punish them for that...if his legs worked. Nothing moved. He tried to move his arms, but only one of them responded, and it weighed a ton. He tried kicking, but he only had the sensation in a few of his toes. He began to panic, head twisting left and right before it would only twist to the right. Sharp spasms of pain came to meet him, making him hiccup in between every excruciating roar.

At last, one man stopped beside him. Though he didn't look like he was in the mood to do much helping. When did he ever?

'Lobates,' Bellerophontes tried to reach for him. 'Lobates, I can't move!'

Lobates didn't exactly move either. His face was like granite, nothing there but a grim sternness that betrayed nothing of his thoughts.

'Lobates!' Bellerophontes harkened. 'Lobates, help me.'

The man lowered his head, but instead of reaching down to assist as was expected, he merely turned on his heels and walked away.

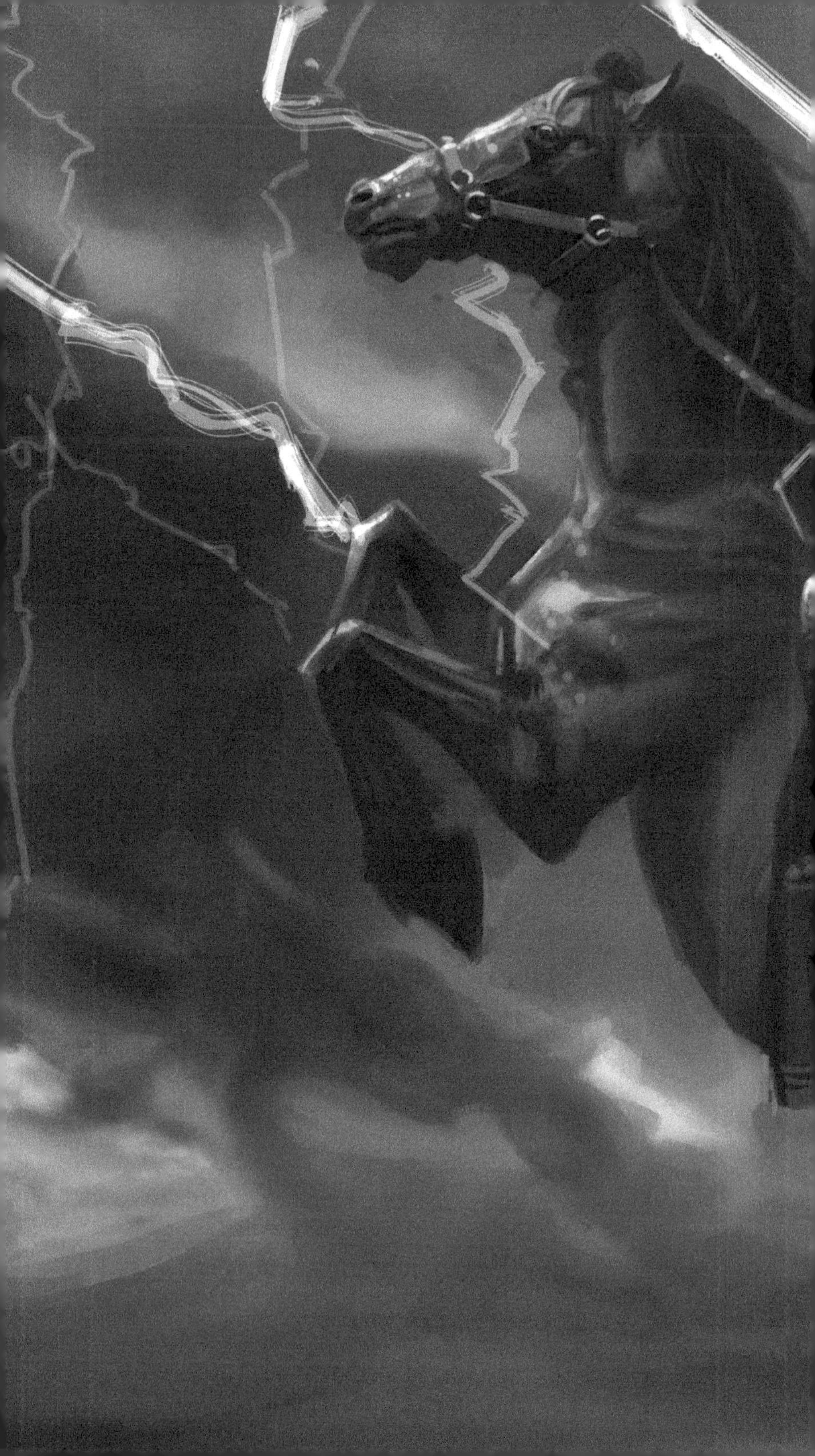

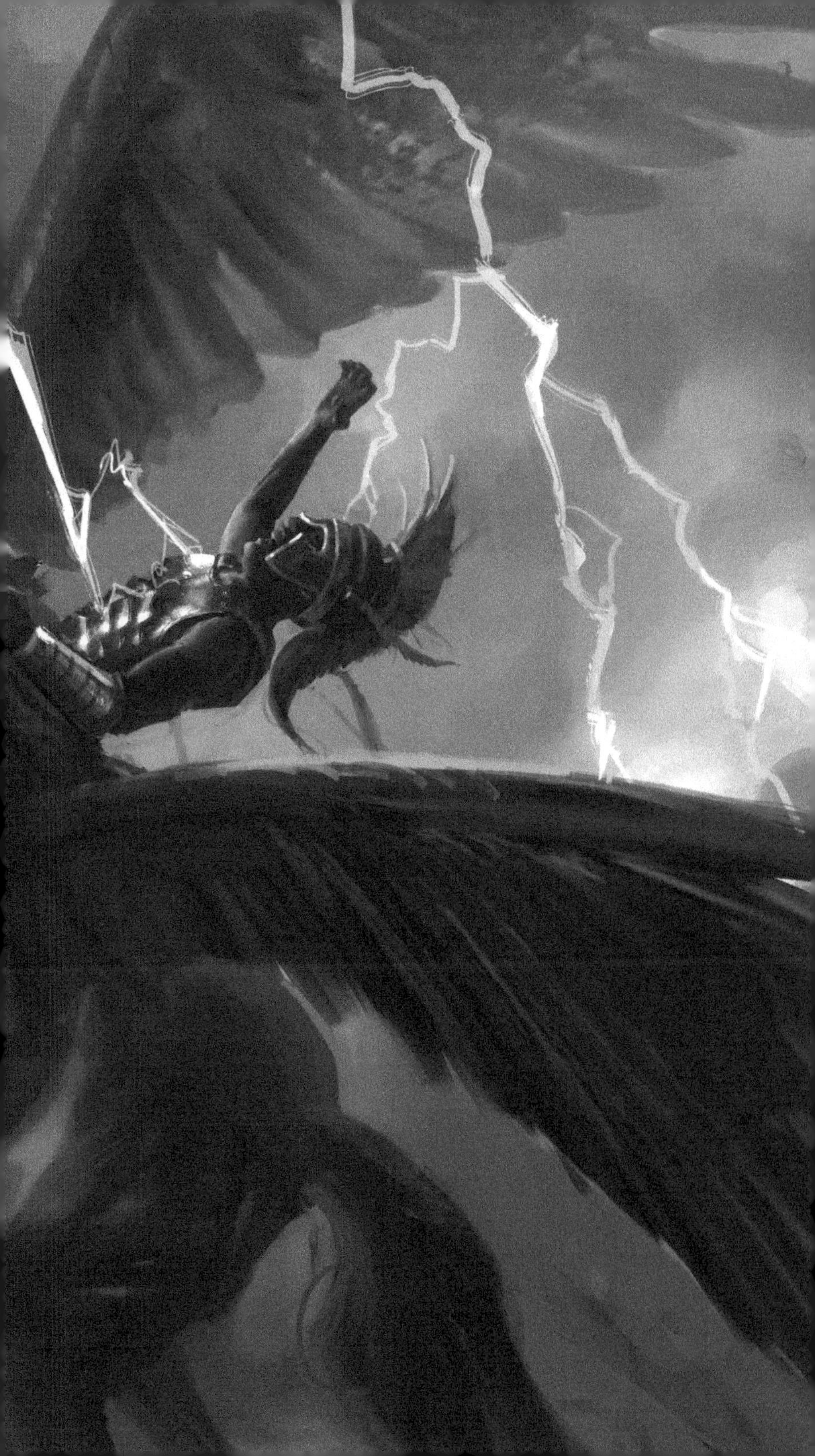

XIV. The Son of Poseidon

Pain shot through his neck. But Bellerophon was used to the shooting, stabbing, chilling pain upon his every waking moment. Well, perhaps not used to it. He would never get used to it. But he tolerated it. He had no choice but to. His new home had its perks, for one he didn't have to eat that awful soup that the cook made. In fact, he didn't have to eat anything at all. He wasn't in a position to. His home was cold though, on account that it was outside in the courtyard. Under a bench.

He lied still for a moment, blinking up at the wooden plank above him where a child was sitting, his shoes dangling right above his face.

'Son,' his mother shouted at him from across the way, 'get away from that man, quickly!'

The boy leapt off the bench and landed in a puddle sending specks of dirt in his face. Of course, Bellerophon couldn't feel it because one half of his face was still numb—seven years later. He cautiously moved his right arm only to find that the mere movement had him lost for breath. He tried to pull himself out from under the bench, but then his legs woke up—or at least, one of them did, alive with a sharp needling at his knee. He crinkled his nose as he shifted, for he smelled something foul in the air.

Oh, he thought with mild annoyance. *I've soiled myself again.*

That was the problem with being crippled. It wasn't the lack of movement that haunted you, but more so the involuntary movement. His grotesque, mangled foot was twitching with excitement but the other one was about as alive as a brick. By the time he'd pulled himself out from under the bench, he was sweating like a worn dog, despite the fact that it was cold and soon set to snow. *Just what I need, a chill in the bones to go with the pain.*

He massaged his withered thighs until he was confident enough to pull himself to a seated position. Once there, he grabbed hold of the bench and very gently pulled himself up, doing what he could to ignore the smell of his pants and the stabbing pains in his lower back. Once he was on his own two feet, he felt relief. But that wouldn't last long, for he felt a heavy pair of hands grab him from behind and shove him over into the puddle.

He heard them laughing at first as he spat the rainwater through his blistered lips. One side of his mouth didn't open properly, so he had to wedge it open with his fingers and let the water drain out on its own. It did not taste nice. There came that horrible moment between the fall and feeling the pain. It stretched out for a good few moments—the final fleeting moments of bliss and then...he was screaming through gritted teeth. It was blinding agony, a searing jolt down the left side of his body from jaw to knee. He surrendered an awful sounding moan. *But now the real fun begins.*

'Hey look,' one of the nobles who pushed him was prancing about, 'it's Bellerophontes! You remember him? The one who thought he was a god!'

'I do remember him!' Another came over. 'And look at that—he soiled himself!'

Bellerophon tried pushing himself up, but his shoulders betrayed him and he damn near pitched on his face. It didn't matter anyway. One of the nobles delivered a foot into his side and that had him flopping over and onto his back. Worse thing was, he remembered these two men. He'd come across them upon his arrival in Lycia when they were picking on some old man.

'You bloodied my nose,' one of them said accusatorily. 'It never was the same after that, look at it.'

'Looks better than mine,' Bellerophon grunted.

'And me!' the other came storming over. 'You embarrassed me in front of everyone. Threw me onto my back, you did.'

It seemed like such a long time ago. Probably because it was. Back when he was a man and not this poor, shrivelled soon-to-be corpse. He wondered what ever happened to that old man they had harassed. He probably died from the cold. Some were lucky like that.

'Not so strong now, are you? So-called son of Poseidon,' they snickered and continued to kick him.

'I am the son of Poseidon,' he growled through his teeth. He had made a mental note to stop saying that now that he was nothing more than a shell of man, but old habits died hard.

'Some say you were shot by Zeus' lightning,' one of them stopped to yell in his face. 'Is that true?'

'About as true as the pain,' Bellerophon replied, but he was sure they didn't hear him. They just kept kicking him, every strike sending shocks down his body until he was coughing blood at the mouth.

'See you soon, Bellerophontes!' one of them hollered as they skittered off on their business.

'Just Bellerophon will do,' he groaned out the side of his mouth and crawled back under the bench.

THE STORY OF BELLEROPHON EXPLAINED

When we think of heroes within Greek mythology, we think of Perseus, the slayer of monsters; Heracles and his twelve labours; Odysseus and his epic voyages; Jason and his Argonauts; and of course Achilles, the greatest warrior of all Greek myth. Despite Bellerophon having a great story, he never really emerges from the shadows cast by the other heroes and demigods which is a real shame as there's much that can be learnt from his rise and fall. As I'm sure most of you are starting to realise, Greek mythology is full of tragedy and Bellerophon is very much a tragic hero. Much like Perseus, Bellerophon was born long before the days of Heracles. Born in ancient Corinth just west of Athens, he was sometimes attributed as the son of Poseidon, god of the sea and the Oceanid Eurynome. Other times he was the son of Glaucus who may have been mortal but after eating a magical herb while fishing, became a god. Regardless of who his father may have been, Bellerophon was different. He was born a demigod, something he would only discover later in his life.

The journey of Bellerophon begins with the murder of a family member often said to be his brother. The exact reason and method is seldom mentioned so we are left wondering whether it was a drunken accident, a calculated murder or if there was foul play from the gods. After his actions, Bellerophon was taken before King Proetus who cleansed him of all his crimes. He may have been pardoned of his crime, but his troubles had only just began. When Stheneboea, the wife of Proetus, saw Bellerophon, she took a liking to him and attempted to seduce him. Being a man of honour and not wanting to anger the king who had just given him his freedom, he rejected her advances. Stheneboea was furious that she could not have the young warrior and returned to her husband and recounted an altered version of the events that took place. Proteus did not hear of his wife's attempts to seduce another man, he heard a tale of an ungrateful man who attempted to rape his wife. With Bellerophon pardoned, he was now a guest, and as furious as Proteus was, he could not kill a guest in his kingdom for fear of angering the gods. He would instead send our hero to his father-in-law in Lycia, passing the burden of punishment over to him.

When Bellerophon arrived in Lycia, he presented King Lobates with a sealed message explaining that he was to be executed for attempting to violate his daughter. However Lobates was faced with a dilemma of his own. The people of Lycia were being terrorised by a fire breathing hybrid beast known as the Chimera. To him, it made no difference how Bellerophon died, so he sent him to slay this beast under the assumption that he would most likely meet his end. Bellerophon, still seeking redemption, accepted Lobates' challenge. Before setting out, he visited the seer Polyeidos who told him that in order to defeat the Chimera, he would need the help of the winged horse Pegasus. Polyeidos suggested that everything would become clear once he spent a night in Athena's temple. Just as the seer predicted, Athena came to our hero in his sleep and offered him a golden bridle that he would use to tame Pegasus, a majestic winged horse in Greek mythology.

With his new found steed, he travelled to the countryside of Lycia and faced the Chimera, but even with Pegasus he could not harm the Chimera. Being able to fly made it so the Chimera was limited in its choice of attacks as it was incapable of flight itself. There were, however, myths of the Chimera in the years that followed that claim the Chimera had wings and was indeed capable of flight, but it appeared to remain grounded in its duel with Bellerophon. Eventually, Bellerophon came up with a plan that he thought might kill the Chimera. He attached a large piece of lead to the tip of his spear and rammed the spear into its throat. The large piece of lead became lodged in the creature's throat, and when the Chimera attempted to once again breathe fire, the spear blocked the fire from leaving the Chimera's body. Eventually, the fire melted the spear and the boiling hot lead poured down the Chimera's throat, causing it to suffocate. To Lobates's surprise, Bellerophon returned victorious. The boy who had lived the majority of his life in obscurity was now a hero. It was here that Bellerophon began to realise that he was capable of things beyond the wildest dreams of any mortal.

It was clear to Lobates that Bellerophon could be of further use to him, and rather than executing Bellerophon as he originally planned, he instead gave him another task. There were two tribes that were at war with

Lycia at the time. The Solymi and the all-female Amazons. Bellerophon was to go and squash an uprising that was taking place amongst the Amazons, for they were fierce warriors and not opposition that Lobates himself seemed keen on engaging. With the assistance of Pegasus, he was able to defeat both tribes, most famously by flying above the Solymi and dropping boulders onto them, quite literally squashing their rebellion. During his travels from the Solymi to the Amazons, Lobates had several assassination attempts made on Bellerophon's life for he began to grow weary and paranoid over his uncanny power, but none were successful. It is here that many believed Poseidon made it known that Bellerophon was indeed his son, helping him repel the assassins' attempts. When both tribes were defeated and Bellerophon returned to Lobates, he once again attempted to kill him. But this time, Lobates would be more audacious and dispatched his own guards to ambush Bellerophon before he reached Lycia. Once again, these attempts were futile and did nothing but anger our hero and cause him to demand an explanation for such a betrayal. Lobates, realising that he could not slay Bellerophon, instead gave him political power and wealth by allowing him into his family.

The reputation and popularity of Bellerophon grew by the day, but unfortunately so did his ego and hubris towards the gods. He had become bored of his life amongst mortals now knowing that he was a son of Poseidon; he started to believe he belonged with the rest of the gods on Mount Olympus. When he finally grew tired of the mundane life of a mortal, he decided it was his time to ascend to the heavens. He mounted Pegasus and began his journey to the home of the gods. However, Zeus was watching from above and he was not impressed. He did not take kindly to the hubris shown by Bellerophon. After all, he was still only a demigod, and in the eyes of Zeus, he had not done enough to earn his place on Olympus. Zeus sent a gadfly to string Pegasus, which caused the horse to buck and send Bellerophon falling back down to earth. Pegasus continued to Olympus where he would be welcomed by Zeus and would even go on to carry Zeus's thunderbolts across the sky from time to time. The fall of Bellerophon would eventually come to an end, and in some tales, he died immediately upon hitting the earth. Other stories believed he survived the fall but he was crippled, cursed to roam the Earth for eternity as a shadow of the man he used to be, hated by both gods and mortals.

The story of Bellerophon is truly a tragic tale. We all love stories where a nobody becomes a hero, but this is a tale that warns of how the fame and glory may change an individual. Bellerophon began his life as a man with no particular reputation. He then committed an act that led to him seeking redemption and atonement. When Stheneboea thrust herself upon him, he rejected her advances and we start to see the type of person he truly is. When taken before Lobates, he could have easily rejected the king's proposal and asked to be executed as was intended. Instead, he saw the opportunity to save the lives of many while atoning for his crime, and he did exactly that by slaying the Chimera and becoming 'Bellerophon, the Slayer of Monsters.'

Learning the identity of his father may have been the catalyst for the change in his behaviour, but living a normal life after slaying a beast such as the Chimera must have been no easy task, especially considering that he was capable of so much more. Eventually, he was overwhelmed by his desire for greatness and his inability to live a normal mortal life. This desire is one that may have come across as arrogance in the face of the gods, and seeing as Zeus and his fellow Olympians did not tolerate hubris, Bellerophon was cursed to live an eternity contemplating the error of his ways.

Stories of Bellerophon were largely replaced by those of Perseus and much of this could have been down to Bellerophon's story, ending with him becoming a disgraced hero. We can argue that his story paved the way for future heroes to come, the story of Heracles is largely about atonement and redemption. We're so used to stories of famous and celebrated heroes that sometimes it's important to remember those such as Bellerophon who show us that heroes, no matter how good or pure their intentions maybe, can still make mistakes and ultimately fall. Part of what makes many of the Greek heroes so interesting is that they are still capable of making mistakes and they are far from perfect. Sometimes your greatest enemy is not the person you despise the most, nor is it one of the monsters or demons you slay. Sometimes, it is yourself.

ICARUS

I. Bound

Daedalus stared at his son for the longest time. It wouldn't be the first instance he caught Icarus, now sixteen years of age, gazing out across the ocean. The sun was descending over the mountains, but the sky remained rich with vibrant pink hues that would soon give way to the coming night. Daedalus supposed his son should've been out there by the shores, his feet in the sands with perhaps a girl by his side. But no, he was stuck here in this accursed tower, bound to it, deemed to share the same fate as his old man.

'I hate this tower. I hate the king. And I hate you,' Icarus told him a day prior, and those words still rung in his ears, plaguing him at times so that he could hear nothing else.

Daedalus opened his mouth to speak, but what else could he say to his son that he had not already said? So instead, he lifted the morsel of unsavoury cheese the guards brought and stuffed it in his mouth. He clenched his fists as he chewed, thinking about all the inventions he had built King Minos. He'd even gone ahead and built the most complex and detailed containment known as the Labyrinth for which to seal the Minotaur, a crazed part-man part-bull beast that plagued the island of Crete. Yet, King Minos repaid him with hard cheese. For just a moment, he caught the saddened sideways glance that Icarus gave him and couldn't help but feel his heart tear in two.

It was a tragic fate. To think, he was an inventor of the greatest creations—perhaps the greatest creator who ever lived. Yet, he could build or conspire nothing of an escape for his son, perhaps the only creation he would give his own life for.

Daedalus felt his stomach rumble. By the gods, it had been a while since his last proper meal. He couldn't imagine how Icarus must've felt, for a growing lad needed his food. But if Icarus was hungry, he showed no sign of it. All he did was hang by that window, watching the waves crash back and forth. Daedalus closed his eyes and tried to think back to a time where he was happy, but soon his dreams took hold of him and he was brought back to that fateful day.

II. An Idea

He pressed the ball of yarn into Ariadne's silky, soft hands. She was King Minos' daughter after all, so when she came to him for help, he hadn't hesitated to offer his services. In truth, he didn't know why he was helping her. Perhaps it was a sense of duty to his kingdom, or perhaps because he took pity on her predicament. She looked up at him with her eyes wet with tears and had a strange sort of expression, like she couldn't afford such a gift and therefore shouldn't take it. But Daedalus gave her a reassuring smile and she soon conceded, accepting the gift as she held it close to her heart.

'One can really navigate the labyrinth with this?' she whispered as if she couldn't believe it.

'Of course,' Daedalus assured her. 'I built the labyrinth, did I not? Certainly only I would know how to overcome it.'

'My father would be most displeased to learn that you have aided me,' she said with concern and the light in her eyes dwindled a slight.

A chilly breeze blew through the street in which they stood, cloaked in shadow and mist.

'Best he doesn't find out then, Ariadne.' Daedalus smiled again, but there was something in his gut that knew King Minos would find out and the results would be devastating. Nothing got past him.

'I must go then,' she performed a short curtsy. 'I must pass this onto Theseus so that he might find his way out of the labyrinth.'

He still has to kill the minotaur before he even thinks about making his way out, Daedalus thought to tell her, but decided not to. There was colour in her cheeks and a certain giddiness to her step as she slipped away and into the night. She was in love, the fool. Daedalus didn't want to be the one to burst her bubble. But surely, she must've known that the minotaur was invincible. Theseus didn't stand a chance.

Daedalus woke from his dream and was greeted by the same grey ceiling he was always greeted by. Cobwebs were wrapped around the beams of the roof and a large patch of damp was beginning to form on the ceiling. Sunlight cascaded in from the open window, and there was the sound of gulls outside, squawking to the rolling of the waves. Daedalus lifted his head only to find his son standing in the exact same spot he had been in the night before, mesmerised by the outside world.

'How did you sleep, son?' Daedalus asked, hoping that his son had actually slept.

Icarus didn't say anything at first. His face was slouched against his fist as he stared and stared and stared at the distant horizon.

'I dreamt I was a bird,' he said without taking his eyes off the gulls outside.

It wouldn't be the first time his son dreamt that. Daedalus approached the window and put a tentative hand on his son's shoulder, half expecting it to be shrugged off. There on the window sill were a few feathers that were shed by the gulls. Daedalus didn't think much of it at first. He watched one bird soar across the sky, its wings so perfectly placed that nothing could disrupt its flight. It was accompanied by a second bird, and together, the two birds drifted out of sight.

'Why are we here, father?' Icarus asked like he hadn't asked it a thousand times.

Daedalus replied like he hadn't answered it just as many.

'King Minos found out I gave the ball of yarn to Ariadne and that she used it to help Theseus escape the labyrinth that was keeping the minotaur imprisoned.'

Icarus sighed, 'But why did you have to give her the yarn in the first place?'

'I don't know, son.' Daedalus clutched one of the fallen feathers that sat on the window sill. 'I didn't know Theseus was capable of killing the minotaur, nor did I know he would take both of the king's daughters and elope. I suppose it was an act of kindness. I did not think it would come to this.'

'King Minos imprisoned both of us for a betrayal *you* committed,' Icarus stormed away from the window and found the furs he had been sleeping on. 'You were his most trusted inventor, father, and I your proud son. Now we are both nothing.'

He felt his son's eyes bore into him, but he didn't have the heart or the courage to return his stare. He just fixed his attention on the white feather that he fiddled with his fingers. He began to ponder on the anatomy of the wing and how a hundred little feathers just like the one in his hand could make a bird glide across the air like it was nothing. He pulled the feather close to his face, studying every inch of its detail. A bird sounded off right ahead of him and dove dangerously close to the waters before pulling up at the last second, its tiny feet trailing against the waves.

Daedalus put the feather in his pocket. He had an idea.

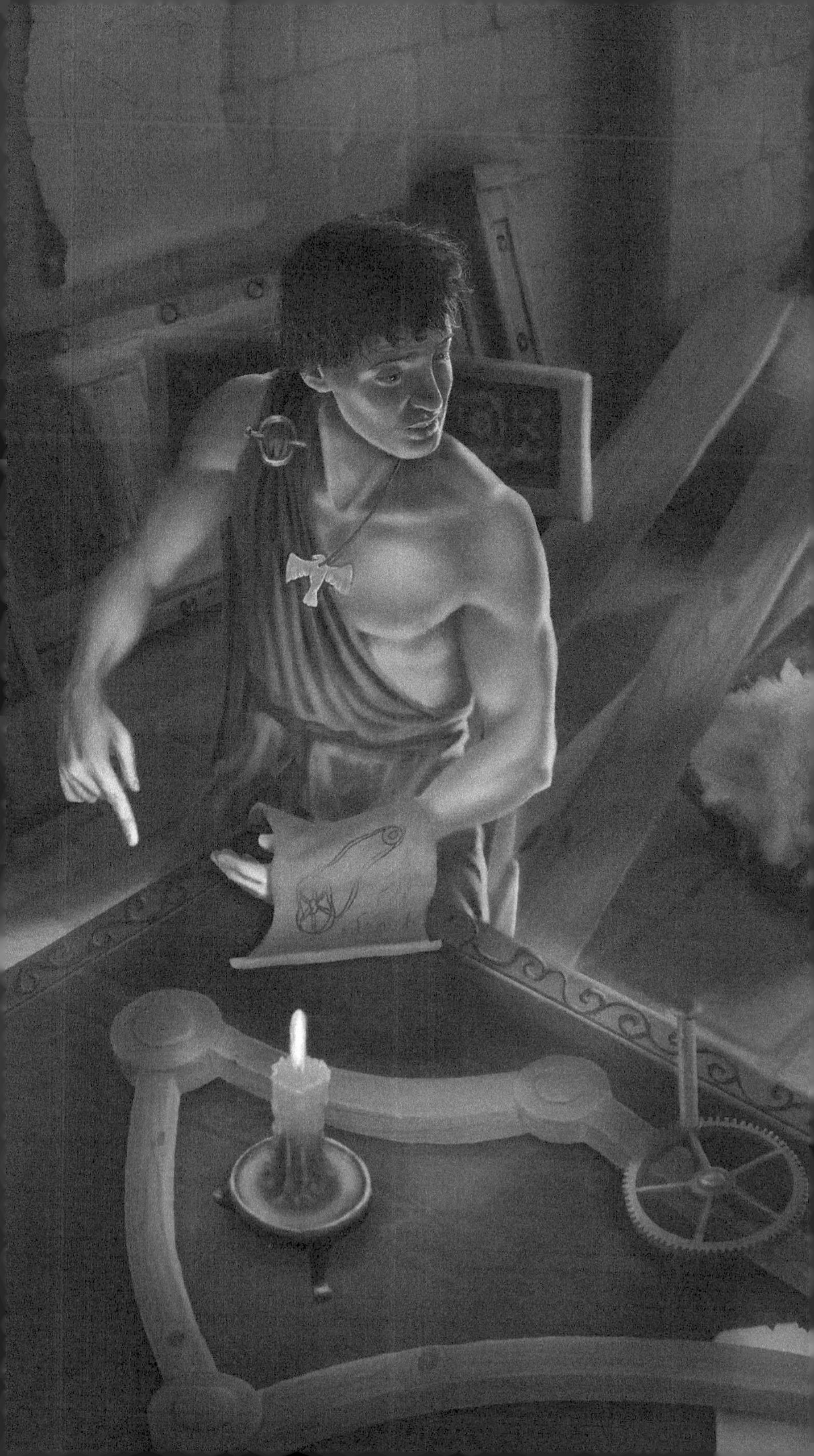

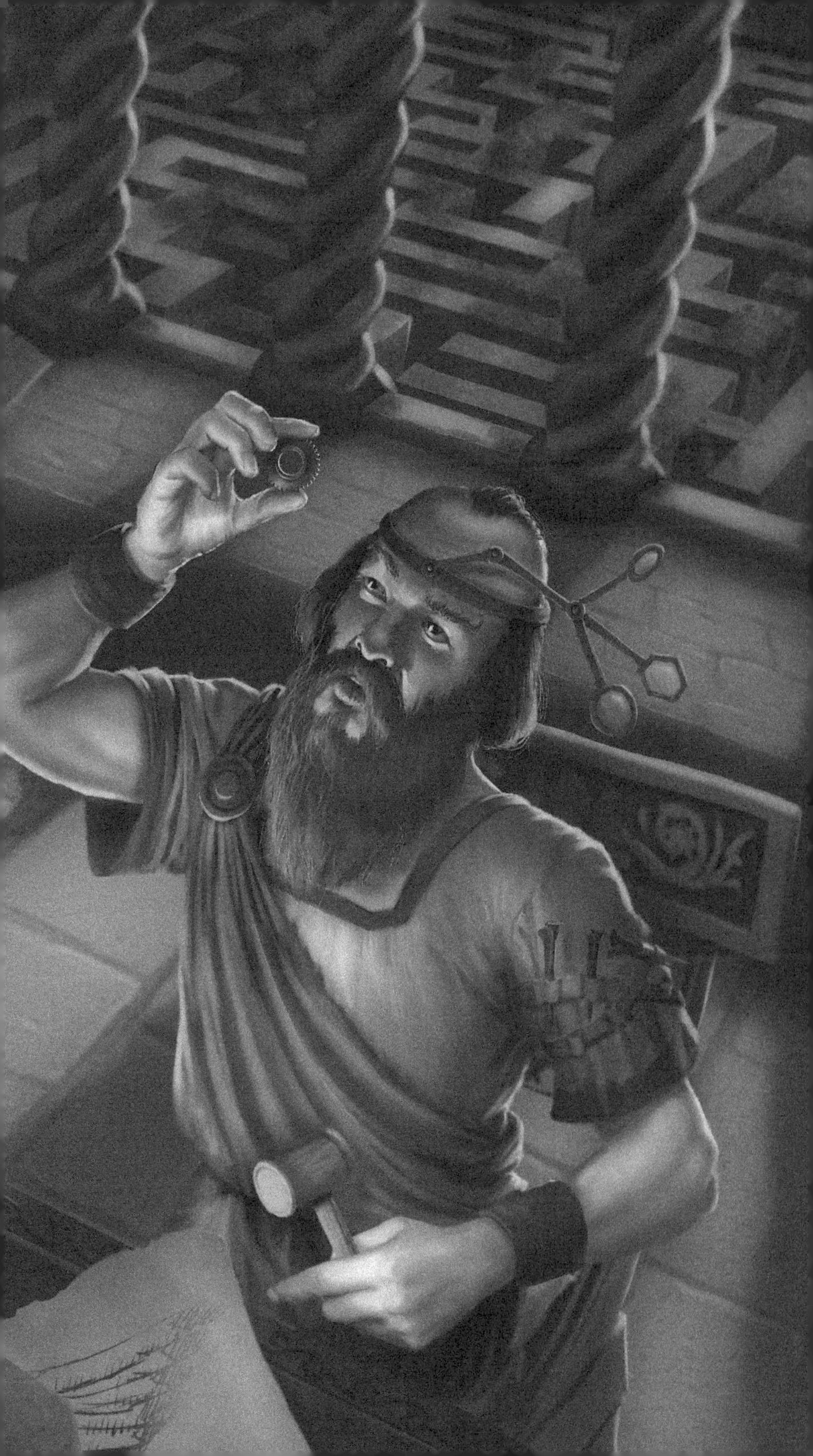

III. A Father's Pain

Months would pass before Daedalus would have enough feathers to start building his next creation. He used wax to put the feathers together, and by no surprise, he was able to construct a pair of fully functional wings. His son watched him every moment during his work with eyes as eager as a hawk. It had been so long since Daedalus had seen his son so excited that he'd almost forgotten what his smile looked like.

'Father!' Icarus would shout every morning. 'Are the wings ready?'

'No, my son.' Daedalus would laugh. 'We still need many feathers before they are able to take our weight.'

But the day soon came where Daedalus had more than enough feathers to complete the wings for both himself and his son. He attached the wings to his son's back, inspecting each and every feather to ensure they would function as intended. He could barely keep Icarus from lunging out of the window, but he held his son steady by the shoulders.

'I know this is an exciting day, Icarus. But this invention of mine has never been tested. Remember to do exactly as I say.'

'Yes, father!' Icarus nodded, his eyes wide and his face alight with excitement that Daedalus admitted he would not tire of seeing.

Daedalus strapped his own wings to his back and approached the window. The fresh sea breeze greeted him, blowing hard enough to take his breath away for a moment. He was a mad man, surely. Who in their right mind would willingly jump out of a window with wings they constructed themselves? Daedalus had an urge to set the wings aside and think of a more rational plan. But then he looked back at his son and saw that fulfilled, animated expression. Why, the boy could hardly keep still he was so raring for his life to begin again. So Daedalus pushed the doubts aside, stepped onto the window sill and took a deep breath.

'Remember, son,' he turned to Icarus, 'the feathers which form these wings are glued with wax. You must not fly too high, otherwise the heat from the sun will melt the wax and the feathers will become undone.'

'I understand, father.' Icarus nodded, though Daedalus wasn't sure he did.

'Stay on my level,' Daedalus warned him. 'Don't do anything that I do not do myself.'

'Yes, father,' Icarus leaped to his side. 'Can we go now?'

Daedalus wanted to say no. What would King Minos do when he found out that they had escaped? Then again, what would Icarus do if he stripped his wings away after all this time and told him he had to stay a prisoner? *I hate you*, the words from that night rang in his ears again. No, Daedalus had no intention of suffering that painful sentence again.

'Follow me exactly,' Daedalus put a hand on Icarus' shoulder and gave it a slight squeeze.

Then he took a deep breath and leapt from the window.

He was falling. The realisation of plummeting to his death hit him hard—so hard, that he almost forgot to flap his wings. He gasped and begun moving his arms up and down, furiously thrusting his arms until they began to hurt. The ground below rushed up to meet him, the air chafing against his face making it hard to breathe. He shut his eyes thinking himself a fool when suddenly...he was flying.

'Father!' Icarus called beside him and though Daedalus didn't want to, he forced his eyes open.

There was Icarus by his side, his arms moving just as Daedalus had shown him, wings flapping back and forth. He was laughing and it was perhaps the most beautiful sound Daedalus heard in quite some time. It was infectious, and before long, Daedalus was laughing as they put more and more distance between themselves and the tower they had been bound to.

'We did it!' Icarus called over the sound of the waves. 'We escaped King Minos! Now we can live our lives, can't we?'

Daedalus glanced back at the tower and the island of Crete in which they once lived. It grew smaller as they progressed, but the tower itself stuck out like a sore thumb. Daedalus didn't look back a second time. Instead, he let himself bask in the sunlight and the endless blue sky that was cloudless and brilliant. Indeed, they had done it and before long, they would be out of King Minos' reach forever.

Icarus whooped with excitement and then his wings were flapping more than before. He was ascending upwards with a dreamy look on his boyish face. It was almost as if he was being called by someone that Daedalus could not hear.

'Icarus!' Daedalus shouted. 'Remember what I said! Do not fly too high!'

But Icarus was transfixed and he was soaring upwards, his wings beating faster and faster.

'Icarus!' Daedalus screamed. He tried to reach an arm up to grab his son's ankle and pull him down, but realised he couldn't without compromising his own flight.

'It's fine, father,' Icarus called back. 'Don't you see? We're free now!'

Icarus kept on going and while Daedalus screamed with all his might, his son did not heed the warning. Before long, Daedalus began to ascend if only to keep within earshot of his son, but then he noticed something that made his heart stop. A lone white feather trailed off from Icarus' wings followed by another and another and another.

'Icarus!' Daedalus beckoned with horror as his son's feathers began to shower down around him.

Icarus made a grunt like he wasn't sure what was happening all of a sudden. His wings were threadbare and the feathers were now taken by the wind, tossed and billowed about like snowflakes. Icarus flapped his arms desperately, but then he was falling.

'Icarus!' Daedalus lunged to reach for him, but it was too late. It all happened so fast. He caught a glimpse of his son's face as he fell from the sky, arms still wringing this way and that before he let out a terrified cry. Before Daedalus could blink, Icarus plunged headfirst into the waters.

Daedalus screamed a desperate wail and flew low to the waters in the hopes of seeing Icarus resurface. He scanned the waters a thousand times, circling the point of his son's impact until he was dizzy. The waves were aggressive and shifted in and out, making it hard for Daedalus to keep track of where his son even landed. It wouldn't be too long before he let out a resounding cry at the realisation that his son was gone, taken by the ocean.

Where there was once the sound of his son's laughter, there was nothing but the growl of the sea and the harping of the birds. He wanted to stay and wait in case the ocean spat his son back out, but his own arms were beginning to tire and he still had a lot of flying left to do. He shut his eyes once more, his heart heavy now with anguish as he took to the skies.

More than once, he thought he heard his son as he continued his journey. His voice haunted him—the laughter and excitement Icarus expressed spilled into his ears, making the hurt of his loss all the more painful. He could hear his son's dying wail and the sound of his body crashing into the waters below. He could see Icarus' face every time he closed his eyes and the terrified expression his son made was burned so vividly into his mind. Then he heard the words that chilled him to his core and would continue to plague him for the rest of his days.

I hate you.

Daedalus flew on.

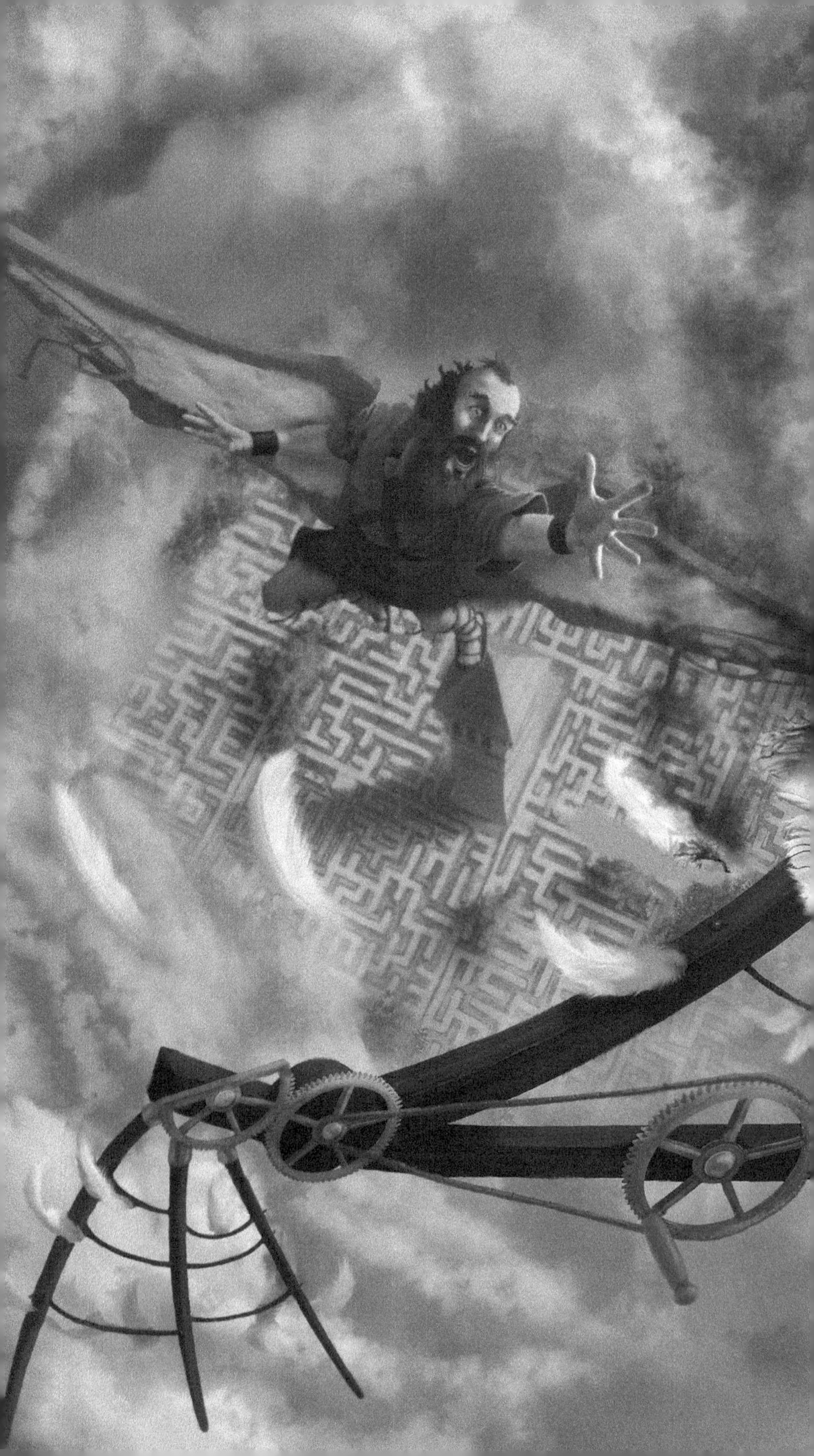

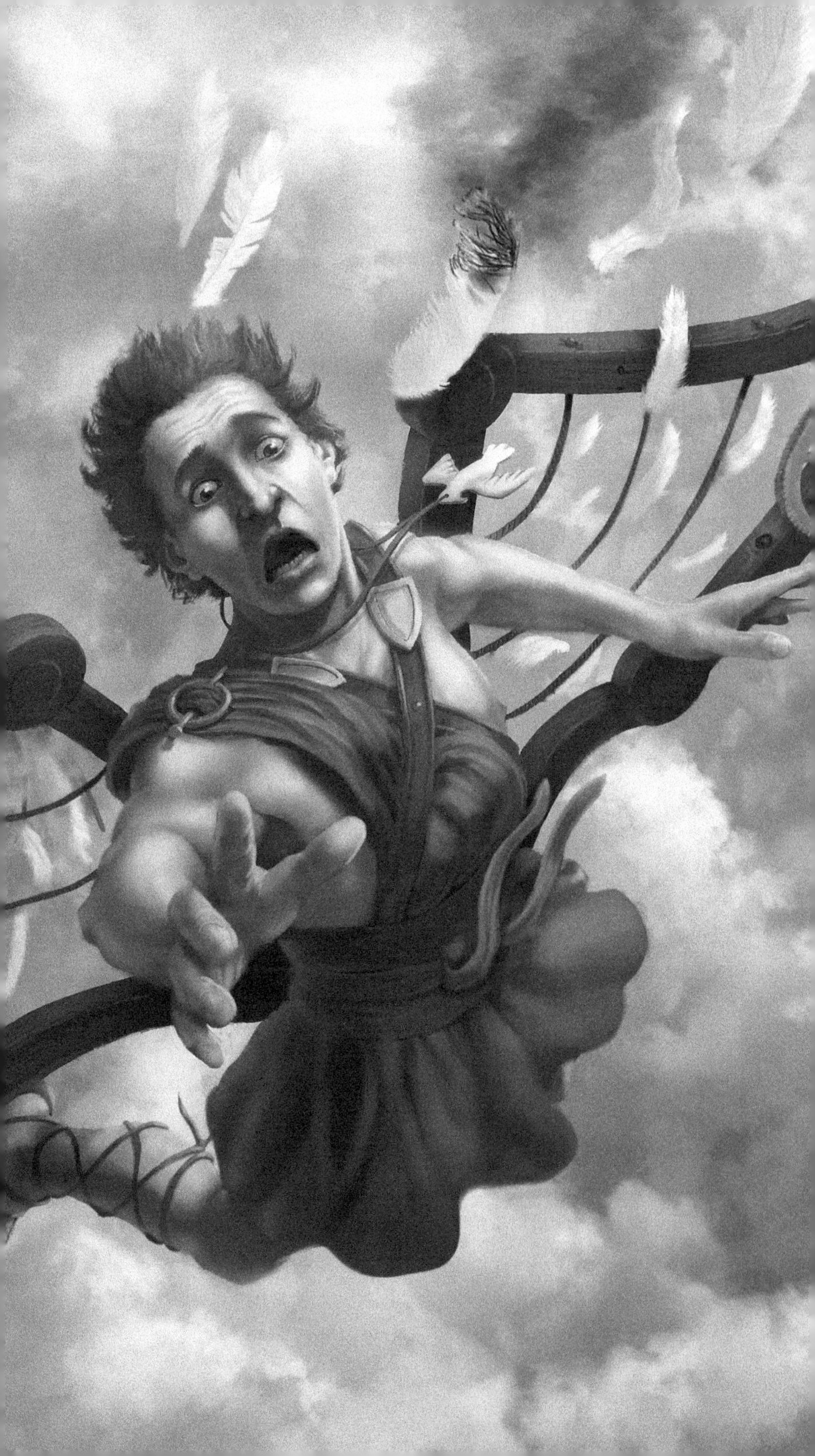

THE STORY OF ICARUS EXPLAINED

The story of Icarus and Daedalus takes place shortly after the events of Theseus and the Minotaur. The island of Crete had been plagued for years by the half-man half-bull monster. In order to contain the beast, King Minos had his most trusted and talented inventor create a prison to house the Minotaur. That inventor was indeed Daedalus and his creation was the great labyrinth of Crete. Daedalus had gone from a servant to a trusted member of Minos' house, and once the labyrinth was constructed, his position was firmly established. He was given his pick from the servant women and one would give him the child he desired, a son that he would name Icarus. However, as with most tales in Greek mythology, Daedalus' streak of success and good fortune would not last long.

After being responsible for the death of Minos' son, Athens would send an annual tribute of children that would be sacrificed to the Minotaur. Over the years, the city of Athens sent dozens of men to kill the Minotaur and release them of the yearly burden. But none were successful. When the Athenian hero Theseus, the son of the king of Athens, King Aegeus, set sail for Crete, he promised his father that he would finally slay the beast that had plagued Athens fall all those years. Upon reaching Crete, Theseus would meet both of Minos' daughters Phaedra and Ariadne who were captivated at the sight of him. Despite both Phaedra and Ariadne falling in love with him, Theseus was more concerned with the task at hand, slaying the Minotaur. Not being able to cope with the fact that he could be slain by the Minotaur, Ariadne visited Daedalus and begged him to help her ensure that Theseus would return from the labyrinth.

There isn't much said about the relationship between Ariadne and Daedalus, but with him being so willing to help her ,we can perhaps assume Daedalus was rather fond of Ariadne in the same way a mentor becomes fond of a student. Daedalus knew that King Minos despised the Athenians and would love nothing more than to see Theseus slain by the Minotaur. Despite being aware that no good could come from helping Ariadne, Daedalus still chose to do so, giving her a ball of yarn allowing Theseus to map his route through the labyrinth and avoid becoming lost.

When Theseus managed to slay the Minotaur, he hastily set sail back to Athens, but on board his ship were both Phaedra and Ariadne.

As you would expect, King Minos was furious having been bested by a man from Athens and losing both of his daughters to him was the last straw. Naturally, the only person left to blame was Daedalus, considering his involvement was instrumental in Theseus' success, and so both Daedalus and his son Icarus were imprisoned. The terms of their imprisonment is something that does vary in the tales and there are two popular myths of what happened to Daedalus after the Minotaur was slain. The first states that King Minos locked Daedalus and Icarus away in the labyrinth as punishment, but also as a precaution, so that Daedalus would never create anything like the Labyrinth for anyone else. They would eventually be freed by Pasiphae, the wife of King Minos, and Daedalus would construct his iconic wax wings to escape the Cretan fleete. The irony of Daedalus being locked away in a prison that he created is not lost on me, but there are some inconsistencies to this story that lead to me favouring the second variation.

If anyone would be able to escape the Labyrinth, it would be its creator and the smartest man in Crete, Daedalus. This makes Minos' decision to lock them away in the Labyrinth quite questionable. Being freed by Pasiphae and then constructing the wings out of confinement makes what we can consider Daedalus' great escape seem far less great. The second variation of myth involved Daedalus and Icarus being locked away in the tallest tower in Crete with only one window as a way of escape. Here we see Daedalus and Icarus scavenge materials, using the wood from tables and chairs, the wax from their candles and slowly and arduously collecting feathers from birds that would perch on their window. With no outside assistance, the father and son essentially performed the impossible, not only escaping the tower safely, but also flying over the Cretan flete that awaited them.

Throughout the story, we see the fractured relationship of Daedalus and his son. We're never really told the exact age of Icarus but we can assume he was fairly young—most likely in either his early or late teens—which makes the anger and frustration he felt towards his father quite understandable. If we approach this story from the perspective of Icarus, he had been forced to spend the majority of his childhood locked up in a tower because of the actions of his father, the sins of the father being a theme that runs all through Greek mythology. It would almost appear to Icarus that his father chose Ariadne over his own son, which was never the intention of Daedalus. It's likely that Icarus, in all the years he spent in confinement, would have gone over the actions of his father in his head hundreds of times until there wasn't much left but anger, bitterness and resentment. Daedalus knew the only way he could win back his son was to escape Crete and attempt to make up for all of the lost time between himself and Icarus. This is why we see Daedalus so eager to formulate a plan to not only escape Crete, but also to win back his son.

A possible explanation to Icarus ignoring the warnings of his father when taking flight was because he had already missed so much of his life having been imprisoned for so long. When he was finally free, he was so overcome by elation that he forgot his surroundings and lost control, which as we all know would eventually result in his tragic death.

Over the years, people have taken dozens of meanings and morals away from the story of Icarus. On a very basic level, the story essentially tells us to heed the advice of those older and much wiser than ourselves. However, if we choose to delve deeper, we can see the story means so much more. It highlights the carelessness of youth and some of the consequences that it can bring. Icarus disregards everything his father tells him, which eventually results in his fall. We can also potentially view the death of Icarus as a punishment from the gods, as in their eyes man was never meant to fly. Daedalus' invention would have been seen as man soaring to heights that were previously thought impossible. The gods would have interpreted this as mankind attempting to elevate themselves to an equal level.

Naturally, this idea would not be tolerated, so Icarus would die and Daedalus would be forced to live a life of guilt and regret. There is a variation of the story where the god Apollo came across Icarus while riding his chariot in the sky. He watched as the boy plummeted to his death, refusing to intervene and offer any assistance. You could argue that the gods not wanting to intervene in the affairs of mortals, especially when they needed help, was fairly normal. Or you could make the argument that Apollo and the other gods chose to make an example of Icarus, making it very clear what fate awaited those who attempted to defy the natural order.

A more modern interpretation of the story that certainly relates to the society that we live in today discusses the pursuit of instant gratification. We now live in an era where everything is so readily available. We rarely have to wait longer than a few days for anything we desire. This can lead to many focusing on short term benefits and forgetting or refusing to acknowledge the long term benefits that actions can have. We can view Icarus's story in a very similar manner. Daedalus had created an invention that was unheard of at the time. There is nothing that would suggest that once they had escaped, the wings couldn't be used again. When Icarus takes flight, the experience is exhilarating, a feeling that he has never felt before. It's very likely that Daedalus felt the same, but in all his years of experience and knowledge, he was able to prioritize escaping safely over his own enjoyment. Icarus became so overwhelmed by the feeling that he lost sight of the long term plan of escape. If he was able to remain level-headed, he would have realised that once they were safe, he could use the wings again, repeating his personal euphoria multiple times. As many do, Icarus fell victim to the allure of instant gratification, only focusing on his present situation. He would then go on to ignore his father and any notion of the future at his peril.

The flight and fall of Icarus is a tragic but necessary tale of moderation and caution. It serves as a reminder to us all, not to forget our dreams and aspirations by flying too low to the sea, whilst also reminding us not to get carried away and lose sight of our objective. It's important to maintain a happy medium by dreaming big and living for today while remaining grounded and planning for tomorrow.

MEDUSA

I. The Birth of a Hero

Medusa breathed in deep, enjoying the familiar feel of the summer-time breeze on her bare arms as she took in the sight of it all. A throng of people danced in the courtyard of the temple, a myriad of multi-coloured fabrics mingling, and everyone laughed with chalices full of wine. A fanfare of music sauntered through the air from the bands littered about here and there, a collection of wind and brass instruments bringing with it a jovial wave. Children were running in and between the crowds of their parents like mice, lunging and catching one another with giggles and joy. The smell of roasted meat caught her nose soon enough, and it had Medusa watering at the mouth. How long had it been since she'd last eaten?

'I must say, priestess,' one stout woman touched her by the elbow as she downed her chalice of wine rather un-lady like. 'You have well and truly outdone yourself this time.'

Medusa laughed, particularly when the woman gave a quiet burp and wiped her mouth with the back of her hand. 'You do me too much kindness, Cassandra.'

'Nonsense,' Cassandra took another swig from the glass, realised it was empty before dripping the last dregs of red on the floor. 'This year's festival is easily your greatest festival yet.'

Perhaps it was, Medusa considered as she held her hand up at the hovering sun. It truly was a marvellous day with golden rays blasting down upon the city of Athens, wrapping it up in their warm embrace. She couldn't see a discontent face as she scanned the bevy of people, all of them now engaged in some merry dance or trading some amusing anecdote. Even some of the older gentlemen had forsaken their canes and were stumbling about, laughing as they bumped into one another in some clumsy attempt at dancing.

'Do you reckon she'll show up?' Medusa turned to Cassandra, and for just a moment, she felt a pang of sadness. How many festivals had she organised in the name of Athena, only for the goddess to snub the event?

Cassandra's big eyes narrowed a slight, but her smile remained all the same. 'Now, don't you go worrying your pretty little head about Athena.'

'But—'

'Enjoy the moment, Medusa.' Cassandra swung her heavy arm around her. 'Every year you worry about whether Athena will come, and when she doesn't, you get into a bother.'

'It's just...it would be good for us to see her, don't you think?'

Cassandra made a face at her, 'Do you think these people are worried about Athena?'

Medusa scanned the crowd once more and saw women arm in arm, dancing around in a circle with men chasing them to keep up. The children were still zipping here and there, all of them as agile as any squirrel she'd ever seen. Even the hardened looking warriors who sat at the tables playing backgammon were pointing and laughing at each other, big smiles on their weighty faces.

'I guess not,' Medusa shrugged.

'I'll prove it to you,' Cassandra, grabbed hold of the nearest man— literally grabbed him by his tunic and pulled him over.

Medusa moved to protest, 'Cassandra you don't have to—'

'How do you feel about Athena coming to visit?' she snapped at him quite pointedly.

The man recoiled at first, lines in his face darkening. But then he let out a nervous laugh and bowed his head at Medusa. 'It would be grand if our goddess would join us, but I am equally happy to bask in the greatness of you, priestess Medusa.'

'Oh,' Medusa went warm at the cheeks. 'I—'

'And what about me?' Cassandra put her hands on her wide hips.

'Oh, of course,' the man bowed his head even lower, 'Priestess Cassandra, you are to be treasured as well.'

'Heh,' Cassandra snickered. 'Get out of here you charmer.'

The man bowed his head again and scarpered off, lost in the fray of bodies before them.

'You see, girl?' Cassandra rather unceremoniously slapped Medusa on the back, almost knocking her over. The woman didn't know her own strength half the time.

'Yes,' Medusa replied, rubbing her back. 'Indeed I see.'

Perhaps Cassandra was right though. Who cared if Athena didn't come to the festival? Everyone looked as if they had forgotten who the patron of Athens was in the first place, and even if they hadn't, what did it matter now? Medusa glanced at the olive tree in the centre of the courtyard. It was a truly beautiful thing with the vibrant glow of a firefly, the emerald coloured leaves nudged by the wind, the bark of the tree as thick and dense as a giant's thigh.

'You're staring at that tree again, aren't you?' Cassandra nudged her.

Medusa sighed, 'Why would Athena gift us something so gorgeous and then desert us?'

'She has not deserted us,' Cassandra grabbed her roughly by the arm. 'She's there. Perhaps we as priestesses are doing such a grand job that she doesn't feel the need to watch over us so protectively.'

'Do you really believe that?' Medusa asked in all sincerity.

'Of course,' Cassandra nodded her head all matter of fact now. 'You know what your problem is?'

'Do tell,' Medusa said dryly, for she'd heard it a dozen times already.

'You don't believe in yourself,' Cassandra prodded her. 'You are a beautiful woman with the head as strong as a bull. You could do anything, Medusa. Anything!'

'Yes, yes.' Medusa rolled her eyes. 'Save your flattery.'

'You really think I'm talking nonsense, don't you?'

'Why you, Cassandra?' Medusa made a sarcastic sound. 'Never!'

A sly smirk came upon Cassandra's chubby face, and her eyes lit up. Then she daintily hopped up onto a large step for a woman so round and cleared her throat.

'Eh?' Medusa felt a shiver of nerves then. 'Cassandra, what are you doing?'

'Can I have your attention?' Cassandra roared across the courtyard. Say what you will about the plump priestess, she sure knew how to make her voice heard.

'Cassandra, what are you doing?' Medusa went to pull her down from the step.

'Proving it to you,' she gave her a friendly wink.

'Proving what?' Medusa was pulling at the woman's sleeve, trying to dethrone her from her step. A shiver of nerves became a war of anxious spasms down her back, through her chest and all over. Just what in Athena's name was this idiot doing?

'Thank you all for coming today,' Cassandra bellowed, though Medusa knew she wasn't using even half the capacity of her lungs to shout. The bands began to quieten down, and the chatter amongst the crowds fizzled out like the tide retreating from the shore. 'I just wanted to say a few words on behalf of our dear Athena. I'm sure, if she was here, she would bestow upon us her most favoured tidings and would grant each of us a fair smile and her warmest regards.'

'Why doesn't she then?' A drunken shout came from the crowd and was met with both disgruntled utterings and guilty snickers.

'Our patron is very busy,' Cassandra took it in her stride. 'Besides, do we really need Athena to bring us joy when we have a priestess as beautiful as our Medusa?'

Medusa was about to bury her head down her chiton and stay there forever out of embarrassment. Was Cassandra a fool? She was a fool, wasn't she? She was definitely a fool. But then a roar of cheers flooded the courtyard and Medusa darn near fell over at the sound of it. All around her the people were clapping, all of them cheering and whistling like she'd just put gold in all of their hands.

'It is because of Medusa,' Cassandra went on, 'that we have days like today—days where we can celebrate in the name of Athena!'

'Let's just worship Medusa instead,' another drunken shout came; this one was met with another roar of approval where chalices were slammed together, cheers of concurrence swept across the bevy and even the children were pointing and waving at her, signifying their agreement.

'Our dear Medusa!' Cassandra held up another chalice of wine. Where she'd gotten that from, Medusa couldn't say.

'Our dear Medusa!' the crowd beckoned back in unison followed by a few drunken echoes.

They were cheering her name now, chanting it through the courtyard with enough excitement to wake the dead. Why, Medusa was sure you could run down to the beach and hear it in all its clarity. It was only then she realised she'd been standing there like a scarecrow, bottom lip hanging low.

'Medusa, the patron of Athens!' one man shouted in the centre of it all, threw his chalice in the air and caught it, despite the wine spilling over his hair.

'Medusa, the patron of Athens!' a whole group of them spouted and then did the exact same thing, some of the catching their glasses and the others forgetting about them entirely as they rained on the floor.

Medusa brought her hand to her mouth. She knew she shouldn't have enjoyed this, but seeing them all but bow before her did put a wide smile on her face. She held her jaw hard to stop it from enveloping her face. She didn't wish to rule them, no. But she did wish to protect them all. It was why she'd become a priestess in the first place—to offer solace and wisdom to those who needed it. But if she was their patron—a goddess like Athena—why she'd be able to save them all, surely? With Athena's wisdom, she could bring council to those who needed it and with Athena's strength she could protect them from harm. Why, she could—

'Hello?' Cassandra was shaking her by the shoulders. 'Anyone home?'

'Uh...'

'What did I tell you?' Cassandra was grinning from ear to ear. 'They love you, Medusa.'

Medusa shook her head free of her thoughts, 'I guess I never realised how much so.'

Cassandra's smile remained for a few more moments, but then it gradually slipped from her face as her tone went grave, 'You know they'd make you their goddess if they could.'

Medusa made a nervous laugh, 'That's ridiculous.'

'Is it?' Cassandra raised an eyebrow.

They were still chanting her name, perhaps louder now as they raised their chalices, raised their fists and some of them even raising their children, offering them up like a sacrifice. The musicians were on their feet, skipping about the crowd with their instruments in hand, playing as passionately as she'd ever heard them. The hardened warriors might've remained seated, but they were eyeing her with a grizzly respect. Some of the elderly had even fallen to their knees. Either that or they had actually fallen over in the excitement, but they weren't in a hurry to get back up as they watched her with a glazed look in their eyes.

'Aye,' Cassandra nudged her back to her senses. 'Best to stay grounded though, eh? You know what they say happens to those who fly too close to the sun.'

'I do,' Medusa pulled her gaze away from the crowd and tried to focus on Athena's olive tree, if only to remind herself that she was nothing more than a servant to the goddess.

But for some reason, it had lost its glow.

Something else caught her attention though after a loud smack resonated through the air. A few gasps sounded off around the area and then there came the crying of a child.

'Don't you ever tell me I've had too much,' a man was slurring at a small girl who now had a red mark on her face, courtesy of his fat hand that was now clenched around a bottle.

'Brute,' Cassandra hissed quietly enough that the man wouldn't hear.

There were mutterings of disapproval from the crowd—men and women shaking their heads but for the most part turning away and pretending they couldn't hear.

'I'm sorry father,' the girl cried.

He brought his hand down on her again, this time the back of his knuckles cracking against the side of her face. Her whole body lurched to one side, but to give the poor girl credit, she stayed on her feet despite the blood dripping from her nose. Medusa decided she'd seen enough as well.

'Hey!' she shouted and marched her way over to the man. He stank of wine, that much was true. He had a rotten look to him with stained teeth, a hard set of eyes and an unkempt beard that was mottled with white and grey. He stood at least a head higher than most of the other men at the festival with a brawny frame and two fists the size of fruit bowls.

'What are you doing?' Cassandra grabbed her, perhaps the only time the woman had ever looked nervous. 'Look at the size of that man. I'm all for the child's safety but maybe choose a better time to go about being a hero, eh?'

The girl stood there with her head hung low. She was a mere ant in the presence of her giant father who was now scanning the crowd with his angry eyes, daring anyone to come and have a word so that he might do the same to them. A few of the men in the crowd looked compelled to oblige him, but their bravado soon faltered when they caught the tensing in the man's shoulders and the savage way he held his jaw.

But Medusa couldn't just stand there like the rest. No, she was the high priestess of Athena. What kind of high priestess stood around and watched such unkindness without acting upon it? Cassandra was more than happy to pretend sipping her wine, but perhaps that was why Medusa was the one who held the highest rank of Athena's temple. Everyone else had the same idea as they resumed their conversations, albeit guiltily as they feigned laughs and pointed in other directions at things that didn't matter.

But not Medusa.

She marched her way up to the man who had his hand raised again as he stumbled left and right, swinging for his daughter who stood there ready to accept the blow. She made a final lunge against the cobbled street and darted right before the girl, shielding her from the blow as the man's hand came thundering down.

She shut her eyes at first, but when the blow didn't come she opened them just as quickly and found the man's outraged face glowering at her, his hand frozen inches above her head.

'Lay your hand on that child or anyone else again and I will have you tossed into the prisons, am I clear?' she lifted her chin to meet his face, which was still short by a mile.

He breathed loudly through his mouth, his breath like the air in a wine cellar, strong and scented but awfully sickly too. The anger in his eyes was still present, the creases around his eyes twitching and darkening all the same. But his hand grew limp in the air and he seemed shorter all of a sudden as he took a step back, glanced about the crowd and realised that everyone was staring at him with shame.

'Who do you think you are?' he slurred, his head moving from side to side, eyes slanting back and forth now.

'I'm Medusa,' she said, poised. 'The high priestess of Athens. To defy me is to defy Athena. Now return to the hole you crawled out from and do not return here until you are sober.'

He looked at her for the longest time, but she stared right back at him, hoping he didn't reach out and smack her the way he'd done to his child. She wondered that if he did, whether the onlookers would jump into help? Or would they pretend they couldn't hear that either? Surely Athena would intervene at that point, wouldn't she?

She folded her arms tight and didn't rescind from his stare down. It might not have changed anything in the long run, but he needed to know he was wrong for striking his child in such a manner. More importantly, she needed to know that she would stand up for any member of her flock, regardless of what the consequences were.

'You got balls lady,' the drunk grunted and there was a grin on his chiselled face as his eyes closed and he began to sway left and right.

A woman who had a striking resemblance to the girl swooped in and carried the girl off into the crowd and out of sight. But if the father had any inkling of his daughter's disappearance, he didn't show it. Perhaps he didn't care.

'Leave this festival and you won't have to answer to Athena,' Medusa said with a strict nod, hoping and praying that he would heed her words and turn away. It took all the strength in the world to stop her jaw from rattling and her knees from shaking.

'Fine,' the man burped and then, to her relief, picked his way through the crowd and stumbled off down the street.

A set of cheers went up from the crowd again as soon as he was out of sight and it was so loud that Medusa felt her heart rocket into her throat. Everyone was clapping once more, chanting her name in the same way they had done moments ago, only now with all the more conviction. Confetti was tossed around, and they all broke into a dance as if she had just destroyed every evil in the world.

'That's why they look up to you,' Cassandra trotted over, looking flushed in the face. She kept looking over Medusa's shoulder, cautious in case the man came storming back. 'That's why we all look up to you, Medusa.'

'It was nothing,' she shrugged. 'I did what Athena would've done in someone's time of need.'

'Hmm,' Cassandra smirked and shoved a chalice in her hand, 'to Athena then.'

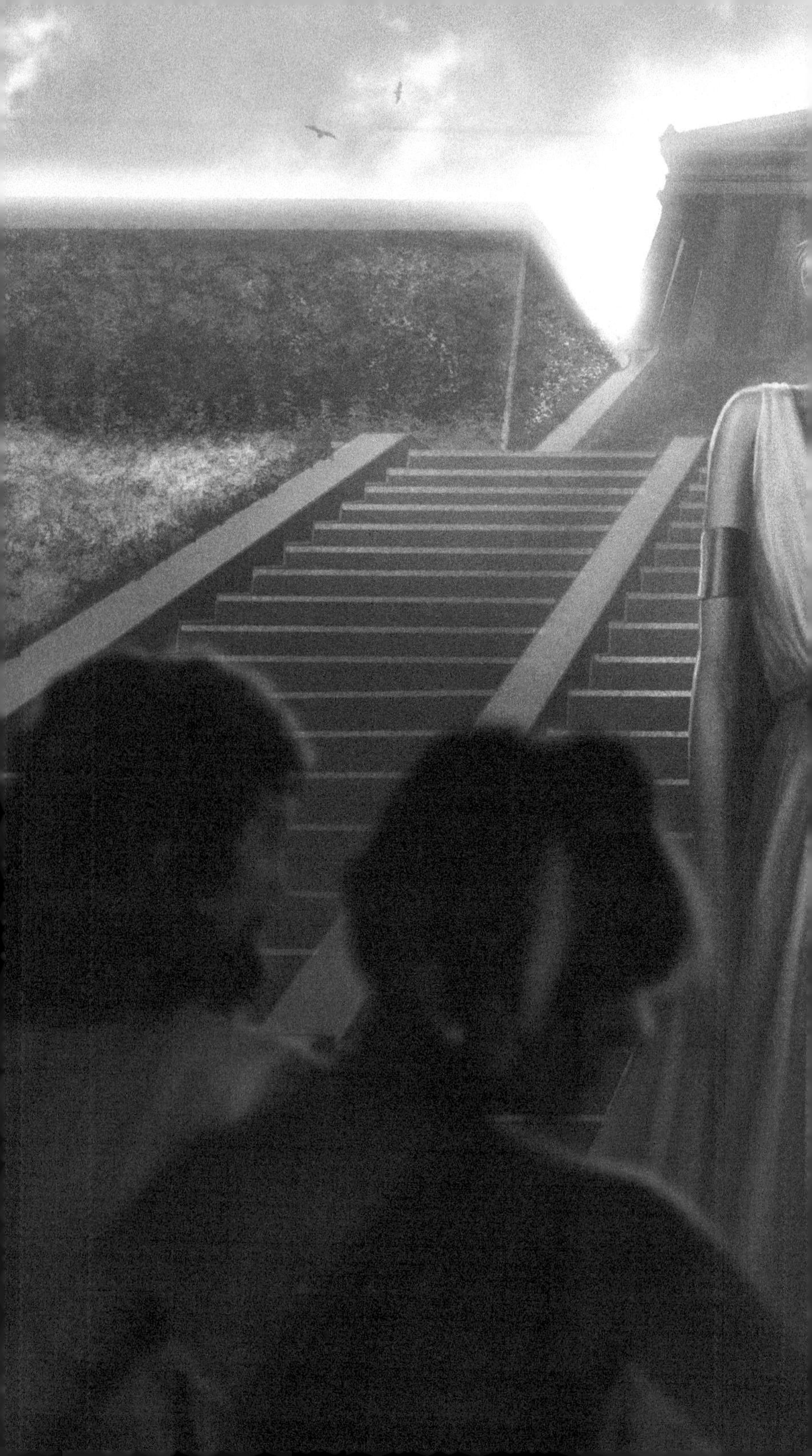

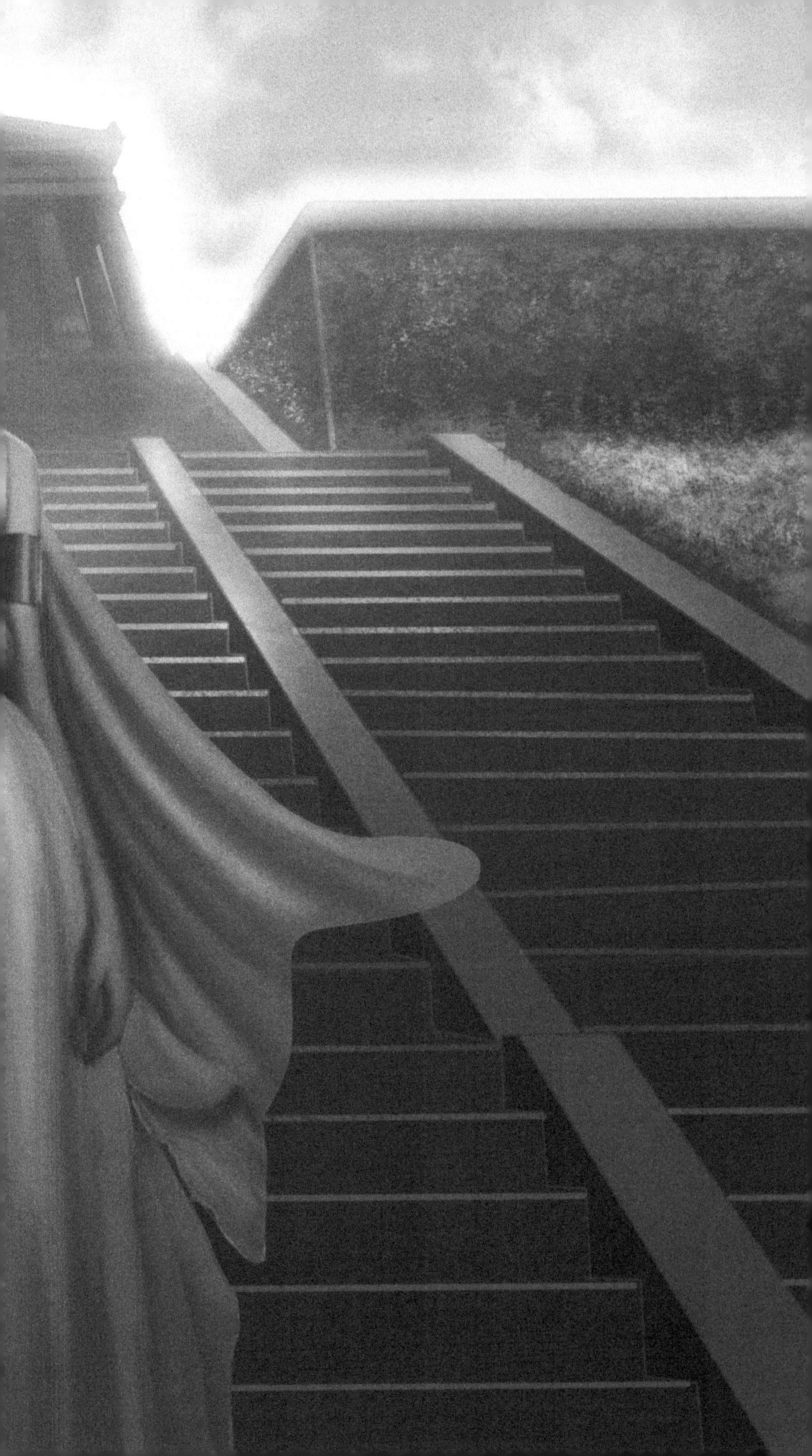

II. An Unlikely Guest

She'd come down to the beach in the thick of the night, though she could still hear the celebrations like a ghostly whisper somewhere beyond the cliffside where the festival lived on, if only through drunken ramblings and the sorry few who didn't know when to call it quits. Medusa had seen Cassandra sneak off with a handsome looking gentleman, and though she, like Medusa, had sworn an oath to remain pure for Athena, it seemed like even a priestess was human in the end.

I've got needs like everyone else, Medusa recalled Cassandra telling her once. *Don't tell me you've never...* She had trailed off after that, widening her eyes and making gestures with her hands, but Medusa simply went red in the face and switched the conversation as quickly as she could.

The smell of the salty air hit her hard, and the sound of the restless waves ironically brought her a sense of calm. She felt the sand between her toes as she set her sandals to the side and skipped here and there between the odd pebble until the cold tide slithered up to meet her, swathing her ankles and bringing with it both foam and seaweed. She cupped some of the water up in her hands, splashed it over her face and felt immediately revitalised. Something about the salty water always made her feel alive again, even after such a long day of planning, cooking, dancing and being momentarily worshipped.

A loud set of cheers went up over the cliffside, and if she looked carefully, she could make out the temple cut out against the night's sky, one side of it concealed by the dark, but the other lit up by the moonlight. Medusa wondered if someone had fallen over or if a fight had broken loose, hence the sudden cheers. But then it went silent after that, and only the arguing of the waves met her ears and the hiss of the tide as it shouldered against the coast.

You know, they'd make you their goddess if they could.

Cassandra's words crept into her head as vividly as if she had just whispered it by her ear. She tried to shake the thought loose, but the more she tried, the more it stuck there like a fly trapped in a bottle. Not only was it a blasphemous thought, but it was a stupid one too. She could no more be a goddess than a crab could be a gull. She paced her way out of the tide's reach and back to her sandals where she got down to her knees. Looking up at the sky, she took a deep breath and considered the subtle purple streak that was spread against the darkness, littered by a thousand stars. She supposed she couldn't have asked for a more perfect night.

'Why didn't you come?' she started, quiet at first and then louder. 'Why didn't you come?'

There was no response, only the waves muttering as they sloshed back and forth. Medusa liked to think they did so in agreement, for surely everything in Athens would benefit from Athena's presence, no?

'I thought that this time you would grace us with your presence for sure, but again you keep us waiting. Have you forgotten us? Do we mean so little to you? Or is there a plan at work here, Athena? Is all as it should be? Then why can you not tell me, so that I might tell the others.'

Still there was no response, just the howl of the salty wind as it whipped at her hair.

'Athena,' Medusa lowered her head, 'if I am on the right course...if Athens is on the right course...if...if you are even there still then please, give me a sign.'

She stared up at the sky waiting—waiting for something that might've been a message. A flash of light? A shooting star? Perhaps a change in the waters? But no, everything remained as it was if not for the chilly wind that snuck up around her shoulders and slithered about her neck.

Medusa sighed, gathered her sandals and was about to head off back to her chambers, but then she heard laughter not too far off. Two figures emerged at the far end of the shore, one of them more composed in his strut, the other less so as he fumbled about, dropping to his knees from time to time. She couldn't see their faces, for they were entombed in the shadows that gathered on that side of the beach, but as they came closer she could hear their slurring, could hear their crude utterings and the cackling laughter that came with it.

A part of her told her to run for some reason. Perhaps it was the realisation that she was far enough from the temple now that they wouldn't hear her scream. Even if they did, they'd probably think it was some drunkard from the festival, wouldn't they? She struggled to get her sandals on, slipping them on the wrong feet before frantically working to change them round. She glanced up and saw them coming, no longer stumbling. One of them had a grin that was illuminated by the moonlight, the other looked like a dullard, face fixed with a lifeless expression.

Surely she was panicking over nothing, right? It was just two men out for a midnight stroll on the beach. There was nothing surreptitious about that, was there? The one with the grin had a mess of greasy hair and was wearing a dark blue tunic. His expressionless friend had a patchy beard, his head too large for his body with a brown tunic that was sullied by something he'd spilled on the front of it. They'd seen her, there was no doubt about that as they stopped to mutter at one another. Then they were pacing towards her, the grinning man all eyes and teeth while the other was mute and void.

She finally got her sandals on and hurried to her feet, kicking pebbles as she spun on her heels and started back the way she'd come. She could see the small incline she'd scaled down and knew once she reached there, she could run into the city centre and work her way back to the courtyard in safety. But then she heard the pebbles being crunched behind her and she knew they were picking up the pace.

Athena, Medusa mouthed in silence. *Athena, if you're there you'll protect me, won't you?*

The only answer that came was from the breathy grunts of the man behind her, probably the larger one with the vacant face. Each of his hurried footsteps were accompanied with an unflattering moan, like an ogre who'd stubbed his toe. She picked up the pace, working her legs faster and faster until she could see his shadow ahead of her in the moonlight, growing taller and taller until it enveloped her entirely.

'You in a rush there, priestess?' The grinning man spoke beside her right. He wasn't lumbering along like his friend, but instead seemed much less exerted.

She herself was breathing hard, her heart pumping in her chest as she slowed to acknowledge him.

'Yes,' she gulped. 'I have things I need to take care of.'

'Well, surely they can wait,' he said with that salacious grin growing wider. The moon emerged behind him, unclothed by the parting of the clouds. He might've been smiling, but there was a mean look in his dark eyes as he began rubbing his hands together.

'What do you want?' she asked and looked to the rounder man who was dribbling at the side of his mouth, the patch of hair around his lips wet and lying flat against his face.

'Just a few moments of your time,' he shrugged and pointed to his friend. 'My friend here really likes you.'

The drool glistened down his chin, but he made no effort to wipe it. There was a noticeable swelling at his groin that she regrettably noted, and he was beginning to breathe heavily through the nose, wafts of air going in and out.

'Me like,' he nodded and pointed to himself with a stubby, hairy finger.

'Charmed,' Medusa receded, 'but I must be on my way.'

'Not so fast,' the other man lunged for her and caught her by the wrist. 'My friend is a good guy.'

'Let go of me,' she tried to pull her arm away, but his grip was true and she could feel his nails digging against her skin. His breath stank of wine and now that she was this close, she noticed specks of it on his tunic.

'But my friend would be most disappointed if he didn't get what he wanted,' he snickered. 'After all, I had my way with a priestess not too long ago and it was the greatest thrill of my life. My friend is just like you. He's never lain with anyone either. I just want the best for him.'

'Unhand me, you fiend,' Medusa hissed at him. 'I'm a priestess of Athena and if you do not let me go then she will—'

He slapped her.

The world was a blur of dark colours as her head whipped to one side. She didn't feel pain at first. She didn't feel anything at all. But then she remembered to breathe and she was suddenly gasping for air, a stinging at her lip.

'Your Athena is gone,' the man was saying and she noticed a spot of blood on his finger—her blood. 'Do you really think she gives a damn about a mere priestess like you?'

'Me like,' the other man droned on. 'Me want.'

'Then you best have,' the other man snickered. 'The priestess said she's busy so you better be quick. Though I'm sure that won't be a problem for you.'

She'd heard enough. She yanked her arm free of the man and bolted across the pebbles, back the way she came, but trust one of them to unsteady her gait. She wobbled to the left, felt herself falling but managed to regain her balance. She could hear him grunting behind her. The pebbles were dashed in the mad frenzy of his pursuit. She screamed for all the good it would do as she felt him reach out for her. The other man was shouting something, goading him on, but she didn't catch it over her own terrified gasps. She kept running, the animal sound from his throat closing in on her from behind.

Athena, please help me.

She wailed and made a strange guttural sound when she felt his hands thrust upon her waist. Surely, she couldn't have made such a hopeless sound. She tried to break free of him, tried to keep running despite the horrible embrace in which he held her. Before she knew it, the grey sand rushed up to meet her and she hit the ground hard.

She didn't want to open her eyes after that. She didn't want to see what came next. But it came all the same as he sunk his entire weight on top of her. He grabbed her by the wrists, pinned them by her sides and stared down with that same gormless expression, saliva coating his lips.

'Me like,' he said with a strange twitch of his mouth. It might've been a smile, but his eyes remained these two dark pits of nothing.

'Get it over with before someone comes,' the other one snapped.

'Who comes?' the oaf looked up.

'Well, with any luck it'll be you, you big idiot. Now hurry up!'

What does he mean, she thought. But she knew that was stupid when she saw the look on his face. She'd heard about that look. He tore at her robe, ripped it with both hands down the middle exposing her breasts. His eyes lit up for the first time, and somehow they were even more menacing than before. She reached out and smacked him, though not nearly hard enough to do much more than make him blink. He smacked her back a thousand fold with his meaty hand. Her whole head whipped to the side and she felt her skull burning afterwards. She caught the other man's face in her sights for a moment as her head lolled to the side, but he looked away with his hands in his pockets.

'Don't do that again,' he growled by her ear, but she could only whimper in response. He still sounded like a dullard, but his words were peppered with something dark. She tried nodding her head, but he had struck her so hard she could hardly feel it. This couldn't have been happening to her, could it? She was a priestess of Athena. She could not be harmed by mortal men. Athena would protect her, would she not? Athena would protect them all from such horrors.

She shut her eyes tight, hoping to all the gods that this was just a terrible dream as he plunged his face upon her chest, savagely smothering her with his diabolical lips. She grabbed his head and went to push him away, but she didn't want him to hit her again. So she just lay there crying, wishing Athena would somehow materialise and save her.

But Athena didn't show.

He started biting her, his teeth relentless, like he was dining on meat. She sobbed for all the good it would do, but there wasn't much good coming for her. She managed to pry one eye open and caught his hair in her face, his scalp rubbing against her nose as he breathed all over her, licking her, kissing her. Still Athena didn't come. Maybe the other man was right. Maybe all this time she was just a lowly priestess, a common worshipper in the end. A nobody, just like the rest.

'There's something in the water,' the other man declared, a hint of panic in his voice. Was it Athena? Had she come? Had she really come? It had to be, didn't it? There was no way the goddess of wisdom, the patron of Athens would allow for such a diabolical act to befall one of her own people. Medusa held her breath, waiting for that moment where Athena came storming across the sea to save her.

The big oaf was too busy with her nipple in his mouth to respond, sucking like a starved fiend to the point she was sore and she wished she could die. Death was surely better than this. But Athena would make everything better, wouldn't she? Athena would banish these men so that no woman would suffer this. Athena would put her back together again. Athena would—

'I don't like this. The water is acting weird, let's go.'

The big oaf took a moment to glance back to the ocean. He clearly didn't notice anything irregular because he was back to her just as quick, his mouth bloody from where he'd broken her skin on his fangs.

But then something thumped into the other man. Medusa couldn't say what, but she heard the startled grunt of the man before he hit the floor. It looked like something was sticking out of his chest, a long shining spear of a kind that looked like...like a trident.

'Eh?' the big oaf lifted his head and scrambled off of her. He ambled his way over to his friend's side and touched the trident with caution as if it was made from lava.

'Oi?' he mumbled, and the realisation set in. Medusa managed to sit up despite her dizzying sights and scurried back on her hind, willing her legs to move. She got to one knee, brought the other up but stumbled and fell on her face in the panic. On hands and knees she scrambled for the sandy knoll, desperately crawling to find egress.

'Oi, you!' the big oaf beckoned, but Medusa didn't look back. She didn't need to look back to know he was marching his way over to her. She tried to stand up, tried to get her legs to respond but they wouldn't. She stumbled forward, moving like a toddler who'd just started walking, barely even able to stand on her own two feet.

Get up! Get up! Get up! She silently begged herself as his sandals crunched the pebbles. She sprung forward, but he caught her again, this time by the hair. She tried to wrestle free, but he wrapped a chunk of her hair around his fist and dragged her onto her back, holding her in place and at his mercy.

'What you do?' he smacked her with the back of his freehand. 'Why friend dead?'

'I don't know,' she blurted out. 'Please. Please I don't know.'

'You bring Athena?' he roared in her face.

'Stop,' she cried. 'Please, if you stop I won't tell anyone.' And she was sincere about that. How could she tell anyone about this? How would anyone look at her the same way? They'd think her a monster, wouldn't they? Athena would cast her out for being sullied. She'd lose everything if they knew.

'Athena do this?' he said whilst spitting all over her face, grabbing her by the hair. 'Athena here now?'

'What makes you so sure it was Athena?' another voice rumbled from behind. Medusa saw the crazed look in the big oaf's eyes refocus on the source, and just like that, the vengeful fire began to falter, the violence in his aura seeping out of him like ale from a barrel.

'Who you?' he tried to sound brave, but Medusa could feel his hand quivering in her hair. She managed to turn around, neck burning with teeth marks as she spied the stranger walking out from the ocean, dripping wet.

He was a tall man with a pilose beard, silver and soaked along with his free flowing locks. He had no expression, if not one of mild boredom for someone who just tossed a trident at a man and impaled him dead. He was rippling with muscle, every inch of him sinewy with veins down his arms.

'Who you?' the oaf grunted again.

'I'm sure not Athena, am I?' the man spoke, his voice rumbling with the now angry waves. It was like the water had come alive all of a sudden.

'Y-you killed friend,' the big oaf pointed at the grinning man who most certainly was not grinning anymore.

The stranger didn't seem much bothered by that accusation. He just carried on walking towards them, not like a hero as Medusa would've liked, but more like he had some place to be and they were in his way. He retrieved the trident from the grinning man's corpse; it made a squelching sound as it came free of his chest, blood splattering on the sand and glistening on the trident.

But where's Athena?

'You hurt friend,' the big oaf made a groan. 'Now you will—'

'Do you swim?' the man asked him in a cool, calm voice. He marched towards them until he was just a few feet away. Medusa couldn't help but feel suddenly overwhelmed by his presence, his sheer size shadowing her made her feel less saved and more scared.

'Uh...' The big oaf stammered and Medusa felt his grip around her hair begin to loosen even more.

There was a twitch of annoyance on the stranger's face as he asked very pointedly, 'Do you swim?'

The big oaf gulped, 'You ask dumb question.'

The stranger snatched him by the neck and lifted him off his feet. Medusa got free of his grasp and scuttled away from him, throwing herself behind a rock only to peak out and see him struggling for air. The stranger held the oaf with just one hand like he weighed nothing and didn't seem like he intended to put him down anytime soon either.

He brought the big oaf closer to his face, close enough that he could have whispered as the oaf kicked and writhed in his grasp. 'Do. You. Swim?'

'No,' the big oaf squeaked. 'Can't.'

The stranger smirked, 'Best learn then.'

Without any effort at all, he launched the big oaf behind him. But he didn't land—not right away anyhow. Medusa slammed her hands over her mouth and watched as the big oaf flew for a good twenty seconds, a silent body soaring across the waves before plunging into the water with a quiet splash in the distance. The stranger didn't even look at him, but instead just carried on walking like nothing had happened.

'He'll drown,' she gasped. It was a stupid thing to say, she knew that. But short of her sobs and cries, there wasn't much else coming out. She was still glancing around, head on a swivel as she kept her eyes peeled for Athena.

'Exactly,' the stranger made a click of his fingers and pointed at her as if there could be no other answer, 'he'll drown.'

'Who are you?' she held herself tightly, clutching the front of her torn robe to protect the last shred of modesty she had left.

'I'm here to see Athena,' he declared the way he might've declared his name. 'You're a priestess. You can bring her here to me, no?'

'What?' She shook her head, none of this made sense. She tried to fix her attention on him, but all she could do was wheeze and choke, the image of the big oaf on top of her burned into her mind forever.

But the stranger wasn't compassionate. He simply rolled his eyes at her as if she had fallen over and scraped her knee. 'Beauty, but no brains. Why am I not surprised?'

'I don't understand,' she sniffed.

'Shocking.'

'Who are you?' she squeaked, bringing her knees close to her chest, hiding behind them and the rock as best she could. 'Did Athena send you? She sent you, didn't she?'

It was clear by his strength alone that he was no mortal, and the presence he brought with him was otherworldly in itself. He couldn't have been from around here, no. Athena must've sent him, surely.

'No child, she did not send me.'

Medusa deflated, 'Then who are you?'

It was only then that she considered the now turbulent waves, the bubbling of the waters and the trident that he slung over his shoulder.

'At last the pin drops,' he looked up at the night sky.

'Y-you're Poseidon,' she took a moment to swallow, her breath only becoming all the more unsteady.

'And you're a priestess of Athena. Now summon her.'

She didn't know what to say. She willed her mouth to open but her trembling lips disobeyed her and she could no more speak than she could stand up and run. The more she tried, the more she could feel the big oaf's hands on her, could feel his teeth on her flesh, could feel it stinging, could feel his saliva dripping off of her chest like sweat and—

'I don't have all evening, mortal. Can you grant me an audience with Athena or not?'

'Y—you're Poseidon,' she stammered.

He let out an irritable sigh, 'Nothing gets past you, does it?'

'I mean...you're Poseidon,' she trembled. 'You're the god of the ocean. Surely you don't need a mere priestess like me to see Athena?'

'No,' Poseidon shrugged. 'But I believe it's the only way she'll agree to see me after...well, I'm sure you know.'

'You two fell out after the contest to decide the patron of Athens,' she noted.

'Suppose you could put it like that,' he said. 'I won't ask you again, girl. Bring me Athena so that I might speak with her.'

Medusa opened her mouth to speak, but she couldn't get the words out. How was she supposed to tell him that she, a priestess of Athena, could no more summon her than a tiny insect could. His eyebrows were drawing together and there was a twitching muscle at his jaw. Indeed, he was growing impatient and it would no doubt be soon that she incurred his wrath.

'Well,' he beckoned, 'can you summon her or not?'

'No,' she blurted it out. 'No I can't.'

A shadow came about his face and his eyes flared for a moment, tiny bolts of light giving way to one hell of a glower.

'What kind of priestess cannot summon her goddess? Do you not at least commune with her?'

'You don't think I've tried?' she wiped her hand over her face, frustrated. 'I've dedicated my life to serving her, and she has not once returned since gifting us the olive tree.'

Poseidon smirked at that, 'I bet you wished you picked another patron. One who actually saved you, perhaps?'

She wondered then how differently her life would've been if it was a god like Poseidon watching over Athens. All her life she'd been taught to be weary of one such as Poseidon, but how was it him who had come barrelling out of the water to save her? Where was Athena? Why hadn't Athena come?

'Take me to the temple,' Poseidon muttered. 'My mere presence will anger her enough to warrant a visit.'

'Do you really think that will work?' Medusa wasn't convinced. She'd held festival after festival for her, brought her gifts and fallen at her knees for her, but still Athena had remained missing. Surely Poseidon's presence alone would not bring her out of hiding.

'It will,' he said all-knowingly.

'And if it doesn't?'

'Then I start smashing things,' he chuckled, though she was certain he wasn't joking.

'I can take you there,' she lowered her head.

'Best be on our way then,' he offered her his hand.

She stared at his hand for the longest moment. Moonlight gathered in the palm of his hand—that same hand that had tossed the big oaf fifty feet across the ocean. She took it hesitantly, his skin oddly soft for such a hardened figure. She wondered what it was like to be one of them—to have that power to stop evil in its tracks and dispose of it as simply as one might dispose of a fly. She looked up into his icy blue eyes and sensed his power, a power that made Athena's pale in comparison.

She took it, although reluctantly as he hoisted her up to his feet. Her legs were like jelly, every footstep an ordeal where she wobbled left and right. Poseidon seemed to know the way, for he led her back the way she had originally come, past the body of the grinning man which was claimed by the tide and back through the pebbles, up a sandy incline. She took one last look over her shoulder at the night sky and saw the moon once more, robed by a thick set of clouds.

Did you not hear me, Athena?

The waters were suddenly quiet.

III. A Simple Thank You

Medusa had to hold the front of her tunic up with one hand from where the big oaf had ripped it. Thankfully, many had retired from the city, and while there were a few stragglers lingering here and there, most were drunk from the festival and either lounging about on the floor or puking in the corners. Either way, none would approach her now—not with Poseidon staring death into anything that moved. It was like he wanted someone to come up and fight him.

The temple stood as proudly as it always did, a little further up from where Athena's olive tree swayed in the midnight breeze. Poseidon regarded it with contempt, and if she wasn't mistaken, she could see the veins in his arms begin to bulge. She wouldn't have been surprised to see him leap at it and rip from its roots. The temple had eight pillars at its face, all of which were made of white-washed stone, polished and cleaned every morning and every evening. A triangular gable sat atop its regal head with an intricate pattern inspired by Athena herself.

'Artsy crap,' Poseidon muttered. 'If it was my temple, it would be an imposing thing. It would be made of gold and would be twice the size.'

She didn't respond, for she was still subdued—though not from the attack. No, she was feeling sour because Athena hadn't lived up to her promise. She'd prayed to Athena every day—had prayed for her to come save her—still she'd been ignored. It wasn't as if she was a sinner or even some common folk calling with favours, no, she was the high priestess. And she deserved better than this.

'Why are you snivelling?' Poseidon snapped at her. 'I saved you, didn't I?'

She hadn't realised her nose was running, nor that her eyes were wet with tears.

'I'm not snivelling,' she snapped back. Though she wasn't sure how wise it was to snap back at a god.

'Ha!' Poseidon remarked. 'Are you sad that your precious Athena wasn't the one that came for you?'

'No!' she shot a look at him, but when he returned it, she felt compelled to look away and down at her feet.

'Cheer up child,' he said. 'With any luck, you won't have to worship her anymore.'

'What's that supposed to mean?' she asked him, but he merely flicked his nose in the air and was quiet after that.

As they entered the temple, Medusa was met by the familiar aroma of burning wood from the two furnaces on either side of the room. A warm orange glow from the flames was strewn across the floor, spilling in between several pillars. Medusa moved silently, but Poseidon's sandals click-clacked on the mosaic floor, loud enough to wake the sleeping drunks outside. He didn't share the comfort she found in the room with its dome shaped ceiling and the decorative beams fixed high above. Moonlight seeped in from the open slits in the wall and onto Athena's statue. Poseidon looked quite repulsed.

'Tacky,' he muttered under his breath.

She had half the mind to scold him, but she didn't have the energy left to speak even a word to him. She simply carried on, feeling the glares from the statues on the left and right of her, all of them as stoic as they ever were.

'Who are these meant to be then?' Poseidon stopped before one of them, stroking his beard as he leaned in close to one.

'That's Zeus,' she made a sideways glance at it.

'This is Zeus?' Poseidon guffawed. 'Well, they got his massive nose right at least.'

The grandest statue of all awaited them up ahead, situated on its own ivory podium and granted an aureole, courtesy of the moonlight from above. Athena looked as fierce as ever, dressed in armour with a halberd in one hand and a shield in the other. A circlet sat upon her head and she wore a large necklace to match it. As always, Medusa sank to a knee before it and thought about ushering Poseidon to do the same before thinking better of it.

'You still kneel to her?' Poseidon made a disgruntled sound. 'You truly are blind, young priestess.'

'Athena is still my patron,' Medusa said. Though it was clear in her voice it wasn't nearly as compelling as it was a day ago.

'If you say so,' he shrugged before striding closer to the statue than she would ever dare go. He stared up at her for the longest of moments, probably without blinking, with those cold blue eyes of his. Now and again, he would scratch at his beard and glance from side to side as if he was hearing voices from the other smaller statues.

'You're wasting your time,' she spoke up at last. 'Athena will not come here. She has not come here in so long. Why, I was but a child when she was last here and—'

'Enough,' he held up his hand. 'Stop making sounds. You've done that quite enough for today.'

She was about to hark at him for such a rude comment, but then something moved in the corner of her eye. Her breath caught in her throat when she saw Athena's statue begin to twitch, and while its body remained still, the nose was crinkling like it was about to sneeze. Athena's eyes were blinking as if she'd just woken from a slumber and they soon fixed on Poseidon.

'How dare you come here,' the voice was sharp and it poured out of the statue's mouth. 'Who do you think you are?'

He shrugged like he didn't care, 'I'm Poseidon.'

'Oh, don't we all know that,' Athena made a pained expression.

Medusa couldn't believe it. She sunk to her knees right there on the spot, lowered her head and said, 'Athena! You have finally—'

'Be quiet, child!' Athena hissed, her head snapping to face her for just a moment before whipping back to Poseidon. 'Why are you here?'

'Simple, really,' Poseidon took his time as he began pacing up and down, 'I saved your priestess from two attackers and have returned her quite safely.'

Athena flicked an icy stare at her, and Medusa was almost crushed under the weight of it. Then she looked back at Poseidon, just as bitter.

'With what catch?'

'Catch?' Poseidon held his hands out as a mischievous grin came upon his face. 'There is no catch. I merely came for a sincere thank you.'

'You acted on your own whims,' Athena snapped. 'My priestess owes you no thanks.'

Poseidon smirked, 'It wasn't she I came to receive it from.'

A pregnant silence ensued where Athena's eyes were fixed on Poseidon, neither one of them breaking their gaze. It was as if doing so would be to forfeit some honourable battle. Medusa felt out of place all of a sudden, like she shouldn't have been within a mile of the temple— as if the gods were about to lunge for each other and tear each other's throats out.

'You'll get no thanks from me,' Athena finally declared.

Medusa felt a pang of distress, for surely her life warranted more than this petty argument between the two. The pair of them had all the power in the world, and yet they were squandering it right before her eyes, bickering about nothing at all. Why, if Medusa had that sort of power, she sure wouldn't have wasted it like this.

'I can see she means a lot to you,' Poseidon remarked sarcastically. 'Are you sure I don't warrant perhaps even a mere nod of appreciation, or even a slow clap for that matter? You're lucky I'm not asking for a slice of Athens. I only ask for your sincerest gratitude so that I may cherish in my mind the day Athena was in debt to Poseidon.'

'Your ego by far exceeds even that of my father,' Athena sneered. 'Now begone.'

'I'm still waiting, Athena,' Poseidon was grinning. 'Say you're thankful for me.'

'Get out!' Athena demanded.

'Last chance,' Poseidon waved his finger.

'Get out!' she roared.

'Fine,' Poseidon bowed his head, all smug and pompous. 'Remember, you did this.'

He ambled his way towards the exit, trailing his hand against the statues as he went past, but not before he stopped at Zeus and let out another laugh—a fake one at best. Then he flicked the nose on the statue and marched his way out, disappearing through the doors.

Medusa was still on her knees, still clutching at the torn fabric at the front of her tunic. She was about to stand up, but then Athena's head whipped around at her, a deep frown on her stony face.

'You dare come before me dressed like that?' Athena tutted.

'I was attacked,' Medusa took a moment to swallow back her embarrassment. 'Two men, they—'

'Get over it,' Athena hissed. 'You are a priestess of mine, are you not? This is a life you have chosen. As a priestess, you are to be pure, and as a pure vessel, there are those who will seek to sully you. This is to be expected. Stop snivelling on your knees, girl. What you've experienced is not remarkable.'

Medusa held her jaw shut, not because she was in the mind to answer back, but because if she didn't, she would unload a volley of tears. Was this Athena? Was this heartless and cold statue before her really Athena? No, it couldn't be. The stories always said that Athena was compassionate, kind, warm and generous. This...this couldn't be.

'Well, girl?' Athena roared at her. 'Did you hear nothing I said? Quit your snivelling and get out of my sight.'

'But—'

'Don't make me repeat myself,' Athena warned her, and if her tone wasn't deadly enough as it was, it now came with an icy edge.

Medusa scrambled from her knees and all but ran out the temple doors. It was only when she reached halfway did she realise that she had forgotten to bow and bid the goddess a fair evening. She glanced over her shoulder, but if the statue-goddess gave much mind, she didn't announce it. So Medusa hurried on and didn't stop until she was standing outside in the dark.

Alone.

IV. Poseidon's Offer

'I can't believe you actually spoke to her!' Cassandra's eyes were wide with excitement. She was so enthralled by the story that she hadn't noticed the thick bit of seaweed that was tangled about her foot.

'Neither can I,' Medusa replied, though not nearly as excited as Cassandra. After all, her meeting with Athena had not been what she'd expected.

The sea was glowing, courtesy of the sun beating down on the waves, and the tide came in slow, sweeping up pebbles and sand as it loitered about their ankles before retreating back. Seagulls sang tunelessly, making for quite the racket against the crashing of waves.

'Well, did she not say anything else?' Cassandra was shaking her for details.

'No,' Medusa shrugged. 'She just yelled at me and that was it. She didn't ask if I was okay, didn't ask about Athens, didn't ask about anything. She just told me what she told me and that was it.'

'Hmm,' Cassandra deflated before applying a hand on her shoulder. 'There, there. At least those two fiends got what they deserved, eh? If I was there I would've—'

'I wish you were there,' Medusa sighed. She knew Cassandra had gone off with one of the men from the festival, but she knew better than to confront her about it. She'd had all she could take of confrontation.

'I'm sorry,' Cassandra smiled sadly.

'It's not your fault,' Medusa shook her head. 'It's Athena's!'

Cassandra gasped, 'You can't go around saying things like that, Medusa. What if she hears?'

'She isn't listening,' Medusa balled her fists. 'I begged her to come save me last night, and she didn't. She didn't even know I was being... anyway...the point is that there is no point.'

'No point?' Cassandra looked confused. 'What do you mean no point?'

'There's no point in anything,' Medusa clarified. 'Athena doesn't care about what we do. She seemed right inconvenienced that she'd been summoned at all.'

A gull soared across the waters, its feet gliding against the waves as it stopped to nip at a fish, only to miss and hark at it from above. It flapped its wings furiously before scanning elsewhere for its meal. Medusa couldn't help but feel for it. It must've been almost as disappointed as she was to have finally found something only to lose it all the same.

'Maybe you should think on it for a while,' Cassandra suggested. 'Who knows, maybe Athena was just having a bad day. We have no idea what she does outside of Athens. Maybe she's just really busy? Maybe the fact that she doesn't visit is because you're doing such a great job here keeping everyone safe.'

'I couldn't keep myself safe,' Medusa shrugged. She wished she had the power of Poseidon. He'd dealt with those two vile men without even breaking a sweat. If she could do that, she'd protect the entirety of Athens from even the smallest of threats. Why, if she had that kind of power she'd see to it that no one was bitten by an insect or even threatened by a shadow.

'Don't give up on Athena,' Cassandra advised her. 'She might not be much, but she's all we have, right? And I'm sure when it comes down to it, she'll be there for us.'

Medusa shrugged, 'We'll see.'

She looked up to see if she could still see the gull patrolling the waters, but instead she found something she hadn't intended on seeing ever again. He stalked out from the waters much like he had done the night before, unburdened by the waves as they moved to avoid him. He still looked bored, but upon seeing her his pace quickened.

'Wow, who is he?' Cassandra bit on her lips and leaned forward.

'That's uh...' she stopped to think about how best to explain it to her, 'that's Poseidon.'

'What?' Cassandra choked. 'You mean *the* Poseidon?'

'Well, there isn't another one, is there?' Medusa remarked.

He had his trident on his back, that same trident that had speared the grinning man in the chest and pinned him against the sand. For someone who had just walked through the ocean, he certainly didn't look that wet. His beard wasn't flattened against his chest, but merely damp and dark. His trousers were scaly, like that of a fish, but a deep, glistening sapphire. He was shirtless, just like before, every inch of him loaded with muscle. Medusa didn't much like the way Cassandra was all but drooling at the mouth for him. Then again, she herself felt her lips were a little damper than usual.

'Will you introduce me?' Cassandra grabbed her by the arm.

Medusa sighed, 'He's really not that much of a people person.'

'So?' Cassandra snorted.

'To be honest, he's really not that nice either.'

'Oh how bad can he be?' Cassandra asked.

'Be gone,' Poseidon waved his hand at her as he drew near.

'I told you,' Medusa smiled wanly.

'Oh...' Cassandra got to her feet. 'Oh, I'm—'

'Don't care,' Poseidon shrugged. 'Be gone.'

Cassandra opened her mouth to say something, but Medusa held up her hand and shook her head.

'Just give us a moment?' she told her.

Cassandra gave Poseidon a weary glance, but then she nodded and said, 'I'll just be over there by the rocks, talking to the crabs.'

'Try not to eat any of them,' Poseidon muttered under his breath.

Medusa waited until she was sure Cassandra was out of ear shot before she turned to Poseidon. 'That wasn't very nice of you.'

'What?' he frowned. 'I was serious. If she eats any more she might be bigger than...bigger than...'

'Zeus' nose?' Medusa finished for him, though in mocking.

'Ha!' Poseidon bellowed as he slapped his knee. 'You have a gift with wit, mortal.'

'That's funny,' Medusa glowered. 'Yesterday I was just beauty and no brains.'

Poseidon surrendered a short smirk, 'Perhaps I was wrong about you.'

'What makes you say that?'

Poseidon's eyes narrowed a slight, his lips still fixed in that cocky manner, like he had all the answers and was shifting through them all, preparing his mouth to fire the best ones off.

'I've found out something about your lineage, dear Medusa,' he said whilst folding his arms in front of his broad chest.

'My lineage?' she frowned. *What did that have to do with anything?*

'You never knew your parents, did you?'

'No, I—'

'They were ancient deities, Medusa. Powerful primordial deities of the sea that preceded the Olympians—the ones who came before Zeus and myself.'

'Impossible,' Medusa shook her head. There was no way her parents could have been gods. No, she'd have known such a thing, surely.

'How do you explain your fair beauty?' Poseidon took a step towards her and she took one back just as quickly. 'How do you explain your way with people, your rapport with them, your ability to get them to chant your name. Tell me, do you hear them chant Athena's name?'

It didn't make any sense to her. The primordial gods had rarely ever been seen or spoken about since the times of old. As far as she knew, there were no remnants left of the primordial gods after Zeus created Olympus. Was Poseidon right? Was that the reason why her looks were so fair and why the people of Athens were so naturally drawn to her? She realised her hands had gone sweaty, her heart was racing and she could feel the heat from the sun intensify as her cheeks began to warm.

'Why are you telling me this?' Medusa touched her head. 'Even if I was a descendent of the primordial gods, what does that matter now?'

'It means you are worthy,' Poseidon said like it was obvious.

'Worthy?' Medusa looked around. 'Worthy of what?'

'I can make you a goddess,' Poseidon said, his eyes widening.

Only the waves made sound after that, crashing against the shore all the more violently. Gulls were squawking and Medusa noticed one snatch a fish from the water, stuff it in its beak and soar off. It seemed like everyone was getting what they wanted.

'I don't know what you're talking about,' Medusa went to turn away, but Poseidon reached out and grabbed her.

'Think about it,' Poseidon spoke low, like he didn't want to be heard all of a sudden, his voice gently nudging her into quiet submission. 'You could save people from having to experience what you did last night. You could protect the whole of Athens, maybe more. You could prevent bad things from ever happening to anyone ever again. Who better than you? Athena sure doesn't care. But you? You're more compassionate and thoughtful than any goddess I've ever come across.'

'N-No,' she shook her head. No she couldn't be doing any of that. Indeed, there are certain things she could definitely do better than Athena, and she knew that if she had such powers, she could protect other women from predators like the ones she'd encountered. But at what cost? Would this not be a direct betrayal of Athena if she suddenly became the worshipped entity of Athens? The new patron, so to speak.

'No?' Poseidon winced. 'You willingly throw away the gift I offer you? I can make you so much more, child. I can make you stronger than Athena, seeing as the blood of the primordial gods flows through you. You could be the patron that Athens deserves. You could right the wrongs of all the Olympians and lead this great city into a place of peace and love. Isn't that what you've always wanted?'

Of course it was, but she'd never believed that she could achieve that. Not as a mortal, anyway. She bit down on her lips, her heart racing even faster than before as she felt a shiver go through her chest. Blood was pumping in her ears, her legs weak at the mere thought of all that power.

'How?' she ventured. 'How could you make me a goddess?'

An ear to ear grin exploded onto his face as he came quite close to her, 'Tell me...have you ever lain with a god?'

Her hand met his face. The loud echo of her sweaty hand hitting his cheek boomed across the shore, hushing the waves for a moment. His head had all but whipped to one side, but that smile on his face was only animated further. If she didn't know any better, she'd say he quite enjoyed that.

'I suppose I'll take that as a no,' he touched his face and inspected his fingers for blood.

'I'm a priestess of Athena,' she said through gritted teeth. She had to keep her jaw locked tight to stop it from chattering—to stop her entire body from exploding with adrenaline. 'I can lay with no man.'

'Your loyalty to Athena is misplaced,' Poseidon eased back and began treading his way back to the shore. 'Should you change your mind child, come find me. Athens needs a woman like you.'

She watched him amble his way back into the water, treading through it as easily as any man might walk through tall grass. The way he moved was as if he'd received the exact answer he came for, so sure and proud. It wasn't until Cassandra came tumbling over that Medusa pulled her gaze away from him.

'By the gods, Medusa!' Cassandra was panting. 'You slapped him!'

Medusa looked down at her shaking hand, unsure of where she gained the courage to do that. 'I did,' she said with disbelief.

'Why would you do that?'

'He made me an offer,' she said with a sigh.

'And you didn't take it?' Cassandra boomed like she was mad. 'He's Poseidon! He's a god! He's—'

'Just another man,' Medusa shook her head and began walking away. She'd had enough of the sun for one day—had about enough of everything.

'Won't you at least consider it?' Cassandra harkened after her.

'I did,' Medusa said, but not before she paid Poseidon one lingering glance before he disappeared into the waters, 'the answer is no.'

And that was that.

V. Taboos

It was dark by the docks—dark and filled with the stench of old salt water, rotten fish, some sickly rusty odours and gods knew what else. Usually the docks were alive with shouting merchants, labourers who were hissing and barking at one another, carts rolling to and fro, anchors splashing in the waters, nets bursting and squelching fish spilling all over the deck. But tonight it was silent, perhaps more silent than a cemetery. Even the waters were still.

'I don't like this place,' Medusa shuddered. It had always given her the creeps during the day, but in the thick of night, it served to keep her on her toes all the more.

'Relax,' Cassandra replied, rustling a bag by her side. 'I had to get more fish to replace what we used in the festival, didn't I?'

'I don't see why you couldn't just get it tomorrow,' Medusa bristled.

'Oh hush,' Cassandra waved the bag of stinking fish she'd purchased as they moved towards the shadowy mouth of a narrow alley. 'Come, let's go this way.'

'Eh?' Medusa stopped. 'Let's just go around.'

'That will take ages,' Cassandra replied. 'You really want to be inhaling this rancid air any longer?'

Cassandra had a point. The waft of stenches were now burning the back of Medusa's throat, and if that wasn't bad enough, the smell of rotten fish made her eyes water.

'Fine,' Medusa conceded. 'Let's go.'

'Atta girl,' Cassandra nudged her. 'You know what your problem is? You don't take enough risks, Medusa.'

She could hear rats squeaking in the dark, could hear them scurrying over piles of rubbish and rustling in the waste.

Medusa put a hand over her nose, 'I imagine that's why I'm the high priestess and you, my dear, are not.'

'Now that's just rude,' Cassandra rolled her head back with laughter.

'You're also a tad too abrasive at times, did I mention that?' Medusa added. 'Maybe you'll do better service to the temple if you started taking less risks.'

'Fair enough,' Cassandra said, her large sandal heedlessly squelching something. 'How about I start taking less risks and maybe you start taking more? It might be good for you.'

'Elaborate, dear.'

'Why, look what happened on the beach. That was Poseidon—Poseidon himself! And you turned him down!'

'As is our duty,' Medusa remarked as sternly as she could, but Cassandra's face was a ball of amusement and energy.

'Poseidon!' Cassandra laughed into the night. 'What type of woman turns down a man like him?'

'This kind,' Medusa snapped. But Cassandra was giving her a mischievous looking grin.

'Oh, you can hide behind that façade all you want,' Cassandra was saying as they pressed on through the alleyway which was beginning to widen so that they could walk side by side without bashing their elbows on the walls.

'What façade?' Medusa frowned.

'I saw the way you looked at him,' Cassandra made an evil sort of giggle. 'You definitely wanted him.'

'I did not!' Medusa snapped, though she couldn't explain why her cheeks were suddenly hot and her heart was beating a little faster.

'Hmm,' Cassandra mumbled, doing what she could to fight the smile on her face, but losing terribly.

Cassandra strolled into a ford of gods knew what—probably water, hopefully water. She made no indication that she'd even realised as she strode out the other side, one eye fixed rather promiscuously on her.

'What?' Medusa challenged her and gingerly manoeuvred around the ford, holding the hem of her dress in one hand.

'Just thinking about all the powers you'll have if you do take him up on his offer,' she shrugged.

Medusa opened her mouth to berate her friend, but then she, too, saw the image in her head. She imagined herself flying—soaring the skies before landing to the uproars of the people of Athens. She imagined having the strength to waltz up to any would be attacker and launch him into the ocean the way Poseidon had done. She imagined kissing him then—imagined his big hands around her hips as he—

'Like I was saying,' Cassandra was speaking, 'you don't take enough risks.'

'I...' she had to stop to clear her throat, 'I take plenty of risks when necessary.' Why were her hands so suddenly clammy? And why was her neck burning up at the thought of that mean, arrogant idiot?

'Oh?' Cassandra snorted. 'Give me an example?'

Medusa had to think on that, 'Well there was that one time I...well I mean I almost...do you remember that time when...Regardless, I am not obligated to answer to you, Cassandra.'

'Exactly,' Cassandra said with triumph. 'You should find Poseidon. It's like you said yourself, Athena isn't even watching half the time.'

'I mean,' Medusa's mouth had gone dry, 'even if I did, I'd only be doing so for the powers.'

'Liar,' Cassandra snickered. 'You quite fancy the look of Poseidon, don't you?'

'No, I don't!' Medusa stormed ahead. 'Now if we're quite done discussing this taboo, I'm going to retire to my chambers.'

'Heh,' Cassandra laughed, 'I bet you are.'

'You're insufferable at times,' Medusa replied and swung around to glower at her.

'Come on,' Cassandra took her by the arm. 'I'll walk you back. Can't have a gorgeous lady like you strolling about the streets at this hour.'

'And what about you?'

'Me?' Cassandra frowned. 'Mercy on the man who starts trouble with me.'

By the time she returned home, Medusa was knackered. She slipped her sandals off by the sturdy door of her chambers and then collapsed onto her bed, a single candle lit at the far end of the room billowed gently. She hoped Cassandra was okay walking in the night alone, but as the woman said, it would be an unlucky man who came upon her expecting anything more than directions.

She stared up at the dirty ceiling eyeing every dark and mouldy patch, wondering guiltily if they'd repair those ugly cracks and that ghastly tone of paint if she were to become a goddess. She craned her head forward and stared at the crooked bedside table, one leg rotten and the other three splintered. Then there were the walls—craggy, grey cobbles that were prone to allow the cold winds to slither through the cracks. She wondered if they'd build her a brand new home if she was a goddess—wondered if they'd build her a temple like Athena's.

What is wrong with me? She shook her head abruptly and turned on her side, facing the side of the room that was cast in shadow. At least she could get no ideas staring into the shadows now, could she? She closed her eyes soon after and waited for the clutches of sleep to claim her, but it did not come.

She flopped onto her back again, tussling in the sheets thereafter as she crossed her arms. It might've been because she was hungry, or perhaps thirsty? But the more she thought about getting up to fetch a snack, the more she felt content to just lie there, staring up at that ghastly ceiling with its blotchy, scarred texture staring back at her. She sighed loudly and allowed herself just a few more guilty thoughts: what gifts would they bring her if she were a goddess; what songs would they sing about her; what Poseidon's hands would feel like against her—

She gasped out loud, heart thumping against her chest. Her breaths were shallow, sweat brimming at her forehead, toes twitching with excitement as she placed her hand at her chest. It was decidedly warm there, perhaps warmer than it should've been considering the cold whips of wind that siphoned through the cracks of the walls. The thought of Poseidon made her giddy all of a sudden, and while she found his rude shortness disdainful, she couldn't help but get the image of his flesh out of her mind.

She was about to ask Athena for strength, but that seemed like a futile thing to do—especially now that she was burning up between the legs just picturing him storming out of the waters, unburdened by anything, stalking his way towards her with that grim cockiness of his.

You don't take enough risks, Cassandra's words were in her ear, repeating over and over until they weren't Cassandra's words but Poseidon's instead. She shivered at the thought of it, for it was so vivid, that it was as if he was beside her right now, his warm breath stroking her lobe. She moved her hand over the curve of her belly, palm sliding over the edge of her hip, lower still against her thigh. She bit her lips and closed her eyes, hardly feeling guilty at all anymore.

VI. Not Pretty Enough

There came a knocking at the door the next morning—a fierce sort of knock that immediately filled Medusa with dread. She'd only just finished her morning bath and slipped into a fresh tunic, but there it was—the rasping of knuckles drilling on the door. Impatient ones too.

'All right, I'm coming!' she beckoned, but the knocking persisted until she yanked the door open and another priestess came almost stumbling in.

'Medusa,' she blanched, teary eyed and a complete sweaty mess. Her auburn hair was plastered against one side of her face and she looked like she was about to spill her guts on the floor. 'You must come quickly.'

'Whatever is the matter?' Medusa shook her head at the mess of a girl. She was about to offer the poor woman a glass of water and a seat.

'You must come,' she breathed heavy. 'You must come now! She isn't in the best state.'

'Who isn't in the best state?' Medusa felt a pang of dread.

'It's Cassandra,' the priestess took a moment to gulp, 'she was attacked last night. She's awake but—'

Medusa didn't mean to brush past the woman. She didn't even think to close the door behind her as she darted into the street, right in front of an oncoming carriage. The horse reared behind her, but she paid it no mind as she bolted up the street to the echo of a disgruntled carriage driver. She caught the glances of men and women in her sights as she barrelled past, most of them greeting her with smiles and good tidings. She returned none of them. Not now.

It was all her fault. If only Cassandra hadn't walked her home then maybe, maybe she would have gotten home safely. Medusa hoped her friend was okay as she rounded a corner and sprinted her way through a cluster of merchants who were gathered like a pack vultures at a recent battlefield. They grabbed at her with offers and bargains, but she slipped past them as rude as Poseidon might've—batting their hands away and storming onwards to the small house at the end of the road.

Much like her own dinghy house, the windows were black with a rotten frame that was once white or lighter in colour. Now it was all grey. The entire building was just a lump with swirls of moss caked around the roof and speckled with white bird droppings. The door was hung ajar, and Medusa wasted no time bursting through it, the hinges screaming in rebellion as she stood there searching the darkness.

Only thin rays of sunlight slithered in from the slits in the ceiling, but that was enough to make out the lumpy shape of Cassandra sitting in the bed, cast in shadow.

Medusa moved towards her immediately but was stopped in her tracks.

'Don't!' came Cassandra's voice, a strange sounding growl from a woman who was otherwise so bubbly.

'Cassandra,' Medusa took a step forwards. 'Cassandra I—'

'I said don't!' Cassandra barked. 'Don't come near me.'

'Cassandra, it's me...' Medusa stammered. 'What happened?'

Cassandra spat over the side of the bed into a bucket that Medusa noticed had a bloody rag dangling at the rim.

'I was attacked,' she said with a grunt. 'One tall savage with a mean right swing. He didn't even take anything. He just beat on me until I blacked out.'

Medusa sighed and charged forward, 'Cassandra I'm—'

'Don't!' Cassandra screamed, but it was too late. Her face caught the sunlight and Medusa saw just how mangled it was.

Both of her eyes were swollen shut and there were dark purple rings around her sockets. The left one was particularly bad; that entire side of her face had been sunken in. A large bump swelled at her forehead with several bloody gashes to accompany it, most of them dried and crusty. Her lips were swollen and blue, her bottom lip so savagely beaten it looked as if it was hanging off her mouth. She was missing her two front teeth and one on the bottom row. It had her making a strange whistling sound as she breathed.

'Cassandra, I'm so sorry,' Medusa fell to her knees beside her. 'It's my fault. You should never have walked me home.'

Cassandra swung her head away. 'That isn't the reason why this is your fault.'

To hear that it was her fault at all made Medusa's heart sink.

'Walking you home is what a good friend would do. I was protecting you. I felt bad I wasn't there when you were attacked on the beach, but you could've protected me. You could've saved my face.'

Medusa felt tears in her eyes, 'If I was there, I would have! I would've thrown myself at them and—'

'All you had to do was spend one measly night with Poseidon,' Cassandra hissed through her teeth. Or whatever was left of them. 'That's all you had to do, and you would've had the power to stop this. You'd have had the power to stop this from happening to anyone ever again. But you won't! Because you're a coward. Just like Athena!'

That took Medusa right in the chest. It felt like a thousand daggers had just been thrust upon her, sharp pains sidling up and down her sternum as a weak hiccup escaped her mouth. She could hardly believe the words she was hearing, and yet...they were true, weren't they? If only she'd have taken Poseidon's offer, then maybe she could've stopped this from happening.

'Say, you were right about one thing,' Cassandra chuckled although it sounded like it pained her to do even that, 'Athena certainly is gone. I prayed when his fists came reigning down on my face, but she didn't come. I begged her to come save me, but she never did. Only difference between me and you is that Poseidon didn't come either. No one did! I suppose I wasn't pretty enough, eh?'

'Cassandra...I—'

'Save your words,' Cassandra laid back, deflated, 'and close the door on your way out.'

'Cassandra, I can fix this,' Medusa said, though her words were panicked and she knew deep down there was nothing she could do now. Cassandra's face was ruined. No amount of saying sorry or begging her forgiveness was about to change that.

'Fix this?' Cassandra touched her cheek and winced. 'I'd have better luck fixing my eating habits.'

'I'll get Athena,' Medusa was rocking her head back and forth. 'That's right! I'll get Athena. I'll do whatever it takes to bring her down here and heal you.'

Cassandra turned her head slowly back around and gave one last hateful look at Medusa, the lower half of her mouth fixed into a horrible snarl.

'To hell with Athena,' she said, looking away for good this time.

VII. Be Careful What You Wish For

'Come out!' Medusa demanded as she burst into the temple, locking the doors behind her. 'Show yourself, goddess, so that I might speak with you!'

She wasn't expecting a response. Not that easily, no. She marched her way up to the statue of the goddess—the same statue Athena had manifested inside of when Poseidon was present—and stared up at it, breathing hoarsely.

'I won't ask you again!' Medusa screamed. 'Show yourself or I will burn your temple to the ground!'

There was silence, only the crackling of the furnaces on either side. Flames flickered from the many candles placed around the altar which cast shadows this way and that. There was no moonlight cascading down from the windows above tonight, for the night sky was full of dark grey clouds and threatened to rain. One side of Athena's statue was cast in darkness, the other illuminated with a deadly orange hue.

Medusa was beyond being scared.

'Athena!' she roared at the top of her lungs, so loud that her voice bounced around the room. 'Athena, answer me!'

She waited until the echo of her voice had drowned out before stepping on her tiptoes and shouting from the pit of her lungs, 'I hate you!'

Medusa saw the broom from the corner of her eye. She would've preferred a mallet, or a sword for that matter, but the servants of the temple weren't known for carrying those. So she snatched the broom up from the floor, marched her way and lifted it high above her head.

She slammed it against the base of the statue first, hammering it down against Athena's toes with such a force that there was a crack in the stone. Say one thing for the broom, it was sturdy. She drilled it against Athena's leg, relentlessly hacking away at her as she screamed and roared and hissed and cursed until her lungs burned. But she didn't stop. Even when the broom head went flying off and she was left with just a stick, she whacked it against the statue, hot tears streaming down her face.

And then she felt the statue rumble.

'What are you doing?' Athena barked at her from above, staring down at her like she was an insect who had the nerve to bite her.

Medusa opened her mouth to answer, but all the witty words she'd lined up to spout were suddenly lost. She racked her brains for the moment, but all that came out was the same tired line: 'I hate you!'

Athena didn't show much of a reaction, barely even a shrug. 'Explain yourself.'

'You were supposed to protect us,' Medusa smacked her again with the stick. 'You were supposed to make sure bad things never happen to us, but now she's lying in bed with no face left!'

Athena had the nerve to roll her eyes, 'Who has no face left?'

'Cassandra!' Medusa cried. 'I bet you don't even know who she is, do you?'

'I'm going to make a guess and say she's a friend,' Athena muttered. 'People get hurt, child. The world doesn't stop. Her fate came for her. What will you have me do? Reverse time?'

'If you were watching over us like you promised to,' Medusa's voice turned dark, so dark she could barely recognise it, 'none of this would've happened. I wouldn't have been attacked and Cassandra wouldn't have her life ruined.'

'I do not control the fate of every person in Athens. It is unfortunate what has befallen your friend, but it is also beyond my ability to fix every single wrong,' Athena muttered. 'You, on the other hand, are my priestess. You are to expect such advances from men and deal with them accordingly. I am not here to fight your battles, girl.'

'You abandoned us!' Medusa hissed.

'I will hear no more of your judgement! You may be a priestess of mine, but you are also a just a mortal woman. Remember your place.'

Medusa curled her fingers tight around the wooden stick. Staring up at Athena's impassive face made her blood boil all the more, and while she knew it was a bad idea, she couldn't stop herself.

'I wish Poseidon was our patron!' she roared and threw the stick hard. It hit Athena in the mouth before clattering loudly on the altar, knocking over some of the candles.

Athena didn't move. If the stick had hurt her stony form in any way, she didn't show it. But then her eyes widened, coming alive like two burning stars in the night sky. Her mouth opened wide and where her teeth should've been was just a dark space, growing wider and wider.

'You dare insult me?' Athena thundered so loudly that it came with its own gust of air—a force so strong it knocked Medusa off her feet and spun her across the floor. 'Show me such disrespect again, girl, and I will see to your punishment myself. Is that clear?'

Medusa wasn't sure which way was up for a moment as she lay there, blinking up at the ceiling. She craned her head forward and saw Athena's face come alive with as much emotion as a statue could. She forgot to exhale, holding the breath tight in her throat. But when she realised this, she spat it out and shrieked on the ground like a spanked girl, the anger all but leaving her as fast as it had come by.

'Is that clear?' Athena screamed.

Medusa wanted to tell her how she really felt. She wanted to continue screaming at her, insulting her, hurting her for her lack of compassion. But it was foolish. She couldn't fight Athena. She could barely even fight off two fiendish men on the beach. She felt her cheeks grow hot and she slumped on the floor, too weak to stand up.

'Is. That. Clear?' Athena barked again.

'Crystal.' Medusa swallowed what was left of her defiance.

Athena made a self-satisfied grunt and then she was still again, her face returning to the original astringent expression she always wore. Medusa would've gotten up if her legs weren't suddenly like paper. She tried to push herself up, but when she couldn't move, she simply let her head fall against the cold ground, crying for all the good it would do.

You're a coward, just like Athena.

She grabbed hold of her head, jamming her fingers in her ears to stop the sound of Cassandra's voice. It was inside her skull, slithering about like a worm in soil. It was her fault. She should've just taken Poseidon's offer and become a goddess. She could've used her powers to save Cassandra, to save Athens, to save everyone! Now what could she do? Pine for her losses like a no-good gambler who'd bet on the wrong fighter, wishing she could go back and change her mind?

'It's not too late,' a voice made her sobs stop short.

She looked up and saw Poseidon leaning there against a pillar, pondering on his fingernails as he blew dirt out from underneath them.

'It is,' Medusa was about to spit again but thought better of it.

'So I hear your friend was beaten up,' Poseidon ambled his way towards her, and in a tone that wasn't very sympathetic at all, merely muttered, 'Sorry to hear that.'

'I could've saved her from that,' she grabbed hold of her hair, fingers tightening around her skull. She wondered if she could dig out the sound of Cassandra's hurtful words, if she could dig a whole bunch of stuff out starting with Athena.

'And I could've been the patron of Athens,' Poseidon mumbled, flicking something from his teeth. 'We don't all get what we want.'

'She didn't even care,' Medusa glanced up at the statue. 'She didn't even know who she was.'

'Classic Athena,' Poseidon shrugged. 'But you should know, others will follow the same path as your friend.'

She didn't like the way he said that. 'What's that supposed to mean?'

'It means what it means,' Poseidon replied as he paced his way around her, slowly orbiting her with his hands clasped behind his back. 'Unless, of course...you were to suddenly become a goddess yourself.'

His words hung in the air as he made his way around her once, twice and then a third time. His sandals kept smacking the back of his feet in a slow, droning fashion—clap...clap...clap. She'd never been with a man before. She'd never even kissed one—never even held hands with one. Once upon a time, before she became a priestess, a boy asked her to dance and slipped his hand around her lower back as they moved into each other, momentarily lost in the music.

But then, as the years went by, she had become increasingly more beautiful, and soon learned that good looks didn't always attract good men. In fact, it seemed to make them all the more scarcer. She allowed herself a brief glance at Poseidon who was still pacing around her and allowed herself the smallest thought of his arms around her.

'No!' she shuffled back against one of the pillars, as far away from him as she could manage, which wasn't too far at all.

'Don't you want to protect what you have left?' Poseidon asked.

'Of course I do,' she snapped. 'But it's just...'

'Just?'

She sighed, 'I've never...'

Poseidon snickered, 'To lay with me is not such a bad thing. In fact,' he cleared his throat, 'it's quite the contrary.'

'I wouldn't know what to do,' she felt herself blushing, felt herself suddenly hot at the neck and the chest.

'It's instinctive,' he made for what she supposed was an oddly reassuring voice as he drew near, lowering himself by her side. 'Afterwards, you won't have to worry about feeling weak. You won't have to worry about your friend ever being hurt again. You can protect Athens the way it deserves.'

She looked up into his blue eyes half expecting to feel that usual grim chill that he gave off. But this time it was different. There was a wet veneer to his eyes and something dwelling there that she hadn't seen before.

What was it? Compassion? Surely not. Not from Poseidon of all people. He didn't press her after that, but merely slid one hand against her arm, chilling her to the bone. But strangely in a good way. She took a moment to clear her throat before meeting his eyes again and was only just aware of her heart thudding against her chest, savagely throwing itself at her ribcage as if trying to escape into his lap.

'If you don't want to,' he whispered by her ear, 'say the word and I'll be gone.'

'No,' the word flew from her mouth faster than she thought it would. If he left, then she'd be alone again, wouldn't she? Cassandra wouldn't see her now. Besides, she was probably too busy cursing her for being such a coward.

'No?' he tilted his head with what looked like an uncertain smile on his rugged face. It was strange to see him look so uncertain, a touch of vulnerability shining through his otherwise hardened face. She felt drawn to him now, her head gently nudged by some unseen hand until her lips were drawn closer to his, her eyes closing a slight, scared she might miss.

'This will definitely work, won't it?' she whispered.

'I'm a lot of things,' he whispered back, she could feel his hot breath against her mouth, 'but I am no liar.'

She took one last look at his eyes and knew he was telling the truth. Somehow, she just knew and she slipped her hands against his arms, gently pulling him closer. Perhaps it was instinctive after all as she received his lips, kissing him slow at first, but quickly liking the taste of him. She forgot about Cassandra, if only for the moment as he brushed a soft hand through her hair, his other hand fixed at her jaw, massaging her cheek with his thumb. It was silent in the temple and nothing but the sounds of their lips wrestling with one another.

Soon, even Athena was just a grey and blurry memory as Poseidon grabbed her by the waist, pulling her into him. She felt his tongue in her mouth, strange at first, but equally welcomed as she wrapped her arms around his head, quite content to keep him there as he pulled at her tunic.

'Come here,' he grunted and guided her up to her feet.

'What are you doing?' she asked, flustered and panting and suddenly longing for his mouth again. 'Why did we stop?'

He didn't answer her, but simply marched her over to Athena's statue above the altar. Before she could ask him anything else, he slid one arm around her lower back, moving it like a snake across her abdomen and then southward, lower and lower as he brought his lips down on her neck. She gasped, heart racing as she moved to break free from him. But then she stopped herself. She wanted this. It almost made receiving power redundant.

He shoved her forward and bent her over the altar without much hassle. She opened her mouth to speak, but then his hand was an adventurous thing, grabbing the hem of her dress and sliding it up her thigh, higher and higher, until it was at her hip and she was all but naked below.

'Uh—' she said, though weakly—weak enough that he knew it wasn't a protest of any sort. Damn it, maybe they should've found somewhere more secluded to do this. Maybe to deface Athena's altar in such a way wasn't the best idea. Maybe they should've—

He ripped her dress with one swift tug, tore a chunk of it off and tossed it away. She was about to turn and shout at him for such savagery, but then his hand found its way to hush her, his fingers sweating as they trailed her inner thigh, making her giddy and ticklish. He slid the other hand across her waist, held her tight, making sure she wasn't about to go anywhere. She squirmed at his touch, gyrating her hips against him as he worked her with his fingers, breathing heavy by her ear as she submitted to him. She groaned, though she felt guilty to do so right there in front of Athena. She bit down on her lips to suppress it, but he must've seen it as a challenge because he grew all the more rigorous, moving his fingers in all the right places, faster and faster until she was hissing through her lips.

She howled for him. It was all she could do when he grabbed a fistful of her hair, shoved her face down onto the altar and slapped her like she was cattle—like he owned her. Athena didn't need to know. Medusa could keep her powers hidden, she could keep this lie hidden. It would be her secret. No one would know. No one would...

He kicked her ankles away from one another, smacked her once more

GREEK MYTHOLOGY EXPLAINED

so she knew he was in charge and she squealed. He grabbed her by the hips at first, toying with her as he rubbed himself against her, grabbing and feeling her, enjoying every inch of her like he had all the time in the world. And to hell with it, he did. Athena could walk in now and she daren't think he'd stop. She didn't want him to. Athena could stand outside and wait if she had to.

He slipped himself inside of her, grunting as he did and she gripped the wood of the altar tight, tight enough that her knuckles turned red. It hurt, if she was honest, and it wasn't exactly the great feeling that she'd read and heard Cassandra spout about. It hurt enough that she was pulling away, but he held her fast, pulled her back by the hair and gave her a smack again. She cried out as he let out a sigh of relief, fully inside of her now.

He thrust slow at first, slow enough that she felt every inch of him glide back and forth. A pleasing sound escaped his lips and it made her all lightheaded with the realisation that a god was having his way with her and liking it too. She moaned low, one side of her face pinned hard against the wood of the altar. He was thrusting faster, her whole body moving with him as the altar creaked and the candles began to rigorously billow.

He was merciless, never once stopping to give her a moment of respite. To be honest, she didn't want it. He grew more aggressive, both of his hands fixed around her waist as he ploughed away at her, getting her to lift her head and groan into the air as freely as she'd like. She couldn't help herself. She was breathing fast, groaning hard, caught between doing a mixture of the two as her whole body began to convulse and spasm.

She didn't know what was going on at first as she lost control of her body. She shrieked into the air, her back arching as her entire body was flushed with a surge of energy. It made her arms weak, so weak that she could not prop herself up. She just flopped on the altar like a caught fish, wailing and gasping as her body twitched with excitement. She made one final roar as he spilled his seed and he growled with her, grabbing her by the back of the neck and forcing her down again, filling her up with the final few thrusts.

She collapsed onto the altar when he withdrew, one of her hands flapping uselessly at the side of the wood, trying to find purchase on something—anything. Her other hand felt for her dress, trying to pull it back down, but failing. He didn't say much afterwards, but instead stood there catching his breath with the occasional throaty grunt. She could hear him adjusting his loosened trousers before he gave her a playful prod.

'I don't feel any different,' she panted.

'You mean you didn't enjoy it?' he made to sound offended, but his tone implied he didn't much care whether she enjoyed it or not.

'No. I mean, yes. But…I don't feel like I have powers,' she still panted, finally bringing herself up to a seated position.

'Pity that,' Poseidon shrugged.

'What do you mean?' she snapped.

The door was kicked opened so savagely that it smashed against the wall, coming loose from its hinges and sending splintered wood into the air. Medusa felt the need to scurry under the altar, but she could no more move than a squashed fly, twitching after the impact. Athena stood there red in the face, her shoulders boxed, rising and falling with her unsteady breaths.

'You!' she roared at Poseidon and went for a knife at the belt on her hip, only to stop short of him.

'Don't worry about that thank you,' Poseidon placed a heavy hand on Athena's shoulder before shooting a glance back at Medusa. 'Your priestess did that plenty enough.'

Athena gave her a sharp look, but it faltered as tears formed in her eyes, and she let out a horrified sort of squeal. She brought a hand to her heart as if she'd been stabbed, the other hand covering her mouth as her eyes began to judder.

'Athena,' Medusa got to her feet, 'it's not what you think.'

'It's not?' Athena bristled. 'You will lie to me as well as break your vow?'

'I…I didn't break the vow,' she lied.

Athena looked to Poseidon, but the man merely offered up a coy smirk.

'Is her vow broken?' Athena hissed at him.

'Shattered,' Poseidon winked. 'Be seeing you both.'

'Wait!' Medusa lunged for him. 'What about my powers?'

Poseidon was already heading for the door but he stopped to throw a triumphant glance over his shoulder before uttering, 'I lied.'

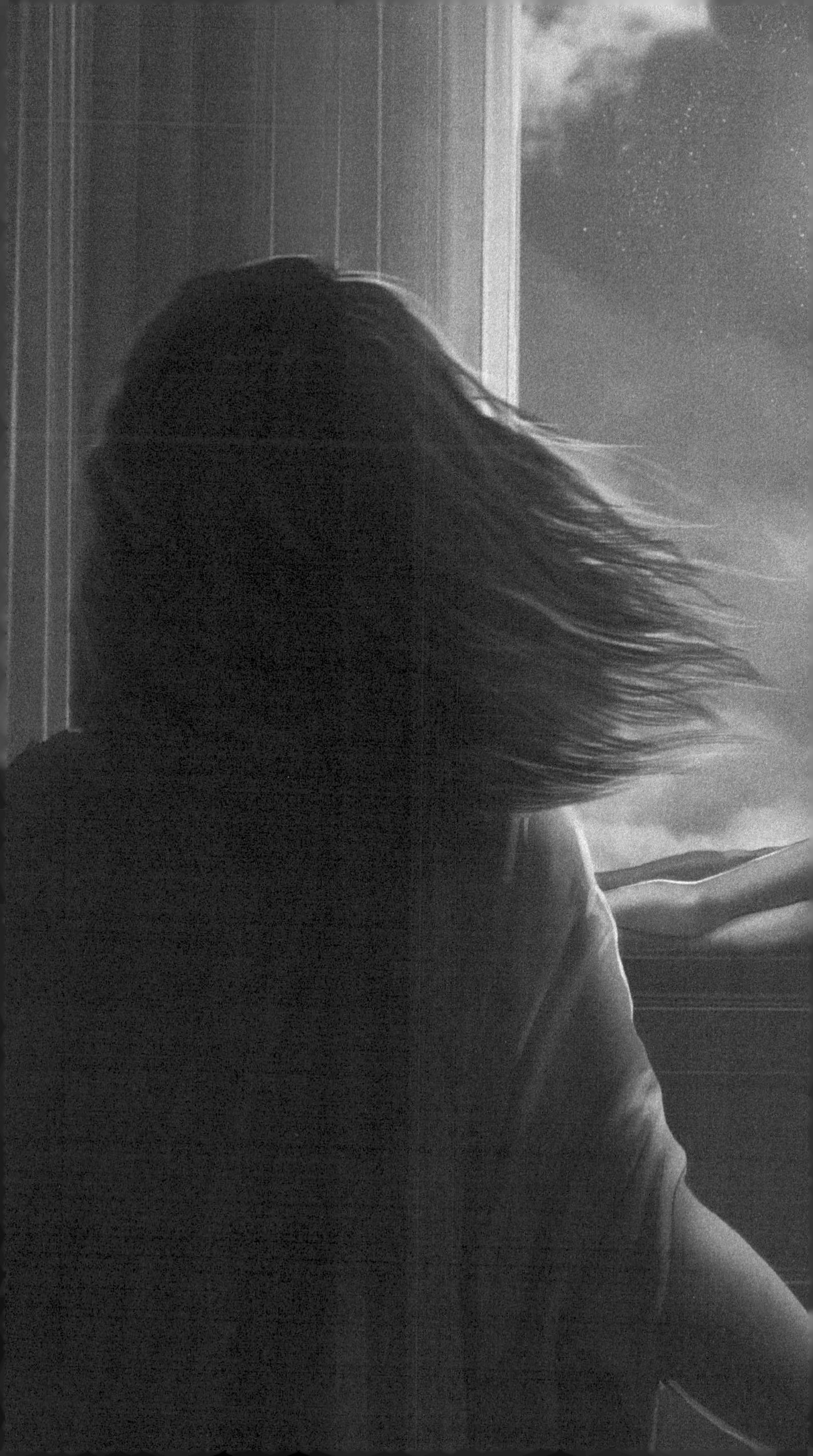

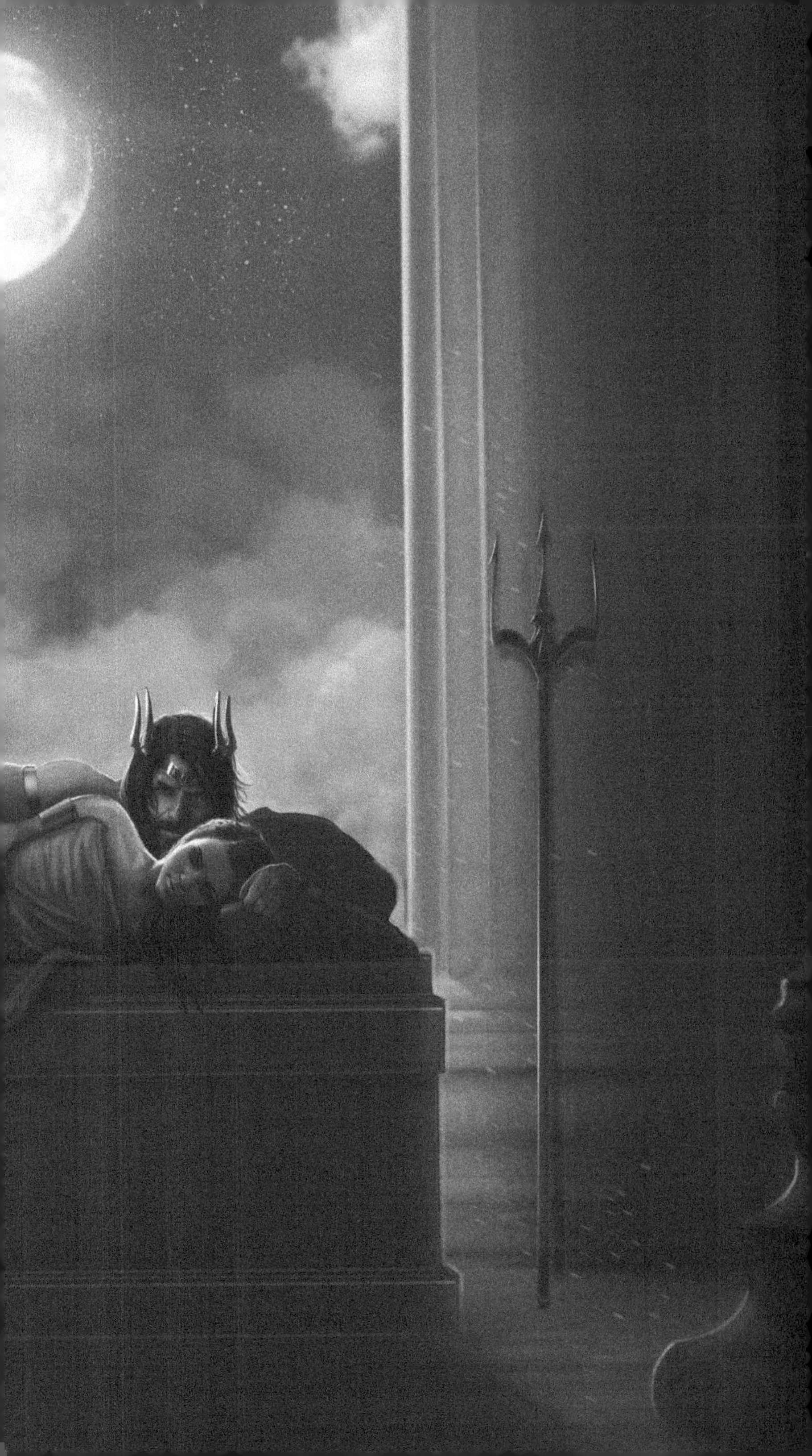

GREEK MYTHOLOGY EXPLAINED

She didn't see him again.

In fact, she didn't see much else as Athena's hand took her square in the mouth, spinning her upside down as she sprawled on the floor. Something clicked in her neck, and all of a sudden, the room was spinning as she tried to gather her bearings.

'You dare...' Athena was pacing ahead of her, 'You dare throw away everything I offered you? You dare go against me like this and with him? Him of all people?'

'Athena,' Medusa tried to lift her head but it weighed a ton all of a sudden. 'Athena I—'

Athena blasted her in the ribs with her foot and Medusa cried out, crawling into a ball.

'I gave you sanctuary here, treated you like you were my own and this is how you repay me?'

'You wouldn't give me power!' Medusa managed to cry out, though it had sounded far more compelling in her head.

'Power? And you thought Poseidon could?'

'He said if I laid with him he would—'

'He says that to everyone you naïve girl!' Athena looked like she was about ready to come punt her again. 'You've thrown away everything for a lie! You have wronged me for a lie!'

'You should've protected us,' Medusa growled as she climbed to her feet. 'All I asked was for you to give us something to believe in, and you ignored me every time. Can you blame me for wanting power so that I might serve our people better than you could?'

Athena blew out air through her lips, 'You've proven that you are not worthy to hold such power.'

'I am worthy!' Medusa barked. 'Perhaps more so than you.'

'Is that what you think?' Athena let out a shrill laughter. 'You think that you could do a better job than me?'

'I wouldn't have allowed one of my priestesses to have her face smashed in while I sat back and did nothing!'

Athena shook her head, 'If it's power you want, girl, then I will give you power.'

Medusa thought about running then, but how could she outrun Athena? The door was on the other side of the room. Even if she could dart past Athena, surely the goddess would reach out and drag her right back. But before she could move, there was an increasing weight that came about her head.

'What are you doing to me?' Medusa cried out.

'You wanted power,' Athena snapped. 'Then power you shall have.'

Medusa's hair was moving. She could feel it on her scalp slithering this way and that. The hair around her shoulders began to rescind up her neck, stopping just below her ear where a loud hissing came. She jumped at the sound of it and moved her hand to touch it, only to find something bite at her finger.

'Ah!' she gasped as she saw the blood drop from her fingertips. More hisses came from above her head followed by nips of pain. She grabbed hold of her hair, but it wasn't hair anymore. Snakes moved this way and that, hissing and snapping at her arms and her fingers. She caught her reflection in one of the windows only to find a bevy of the scaly creatures shifting back and forth, moving to a silent rhythm with tiny tongues and little black eyes.

'What have you done to me?' Medusa screeched.

Her skin was changing and what was once a pleasant and peachy hue was now a sickly greenish colour. Her eyes were lost of their dark pupils and now there was only a colourless space, just the whites staring back at her. Even her gums were changing and seeping yellow and reddish pus.

Then came the pain.

'What are you doing to me?' she roared, but her voice was different, dark and insidious.

'Nothing that you didn't do to yourself,' Athena shook her head with disappointment.

Medusa fell to her knees. It was all she could do as a surge of agony shot across her back. She felt something gnawing behind the tip of her spine like an unnatural twisting of muscle. She screamed bloody murder for all the good it would do. She heard her flesh rip. She could feel a weight on her back get heavier and heavier as something flapped against her shoulders. Whatever it was, it was bleeding everywhere. Buckets of blood spilled down her sides and dripped on the floor.

She managed to crane her head up only to find Athena standing there with her arms outstretched before her, hands working like a composer, fingers dancing like she was knitting thread. Medusa tried to scramble to her feet and tried to move out of Athena's sights. But the goddess moved after her without any urgency. It was like Athena had her exactly where she wanted, and no amount of running or hiding would spare Medusa from her fate.

She grabbed the side of the window sill, pulled herself up as best she could with the pain in her back. What awaited her had her shrieking along with the snakes, though for very different reasons. Small wings had sprouted from her back—two ugly shaped things all grey and mottled with greenish pus.

'What...' she started. 'What have you done to me?'

'Now you needn't fear about your loyalty to me,' Athena spoke. 'For now no man will ever look at you, and you can never betray me again.'

Medusa was running after that, but even her feet were different. When had they changed? Two sickly coloured talons clacked against the floor with long black nails protruding outwards, curling at the tip. So stunned by it, Medusa almost got them tangled and nearly went flying face first into the statue of Zeus. It wasn't long before her legs moved on their own accord. Hot tears flooded down her face. She thought about running to Cassandra because she always knew what to do. But Cassandra hated her, and she would hate her even more now that she looked like this. Everyone would, surely. She thought about Poseidon, but that only had her heart aching and her chest burning with something horrid.

She brushed past Athena, but it was clear the goddess had no further intention with her. She didn't try to drag her back, nor try to block her path as she headed towards the exit. In fact, Medusa was certain she didn't even watch her leave.

It was true then. Athena didn't care.

Come to think of it, no one did.

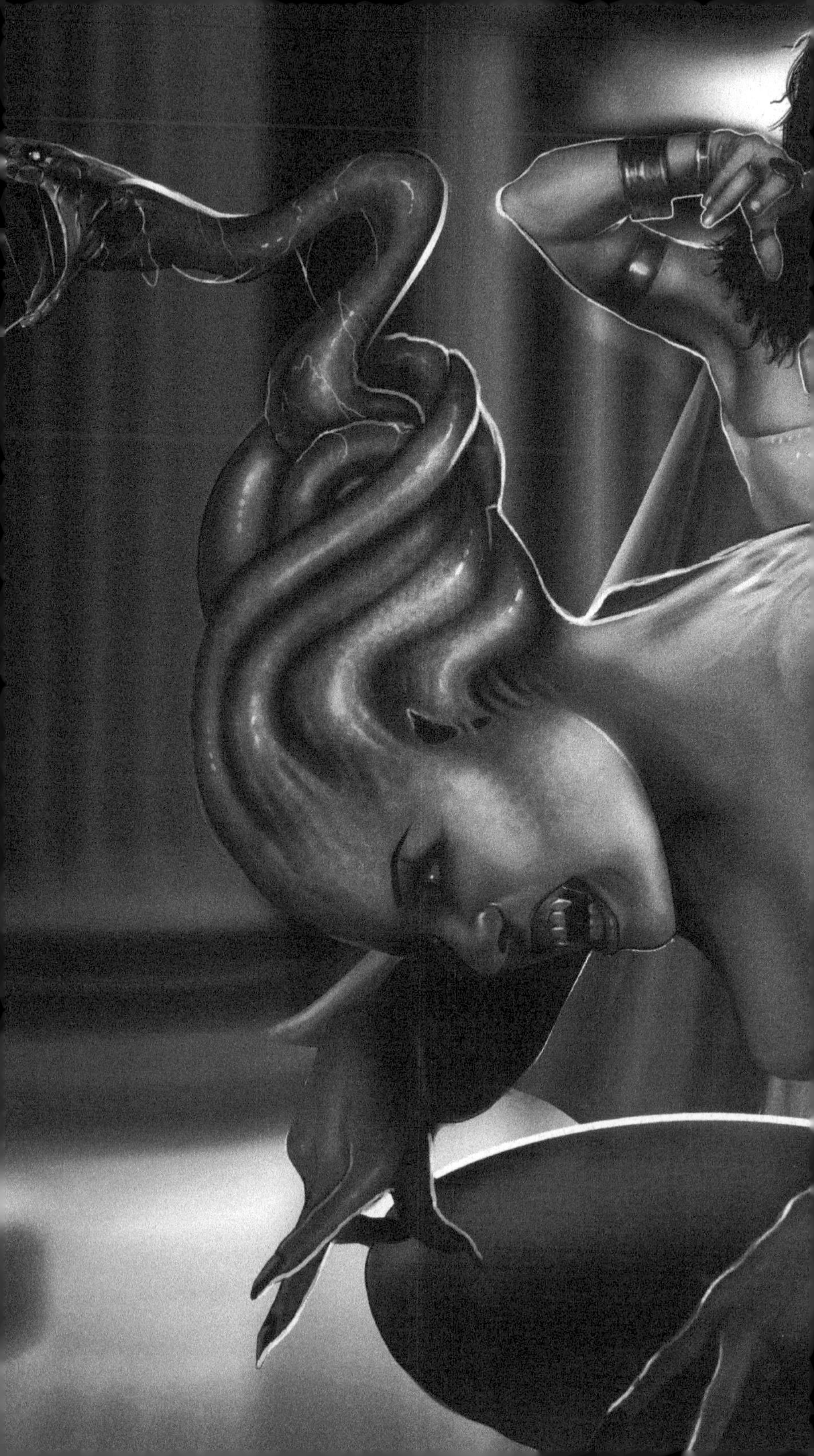

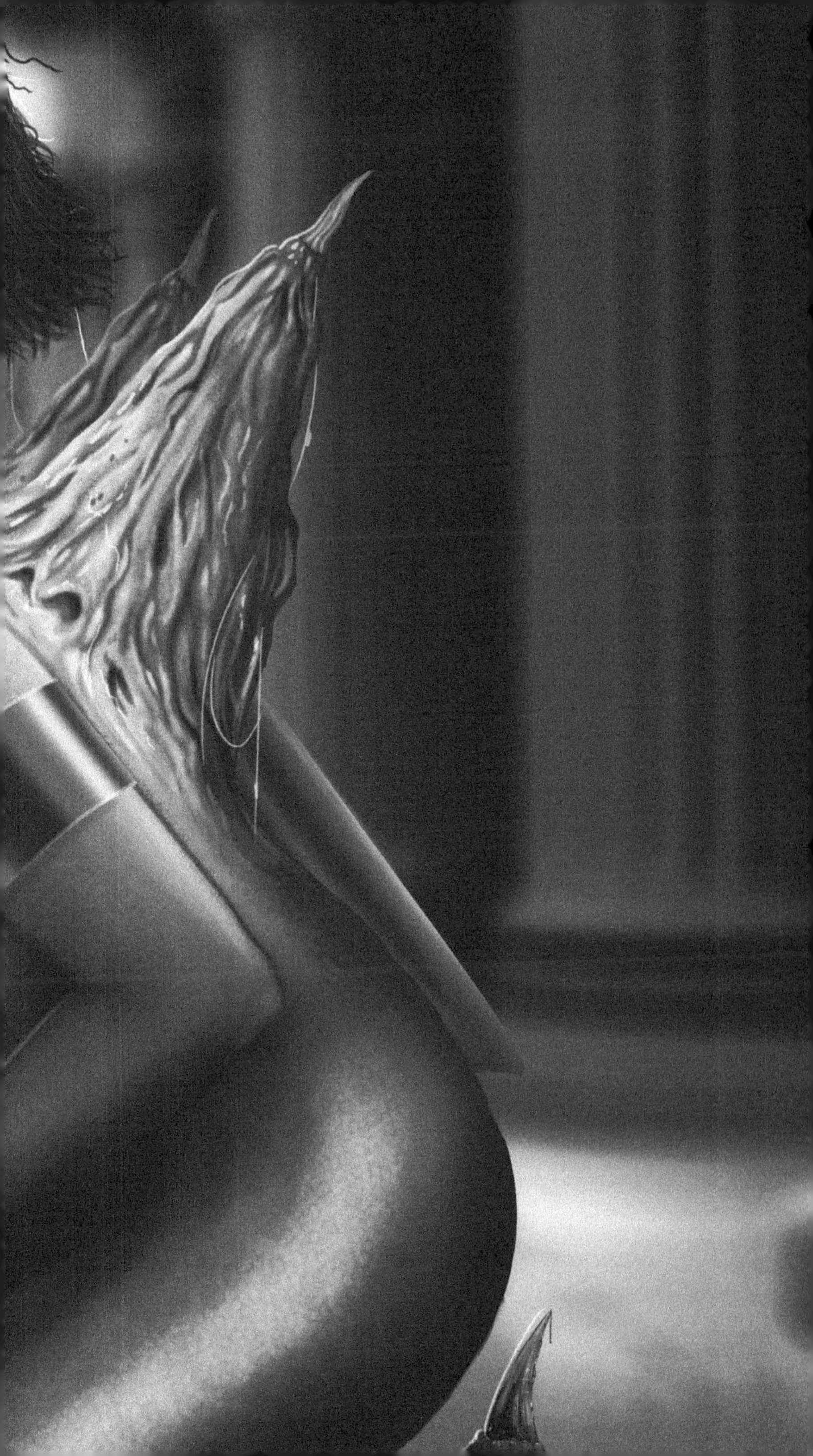

VIII. The Heroes

She'd stopped counting the years since she had left Athens sometime after the second year. Now…well, now she only counted bodies and even that number had come to elude her. Men of all different shapes and sizes had come for her, men of a dozen different shades with different weapons and different accents. The only thing they had in common however, was the look on their faces when they saw her, their mouths fixing into a gaping hole as fear caught in their throats.

There was a small cataract inside the dark pit she resided in where only a slither of light trespassed through the cracks in the walls and the stony ceiling above. Occasionally, there was an evil, golden sparkle from her eyes, but it was gone too quick to admire. It was perhaps the only thing she could appreciate as well considering her eyes were sunken in, the flesh around them was dark and bumpy to touch. She'd never been one for vanity, and while she knew she was beautiful, she had never relied upon her looks. But she sorely missed them now as she ran her thick, draping tongue along her oozing fangs.

The snakes in her hair weren't the worst feeling anymore. They were obedient now. All twelve of the black skinned creatures had become her only company with their burning red eyes and the slow, arbitrary way they moved. Her skin had become as hard as granite with the awful hue of days-old phlegm, all greenish-grey and rough to touch. She brought her slender fingers up to her face, touching the hollow points around her cheeks, and shivered. It was like touching concrete.

She didn't like to think of her life before, but sometimes some things were unavoidable. She scuttled through the sand and it would remind her of the beach, but here there was no sunlight. Nor was there the crashing of waves which she supposed was a good thing, because that would probably remind her of Poseidon and he was the last person she wanted on her mind. She wondered if Cassandra had cried for her and wondered if the woman still thought about her, but who was she kidding? In the end, she supposed there was a bit of Athena in everyone when it came to compassion…or lack of it. But she didn't like to think about it and so she wiped her dry, flaking hand across her bumpy face and sat down on a slab of slate.

It was the fourth tomb she'd relocated to. The first one had been flooded by the men of Athens who had come hunting for her. The second tomb was caved in, though she wasn't sure if that had been deliberate or whether nature had simply turned on her too. The third tomb saw savage, dark skinned men come thundering through the tunnels wielding spears and knives to kill her. Although she supposed she deserved that one. She had slain one of their children who had wandered into her domain, pulled off his head and tossed it outside.

She had tried to live in a faraway forest at one point, but the harpies were keeping her awake. Besides, there were whispers of hunters in the night who were searching for some other foul creature who had wronged the gods. Medusa had heard that this creature lured men into her clutches and then devoured them. She wondered if they might've made good friends, all things considered.

There was movement on the floor above her, and she could tell as dust and sand drizzled from the ceiling that there was more than one hero coming for her head tonight. That's what they called themselves: heroes. She had wondered what was so heroic about a group of men—hunting her down. After all, she was a woman. Or whatever it was she had become. It hardly seemed fair, but when was anything fair?

She sauntered her way through the dark confines of the tomb, twisting her way through the narrow pathways in silence. The snakes didn't hiss anymore, not unless she did. If she was honest, she hardly even noticed them there. Once she was free of the winding pathways, she came to an open space that was cluttered with greyscale statues, all of them men in various poses. Some were drawing their swords, a look of relishing delight on their butch faces. But others looked more worried with their hands drawn up to their mouths or over their eyes. One that made Medusa laugh every time she saw it was in the middle of relieving his bladder with his pants down.

My creations, she mused as she made an almost proud sounding sigh. But she was far from proud. There was a time she made the same sort of sigh while standing in the courtyard of Athens, watching as men and women swung each other around in dance or drank to the name of Athena in jolly moods and big smiles. She was proud of that, most certainly. But not anymore. All she had now was her statues that filled the tomb like a macabre mix of an art exhibition and a cemetery. Either way, it was home now and the statues lived there with her. They had no choice.

The heroes above her were making enough noise to wake the dead. Their armours rattled and they were muttering to one another with contempt, harking insults at the other as they fumbled this way and that. Medusa knew their current path would soon lead down to her and so she folded her arms and set her eyes on the sloping, sandy incline above. Cold blue light emanated from the pinnacle of the slope, but it would serve no one once they came barrelling down towards her. Once they were there, the shadows would claim them and they would be hers. Just like the others.

'We're going the wrong way,' one of them was snapping to the others. 'I told you we should've taken the left at that pretty statue.'

'You thought she was pretty?' another voice muttered. 'You really don't have any standards, do you?'

'Oh and you have standards, do you?' the first man thundered. 'What would you know about standards?'

'Enough to know when a statue looks like a man,' the other said.

'I hate you,' the first one grumbled.

'Keep your eyes peeled,' the second one warned. 'We've already lost one of us. Can't afford to lose anymore.'

They wouldn't find her for another five minutes, the three of them bickering more like a trio of school boys than the heroic men they pretended to be. She'd learned enough about them by merely standing there listening to their voices bounce along the cavern walls down to the pit in which she waited. One of them seemed to be the leader of the group, all boisterous and whiny. Then there was the quieter more sensible version of the leader who she'd decided to nickname Lazy on the account that he was only interested in taking a break. At last there was the third man, one she'd simply name Dopey, on the account that he was undeniably stupid. He was more interested in selling the other two water, but the price seemed to only get higher each time he made a pitch.

The leader emerged first at the top of the slope. He didn't have the look of a hero, though he had the sense to wear a helmet, rusted as it was. He held a sword in one arm and what looked like a map in the other; his arms were like twigs and his chest was like that of an adolescent. The lazy one wasn't faring much better with armour that might've been too small for him for there were noticeable gaps where anyone could've slipped a knife. Finally, the third man emerged, the dopey one, with flasks of water, holding them up like he was offering them to the others, before snatching them away.

'Thirty gold coins and it's yours,' he said with a wink.

'For the last time, I don't want water!' The leader barked at him. He certainly had a temper on him.

'Forty gold coins then,' he waggled his finger at him like there could be no better price.

'You really don't understand haggling, do you?' the lazy one called over the leader's shoulder.

'What's haggling?' The dopey one was frowning and smiling at the same time.

Medusa cleared her throat and that got them to shut up real quick. At first the leader didn't see her and he had to slip a monocle over one of his eyes—his other eye squinting like something was stuck in it. As he leaned into the void, she could see his expressions begin to change from the excitement of having found his glory to the realisation that he was indeed about to die.

'Close your eyes!' he roared at his comrades, but he did not follow his own advice in time.

Medusa had him where she wanted. She could see his eyes begin to dilate, and in that split second, he was hers. She could see him trying to pull his head away from her, but it was stuck now. His skin was turning grey. Dark grey lines spread up his neck, over his chin and up his face. He went to reach for his sword, but his arms were rigid now, barely mobile at all.

'Are you okay?' the lazy one was grabbing him, but upon making contact he recoiled. He put his hand against the leader's now stony face and trembled at the lip.

'Here,' the dopey one tossed a flask at him. 'Give him some water.'

'That's not going to help now, is it?' the lazy one barked at him before tapping his leader's face. 'Can you hear me? Can you hear me? Can you—'

'I don't imagine he'll be responding,' Medusa sniggered. 'Besides, he certainly didn't have the presence to fight me.'

Medusa allowed herself to laugh. Their leader stood there with a fearful expression, like a deer caught in the path of a speeding wagon. He had no glorious beard, nor any physical abundancy or even an air of strength. He was quite plain as far as Medusa was concerned. His companions looked quite out of place too with Lazy trembling at the jowls and Dopey who, if she wasn't mistaken, looked like he was still smiling at his flasks of water.

'You must be today's heroes,' she called up at them, her voice turning them all a paler shade. 'Why don't you come down here so that I might get a better look at you?'

They at least had the sense not to look at her. The lazy one had his hand over his brow while the dopey one stood cautiously behind a large boulder, his arm outstretched to their leader as he tried to feed him water.

'You...you turned him to stone,' the lazy one was sweating now.

'Observant, aren't we?' she said mid-yawn. She half-expected Lazy to bolt the way he came, but to give the little man credit, he stood his ground. It was more than could be said for Dopey who, she had decided, was most definitely an idiot. If she wasn't mistaken, he was still trying to barter with their frozen leader.

'You won't get me,' Lazy beckoned, storming towards her.

Medusa grinned.

He had something of a strategy, at least. He took a bow off from his shoulder and began unleashing arrow after to arrow at her. To his credit, he didn't look at her face. He had his gaze fixed on her guts, aiming for her as best he could whilst running. But most of his arrows went askew, and pretty soon the terrain became treacherous and he had trouble keeping his balance. More importantly, it looked like he was running out of breath.

'Perhaps you should consider another weapon,' she mused as he got to the bottom of the slope. He ran in a straight line towards her, head still down.

He was about to reply, but then stumbled over a rock and with arrow in hand, he managed to land on the steel point with his throat. He thrashed on the floor for a moment, tried pushing himself up, but realised he was too heavy. Instead, he chose to lie there in a pool of his own blood, legs twitching until they were still.

Medusa sighed. She had hoped for a challenge this time.

That left the final hero—the dopey one. The sound of his fallen ally stopped him from his haggling of the flasks. He looked at the bloody puddle in which the lazy one was lying in and recoiled.

'Oh,' he muttered in a voice that wasn't the least bit distressed. 'You killed him.'

She merely shrugged one shoulder in response.

'Then I suppose I shall have the glory of killing you myself,' he reached back over his shoulder and pulled a frightfully large scythe out and into his hands. In all honesty, it looked quite ridiculous. The blade was sharp enough that it may have taken her head clean off with the right swing, but the functionality of the weapon looked quite arduous. To swing it in such a small place was foolish enough as it was, but to swing the thing fast enough that it might catch someone was another thing altogether.

'Why aren't you using a sword like every other hero?' she asked. The lazy one had used a bow which was appropriate enough, but a scythe? Even a spear would've been acceptable. What did he intend to do with a scythe down here? Tend to the weeds?

'I'm not like every other hero,' he said in a voice that might've been dramatic if he didn't have a stupid smile on his face and if he wasn't looking down at the ground.

'Suit yourself,' she shook her head. 'Come and meet your destiny, boy.'

He came barrelling down the slope with the scythe held high above his head, more like a javelin than anything else. She was half tempted to see whether he'd make a decent enough cut with it, but she'd wasted enough time on these fools. Instead, she focused on the movement of his body as he came closer and closer.

'You have strong eyes,' she told him with a purr to her voice.

'I do?' he looked up at her, and just like that, she saw the regret in his face.

'No,' she said and stared deep into his pupils.

His face began to contort and his approach slowed to a mere jog, then a walk and then nothing. He brought the scythe down so that he held it with both hands, but he made no further attempt to attack.

'Is something wrong?' she asked, though she knew all too well. She sauntered towards him as sultry as a lover might, slipping her hands around his face and bringing it close to hers.

'I don't feel so good,' he tried clearing his throat, but his eyes were fixed on hers, staring into them as if he could see into the back of her skull and he was mightily intrigued. All the heroes usually were though, weren't they? They hadn't resisted her eyes when she was mortal and beautiful, now that she was something else and repulsive, they stared all the more. *Funny how that works*, Medusa mused.

The colour on his neck was turning grey before it advanced up his chin, along his cheeks and up the rest of his face. His eyes widened as if they might pop out and he gave that gormless O shape with his mouth as his skin began to harden. But he couldn't look away. She held him needlessly tight around the face knowing that if she let go, his eyes would still be glued to hers. No one could resist her dark powers.

'You won't win,' he croaked out of his mouth. 'There's still one more of us out there.'

'Oh, a fourth man? I look forward to finding him,' she gave his cheek a squeeze.

There was a faint whisper from his lips. A sliver of smoke sauntered out from between his teeth. Something twitched across his nostrils and along his forehead. It looked as if he was about to shout. But after that he was silent, another statue in her collection.

IX. The Fourth Man

She watched the fourth hero walk through the chambers, stalking through the tomb like he owned the place, like a man returning home after a long voyage away. It made her wonder why she was the one skulking in the shadows, stalking after him, waiting for him to let his guard down long enough that she might sink her teeth into his neck. But to his credit, this hero seemed like he knew battle well, and so he didn't give her many opportunities to strike.

He brought with him a strange sort of aura, one of ferocity and strength, but he looked mild for one so generously armoured. His arms were bare, but given how sinewy they were, it didn't look like they needed much protection. He wore a brown breastplate, one that was polished and well-kept if not for the stain of blood on the front and the rather noticeable dent at the side. He kept his sword sheathed in the scabbard that dangled by his legs, both of which were wrapped with steel greaves and heavy looking boots.

He moved quietly for such an armoured man with delicate footsteps that were somehow hushed upon impact. If she hadn't seen him first, he might've been able to creep up on her and do away with her for good. His hair was cropped short, his face devoid of much emotion except for the hawk-like concentration that was permanently in place. It was the first time she wondered about a hero and wondered what his purpose in hunting her was. Perhaps she'd killed one of his relatives and he'd come for revenge. Or maybe he was coming for her head so that he may claim one of the many rewards in Athens.

He slowed when he arrived in an open space filled only by the occasional statue here and there. There were cracks in the ceiling where moonlight spilled through, lighting up what would become his final resting place in an eerie, silver glow. He had his back to her as he pondered the statue ahead of him—a mere boy, as far as she was concerned, whose name she had long forgotten and whose purpose she hadn't cared much for in the first place.

She strolled out from the shadows. Now was her chance to strike. She fixed her eyes on his exposed neck, licking her lips. She traversed across the sand silently. Her heart thumped with a thrill as she came close. She could smell his musky scent as she closed in. She opened her mouth wide, readied her hands to hold him still. She came over his shoulder, went to sink her teeth in.

He smacked her with the back of his hand.

She didn't just stumble back, no. She was tossed through the air, snakes hissing as she flapped her arms about hopelessly. She hit the far wall hard, met the floor even harder as she rolled onto her face.

How?

It was the first thing she thought as she craned her neck up, spitting sand, only to find him still standing there with his back to her. No mortal had ever struck her like that before. Why, it was almost reminiscent of the smack that Athena had given her all those years ago. Her ears were ringing as she pulled herself up to her feet, and for the first time in a long time, the snakes in her hair would not silence.

He only just turned to her, though he didn't look like he was in the mind to celebrate. In fact, he didn't really look in her direction at all. He held his shield up, angled it carefully like he was trying to catch her reflection through it. *So he's wise to my power*, Medusa noted. Most of the brave men she'd faced had met her head on, gazing into her eyes and roaring from their lungs as if doing so gave them an advantage. It didn't. All she needed was for a man to stare into her eyes for merely a few seconds and then they were hers, frozen in time, nothing more than hardened rock.

She could see his eyes in the reflection of the shield and they were a cold set, perhaps dead almost. He held his mouth in such a way it looked as if he was chewing on molten rock but didn't mind the taste. Beyond that, there was no reading him. No fear, no joy, no nothing.

'You have good reflexes, boy,' she spat a greenish goo.

'I've had a lot of practice,' he replied without hesitation, his voice as deep and compelling as his militant stance.

'Why don't you put that shield down and face me?' she tried to work him over into looking at her for just a moment.

But he wasn't so foolish.

'I think I'll keep hold of it,' he said. 'At least for now.'

'Suit yourself,' she said. It wouldn't matter if he didn't look in her eyes. She'd just have to kill him the old fashioned way. 'Do you come here for glory?' she licked her lips, knowing his answer would not change his fate. 'Or is it vengeance?'

He gave her a tired shrug, 'Neither.'

'You must serve someone or something,' she hissed and the snakes echoed her sentiment.

'I suppose I have my reasons for wanting your head,' he answered.

'A man of few words, aren't you? But you should know that serving someone other than yourself is a road to misery. I was like you once, serving a power I thought greater than my own. Look where it got me.'

'They say you were a high priestess some many moons ago,' the young man glanced at her for a moment but looked away too quickly for her to sink her eyes into him. 'They say your beauty was rivalled by no other and that you were a kind and just woman who sought the safety of others.'

Medusa twitched with annoyance. She hated hearing about the woman she used to be. It always made her feel so much less now that she was something else entirely.

'What of it, boy?' she snapped. 'So I was the high priestess of Athens? So I wanted to help and protect my people? Look where that path led me. I wanted to save them, to heal them, to bring them peace and salvation in turbulent times. Look how they repay me. They send boys like you to hack off my head.'

'Life's been cruel to you,' he had the decency to acknowledge. 'But I have my own destiny to fulfill and for that, I must show you yours.'

'Ha!' she cackled. 'You have nerve, young man. I'll give you that.' She spat again, this time red blood which she hadn't seen in quite some time. She wasn't sure if she had bitten her tongue because blood was spilling over her lip and dripping down her chin. Maybe it was from where he'd rather rudely smacked her.

'I suppose I have my moments,' he replied as he brought the shield closer to his face, turning away from her once more as he looked for her in the reflection.

She grinned at that. How many heroes had come her way with less wit than a drowning dog? Indeed, this seemed like it would be a battle worth remembering, and she would store his corpse somewhere she'd be prone to seeing it often.

'Before I send you to Hades, boy,' she said, 'tell me your name.'

It was then that he ripped the sword out of its scabbard and a flash of golden light came away with it, rippling through the air. For some reason, she couldn't help but regret having asked him at all.

'My name is Perseus,' he said and his eyes flickered with lightning. 'Son of Zeus.'

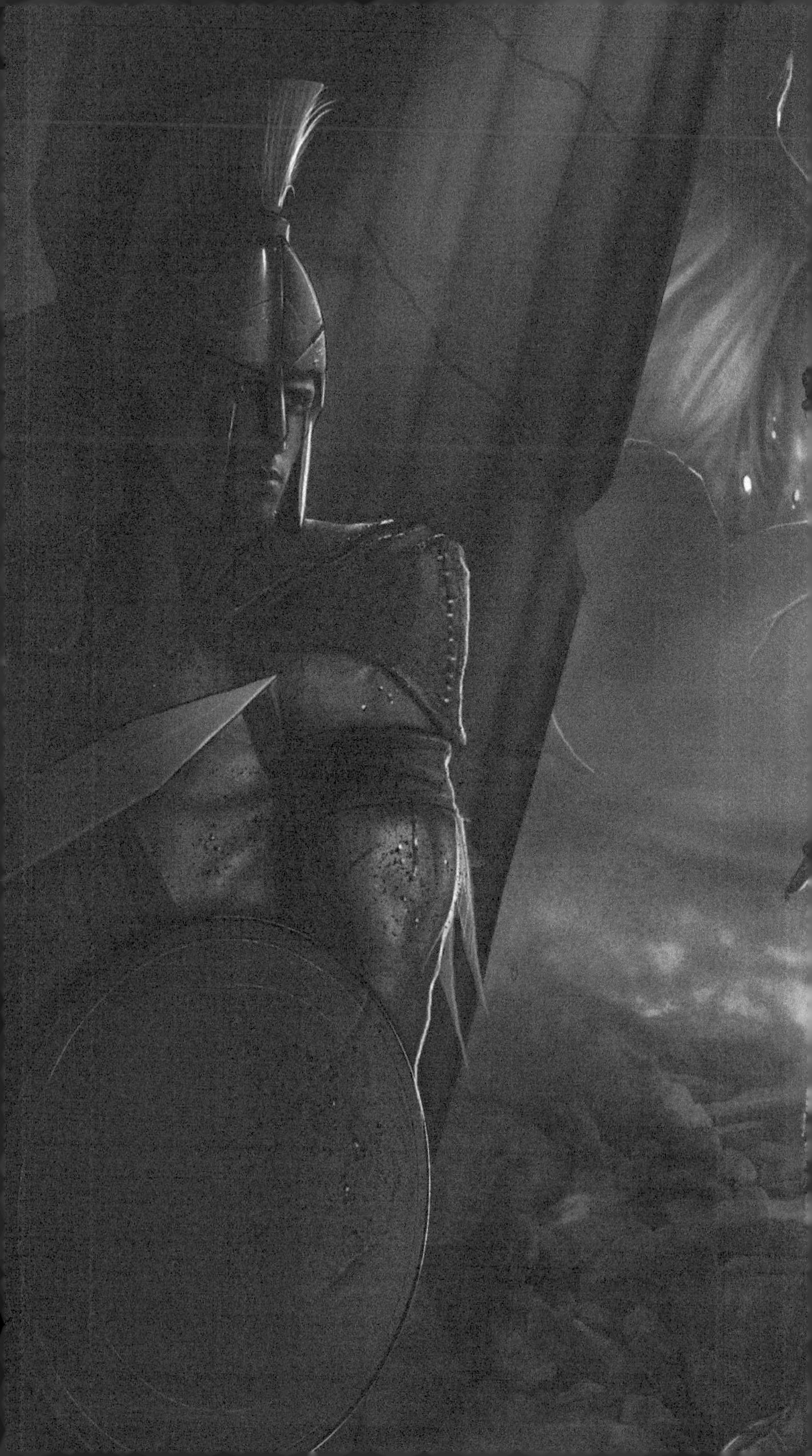

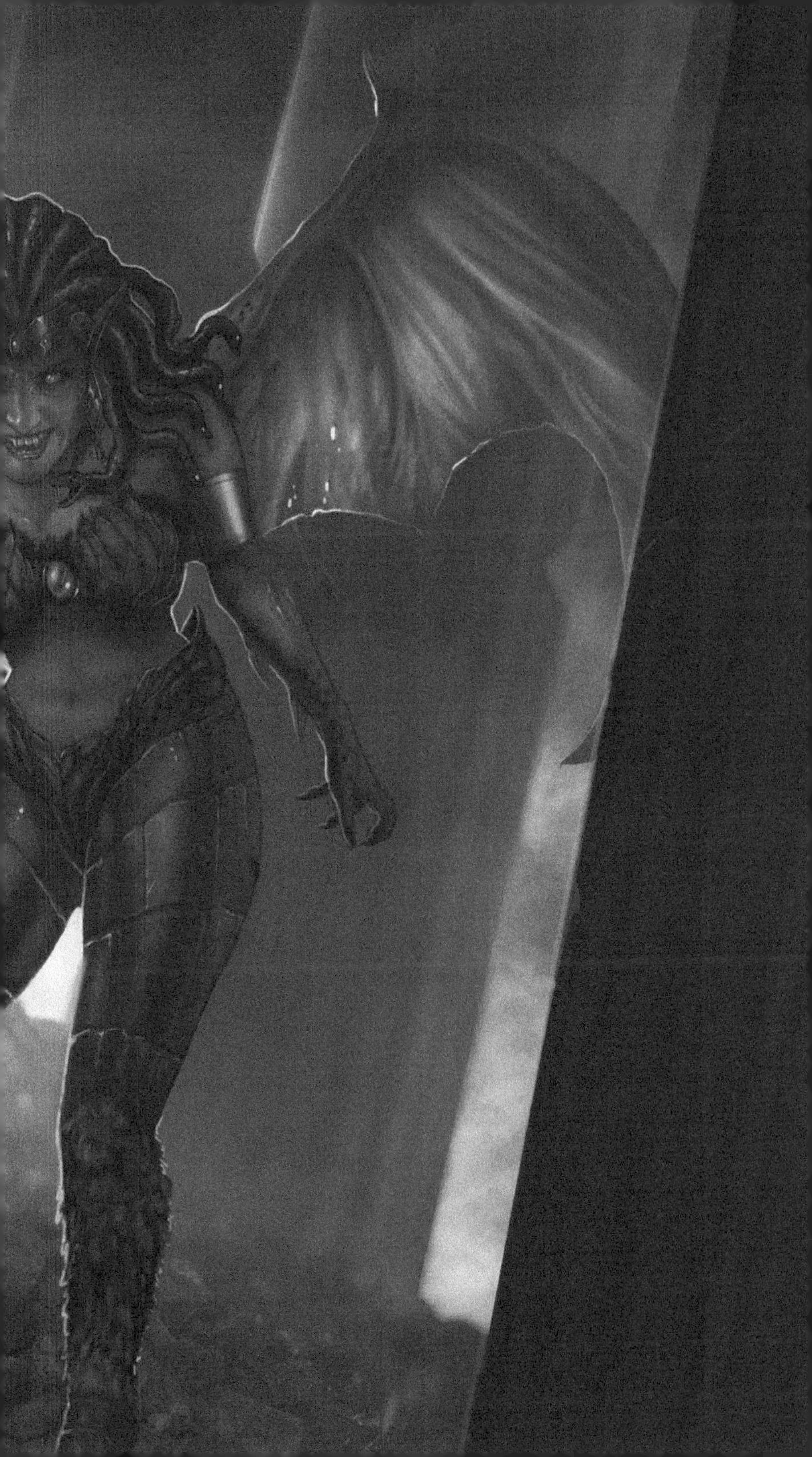

THE STORY OF MEDUSA EXPLAINED

Greek mythology has a plethora of iconic figures that are recognisable even to those who are unfamiliar with any of its stories. Names such as Zeus, Poseidon or Heracles are likely to elicit a nod of acknowledgment from most people, but if you were to show them a picture of a snake haired woman, you'd be hard pressed to find someone who couldn't identify that woman as Medusa. Despite being thrust into mainstream popularity, there is so much surrounding her story that the majority of people are unaware of. The story itself has numerous variations where the actions and motives of those involved are constantly changing. The outcome, however, always remains the same. It's the numerous paths that take us to this outcome that make Medusa's story so interesting.

There are several things that most poets seem to agree on, the first being that Medusa was a beautiful maiden before she was transformed into a Gorgon. The earliest accounts of Medusa and her fellow Gorgons were that of hideous creatures. Over the years, however, tales of Medusa that depicted her as Gorgon from birth began to fade. The notion of her as a beautiful woman became more popular with poets such as Pindaros referring to her as 'fair cheeked Medusa;' this fueled the belief that she became a Gorgon later in her life. It was later believed she was transformed into a Gorgon by the goddess Athena after an encounter in her temple with Poseidon. The reasons behind Athena's decision range anywhere from jealousy and anger to sympathy and the desire to help Medusa protect herself.

The events that transpired in the temple are what makes each version of this story different. In Ovid's variation, Poseidon, after his feud with Athena attempted to seduce one of her priestesses. Medusa rejected several advances from Poseidon until the god had finally had enough and pursued her into Athena's temple. It was here in Athena's temple that Poseidon had his way with her. When Athena saw the two laying together she was furious, but she couldn't punish a god with the power and stature of Poseidon. With Medusa distraught, the only way Athena could ensure that no man would ever lay a hand on Medusa again was by turning her into a Gorgon. Anyone who meant Medusa any harm would look into her eyes and be turned into stone. In this version, it's very clear that Medusa is the victim, Poseidon is the villain and Athena is the sympathetic party. The transformation into a Gorgon is often described as a curse, however, here it's more a gift. If we've learnt anything from the Greek gods, it's that their help often comes with a price or a catch.

Medusa, however, is not always portrayed as a victim in her story. There are variations where she desired the power of a goddess and believed the best way to attain that power was to have sex with a god. This time, when Athena found Medusa and Poseidon in her temple, the anger and frustration are instead directed towards Medusa. To Athena, the actions of Medusa were the ultimate betrayal, for not only did she break her vow as a priestess, but she defiled the temple with a god that Athena was in the midst of a bitter conflict with. The transformation in this story is done very much out of anger and revenge. If Medusa was so willing to break her vow for personal gain by laying with a god, then Athena would make sure that no man or god would ever look at her again. The Gorgon form was not meant to offer Medusa protection, but instead served as a reminder of her actions that night in Athena's temple. Her actions in this instance were driven by selfishness and she would spend the rest of eternity alone.

The story we've tried to tell takes elements from both of these popular versions. Medusa does ultimately succumb to Poseidon, but her need to become a goddess is more for the protection of innocent people rather than for personal gain. Poseidon's actions in every version seem to be the same as he wants nothing more than to spite Athena and Medusa is the instrument he uses to do that.

Medusa would then be exiled into obscurity where she would be hunted and pursued by countless individuals looking to make a name for themselves and become the next hero of Greece. Many tried to slay her and many failed. Hundreds, if not thousands, of statues were scattered throughout her cave or varying habitat, serving as a reminder to all those that entered that there was no glory awaiting them. There was only death.

That is until the hero Perseus was tasked with retrieving her head.

Unlike the others, he had help from the gods. Athena had given him a bronze polished shield that acted like a mirror. Using this shield, he was able to look into the reflection cast by the material, allowing him to see Medusa without being turned into stone. Unlike all those before him, Perseus would not enter the cave blind. He also had the sandals of Hermes granting him flight, a helmet from Hades that would make the wearer invisible and a sword crafted by the god of the forge, Hephaestus. Armed with an arsenal from the gods, when Perseus did finally come face to face with Medusa, he would slay the Gorgon by cutting off her head. Unknown to Medusa, she had fallen pregnant after her night with Poseidon, but the curse Athena placed on her concealed the pregnancy and made it so she could not give birth. Once she was slain, the curse was lifted, and from her open neck spawned her two sons. Pegasus, the beautiful winged white steed, and Chrysaor, a golden giant holding a sword to match. Perseus would later use Medusa's head to turn the titan Atlas into stone during a disagreement, but the main reason Perseus acquired the head was to slay the enormous sea monster Cetus. He achieved this by aiming Medusa's head at the monster and thus turning it stone when the monster returned Medusa's gaze.

With the explanation of the events that took place out of the way, there are several things left to discuss. One of the main misconceptions that exists today surrounds the appearance of Medusa and the other Gorgons. Before we delve into how the appearance changed over the years, we first need to establish where Medusa came from. She was the daughter of the primordial gods Phorcys and Ceto, ancient gods of the sea. She had two sisters, Stheno and Euryale, who were depicted as immortal Gorgons. Medusa, however, was mortal, and unlike her two hideous sisters, she possessed radiant beauty. The eldest tales of Medusa did in fact describe her as being born a monstrous Gorgon just like her sisters. So we know that Gorgons existed before Athena's curse.

So what exactly did these Gorgons look like? If we go by modern day mainstream interpretations that have stemmed from Hollywood, then Gorgons are snake haired women with the lower half of a snake. This, however, was not the case in Greek mythology. The Gorgons are described as winged women with snakes for hair and talon-like feet. They naturally had a deep hatred for men. The name Gorgon derives from an ancient Greek word meaning dreadful, so it's safe to assume that they were certainly never considered a pleasure to be around. There is the belief that the Gorgons existed long before Medusa and her sisters. The oracles of Ancient Greece were said to have been protected by snakes and creatures that bared an uncanny resemblance to the Gorgons.

Athena's role in this story is quite an interesting one because she comes across as the polar opposite in the two popular renditions of the story. Known as a protector of women and goddess of wisdom, she does fulfill her duty, giving Medusa the means to protect herself. In her wisdom, she knew that she could not protect Medusa at all times and so transforming her into a Gorgon was the most logical solution. If we compare this to the interpretation where Medusa's actions with Poseidon were ill-intended, Athena completely disregards her role as a protector and we see that she is driven by her emotions to punish Medusa. Many would argue the actions of the goddess of wisdom should not be dictated by ego or emotion. It's important to note that being wise does not make one emotionless. It becomes very difficult to relate to a character who displays no emotion and whose actions are only dictated by cold, hard logic. The gods and goddesses throughout Greek mythology demonstrate behaviour very similar to our own in the sense that they are emotional—fallible. Just as in the first rendition of the story where we see Athena display emotion in the form of compassion towards Medusa, here she is hurt and angered by her actions, and though the outcome of Medusa's transformation remains the same, the motives behind it are very different.

There is no doubt that Medusa is one of the most misunderstood figures that appears in Greek mythology. She was branded as nothing more than an evil monster that would turn the innocent into stone, and much of this stems from movies and television. Her story is one that has much more meaning behind it than first meets the eye. For the most part, Medusa had only the best intentions but she found herself in the middle of a conflict between the gods and would sadly become collateral damage. In certain renditions of the story, she placed her trust in Athena who ultimately could not protect her, reminding us all that the Greek gods were far from perfect or otherwise omnipotent. They made mistakes, acted out of pride or spite and sometimes punished those who were not deserving.

The meaning does slightly change if we interpret Medusa's actions as being ambitious enough to want to be a goddess greater than Athena for the sake of power. Here it's clear the story warns against greed and hubris against the gods which always ends in either death or transmutation, or in this case both.

Even in death though, the slain head of Medusa would be seen as a symbol of good. The Ancient Greeks would create an amulet with Medusa's head on it called the Gorgoneion. This amulet was used to ward off evil and protect the wearer. It was even described in later stories as being worn by the likes of Zeus and Athena in the years that followed. Medusa's story is a reminder that bad things do happen to good people, but that's not to say the outcome cannot serve as a source of inspiration or hope.

ARTEMIS & ORION

I. Actaeon

Actaeon moved silently through the forest, ignoring the nagging thought in his head, that same gnawing thought that wouldn't leave him be. It wasn't always this way. There was a time he was dashing through the giant trees, running up the barks as quick as a squirrel, all with a wide smile on his face. Now what was he doing? Lumbering through the hard soil, one subdued breath after the other, searching for his dogs. *Why do I even bother?* he thought to himself. His dreams of becoming a renowned hunter were thinning each time the sun set, for even though he lived and breathed the woods, and could hunt anything that had a pulse, none had heard of his name.

It was hot too, and he could feel the stroke of the sun on the back of his neck. He supposed he should've sought out shade underneath a few of the overgrown trees that towered over the nearby riverbank, but then he'd probably fall asleep in the brush. The last man who did that was supposedly carried off by the harpies and torn to shreds, his guts strewn across the forest in one bloody spectacle. It gave Actaeon the creeps, and he suffered a shiver at the mere thought of it as he pressed on, up a steady incline as he blew out a hot breath.

He could hear the river over on his left. Maybe the hounds had gone for a swim? It wouldn't have been the first time he'd caught them goofing off in the water. Bloody dogs. He drew his fingers up to his mouth and was about to blow out a whistle, but he was parched. He pulled the stopper from his flask, brought it to his dry lips and knocked his head back. But there was just a mere lukewarm drop that landed on his tongue and disappeared down his throat, leaving his desert of a mouth wanting more.

'Confound it,' he was about to throw the flask down on the soil, but then he'd have to bend and pick it up again, wouldn't he? And the last time he bent over to grab something, he'd been pounced on by a wildcat that had nearly torn his eyes out. So he squeezed the flask in his hand for all the good it would do and strode his way through the trees, down a muddy slope and onwards until he found the lake.

The water was a tranquil blue and smelled as fresh as it always did. His knees were sore, his back felt stiff and his spirits might've been lower than Hades, but this place put a smile on Actaeon's face. Perhaps the first smile he'd had in quite some time. Trees were scattered around the outskirts of the water; a myriad of auburn and green colours swathed across the leaves. Flowers were growing at the base of knolls in the near distance where clusters of blue, yellow and red petals sprouted here and there. He thought he'd had enough of the sun for one day, but here in this serene outlook, he dared say he quite liked the way the golden rays plunged down onto the waters, lighting up the space between him and the bank.

Funnily enough, he wasn't alone either.

He didn't realise they were naked at first. Three or four women were prancing about in the water, splashing each other and giggling with bright sounding voices. But there was one woman who looked a little more concerned, perhaps vigilant even, eyeing each and every crevice of the forest in the same way he might've done. She drew soap over her flesh, both dark eyes scanning the trees, the rocks, the knolls, the shrubs and then him.

Actaeon felt his chest tighten as his breath caught in his throat. His cheeks grew warm, so warm that he thought his face might explode into flames. What in Olympus' name was he supposed to do now? He coughed into the air to announce his presence and that was met with a collective shriek from the other women who took to submerging in the water. But the vigilant one simply stood there, brow furrowed deep. She made no intention to hide her shame, and unlike the others, she hardly seemed embarrassed at all.

'I'm sorry I've stumbled across you,' Actaeon heard his own voice, but it sounded awfully weak and pathetic. He looked away, held his hands above his head just to show that he was averting his gaze and meant no harm. 'I was just coming to fill up my flask.'

'Pig!' one of the women shouted.

'You should be ashamed of yourself.'

Believe me, I am.

'I wasn't trying to spy on you,' he looked up for just a second out of habit but quickly averted his eyes when they each hissed at him. 'Honestly, I was just trying to fill up my flask.'

'Liar!' came one response.

'I bet he was there the whole time!'

'Disgusting man!'

There's less hostility from the dogs, Actaeon mused to himself. But this was really no time for musings. He allowed himself another look up at the women with the intention of offering one last heart-felt apology before running away. But as he did, he noticed the woman who hadn't moved began to stretch her hands out before her.

'Awful man-pig!' one of the other women hissed from the water.

'I think that's a bit uncalled for,' Actaeon replied. He'd had enough of this. He'd apologised profusely and still they were insulting him. It was an honest mistake to make, was it not?

'Perverted savage,' one of the others snapped.

'It was a mistake,' Actaeon snapped back.

'That's what they all say, rapist pig!'

'Rapist?' Actaeon recoiled. 'But I never even—'

That was when the woman in the middle began to chant something. It was a brief thing—perhaps a mere utterance—but her voice rumbled through the forest, making it seem a slight darker all of a sudden. He allowed himself to take in her features, considering she certainly wasn't shy. Her hair was long and black, dripping wet and scrunched into a long coil down the side of her breast. Her eyes were truly penetrating things, all dark like a murky puddle but yet oddly enthralling at the same time.

He stuffed his fingers in his mouth and blew hard, summoning his dogs. Perhaps it was time to get out of this forest and leave these women to it. They certainly weren't interested in his apologies and he didn't have the mind to stick around and argue with them any further. As always, the two dogs came barrelling through the bushes but this time they were riled, foam at their mouths as they galloped to his side.

'What is it?' he asked them.

But the dogs just glared at the woman across the lake, staring death into her like they could see something he couldn't. He followed their gaze, but he couldn't see anything out the ordinary other than her naked flesh and those poised, sharp eyes.

'You will never speak of what you have seen here to anyone,' the woman spoke from the water, but it was the dogs that answered, barking at her like she'd just yanked their tails.

'Of course,' he thought it best to agree with everything she said as he tried to hush his dogs, but it was no use.

'In fact, as your punishment, you will never speak again or you shall face dire consequences.'

Not speak again? Who did she think she was?

The dogs echoed his thoughts, the pair of them taking a step forward as they growled and barked, both of them leaning forward, inciting her to make the first move. But Actaeon was a better hunter than that. He wouldn't set his dogs on anyone, let alone a naked woman, so he grabbed them quite roughly by the neck and pulled them away, hissing at them to get them to quieten.

'Nod if you understand,' she hissed.

One of his dogs broke forward, but he was quick to pounce on him. He'd never seen the mutts so enraged, so keen to sink their teeth into something. They barked like wild animals, a constant string of throaty woofs that didn't stop until he brought his hand down on the animal's head and shouted, 'Behave!'

'You spoke,' the woman thrusted a finger out at him. 'Now you will face your punishment.'

'Eh?' Actaeon looked up at her. 'What are you talking about, woman?'

He looked down at his legs then, and where there should've been two ruddy boots all caked in mud, there were two hooves. It didn't make sense at first. He just stared at those grey hooves with all the intensity of a man who'd just seen a ghost. He was falling after that. He must've tripped over himself in the panic. He wasn't quite sure. He tried to self-right, a soreness in his back now a hot volcano exploding with spasms in all the wrong places.

He stared up at the trees, too afraid to look down at what was going on with his body. He was thrashing left and right. The pain was too much. He shut his eyes, but they were forced open just as suddenly. The woman was staring at him still, naked and glistening with her hands moving left and right, chanting as she did. He went to swear at her, but his mouth was changing. The entire shape of his jaw morphed along with the shrinking of his head. He cried out, but it was a different sound now, more of an animal's whelp.

There was fur on his arms, fur on his legs—dark, mottled fur all stinking and sweating. He tried to stand on his own two feet. He tried to get up and run. But he couldn't get up. Somehow, he was already standing, but standing on four legs instead of two. His tongue felt heavy and it slipped out of his mouth, hanging by a strange set of teeth on heavy gums that certainly weren't his own. There was something on his head too, a weight of something like a hat, but protruding from his skull, infused with it.

'A stag?' he heard one of the women laugh.

'Such an elegant creature for such a pig,' one of the others hissed.

'A stag will do,' another said. 'After all, you told him not to speak again.'

Stag? Actaeon didn't understand as he stumbled left and then right. He tried to move his arms, but all of a sudden he had two front legs. It felt as if he had been bunched over and while he could still move his head, the rest of his body was this confusing mess of fur, hooves and if he wasn't mistaken, a small tail trailing off his lower back. By the gods, his neck felt massive too. It felt like a terrible tree trunk of a thing nestled under his head.

'You are a stag now,' the woman spoke, her voice still trance-like and deep. It was so deep, it almost sounded like that of a man. 'As a stag, you shall never speak again and therefore cannot possibly relay what it is you have seen here today.'

'Well done, Artemis!' one of the other women shouted in joy.

Artemis? Actaeon found his mouth had become even drier, and where his heart should've been in his chest, it was now unpleasantly beating in his throat. *Artemis? Surely not Artemis, the patron of Sparta?*

'I didn't do anything!' he shouted, but it only came out as a savage sort of moan. 'I just wanted to fill up my flask, I swear it!'

That was when the dogs turned their attention on him. He saw the glint of their four eyes staring back at him, their mouths and snouts wet and shining. The pair of them lunged at him, one black and one brown, with teeth as sharp as anything. You couldn't say they weren't loyal to the hunt, he supposed.

They went right for his face.

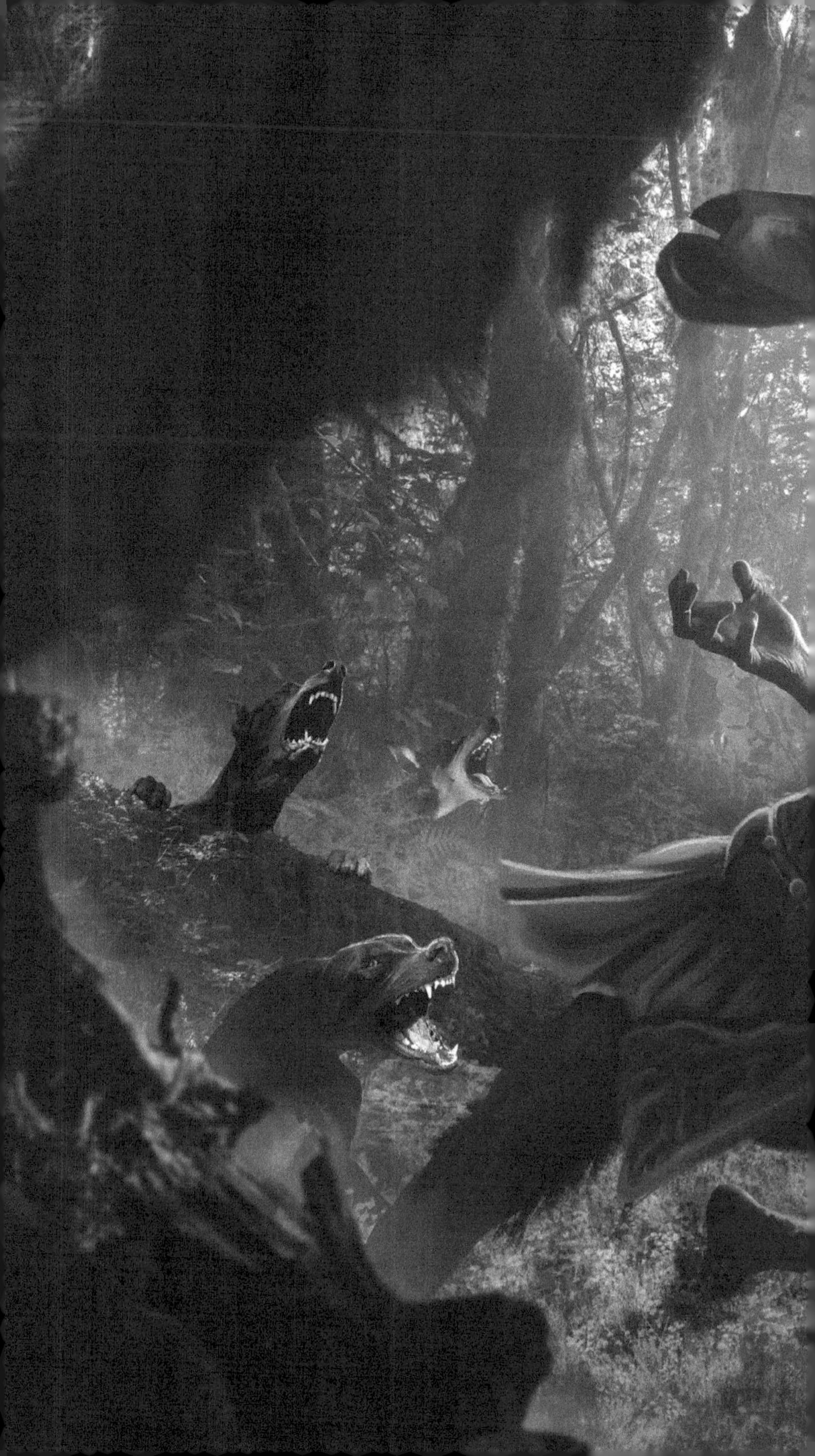

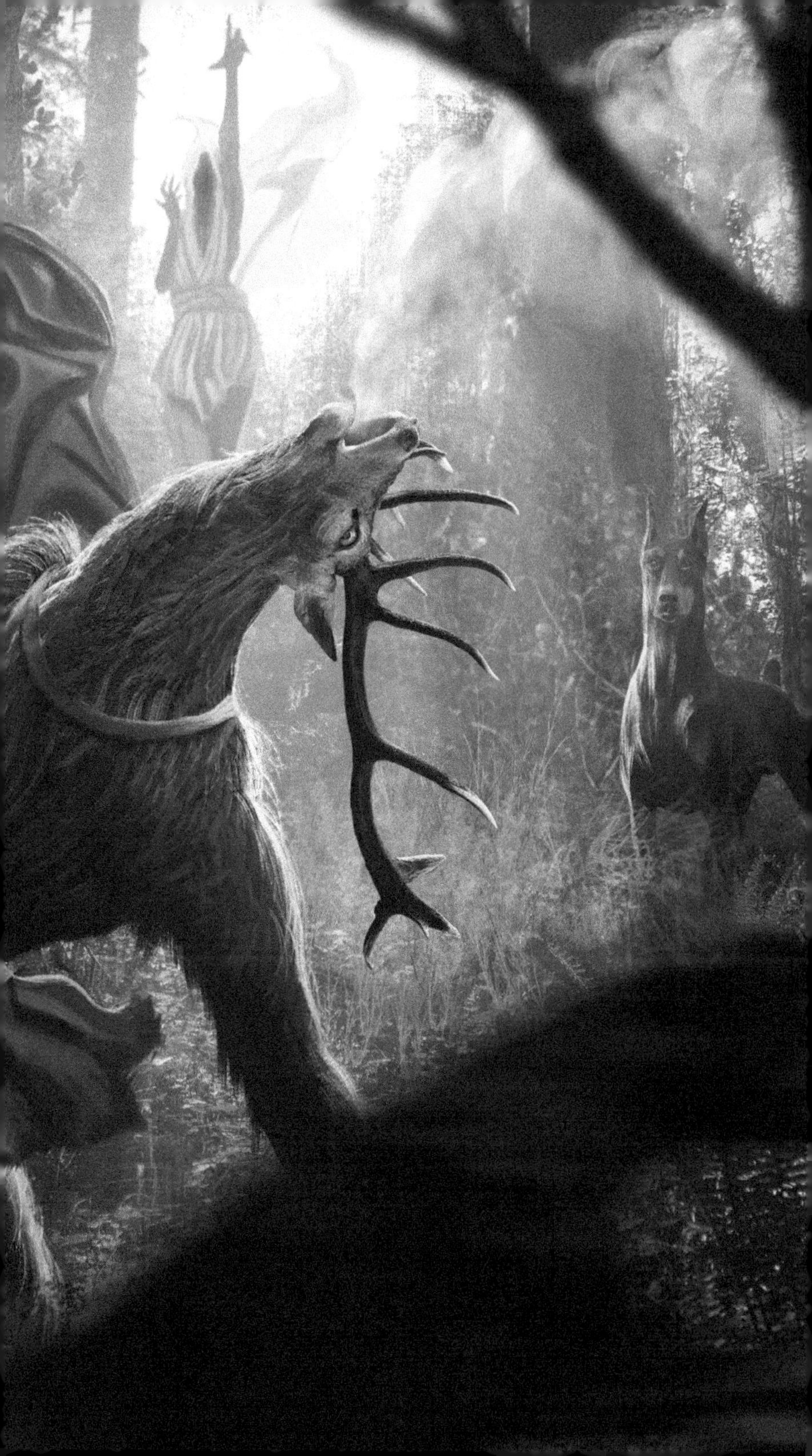

II. An Unfortunate Interference

She tugged on the bowstring, pinching it between her fingers and pulling it back. It made an all too familiar sound. She hadn't nocked an arrow as she stared ahead at the dense yews, a fortress of trees spread before her in the thick of the woods. Any other woman might've turned back at the sight of such an imposing cluster of giant trees, but not Artemis. She checked the dagger at her side, checked the smaller knives in the pouch at her hip and tapped her back to make sure the spear was still there.

Four days had passed since she'd started prowling this far into the woods. She would've liked for the company of the nymphs she'd bathed with at the river, but they were squeamish and cowardly. The mere mention of venturing into the thick of the woods had turned them pale and they'd quickly shoved their clothes back on and scarpered out of sight. It made her think about the hunter who stood before them, eyeing them like the perverted swine he was. Indeed, she'd certainly made the right choice ridding him from this world. His dogs had fed well on him and they'd have no doubt thanked her for it if they could.

She straightened where she stood, wiping the sweat from her face. She squinted up at the sky. The sun was a vengeful thing from above, blazing like her father's temper and sucking all the moisture from the land, drying the blood on the rocks she'd spilled from clipping a deer with an arrow.

But not just any deer. The Ceryneian Hind itself lurked in the woodlands.

She pulled on the bowstring again, practicing that very shot that she'd missed. Any other deer would've taken the fall and tumbled over itself, unable to rise again. But the Ceryneian Hind had landed on its hooves like it hadn't felt a thing as the arrow grazed up against its leg. In fact, it probably *hadn't* felt a thing. It dashed passed her, barely even acknowledging her before darting through the yews and out of sight. She cursed her rotten luck, but the creature had always evaded her, had it not? One day she'd get it. One day she'd—

'Still trying to catch it?' a low rumbling voice came from behind.

An unfortunate interference.

She glanced over her shoulder, none too concerned. Who could hurt her out here in the wilderness? She was the hunter of all hunters. Everyone knew that. She spotted him in the corner of her eye standing there about half the height of the yews. One thing that had always puzzled her was how he had his clothes made so big, for he was a giant amongst men with a chest the size of an entire bull. Not many could sneak up on her like that, and she cursed under her breath knowing that, if he wanted to, he could've put an arrow in her back before she could realise it. Not that she would ever tell him that. The giant was both wise and annoying enough as it was.

'What's it to you?' she swung around, nocked an arrow and took aim at him, drawing the bowstring back in one fluid motion.

A meeker man might've flinched and stumbled over himself like the hunter from before, but the giant, with his infuriating calm face and lacklustre stance, did nothing but stand there as still as a tree himself, unmoved by anything.

'I only wish to help,' he said. Like he'd said a million times before under varying circumstances. Why he didn't leave her alone, she couldn't say.

'I don't need your help,' she snapped.

Only the tweeting of the birds came between them for a moment as they stood there staring at each other, neither one of them too sure of what to say next it seemed. By the gods, he was truly exasperating. Him and his wild, shaggy hair and his sunken face and his irritating jolly little mouth that somehow always managed to find its way to smiling. He towered over her with long, sinewy arms with nothing for weapons save for a small axe at his side. Rumour had it he killed his prey with well-placed chops of his massive hands. How a man that size could creep so quietly was a mystery to her.

'If we hunted it together, we might stand more of a chance,' he said in a slow, deep voice. By Zeus' beard, even the way he spoke got under her skin—so relaxed and poised like nothing could ever shake his nerves. She imagined him giving a monotone sort of response if she had stuck an arrow in his shoulder. Why, he'd probably even compliment her for such a well-placed shot. What a fool he was.

'I don't need help hunting it,' she spun around and started through the yews, following the blood. 'I especially do not need *your* help,' and she stopped to search for his name, only to find she couldn't quite remember it.

'Orion,' he supplied, but if he took offense to her lack of memory he didn't show it. He didn't really show anything either way.

'Good day, Orion,' she said and would've strode off if he didn't stop her in her tracks.

'What was your name again?' he asked.

She nearly dropped her bow at the ridiculousness of it. How did he not know her name? Everyone knew who she was. Not that it mattered much to her, for she'd rather have spent her days in the forests unbothered by the mortals. But regardless, even a dumb giant like him should've known her. Even the hunter from a few days prior recognised her...eventually. It would've been pretty obvious when he realised he had antlers and a tail all of a sudden.

'You don't know my name?' she swung around, trying to hide the annoyance in her voice.

'Er,' he stretched his hands out before him and that stupid, jolly smile only grew wider. 'It begins with an A, right?'

'Artemis,' she snapped. 'Patron of Sparta, the Goddess of the hunt, daughter of Zeus!'

'Not ringing any bells,' he scratched at his face. 'But pleased to make your acquaintance again.'

She opened her mouth to retort, but she'd wasted enough time on him already. She gave him a lingering glance and felt her face scrunching up at the sight of that god-awful smile on his stupid, rugged face. Curses, she'd never met another who'd gotten under her skin like Orion did. She turned and started to march her way through the yews again, eyeing the trail of crimson blood that was spilled in the grass, leaking into the soil.

'That's the wrong way,' he said.

She felt her eye twitch.

'What do you mean?' she replied, biting off each word.

'I'm just saying,' he moved after her, 'if you go that way, the Ceryneian Hind is just going to double back when it gets thirsty and head east for water at the river.'

'So what are you saying?'

It seemed like he left a moment's silence, prolonging the suspense as he revelled in her ignorance. Gods, she was so close to putting an arrow between his eyes.

'I'm saying that if we head east, we can get to the river first and lie in wait for the creature to come to us.'

She shaded her brow with her hand and squinted east. The forest still spread far away into the distance, so far that the river wasn't even visible from this point. There were just trees upon trees with the occasional segue of overgrown bushes, wild and uncut grass, and the deadly patches of bramble. Oh, how she would love to shove him in there. But curses, he was right. Lying in wait for the Ceryneian Hind was a smart idea. It was so smart, that she began to clench her fists because she hadn't thought of it herself.

Worst thing was, it seemed like he knew what she was thinking. 'I'm sure you would've come to that conclusion eventually.'

She gave him the longest, flattest stare, but he only smiled back with his bright eyes sparkling in the sunlight. She would've punched him if she could reach.

'Fine,' she threw her hand eastward. 'Why don't you lead the way then?'

'Oh,' and somehow that smile grew wider. 'So we're working together?'

She felt her eye twitch again.

'If I agree to let you come, will you shut up?'

He let out a gawdy laugh—one that seemed to bring the forest alive with tweets, scurries, flappings and squawks. Artemis wasn't sure if she preferred his stupid permeant smile. At least his smile didn't make noise.

'We have a deal, Artemish.'

'You're pronouncing it wrong,' she growled.

'I know,' he said and laughed again.

...

By the time they made it to the river, the sky was scattered with bright stars and the air had turned cool, perhaps even a little chilly. The river was still and dark. Perhaps dark enough that it could've been mistaken for soil. A cluster of trees were bunched up around the river bed, and a curved line of shrubbery supplied the perfect hiding place to wait for the Ceryneian Hind to come trotting by. If it hadn't already bled out, that is. She liked to think that in a couple of hours, she'd have the beast that had elluded her for so long slung over her shoulder. It would be a truly glorious moment, would it not? Why it almost made the idiot who was crouching down beside her seem bearable. Almost.

'Breathe through your nose,' she hissed at him.

He closed his mouth and started breathing through his nose only to have an accompanying whistling sound. Artemis gave him one hard look, but to Orion's credit, he was more focused on the river, watching each crevice of the bank in the same way Artemis would've normally done. She hated to admit it, but at least he knew what he was looking for.

'It's coming,' he said as he closed his eyes.

'What do you mean it's—'

'Shh,' he held up his hand.

'Don't shh m—'

'Shhh!' he did again, this time holding a finger up.

Artemis opened her mouth to retort, but then she saw movement in the corner of her eye. There was no mistaking the Ceryneian Hind. It didn't move with its usual grace, courtesy of the arrow she'd grazed against its leg, but it didn't limp or struggle either. Its fur was golden and glinted in the night, with matching gilded horns that protruded from its head. It truly was a magnificent beast with dark, expressive eyes and an elongated tail. It certainly would be quite the achievement to tie up its legs and march it on home on her shoulder. She'd brag to her brother upon returning. That would certainly settle who the better sibling was, would it not?

She exchanged a look with Orion and he gave a slow nod. Nothing more needed to be said as the Ceryneian Hind sunk its head down into the water and began to sip. They scrambled out of the bushes in silence, picking their way carefully across the bank, around boulders and dried up branches. The slightest sound would set the deer off and then it would have all been for nothing. But Artemis certainly wouldn't be doing that. No, she might've been able to skip across the water and pounce on a regular deer, but the

Ceryneian Hind was no regular deer, and the pair of them knew better than to take a risk like that here. Well, at least Artemis knew that much.

Orion moved deceptively fast and she found herself taking strides just to keep up with him. She kept glancing at the deer to make sure its head was still submerged underwater. If it looked up, it might not have seen them courtesy of the darkness, but if it looked hard enough it would no doubt make out Orion's lanky frame and her own slender shape skipping over rocks after him. By the time they made it around the bank, she realised that Orion was heading straight for it.

'Wait,' she whispered and grabbed him by the wrist. 'You can't sneak up on it, you moron. Let me shoot it first and then you can grab it when it tries to run.'

She could see him smiling in the starlight. 'It won't hear me.'

He turned to move off, and fighting the urge to snap at him for such arrogance, she crept after him, keeping low to the ground. For just a moment, the Ceryneian Hind looked up, snout glistening and wet. Artemis was sure it would turn and see them before darting off back the way it had come. She held her breath, heart thumping in her throat, but then the deer dunked its head underwater again and drank.

Orion moved to the left, barely crouching as he hopped over a rock and scurried around the creature. He was closer than her now, close enough to the deer that if he threw his axe with enough force he'd be able to stun it. That would give her enough time to move in and sink her weight on top of it before slashing its throat. But he didn't go for his axe. In fact, she was sure he'd forgotten about it completely.

She hissed to grab his attention, sure that the deer would snap its head up and see them.

Orion looked at her and mouthed, 'What?'

'Axe,' she mouthed back, pointing at his hip.

He merely waved dismissively at her as he readied his bare hands. The man was a fool. Indeed, she had deduced that a while ago, but this was idiotic even by his standards. He might've had giant hands, but he couldn't kill the Ceryneian Hind with them alone. She opened her mouth to shout at him, but then slammed a hand over her lips. She could live with him making such a mistake, but her? No, she would not be so foolish. She quietly shrugged the bow off her shoulder, nocked back an arrow with practiced smoothness and took aim at the deer.

'Don't,' he mouthed at her. 'Let me do it.'

'What are you going to do?' she mouthed back incredulously. 'Jump on it?'

'Well, yes,' he mouthed back like it was obvious.

'I've got a clear shot,' she returned, 'just sit there and you can jump on it after I've fired.'

'That's not necessary,' he waved his hands. 'I can do this.'

'You unbelievable idiot,' she mouthed back. 'I've never met a fool so incredibly dense. Are you stupid? You must be stupid. Don't ever follow me again. As the daughter of Zeus, the patron of Sparta and the goddess of the hunt, I command you to leave right this instant you overgrown, deluded, abomination of nature.'

He looked at her for a long moment and then said out loud, 'What?'

The Ceryneian Hind's head shot up and glanced right at her. She saw Orion leap for it, but he was too slow. She let the arrow fly. The deer sprang forward, tried to dart to the left and speed off. But her arrow was faster and it caught the creature square in its rump, drawing a cry from its mouth. Orion landed on top of it. A scuffle broke loose, but the giant was too strong. She could see its legs kicking out from beneath him. It squealed into the night, but there was no rescue coming for it.

'Draw your axe, idiot!'

'No need,' he shrugged and delivered a well-placed chop across its neck. And just like that, the creature was still.

He stood up from it, but gone was his jolly smile and in its place was something sombre. If she wasn't mistaken, there was a tear in his eye. A cold wind blew across the river, ruffling her hair and slithering across her neck. Gone was the elation of having hunted the very creature that had eluded her for so long. In fact, if she was honest, it was hardly a satisfying feeling at all. The Ceryneian Hind hardly looked majestic anymore with one cut up leg, crimson blood surging out from the wound where the arrow was buried into its flesh. Its head was twisted the wrong way and its golden antlers were spoiled by specks of mud and dirt.

'I don't like killing things,' Orion said at last, wiping his face.

'You're a hunter,' she said, perplexed. 'The thrill of the hunt is what we live for.'

'Doesn't always make it right though, does it?' he sighed. 'I mean, did we really need to hunt this creature? Neither one of us are particularly hungry.'

'Yes,' she stammered. 'Well...it's not about eating, is it?'

'Then what is it about?' he turned to face her. 'Why do we do this, when we could just as easily let things live?'

'Well, because...' and she stopped to fetch the answer.

But she couldn't find it.

'Deer is all yours,' he said with the shake of his head and quietly walked off into the forest.

'Wait!' she called after him. 'Don't you want your share?'

'You keep it,' he called back and then he was gone.

That just left her staring down at the Ceryneian Hind. It was a strange feeling to stare down at the creature she'd spent so long trying to hunt, dead and ripe for the picking. She could skin the furs and net a hefty price for such a thing. Or she could sell the flesh and let the simple mortals fiend and relish over such sacred meat. How many times had she dreamt of this moment, after all?

So why did it feel so hollow? Somehow that giant ogre of a man had tainted this moment for her. She should've been jumping for joy and hooting up to Olympus in triumph. But instead, all she could do was question why it was that she felt the need to cut this animal down—or any other animal for that matter. Did they not have the right to live as she did?

The question burned in her mind as she bound the creature's legs and slung the deer over her shoulder. Perhaps, maybe, her brother would raise her spirits when he saw what she'd brought home and she could find some joy again in having achieved her goal. But the creature was a cumbersome one to carry. She'd done it a thousand times before. Sometimes she had carried even larger creatures that felt like they weighed tons.

But this one felt heavier than the rest.

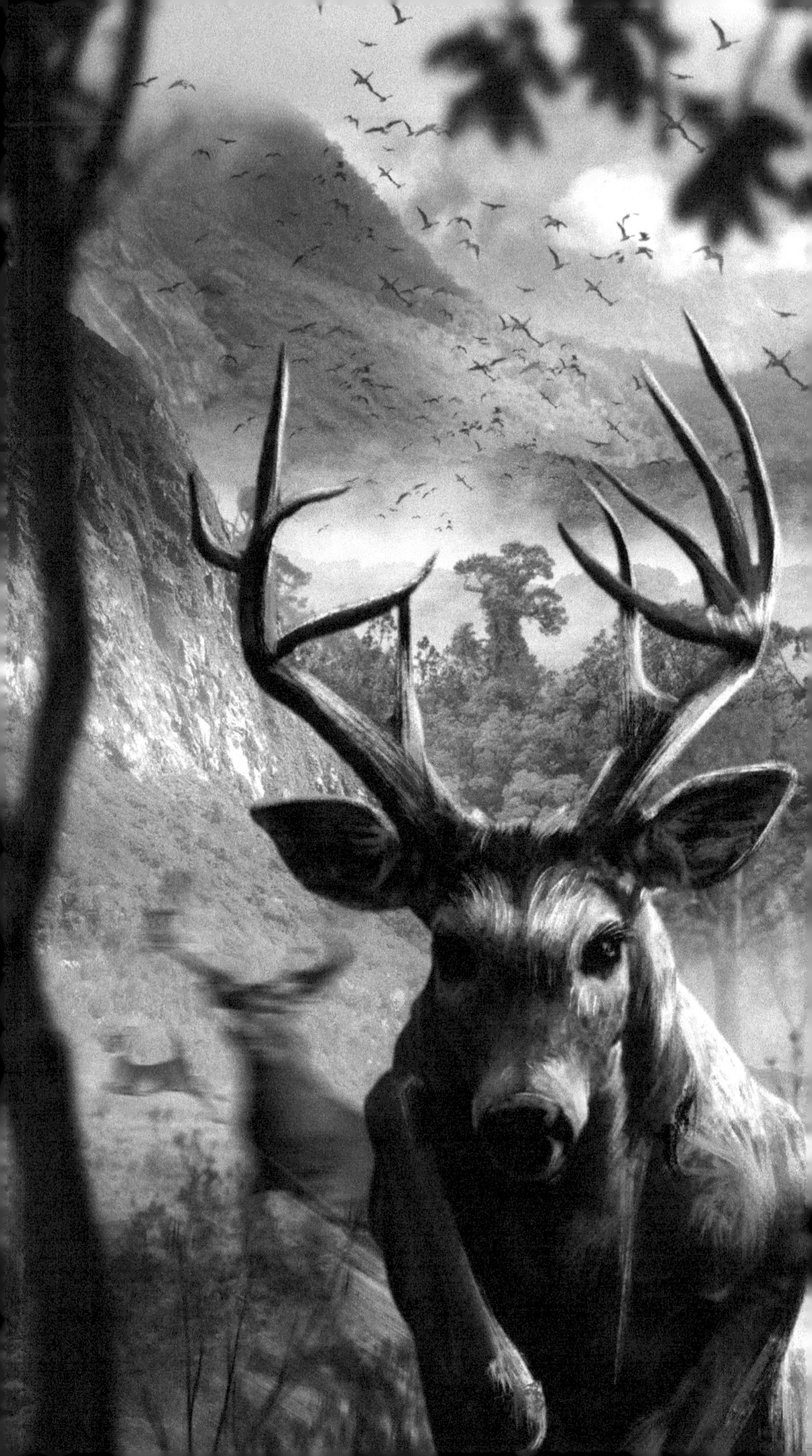

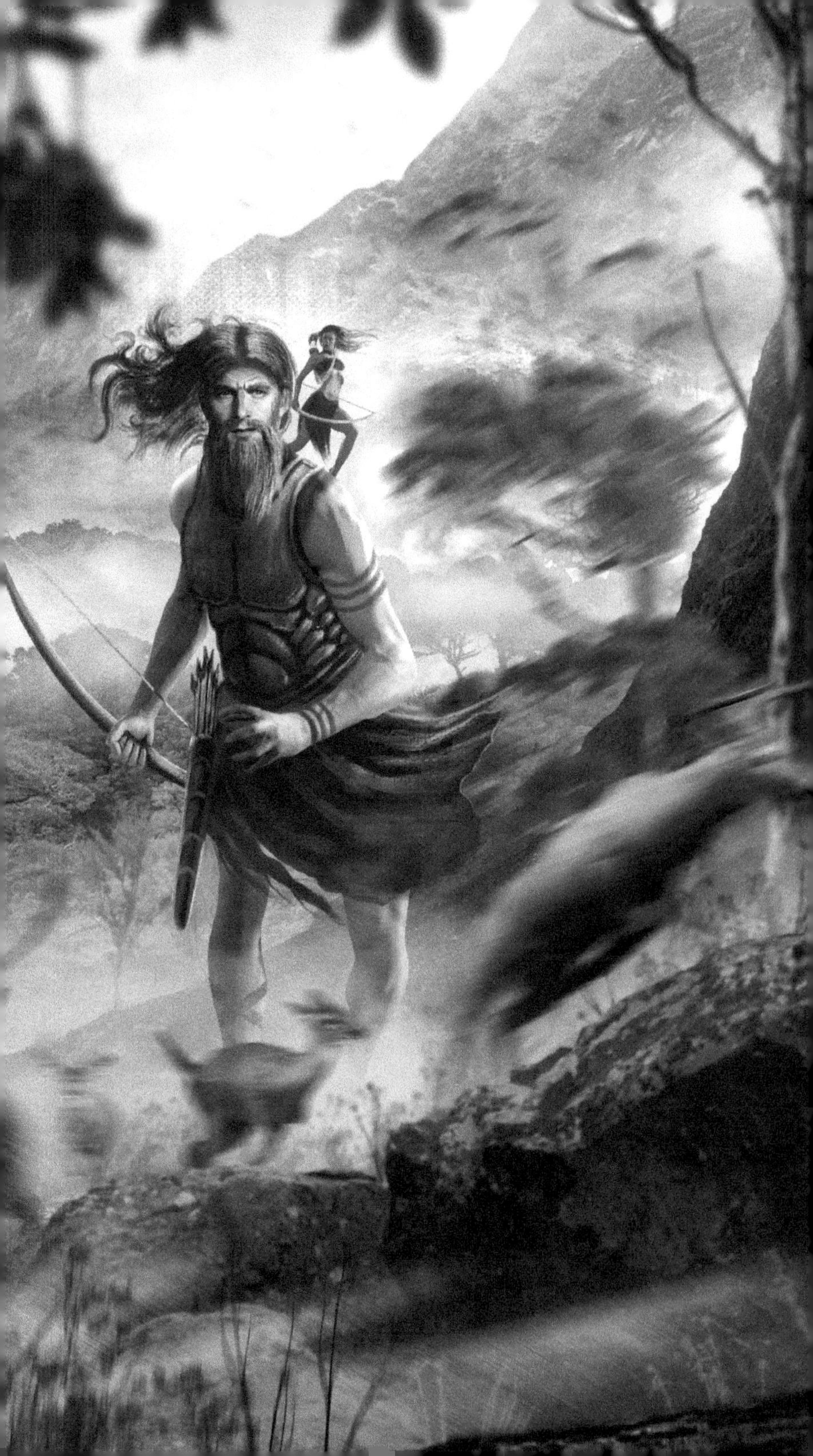

III. Hungry

One bird fell with a thump, the arrow jutting out of its side, pinning its wing against its chest. A sliver of blood drooled out from the wound and spilled onto the grass, turning a small patch of it red. Artemis winced. Far be it from her to ever wince, but when Apollo shot several more out of the trees, it had her grabbing hold of her own head.

A few days had passed since she'd brought back the Ceryneian Hind, and while Apollo was all smiles and joy, she herself found her smile was forced. Killing the deer had only left her feeling hollow. Even watching the birds litter the grass before her made her question why they were doing this. Why were innocent creatures falling right before her eyes with no real purpose?

'Aha!' Apollo rejoiced. 'Did you see that shot, sister? I nailed that one bird with my eyes closed!'

'Good for you, brother,' she intoned.

Just a few short days ago she'd watched him with a certain pride as he leapt about with his bow, flipping and somersaulting more like a performer than anything else. His golden hair flowed angelically. He was a handsome man, her brother. But then again, a son of Zeus would be, would he not? Apollo knew it too. Anyone with a pair of eyes could see that in the regal way he dressed. Even when hunting he wore his golden bands around his wrists and the finest silks and fabrics for his tunic. Even his bow was a large and ostentatious thing dressed with ribbons and feathers.

But now, as she watched him frolic back and forth with his perfectly white smile, did she begin to feel weighed upon by Orion's words. *Why do we do this?*

'You must be hungry,' she called out to her brother. 'You've killed nearly twenty birds this morning.'

'I already ate,' he shrugged and brought down another bird, this time with a nest. There was an unmistakable crunch as it hit the ground.

She winced again, 'Maybe we ought to find something else to do.'

'Something else?' he frowned whilst taking aim at another bird. 'Like what?'

'I hear the mortals are planning the festival in Sparta. As their patron, perhaps we might lend our assistance. You know how traditional they like to be.'

'*You're* their patron,' he said almost bitterly as he brought down another bird. 'If you want to help them, then go do that.'

'Fine,' she grabbed her quiver and slung it over her shoulder. 'I'll see you back at home then.'

'Oh hold on!' Apollo hissed. 'Look up there!'

She followed his gaze and saw a tiny bird teetering on a branch. It had small yellow feathers, squawking loudly for its mother who no doubt probably laid on the ground with an arrow in her stomach, courtesy of her brother's fine marksmanship. It hobbled its way along the branch in an almost comical fashion, stumbling over its own feet and flapping on its stomach in a race to get back up. She'd never really stopped to appreciate such a thing before. The innocence of it even had her producing a limp smile.

Until she saw Apollo take aim at it.

'Wait!' she barked and shoved him to the side.

'What are you playing at?' he shouted back and, together, they watched the arrow climb the sky and narrowly miss the tiny bird who was still clamouring on its stomach.

'Haven't you killed enough of them?' she swung her hand around at the floor.

He frowned and focused on her still full quiver, 'Oh, I'm sorry, sister. I didn't realise I was hogging all the kills. Go ahead.'

'I don't want the kills,' she snapped. 'I'm not hungry.'

'It's not about being hungry,' he laughed.

'Then what is it about?' She pressured him with the same question she'd been asked, but unlike her, he didn't even take a moment to consider it. Only a dark shadow came upon his face.

'This is about what that brainless giant said to you, isn't it?' He rolled his eyes and threw his hands up like he'd told her this a thousand times. Truth was, he actually had. 'We are hunters. This is what we do. Most of these animals will die anyway. All we are doing is fast-forwarding their destiny. They do not feel a thing. There are other creatures out there who will savagely tear them apart. What we do is rather humane in comparison.'

'Doesn't make it right though, does it?' she said and realised she'd stolen the words right out from Orion's mouth again.

Apollo just looked at her with a vacant expression but she returned it with a stern one of her own.

'Fine,' he threw the bow over his shoulder with a huff. 'I won't kill the stupid baby bird. Are you happy now? Are you happy knowing that some hound will come and chew its body up, starting with its legs? As opposed to the quick death I can offer it right this very moment?'

'I'll be happy if you don't undermine me, and if for once in your life, you have some regard for something other than yourself.'

Apollo opened his mouth to defend himself, but only exasperated sounds came out. He lifted his finger up at his sister, but still no words followed as he went red in the face.

'I'm sorry for my harsh words, brother. But sometimes I think we need to consider our actions before we commit to them. If we needlessly slay creatures for fun, does that not make us murderous, or vengeful or wicked for that matter?'

Apollo walked over towards her, lifted his hands close to his face and spoke through them, saying very slowly, 'What kind of goddess of the hunt doesn't hunt?'

She wasn't going to dignify that with an answer. At least, not until she had an answer worth supplying. Instead, she merely inclined her head and said, 'I will see you at the festival, Apollo.'

He merely shook his head at her and stalked away, eyeing the baby bird in the tree as he did.

She let out a sigh. Indeed, what kind of goddess of the hunt didn't hunt? She looked around at the sea of dead birds at her feet and couldn't help but feel responsible. After all, she'd sat by and watched him shoot down those birds. In fact, how many times had she done the same thing with him? How many times had the pair of them pounced on a bear, dissecting it with every unnecessary slash, avoiding its throat so that the thrill of the kill could go on longer. Indeed, she was as much to blame for these deaths as he was.

'At least one got away,' came a voice from behind.

She went for her bow immediately, but stopped half-way when she realised it was Orion's voice. It was hardly a mistakable voice, after all. He loomed out from between two stark trees and paced his way over, his eyes fixed on the tiny bird who had finally gotten off of its stomach and was flapping back and forth, tweeting loudly. Maybe Apollo was right. It had no mother now, no means to gather food and certainly no protection. Had she saved it? Or had she merely postponed the inevitable?

'What are you doing here?' she asked, dragging her gaze away from the bird and on to him.

'Just passing by,' he said. 'Couldn't help but hear your little argument with your brother.'

'The last person I caught spying on me I turned into a stag and his own dogs then ripped him apart,' she said in a tone that should've had him apologising.

But he merely gave off that accursed smile of his.

'Seems like you're starting to see the world my way,' he said as he paced his way around the corpses of the birds.

'No!' she fired off adamantly and then softer, 'Maybe.'

He smiled all-knowingly. It kind of reminded her of her father for just a moment. 'If I didn't know any better, I'd say you were close to making up your mind about hunting altogether.'

'And if I was?' she felt her hand itching to go for her blade to shut him up once and for all.

He held his hand up at her, 'It would make us work better as partners.'

'Partners?' she blushed. Damn it, why was she blushing? Surely not for this annoying fool?

'Yes,' he nodded. 'Hunting partners. For food of course. Believe it or not, I thought we made a good team.'

'Oh,' she cleared her throat. 'Yes. *Hunting* partners.'

'What did you think I meant?'

'Nothing!' she snapped. 'That's exactly what I thought you meant.'

'Oh, okay then.'

There was an ever looming silence that came next. The birds weren't tweeting on the account that most of them were dead, but the trees rustled in the calm breeze. Artemis couldn't quite understand why she suddenly felt so inept in his presence. Why, she'd never felt such a horrible feeling. Her hands were sweating and she nearly dropped the bow because of it. He stood equally shifty too, his head glancing back and forth, unable to meet her eyes all of sudden as his cheeks grew rosy.

'I should leave,' she spat the words out so fast she was sure he wouldn't understand them.

'Ah,' he said, now it was him clearing his throat, 'I thought we might join forces again and venture the forest.'

Her heart was thumping. Why in Zeus' name did she suddenly feel compelled to say yes? Just a night or two ago she had contemplated putting an arrow between his grey, idiot face.

'I can't,' she took a step back. 'I...I have plans.'

'Ah,' he deflated and inclined his head. 'I understand.'

He moved to walk away and she supposed she should've just kept her mouth shut—should've let him walk on and be free of him for good this time.

'It's not because I don't want to,' the words flew from her mouth. 'I have the festival in Sparta to attend.'

'Right, the festival.' His eyes lit up. 'Of course. I hope you enjoy your evening.'

'You're welcome to join me,' she said, her chest tightening, knees rocking back and forth. She'd only ever felt this way when staring down a formidable creature in the wild, and even then, it was a fleeting thing. Whatever this was had her in its grip and it wasn't letting go.

'I thought you might go with your brother,' he said.

'Who?' she asked before shaking her head. 'Apollo! Right, yes! Of course. My brother has a string of women who I'm sure would attend the festival with him. I'm sure he'd rather spend the festival with them than with me.'

'He sounds foolish,' Orion remarked.

'You'll get no argument from me.'

'That makes a change,' he smirked.

'Don't start,' she warned him. 'Don't make me rescind my offer. You helped me claim the Ceryneian Hind, the least I can do to repay you is bring you along for an evening of fun.'

'An evening of fun?' And now it was he who took a step back.

'Yes, at the festival,' she clarified.

'Oh,' he glanced away. 'Yes, the festival. Of course.'

'What did you think I meant?'

'Nothing,' he shook his head feverishly. 'I'll see you at the festival.'

IV. The Perfect Brother

He flashed his own brilliant smile in the basin, staring down at his perfect reflection in the cool blue water.

Indeed, he was blessed with good looks, perhaps even more than his father in his prime. He ran his fingers through his blonde hair, shaping it just the way he liked, combing it with his hand until it was perfect. Everything had to be perfect, especially for today. It wasn't every day that the people of Sparta threw a festival in his honour...well, Artemis' honour. Still, he'd relish in the glory nonetheless. They all knew that without him, Artemis wouldn't have made it this far at all.

'Hi,' he extended his hand in front of his reflection, almost knocking over a candle on the side of the sink surrounded by facial powders and tiny bottles of very flammable liquids. 'I'm Apollo,' he said to his reflection, pretending it was a pretty young lady that he was about to pounce on.

But that wasn't quite right. The tone could've been better and he should've stood up straight, should've smiled a little more and made his eyes widen a slight so they could really appreciate the still, cool blueness that resided there.

'Hi,' he said again, this time avoiding the candle as he reached out his hand. 'I'm Apollo.'

He scrunched his face; that was truly worse than the last attempt.

No woman would swoon for him if he went about spouting a weak and measly introduction. No, there was something missing. He was wearing his orange tunic, one that was sewn with golden thread making for intricate looking patterns on the breast and the sleeves. He'd gotten the fancy sandals out—the ones that had a leather base making them click with every footstep. He smelled divine too, so much so, that he brought his nose down against his armpit and breathed in the aqua freshness. Any woman would be lucky to be in his presence.

'Hi,' he said once more as he reached his hand out and to his own shock, supplied a sly sort of wink that he thought went down a treat. 'I'm Apollo, son of Zeus.'

Perfect!

The door creaked open behind him and he spun around to find his sister trudge through the doorway, boots still muddy from the forest. She wore the same ripped and tattered cloak that he was sure she had on the day before. There was darkness about her eyes, her face speckled with dirt from the forest, and if he wasn't mistaken, she had a musky scent about her too.

'You're not ready?'

'For what?' she slurred as if she was drunk, swinging her bow on the floor and chucking herself into the seat by the window.

He blinked. Surely she wasn't this dense. 'The festival!'

'Oh,' she lifted her head. 'Yes, I'm ready.'

'You're going like that?' he made a horrified sound. Surely she couldn't be serious.

'What's wrong with how I'm going?' she muttered.

'You...you look ridiculous?'

She gave him a long, wavering look. 'So do you.'

'I do not!' he blurted out as he stormed towards her. 'You can't show up to a festival in your honour wearing that!'

'It's better than that ridiculous garment you made me wear last year,' she hissed out the side of her mouth.

He remembered it well: a silk tunic, milky white with a golden strap to keep everything in place. It truly was a magnificent garment when worn with the sandals he'd picked out for her.

'It wasn't ridiculous,' he defended it. 'It was gorgeous and sophisticated and—'

'Brazen!' she snapped.

'So it was a little short on the leg,' he shrugged.

'My entire thigh was exposed.'

'No one said anything,' he noted.

'They said enough with their eyes,' she stood up sharply.

'Well, you sure can't go out looking like that, can you?' he gave her one sorry look, the same sort of look he might've given to a stomped flower. 'Come, if we hurry we'll be able to fit you into something more appropriate of a goddess. Then we can enter Sparta together.'

Her face dropped and a look of apprehension built about her dark eyes.

'What is it?' he touched his face and then his tunic. 'Is there something crooked?'

'Now don't get sensitive,' she stepped towards him.

'Me?' he didn't like where this was going. 'Sensitive about what?'

She made a nervous glance to the side, perhaps the only nervous gesture he'd ever seen her make. She'd always been a pillar of strength. Like a sturdy tree, incapable of showing any emotion other than strength and indifference. But there was only a fraction of that now as she took to fidgeting with her sleeves.

'I've invited Orion to join me this year,' she told him guiltily, like she knew it was wrong.

Snake, he was about to call her. How could she do this to him? How could she go to the festival with someone else? All these years they had done everything together. Why, they'd been through so much that all she should've ever needed was him.

'Him?' he tried to hide the venom from his words, but it was there all right. 'That dumb giant?'

'He's not dumb,' she looked up immediately. 'He's a skilled hunter who—'

'Dumb, stupid giant!' Apollo slammed his fist on the basin and the bottles rattled in the following silence.

'It's just a festival, brother.' Artemis spoke, trying to use that reason in her voice. But that only infuriated him more. It always did.

'Since when do you like men?' he swung his head around at her. 'Bathing with nymphs and staring daggers into any man who looked at you. If I didn't know any better, I'd say—'

'Enough!' she lifted her hand. 'I'll be attending the festival with Orion as I promised. If you are feeling lonely, brother, then I suggest you find someone to go with as well. There are plenty of women in Sparta who will jump at the chance to be by your side.'

'But I want you by my side,' he said with gritted teeth. Why would she do this to him? And with that mindless giant as well? For the longest time she had shared his sentiment and had spoken about what a weird, horrendous creature he was. 'Is that all it takes to win your heart? To be stalked by some odious fool?'

'He is not a fool,' she defended him. 'He's right about quite a few things, in fact.'

'Like what?'

'Well,' she thrust a finger at him, 'you kill too much.'

A smile fought its way onto his face, 'What are you talking about? You mean today with the birds? They're birds! Who cares if they live or die?'

'All we've ever done our whole lives is kill. I never questioned it before yesterday when we caught the deer, but now I can't stop. Why do we do this? Do these animals not have the right to live as we do?'

Apollo couldn't believe what he was hearing. One mere moment with that confounded giant and now she was half the goddess she once was. In fact, to call her a goddess now seemed like a disservice. She sounded ordinary—mortal.

'You shouldn't let the words of a mindless giant cloud your judgement, sister.'

'He is not a mindless giant!' she insisted.

'That's what you always said. You said he annoyed you, that he got under your skin. Now it looks like he'll be getting under you entirely!'

'Why do you care so much?' she roared.

He recoiled at that and found himself back up against the basin, heart beating fast, a sheen of sweat built up around his brow. His head was throbbing at the thought of it—the thought of that lanky, ugly giant with his hand around her waist, whispering in her ear with his dirty, fat tongue. His fingers began to curl around the edge of the dresser, squeezing the wood so tight it almost broke off in his hand.

'I don't care,' he finally said and marched his way off to the window. 'Go on your farce of a date. See if I care!'

He thought she might've come over and given him a hug. That was the least he deserved, wasn't it? She was abandoning him. She was abandoning him for some cumbersome oaf who was half the hunter either one of them was. He was filth. No, he was less than filth. He was nothing. Nothing! But she didn't come over. In fact, she didn't say a word as he listened to her footfalls grow quieter and quieter until she was out of the room.

That made him hate Orion more.

V. The Festival

Artemis felt ridiculous.

She hadn't found anything suitable to wear except for her hunting gear, but she supposed Apollo had a point. The people of Sparta had thrown a festival in her honour. The least she could do was dress for the part.

'You look erm...very beautiful,' Orion stammered, red in the cheeks at the sight of her, one side of his face trying to gawk at her and the other side pulling away out of respect.

She hadn't worn that scandalous thing Apollo brought her last year, but the dress she now wore felt as unnatural as wearing two different shoes. It was made from silk, as far as she could tell, a pale greenish colour that fastened at her chest by a broach, a ruby at its centre. The dress didn't flow down her body the way she would've preferred, but instead stuck to her, supposedly pronouncing her every curve. As far as Artemis was concerned, all it did was make it more prone to rip if she started running.

Still, she was glad she'd made some effort. After all, Orion had thrown on a more dignified looking tunic as oppose to his dirty, muddy cloak and his torn breeches.

'Thank you,' she replied, fighting the urge to smile. What sorcery was this? Just a day ago she was the huntress of the wild. Now she felt like a giggling nymph. Maybe Apollo was right. Maybe Orion had gotten in her head a little too much. But was that a bad thing?

The square was enormous and perhaps wide enough that it would take Orion a good a few leaps with his mighty legs to move from one side to the other. Sheer white buildings towered all around them, glittering with tall windows and artsy gables that were strewn with the faintest touch of creeper. It was crawling with people. There were all sorts of men and women in their vibrant-coloured tunics; a sea of beiges, oranges, and greens spread out all around her. The whole thing made her slightly dizzy.

An army of workmen were still circled around a wooden statue, heaving it up and off of the ground until it stood upright and proud. It was a statue of herself, a statue with a softer nose admittedly, but she could forgive them for that. They'd captured her poised expression well enough.

'Is that meant to be you?' Orion nudged her a little too hard and she stumbled to the right. He made no intention of apologising as he guffawed to himself at the statue.

'Yes!' she snapped. 'The people have spent days making this in my honour.'

'Right,' Orion intoned.

A lane opened up in between the tall buildings where it looked as if a patch of the forest had been scooped up and neatly dumped in the space. But the grass here was a trimmed, vivid green carpet that looked smooth to touch. There were flowers growing in regimented clusters, rows and rows of multi-coloured petals all sorted into a specific grouping. Bushes and trees were squeezed into the area, all of them clipped and assembled in a way too perfect for nature. A pond sat at the inner centre, attracting the company of two dragonflies that hovered over the water, teasing a mean looking frog that glared at them intently.

'What ever happened to the Ceryneian Hind?' Orion asked.

She didn't like to think about the golden deer. It had been easier in the moments before, when the elation of sinking her knife into the back of an animal was still a palpable thing. Now it was nothing but a grey sort of feeling that filled her with dread.

'I buried it,' she said with a tilt of her head. 'It seemed like the most respectful thing to do.'

'I think you did the right thing,' Orion agreed.

'I suppose the right thing would've been to avoid killing it at all. Tell me, why did you help me do that if you feel guilty about killing?'

He took a moment, glancing over at a man who was juggling three or four balls much to the amusement of children.

'If I didn't, then I don't think you would've learned the lesson. It's one thing for me to tell you excessive butchering is bad. But for you to experience that dread yourself? That's more than compelling enough, wouldn't you agree?'

'I wish my brother would feel compelled,' she sighed.

'Put him from your mind for now,' he calmly told her. 'You promised me fun, did you not?'

She smirked, 'I suppose I did.'

It wasn't long before the entire square was swarmed with people. Women were swaddled in elaborate dresses, some young and some old, but both equally merry as they moved amongst each other. The men were less enthused and seemed too busy trying to get out the way of Orion who towered over them all like a great, wandering oak that had broken away from the fixtures by the pond.

Stalls were set up in various sections along the square operated by smartly dressed men selling divine smelling foods, the aromas of spices meeting Artemis' keen nose made her mouth water. A fanfare of string music soon siphoned through the air as musicians took to podiums and began to play in seamless union.

'Seems like they really went all out for you,' Orion mumbled.

She would've replied, but she was soon flocked by her people—all of them surrounding her like buzzards before a corpse. They were cheering her name, most of it all just one blurred echo of noise that came with a hundred smiles on faces she'd never seen before. They shoved gifts into her hands: golden coins, parchments, plates of foods, the occasional chalice, fruits, books and at one point a fist sized diamond.

'Artemis! Look what we've made for you,' some children pulled at her arm. She almost missed them standing beneath her, dwarfed amongst the other adults brushing up to get the best look at her.

'Oh,' she stared down at their portraits. 'Why, they're very—'

'Artemis!' a man shoved his way in front of them. 'Would you do me the honour and turn me into a bird? I've always wanted to fly.'

'I erm—'

'Artemis,' another man shoved him out the way. 'Will you marry my son? He's very rich and—'

'Artemis!' This time a chubby woman with red marks on her face stood before her. 'Artemis, please! You have to help me. I've tried losing weight but I can't, and now my partner won't marry me.'

'I'm really sorry to hear that—'

'Artemis!' Someone barrelled in front of her. 'Artemis, you look beautiful as always!'

'Thanks, I—'

'We love you, Artemis!' two women who could've been twins damn near screamed it in her face.

She stumbled backwards and thought she might fall. But then she felt his hands on her lower back as he effortlessly lifted her up off her feet.

'Oh,' she said, shocked.

'I didn't mean to grab you,' he stammered. 'I simply saw you falling and—'

'No, no it's fine.' She placed a hand on his chest to hush him, her other hand limply held onto the back of his neck. When did that even happen?

'I guess I ought to set you down,' he said, still cradling her.

'Uh, er yes!' she had to gulp before nodding hard. 'Yes, that would be a good idea.' Although she wasn't sure why. A part of her quite liked being scooped up and carried like that.

'Speech!' someone was pulling at her left arm.

'Yes, come Artemis!' another pulled her to the right. 'Share your wisdom with us!'

'She's going to speak!' someone beckoned over the rest.

'Everyone shut up!' someone screamed.

Before long, she was being led away by two priestesses who held her either side, more like guards escorting a prisoner than anything else. Ahead was a gilded podium from where she supposed she'd be making this speech. Yet again she hadn't prepared anything to say. What did any of the other goddesses say to their people anyhow? From what she understood, other goddesses didn't even acknowledge their flocks. What use would she have at this? All she knew was how to kill things, and given how that was going, she started wondering if she was good for anything at all.

'Orion!' she swung her head around to see how far behind the giant was.

'I'll catch you up,' he shrugged as men and women half his size brushed past him while he carefully manoeuverd around them, trying not to crush anyone under his massive feet.

It made her smile how delicate he looked.

VI. Zeus' Son

Her speeches were stupid.

Everyone knew her speeches were abysmal. Apollo sure knew it. He'd heard her recite them before and had to force a smile to receive her monotone voice and dead words. It was like watching wood speak, if wood could be any more rigid and lacklustre that is. He could feel his fists clenching by his sides and had to hold them against his thighs to stop them from shaking with rage.

That was when he saw that imbecilic giant stumbling this way and that as he carefully placed his feet in and around the careless mortals. Apollo knew that, if he was that big, he'd have just stamped them all until they physically began diving out of his way. The giant was too patient—too passive—too flaming stupid. He was bumbling about with that gawdy smile on his face as if he weren't inconvenienced at all. Apollo had seen the way he swept Artemis off her feet, a lusty look in his eye. That horrid, stinking ogre of a man was likely going to sling his sister over his shoulder and have his way with her right in the thick of the woods. Probably in the mud like pigs.

'Savages,' he hissed through his teeth. Not that anyone could hear him. The foolish mortals were bunched up like cattle all around him, staring mindlessly as their precious goddess took the podium. Apollo didn't know why they weren't shoving him up there instead. At least he'd be able to captivate them, to work them, to give them some grand speech to remember throughout the ages. What could Artemis say? *Don't kill animals. Don't hurt innocents. Don't do all the things I've been doing since I was born?* What a hypocrite she'd become.

It was all Orion's fault.

Apollo watched the back of the giant's wrinkled, splotchy head and wanted to spit on it, punch it, kick it. If it wasn't for Orion, then both he and Artemis could've been going on about their lives the way they always had. There would be none of this moral confusion that now stumped his sister. No, it would be as it should've been. The two of them together, forever.

'You,' Apollo hissed again as he shoved his way through the crowd. 'This is all your fault.'

He could hear Artemis giving her speech, but it was just a meaningless sound. Even if he stopped to listen he'd probably had to have strained. The woman muttered and mumbled at the best of times, after all. She had no skill at articulating herself, nor presenting herself. Not at all like Apollo. Why yes, he was smart, sophisticated, handsome and regal. Artemis should've recognised that in him instead of fawning over that mindless, dull, stupid, idiotic giant who—

'Hi,' he turned around with a wide grin on his face and extended his massive hand as fluently as Apollo had done in front of the basin. 'I'm Orion.'

Apollo tried to reach out in that same practiced manner, but his hand felt heavy all of a sudden and he didn't quite like being so dwarfed. He fumbled with his sleeve and looked down at his shoes for a moment too long before sheepishly reaching out.

'Hi,' he mumbled. 'I'm Zeus, son of Apollo.'

'Eh?' the giant raised an eyebrow.

Apollo's heart shot up into his throat and he came horribly close to punching himself in the face for such a blunder. 'I said, I'm Apollo, son of Zeus!'

'Ah, that's what I thought you said.' The giant sniggered and dropped his hand after shaking it just the once. 'Isn't this a grand festival?'

'I've seen better,' Apollo muttered. It was nothing compared to the festivals thrown in Athens in honour of Athena. The priestess there was famed for her beauty and certainly knew how to put on a show. The priestesses here were far less competent and certainly nothing to look at.

'Your sister certainly is beautiful,' Orion bowed his head respectfully. 'You must be very proud of her.'

I was until you came along.

How would he do away with this giant? He couldn't just kill him in cold blood, for Artemis would never speak to him again. He could try and scare the fool away, but Orion seemed like he was too thick for threats in both brain and muscle, even from a god. Apollo would've paid him to leave, but that was too much of a mortal thing to do, was it not?

Besides, his father Zeus wouldn't have gone about paying or pleading people to leave. He'd simply do away with them, wouldn't he? But he'd make it poetic too. He wouldn't have just jammed a knife in the giant's neck, no. He'd make a game out of it. In some ways, Apollo liked to think of his father as an artist—gently applying his brushes as he stirred the paint around the canvas, painting every tragic outcome and picking the one he liked best.

That was when it came to him.

'Orion,' Apollo started. 'Perhaps we ought to get to know each other a little better.'

Orion looked a little taken aback by that, a suspicious sort of look in his eyes. Perhaps not as dull as Apollo had considered.

'I'm sure your sister would like that,' Orion said.

'My thinking exactly,' Apollo said and waved him away from the crowd. 'Tell me, do you know about the spring in the forest?'

He frowned, 'There is no spring.'

'Ah! That is where you are wrong, my friend,' Apollo pointed. 'If you follow me, I can take you there. I assure you the spring is the warmest thing you'll ever step into.'

Orion glanced back at Artemis, uncertain. 'Perhaps we should wait for—'

'Nonsense,' Apollo tried nudging him only to find his arm was like solid steel, probably hard enough to knock him unconscious for a good while. He'd need to play this carefully.

'How far away is it?'

'Not far at all,' Apollo declared and marched away only to find the giant wasn't following. 'Come, Orion, the spring is only warmest at certain parts of the day.'

Orion shook his head, 'I'll wait for Artemis. Then you can show us both.'

Apollo took a deep breath. There was no winning with this block head. He could not be reasoned with and though he was likely witless, there seemed to be no way to work past his thick skull. Apollo thought about killing him right there and then. Perhaps outright blood was the only answer. But no, there had to be something he could appeal to? Every man had his weakness, did they not?

And then it came to him.

'Do you want to ram my sister or not?'

'I...uh...excuse me?'

'My sister has been waiting for a man to put her on her back and ravish her for her entire adult life,' Apollo snickered. 'But no man has been able to impress her enough, don't you know?'

'I don't know what you're—'

'Yes you do,' Apollo grinned and relished in the redness of the giant's cheeks and the shifty way he now held his hands. 'She'll be most impressed with you leading her to the spring that I'm sure she'll spread her legs for you right there and then.'

Orion cleared his throat, 'I'm sure your sister has more self-respect than to simply give herself away like that.'

'Your loss,' Apollo shrugged and began to stalk away. 'If you don't impress her with the spring, then I'm sure someone else will.'

'What do you mean?'

Apollo felt his lips pulling into a smile. 'I mean a goddess like Artemis has a string of suitors, don't you know?'

'She does?' Orion sounded deflated all of a sudden.

'Why yes,' Apollo slowly turned around and prowled his way around the giant, 'she's had several marriage proposals and she's close to accepting one. Maybe even two? But the spring I speak of is a magical place where people are known to fall in love. Should you meet my sister there, she'll be so impressed by your gesture that she'll marry you on the spot.'

'She will?' the giant frowned, working his massive hand against his chin. 'You say this spring is...magical?'

Apollo nodded, fighting back a smile, 'You sure can't make this stuff up.'

The giant glanced back at Artemis who was still fumbling her words at the podium. She'd gone red in the face and her stance was about as flattering as a dried up weed. Her shoulders were all bunched up, she slouched forward, her knees were rocking, and if Apollo wasn't mistaken, her hands were shaking something chronic. Stupid girl could dismantle a boar in seconds, but ask her to speak to more than one person at the same time and she crumbled like paper in a fire.

'I mean,' Orion began, 'if you say she has other suitors...'

'Hundreds,' Apollo lied. 'But you my friend have a real chance if you come with me now.'

'Why would you help me?' Orion asked.

You're a stubborn one, aren't you?

At least he had the giant considering his offer. All he had to do was lure him to the spring and then he'd set the rest of his plan in motion. Indeed, it was a glorious plan. In fact, it was so glorious it may as well have been torn out of the book of Zeus himself. Yes, it was a grand plan. A grand, devious and thrilling plan that made his heart thump with nervous excitement.

'Help you?' Apollo frowned. 'Why, I'm helping my sister. The other suitors she has lined up are not thoughtful or considerate like you, Orion. They share not your compassion or your wisdom. I should not want my sister to end up with one of them.'

The giant glanced back at Artemis once more before shrugging his shoulders and nodding his head. 'I would not want for her to be with anyone else either.'

'Why would you?' Apollo agreed. 'You love her. Why would you want any other man to have his hands on her? Would you not do anything to prevent that from happening? Anything?'

'I would,' the giant nodded.

'So would I,' Apollo grinned. 'Now, are you coming with me or not?'

VII. The Perfect Shot

She'd made a fool of herself, that much was true.

Her people still chanted her name as she scurried off of the podium and through the masses, but she knew most of them had no idea what she'd said. Her cheeks were hot with embarrassment, and though they still clapped at the end of her abysmal speech, she couldn't help but feel their confused and almost pitying stares like a harsh whip against her spine. She paced quickly through the bevy, head down and eyes closed.

'Sister!' Apollo grabbed her by the shoulders.

She almost shrieked because of how fiercely he'd come at her. His eyes were alight with energy and there was a sheen to his face as if he'd been jogging in the heat and had come back sweaty.

'Brother? What's wrong?'

He was erratic. Something had happened and going by the way his eyes were darting back and forth it wasn't anything good.

'Your speech was marvellous, truly marvellous!'

'It was?' she felt herself shrinking all of a sudden. Why was it that compliments made her feel more uneasy than criticism did?

'Absolutely! That part you mentioned about treating animals the same way we might treat each other. Why, it got me thinking...'

'Oh?' she straightened. 'I'm surprised anyone even heard me.'

'I most certainly did,' he said with an air of pride as he swung his arm around her shoulders. 'It got me thinking about our chat earlier and that maybe...maybe I have been killing in excess.'

'That's an understatement,' she muttered and she was sure he paid her a lingering, sidelong glance.

'Anyway,' he shook his head, 'I've been thinking about cutting back, but at the same time...what type of gods would that make us if we are not hunters anymore?'

'We can still be hunters,' she looked at him, 'but only hunt what we need, not what we want.'

'I don't know,' he made a pained expression. 'How about we have a contest to decide?'

He had that suspicious air about him. He liked to think he hid his emotions well, but Artemis knew her brother and could probably tell what his mood was even if they were locked in darkness. He was up to something. That much was true.

'What contest?'

'A target,' Apollo produced his bow. 'We both shoot at something and whoever misses has to concede to the other's will.'

Artemis sighed, 'Apollo, this is ridiculous. What games are you playing?'

'No games,' Apollo held up one hand, 'but a mere contest between the two of us to prove which should prevail: your notion that everything should live, or my notion that we should be allowed to pick and choose as gods do.'

'Fine,' she snatched the bow out of his hands. She'd had about enough of all this. 'What do I have to shoot?'

'Come,' he grinned. 'I'll show you.'

She moved after him, but then she stopped to glance around at the crowd. Orion wasn't exactly hard to spot given that he towered over the rest of her people, but she couldn't see him. She had hoped that he'd heard her speech, tragic as it was. But he understood her in more ways than one. Surely, he'd have appreciated her words.

'What are you looking for?' Apollo bit off each word, suddenly impatient.

'I'm...' she was about to mention Orion, but she caught the way her brother's nose began to scrunch up and thought better of it. The last thing she wanted was him going off at her again. She'd put an end to this debate once and for all with his stupid contest and then she'd go on about her own life, protecting the wildlife with Orion if that was on the cards. 'Nothing.'

'If you're looking for your ogre,' Apollo snapped, 'I saw him limp off during your speech. Yawning, might I add.'

'He left?' she felt her heart sink—a horrible and most unwelcome feeling. A sharp pain drilled its way up her sternum and she was left feeling a tad breathless.

'Yes,' Apollo hissed. 'Told you he was a bumbling oaf. Now, come! Let's settle this debate once and for all.'

He led her through the dense forestry with a certain conviction in his gait, as if every moment of his life had led up to this moment. Why it was so important to him, she couldn't quite say. But he was agitated, perhaps even nervous with a certain crazed giddiness that made his aura darken. He didn't walk with his usual smoothness, but instead had a more robust sort of walk as he brushed past the thick yews. He absently stamped through mud that he otherwise would've hopped across and bared no notice to the army of birds that fled to the skies upon his approach.

'Where are you taking me?' she asked. 'Surely we can just shoot one of the trees as our target and be done with?'

'That's too easy a shot,' he said. 'I want to give you a chance.'

She was about to respond that she was indeed the better archer, but that would only lead to more conflict. He'd grown up believing he was the finer marksman, and she had allowed him to hold onto that belief, if only to save his own ego. Now and again, she'd wonder if it had been better to stamp it out entirely all those years ago.

'What do you want us to shoot at then?' she asked.

'Those rocks,' he pointed as they emerged before a calm body of water.

Sunlight stabbed through the gaps of the trees, coating the greenery that grew around the spring in a golden brilliance. Smoke billowed from the water and a ghostly mist hovered about the area, gently creeping further into the forest. A tiny cataract was formed between the rockery of a small, sloping hill and there were indeed several rocks in the water, dressed with moss.

'Not exactly a complicated target, brother.'

'I bet you can't hit that rock there,' he pointed in the middle of the spring to one pale rock that uncharacteristically stood out from the rest. 'You go first.'

'Fine,' she rolled her eyes and nocked an arrow as fluidly as she ever had. She didn't hesitate. She let the arrow loose and didn't even bother watching it fly until it sunk into the rock. But that was strange. Since when were rocks so soft that they absorbed the head of an arrow?

More importantly, since when did rocks bleed?

'Nice shot, sister!' Apollo gaudily laughed. 'I'm afraid I can't compete with that. You win!'

But his words were just faint sounds now as she watched the blood from the rock spill into the water, the red puddle gradually expanding until she saw his shoulders emerge.

'No,' she said out loud as the bow fell from her hands and thumped on the grass.

'He was getting inside your head too much,' she heard Apollo's words beside her, though they were distant somehow. She could no more conceive them than she could take her eyes away from Orion whose massive back now peaked out from the waters like the hull of a drowned ship.

She couldn't move. She tried to blink, but she couldn't take her eyes away from the scene, unable to even move her head. A bit of saliva dangled from the corner of her mouth, but she could not move her hand to wipe it away. Why was there so much blood? Why was most of the spring now crimson red?

'He was trying to take you away from me,' Apollo was saying. 'He tried to come between us!'

She managed to look down at her shaking hands. She'd done this. She'd killed him. She'd fantasised about this moment before when he was nothing more than a cumbersome nuisance, following her about the forest. But he was something more—a wise and beautiful man with so much to offer. Now, he was nothing. Just a floating bit of lifeless meat with an arrow—her arrow—protruding from his head.

'Say something, sister,' Apollo nudged. 'Say you're glad that we're back together and that you won't leave me again.'

A sob escaped her mouth. That was it. Just a pained, stupid, awful sound. She was breathing heavy now, arms and legs shaking with such an intensity that she was afraid she'd topple over. She could feel her heart being torn in two and her entire chest constricted making it difficult to breath. She would've fallen flat on her face, but Apollo had his hands around her waist now, his mouth close to her ear.

'Why don't we go back to the festival?' he asked her. 'And then maybe we can go hunting again like we used to? Before that fool came and ruined everything that we—'

She drilled her knee into his groin. She made decent enough contact, enough that he crumbled before her, but not enough that he was down and out. He squirmed on the floor for a moment, wheezing and coughing before he scrambled on all fours.

'You ungrateful woman! I did this for you, can't you see?'

Her mouth was open, but the only thing that escaped was this sort of animalistic grunting that she couldn't stop. She grabbed the bow off the floor, nocked an arrow and fired at him, but he spun out of its way and stormed up a tree.

'You're being unreasonable, sister!' he barked from above. 'You and I belong together. Can't you see that?'

'You murdered him!' she screamed as she fired off another arrow that narrowly missed him.

'Actually, that was you.' He gave a brief chuckle before she sprinted up the tree after him.

All she could see was red as she reached out for him. He was quick though, he always had been. He kicked her in the face before she could find purchase on him, and she went tumbling back through the branches. Before she hit the ground, she grabbed hold of one of the thicker branches on her descent and swung herself upwards once more, pursuing him as they went higher and higher.

'I did this for you!' he pleaded as leaves and branches rained down upon her in his mad dash for escape.

'Come and face what you've done!' She roared at him as she ascended up the tree, moving left and right as she darted from branch to branch, chasing him upwards as easily as one might've given chase up a set of stairs.

Up and up they went with the blood pumping in her ears. Branches were snapped, leaves rustled, small fruits dislodged from their hangings and cast down below to splatter. Nests were uprooted in the mad ascent and angry birds hooted upon their emergence. She closed in on him, each branch springing her forward as they climbed higher and higher, onwards and upwards, until they reached Olympus.

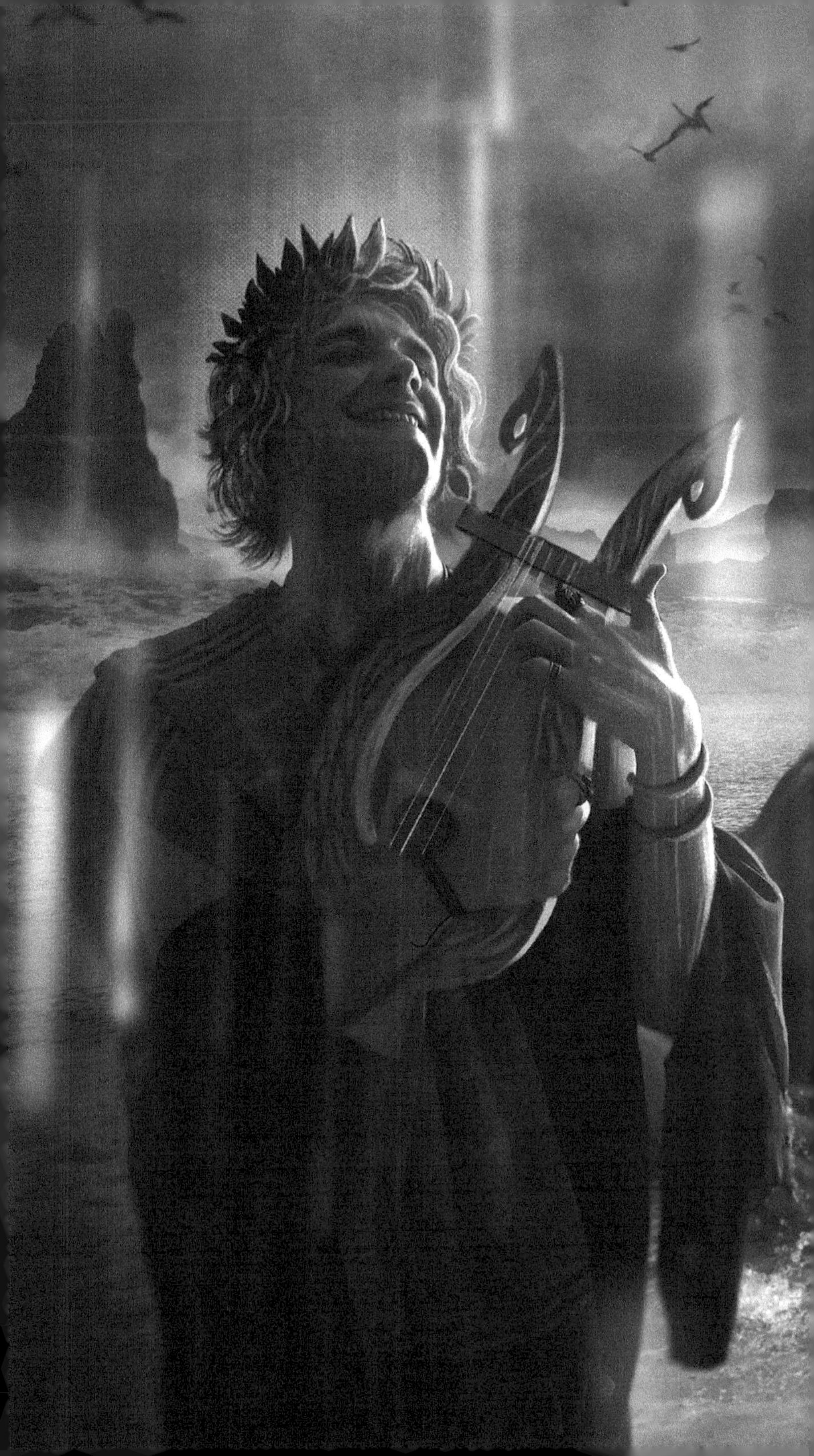

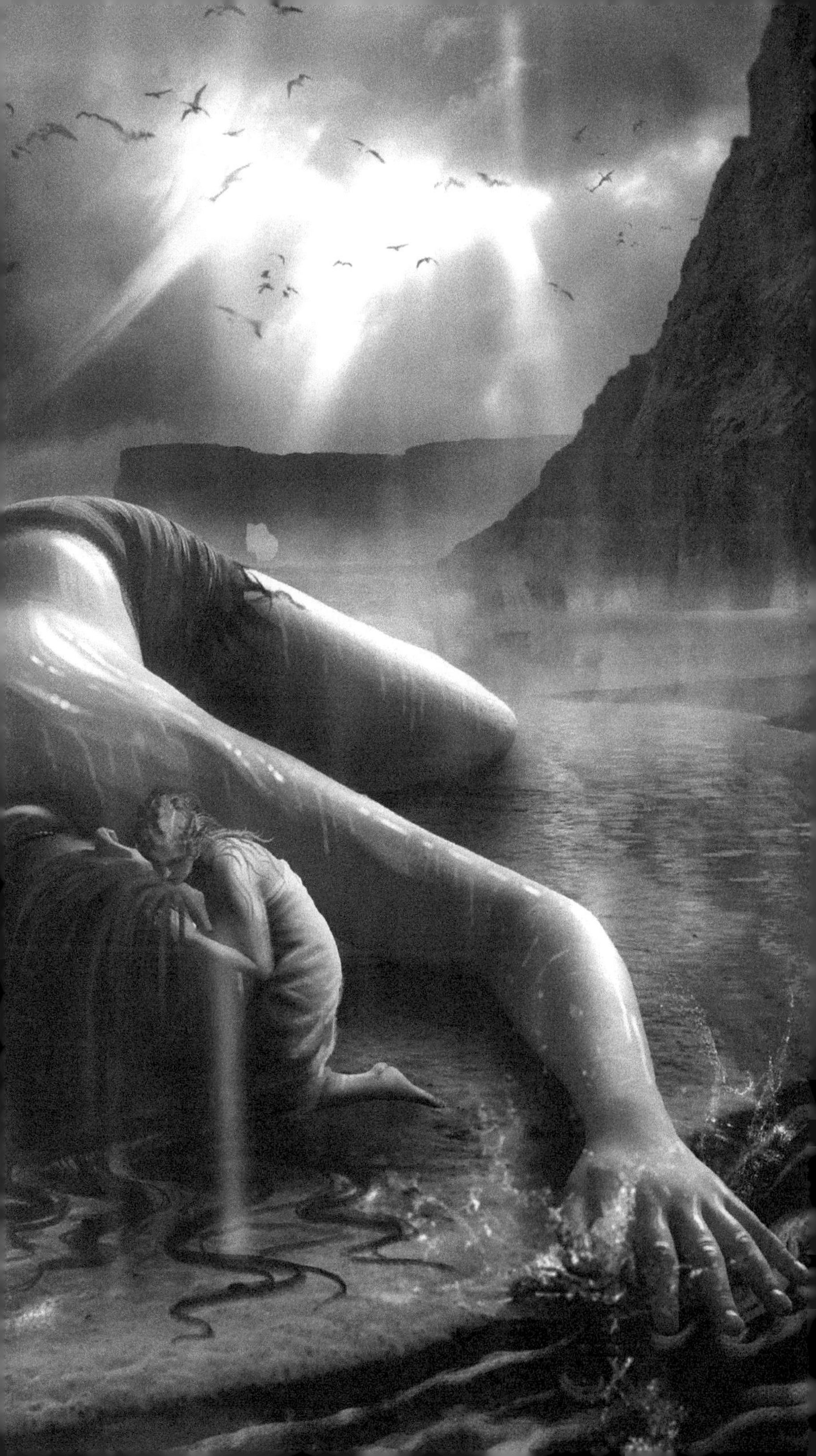

VIII. Family Ties

The skies darkened above Olympus. Dark grey clouds were ushered in by the winds and sat menacingly above the kingdom, threatening to drench it all in rainwater. But that didn't matter to Artemis. The rain could flood the entirety of Olympus and she would shove Apollo's head under the water until he stopped thrashing.

Rows upon rows of magnificent towers spread out before them. It was a forest made up of buildings with spires and domes where each pinnacle was sparkling vividly with gold. The gates of Olympus were set upon the clouds and were dazzling to look upon—at least they usually were, but all Artemis could see was the back of her brother's head as she pressed on after him. Still, it was hard not to take a moment to gawk at the immensity of Olympus as it loomed over her like one giant mountain of architecture. It was Zeus' palace that struck her the most. It was a grandiose structure rearing over everything else in the same way he did, casting a long shadow across everything else below.

'Father!' Apollo was screaming.

But Zeus couldn't save him now. No one could.

She nocked an arrow, took aim at the back of her brother's golden head and released, sending an arrow right for him. But he was always one step ahead, wasn't he? He swung around, saw the arrow and managed to snatch it out of the air, tossing it to one side. She would've fired another, but now the guards from the gate were rushing in with their steels.

'Help me!' Apollo was screaming. 'My sister has gone mad and is trying to kill me!'

The guards moved in to block her way, a dozen of them with their sapphire-blue armour glinting and polished. They formed a formidable enough line to engage her, but as she drew nearer she noticed the tremor amongst them. There was uncertainty on their otherwise impassive faces and the fact that they hadn't drawn their swords only made them look weaker all of a sudden.

'My name is Artemis!' she roared as she made a beeline for them. 'Daughter of Zeus, goddess of the hunt! That man there is my prey.'

She didn't need to say anymore. The three or four guards ahead of her stood to one side and dropped to one knee, the rest of them following suit soon after. She brushed past them unburdened and carried on after her brother as they moved into the confines of Olympus and right for Zeus' home.

'Father!' he went barrelling through the double doors and scattering on the ground.

Artemis moved in a second after, bow drawn as she took aim at her snivelling brother who made no effort to get to his feet. She could've let the arrow fly right here, could've nailed him right between the eyes and be done with it. But that wouldn't be right. That's not what Orion would've wanted, was it? Then again, it didn't matter anymore. He was gone.

'All these interruptions!' Zeus boomed from his obsidian throne. He slammed one fist down against the armrest of his chair and the thump shook the entire room. In his other hand, there was a pale goose that he held by the neck, but after seeing Artemis, he threw it across the floor and didn't pay it a second glance as it squawked out of the room in a hurry. 'First comes that idiot on the flying horse and now my own children are bothering me!'

He hadn't changed at all. He was still the short tempered and peevish man she'd remembered who seldom smiled at anything that wasn't a pair of legs or a pair of breasts. If she wasn't mistaken, he'd been smiling at that goose upon their entrance, but any trace of his amusement was now lost in the grey frown on his face.

'Father,' Apollo climbed to his feet. 'Artemis is trying to kill me.'

'About time,' he snapped his fingers. 'Go on girl. Give me something to laugh at and do away with this prancing fool.'

'You don't understand,' Apollo was waving his hands. 'She was about to lie with a giant! A giant of all things! She would've given up her hunt for him.'

'A giant?' Zeus beckoned, his face now staring daggers into hers. 'You would willingly lie with one those...abominations?'

'He wasn't an abomination!' She roared. 'He was my friend...he was...'

'A lover?' Zeus snorted. 'No daughter of mine is going to be fondling with a giant. Where is this giant now?'

There was a moment of silence and then Apollo squeaked, 'I tricked Artemis into killing him. But I did it only so that our lineage would be kept clean and so that Artemis would remain the goddess of the hunt. Why, that giant was actually convincing her to give up hunting! He was poisoning her mind.'

She was about to lunge at him, but Zeus must've sensed it because he strode between the pair of them, one hand scratching at his mighty beard.

'You mean to tell me that you tricked your own sister into killing her lover?' Zeus towered over Apollo, backing him into the corner of the room.

Maybe she wouldn't have to strike at all. Zeus seemed more than content to do it himself all of a sudden as Apollo cowered like a whimpering dog whipped by his master.

'Yes,' Apollo sobbed. 'Yes, I did it.'

Was this the moment a lightning bolt came thundering down to claim her brother's life? Or was it simply the moment that Zeus grabbed him by his fancy collars and tossed him from Olympus all the way down to the mortal world below? Artemis realised that she was content with either one. But to her dismay, neither came to fruition. In fact, there was only Zeus' vile laughter.

'My boy,' he grabbed hold of Apollo and pulled him into a hug, 'that's the funniest thing you've ever done! Why, I don't think I've felt more pride than this moment.'

'What?' Artemis boomed. 'You condone his act?'

Zeus looked over his shoulder at her, 'You'll get over it, child. Men come and go the same way women do. Love is fickle. You'll meet someone else.'

'You're my father,' Artemis shrieked. 'How can you stand there and accept this behaviour? He killed Orion and he's broken my heart!'

'Yes,' Zeus winced. 'But it's still pretty funny, don't you think?'

She almost collapsed at his words. There he was, her own father with a big, gawdy smile on his bearded face as tears cascaded down hers. Apollo stood in his father's shadow, rubbing his hands together as he nervously laughed.

'Dry your eyes, girl.' Zeus sighed. 'We'll find you another man.'

'I don't want another man,' she hissed and lifted her bow at him. 'I want my Orion!'

Zeus's smile began to fade and his voice went suddenly dark, 'You dare make demands at me, girl?'

'Yes, you dare make demands at our father?' Apollo added.

Zeus looked at him, 'Shut up, boy.'

'At once,' Apollo fell to one knee.

She tried to stop herself from shaking with rage, but she could no more do that then she could stop the tears. Zeus' presence weighed on her so much so that soon she could barely look him in the eyes. Her head felt heavier all of a sudden and she was forced to look down at his sandals and nothing else.

'What will you have me do, girl? How can I stop your tears?' he asked her.

'Bring him back,' she said simply.

'Bring back a giant?' Zeus winced. 'I won't be doing such a thing and certainly not one who it seems has taken away your desire for the hunt.'

'My desire is still there,' she replied, 'but I won't be killing innocent creatures for no reason at all!'

'Pffft,' Zeus rolled his eyes. 'You are ever dramatic, daughter.'

She dropped the bow and sunk to her knees. What else could she do? This was the reason why she had never let anyone get too close, was it not? This is what she had tried to avoid all these years? What was the point of allowing herself to feel for someone when they would only be ripped away from her in the end?

'Please,' she begged and lowered her head to the floor. 'Please bring him back.'

She knew it was futile. She knew no amount of sobbing or pleading would change her father's mind. Stronger women had tried, after all. She looked up with wet eyes at her father, but there was no sympathy on his bored face. It was as if he was looking through her, staring at something in the distance that had caught his eye and was far more interesting than her tears. So she looked to Apollo and felt her hands clenching into fists.

'You did this to me,' she hissed through her sobs.

He withdrew even further into his father's shadow with that, but gone was the wicked smile on his face. For just that moment, he was her brother again with nothing but concern in his bright blue eyes and a tremor at his lip.

'Perhaps, I might suggest a solution to all this...'

'And what would that be, boy?' Zeus looked at him.

'Let me show you,' he said and pointed out the window and up at the sky.

IX. Born Anew

She sat on a hilltop overlooking the rest of the forest, though it was drowned in darkness with only the blinking of stars for company. She didn't want to look at the stars. If she looked at the stars, then she would see him. And then she would miss him. And then there would be pain. She nursed his bow in her lap, stroking her hand against the wooden limb. There was a time the bow had his musky scent to it, but now it had faded. It was a heavy thing too and probably hardly worth hauling around on her back. But she couldn't seem to part with it—couldn't bear to not have it with her.

Artemis had gone back to hunting, for it was the only thing that kept her mind off him. But each kill left her emptier and emptier until there was nothing left. The forest had become her home now, and she sat in her sweaty, stinking slacks with mud on her face, in her hair and down her arms. Her stench had long since stopped bothering her and she no longer felt unclean having bathed nearly two months ago. She was unkempt to say the least. Her body sprouted thick, coarse hairs down her legs and along her arms. But she didn't care as she pulled her cowl closer over her greasy hair. No one needed to see her now.

She could feel him staring down at her from above, and if she closed her eyes, she could hear his laughter gently rolling through the air. She hated him for leaving her. Why didn't he stay with her at the festival?

Why couldn't he move his stupid, giant feet fast enough to keep up with her? Why couldn't he be here now with his arms around her? She wiped her hands over her face, squeezing at her brow as she tensed with anger. There was so much they hadn't talked about and so much they hadn't done together. Everything she imagined with him had already crumbled away, whisked away by the winds and scattered into a million pieces, lost forever.

She wanted to look at him. By the gods, she always wanted to look at him in the end. She could feel her head being pulled up towards the sky where she knew he'd always be now, but what good would that do? It only made her suffer a terrible conniption that she felt through her entire body, tugging at the heartstrings, wrenching them out of place and leaving them tangled. If she looked at him now, she wouldn't look away for a good few hours and then she'd be back in the same place where she'd desperately pine for him.

Let's put his face in the sky, Apollo had said that day. *That way, Artemis can never forget her lover.*

She had begged them not to. She threw herself at her father's feet, and just like that, she had become a little girl again, pleading and crying for him not to curse her to such a fate. But Zeus merely smiled at her, paid Apollo a fatherly glance of pride and then did it anyway. Orion's face watched her every move with that same infuriating smile she had once hated, then loved and now hated again. Never again could she enjoy the sunrise nor contemplate the moon, for it was only his face that awaited her, forever and always.

Alone again then, she thought as she fell back into a slump. She closed her eyes and took a deep breath to calm her thumping heart. The temptation to stare up at the sky was there with a vengeance, and if she wasn't mistaken, a pair of invisible hands were clutched around her head, gently turning her face upwards as she tried to resist.

But she couldn't resist it forever. She knew that much. What was one more look going to do to her anyway? She gazed upon him coyly at first, taking in his rugged features, his big eyes, the stubbly hairs on his cheeks, the creases at his eyes from where his smile dominated his face. By the gods, it still infuriated her, didn't it? It still made her want to punch him, perhaps now more than ever. What she would give to punch him now. She'd swing as hard as she could, for at least she could touch him then. At least she could hear his voice one last time. At least she could tell him how she really felt.

She finally looked away and found her attention on the arrow she had drawn. The metal head glinted and in her peripheral vision she could make out a lone deer loitering in the brush. But it was too far to give chase and certainly too far to shoot. If she was honest, she didn't have it in her anymore anyway. So she simply gave Orion a lingering glance and smiled as she touched the arrowhead against her throat.

Something moved in the corner of her eye. It was a welcome distraction from being tempted to glance up at the sky. At first she paid it no mind, but then she caught the golden dust that trailed off from its body. It stood there on all fours, its giant gilded antlers seated majestically upon its head. Its fur was as bright as she remembered and it had a long, golden tail. Its dark eyes were glued to her, watching her without ever blinking.

'Impossible,' she whispered, for she had buried the Ceryneian Hind after she and Orion had killed it. But it was here somehow, still as a statue.

She slowly sat up into a crouched position, but the Ceryneian Hind must've remembered her, because it stopped in its tracks, watching her with intent. She wondered if it was angry at her for having shot it with an arrow and wondered if it had come for revenge of some kind. Artemis was in the mind to let it have it. But its eyes were different now, no longer black and void, but greyer with a distinct glow of light from within. Something about the way it gazed at her was conversant, and the odd way in which its mouth moved made it look like it was...smiling.

'Orion?' she reached out and the deer moved forward, lowering its head so she could feel the sturdiness of its antlers, the soft fur on its face and the dampness of its snout. She was going mad. She had to have been going mad, hadn't she? There was no way this creature could've suddenly become Orion. In fact, there was no way this creature could've suddenly dug itself up from the grave. And yet, here it was with an awfully familiar energy radiating from its eyes, from its antlers, from its mouth and its hooves and its tail and everything else.

It darted back then and she let out a gasp for fear of having spooked it somehow. Her heart was beating fast and she scuttled after it, grabbing her bow and lunging to her feet. But it didn't appear spooked, nor was it as serious and regal as she had once remembered. Now it seemed playful, perhaps charming and mischievous as it pranced about, luring her into a chase. It gave that same giddy smirk Orion might've given her before it broke into a sprint across the green lands and into a sea shrubbery.

Artemis hurried after it.

THE STORY OF ARTEMIS EXPLAINED

When we think of gods and goddesses, we imagine them to have their own community in the same way we do as humans. Their day to day interaction is mostly amongst themselves, but they do occasionally interact with humans, depending on the situation. Whether it's in the form of a punishment, an act of guidance or in Zeus's case it's likely he found the next woman that he wished to impregnate. There were many deities that preferred the company of mortals, even choosing to permanently live amongst them. This wasn't the case for most of the Olympians and some of their children as they distanced themselves on Mount Olympus. Those gods and goddesses at the top of the hierarchy usually had very little interaction with mortals. The lesser known deities and those who were considered less powerful or significant would often have more interaction with humankind than their own kind.

Artemis is an interesting goddess because she is well-respected and held in high regard by both humans and gods, yet her interaction with both is kept to a bare minimum. Outside of the nymphs who sometimes accompany her, her mother Leto and twin brother Apollo, her interaction remains solely with the wildlife she encounters in her forests. There are two stories in particular that highlight the perils of coming across Artemis in the forest. The stories of Actaeon and the story of Sipriotes. Actaeon was a young hunter who gazed upon Artemis while she bathed in a spring with her nymphs. Seeing the Goddess in all her beauty he was unable to look away. Artemis, furious with the lack of respect shown by Actaeon, told him he was not to speak or she would turn him into a stag. Hearing his hunting dogs nearby, Actaeon called to them and Artemis, keeping her word, turned him into a stag. Sadly for Actaeon, he had trained his hounds too well and even as a stag he could not outrun them. When they finally caught him, they tore him to pieces, mistaking him for a regular deer. Actaeon's death can be viewed as a punishment for his actions, but it can also be seen as a human sacrifice in order to appease a deity which is a belief held by many cultures from around the world.

Similar to the story of Actaeon, Sipriotes was a young boy who stumbled across Artemis while she was bathing in the forest. Sipriotes was then given two choices: he was told he could either live the rest of his life as a girl or simply choose to die. Needless to say, he chose to be transformed into a female where he would then become a follower and companion of Artemis.

The tale of Artemis and Orion, regardless of which interpretation you may be familiar with, is a tragic love story that ends in heartbreak. The biggest point of contention and discussion is the way the story ends and how Orion is killed. The interpretation that we have chosen for our version of the story is one where Apollo's jealousy leads to Artemis accidentally killing Orion. Before understanding Apollo's motives and why he tricked his sister into killing Orion, we first have to establish the bond and relationship between the siblings.

Unlike most Greek deities, Artemis and Apollo were not recognised as divine at birth. Along with their mother Leto, they were cast out and pursued by all manner of creatures sent by Hera who was furious that Leto had given birth to Zeus's children. As a result of their circumstance, Artemis and Apollo were extremely close growing up; they developed a close bond that meant they were far stronger when together. Over the years, Artemis limited her interaction with male suitors and so their bond was never under any threat. That is, until Orion entered the picture. You can view Apollo's jealousy in several ways, perhaps because he sexually desired Artemis. Her relationship with Orion would then ruin the possibility of Apollo courting his sister into a relationship of his own. We can also look at Apollo's jealousy as stemming from a need for power—with Orion and Artemis together, his bond with this twin would slowly diminish, causing Apollo to lose a portion of his power. If we couple the fear of losing his sister with that of losing his power, we then have clear-cut motives as to why Apollo manipulated the situation that lead to Orion's death.

There are several versions of the story where Orion's death was not caused by Apollo. In one interpretation, Orion boasted greatly of his hunting ability, claiming he could kill every living thing. This greatly angered Gaia, the primordial mother of all the gods who has since been described as the mother of earth, whereby all nature came from her. Orion was essentially threatening to kill her children with his boasts about killing everything and so Gaia sent an enormous scorpion to kill Orion. When the giant encountered the scorpion, a battle ensued; the scorpion's poisonous sting would eventually kill Orion.

There are several versions where Artemis intentionally kills Orion. In one instance, Orion forced himself upon one of her handmaidens, and in another, he challenged her to a test of hunting ability from which Artemis emerged victorious.

Artemis, for the most part, seemed incapable of a relationship. She was incompatible with most men, but unlike the other men she had encountered, Orion seemed to care more about the sacred nature of the hunt. Most men saw Artemis as a strong goddess, the daughter of Zeus and a great candidate for a wife. Orion, on the other hand, saw her as a huntress, ignoring her status and reputation. They formed a bond rooted in their love for nature which turned into love for each other. But, unfortunately for Artemis, this would ultimately end in tragedy.

ABOUT THE AUTHORS

Marios Christou

Marios Christou currently runs the YouTube channel *Mythology and Fiction Explained* where he discusses myth, folklore, and fiction from all around the world.

David Ramenah

David Ramenah has been writing science fiction and fantasy books for the past ten years. He currently runs the YouTube channel *Legends of History* where he discusses the deeds and lives of some of history's most iconic, deadly, weird, and violent figures.

Mango Publishing, established in 2014, publishes an eclectic list of books by diverse authors—both new and established voices—on topics ranging from business, personal growth, women's empowerment, LGBTQ studies, health, and spirituality to history, popular culture, time management, decluttering, lifestyle, mental wellness, aging, and sustainable living. We were recently named 2019 *and* 2020's #1 fastest-growing independent publisher by *Publishers Weekly*. Our success is driven by our main goal, which is to publish high-quality books that will entertain readers as well as make a positive difference in their lives.

Our readers are our most important resource; we value your input, suggestions, and ideas. We'd love to hear from you—after all, we are publishing books for you!

Please stay in touch with us and follow us at:

Facebook: Mango Publishing
Twitter: @MangoPublishing
Instagram: @MangoPublishing
LinkedIn: Mango Publishing
Pinterest: Mango Publishing
Newsletter: mangopublishinggroup.com/newsletter

Join us on Mango's journey to reinvent publishing, one book at a time.

CPSIA information can be obtained
at www.ICGtesting.com
Printed in the USA
JSHW020849171121
20510JS00002B/2